Madison Avenue Mediator

LOVE IN THE BIG APPLE
BOOK TWO

NICOLE SANCHEZ

Go fer what you want

To request permissions, contact the author at author.nicolesanchez@gmail.com

First paperback edition January 2023

Edited by Amanda Iles

Cover Art by Angela Haddon Designs

Vector Image by Vecteezy.com

❀ Created with Vellum

For the people who want it all - don't settle for less

One

TWENTY-YEAR-OLD AINSLEY never would have believed there would be a day where she *didn't* need an alarm to wake up, but here I am, thirty-two years old and waking up before my alarm goes off. My arm is folded uncomfortably under me, and my neck is stiff from sleeping in an awkward position. I mentally curse myself, knowing that it's going to be bothering me for the next week. My eyes open and I search for where my alarm clock should be in my room, only to find that the nightstand I'm looking at isn't remotely mine. There is at least a clock on it, and I feel vindicated seeing that I still have ten minutes before my alarm is supposed to go off.

When I reach for my phone, I realize that I'm being restrained by an arm lying heavily on my back. I have to take a minute to inventory my surroundings before I panic. It's not the first time I've woken up in a stranger's bed, and it's always alarming as I try to place the events that led me here.

I'm lying on my stomach, naked, and a man's arm is slung across my back, and that is not my clock. Priority number one is going to be turning off my phone before I wake up the person beside me. I stretch, reaching to my limit to grab it and turn off the alarm.

Awesome. I also neglected to charge my phone last night.

Tequila - 1; Ainsley - 0

The arm around me tightens, pulling me against the rock-hard body that is equally naked and oh, *oh*, very alert, judging the morning wood pressed to my hip. A memory surges up, of me sitting on a counter or a table as someone thrusts inside me. A combination of desire from the memory and nausea from my hangover fight for dominance as the memory unfolds.

Nausea wins.

I curse myself, trying to remember what else happened. I know it will come back to me, slowly, over the course of the day. It's plausible that I might still be drunk.

I try to remember what happened last night. I was at a bar. My Sleepless Nights date stood me up and I was chatting with the bartender. It was Mardi Gras, so there were beads and masks everywhere. We were commiserating over the woes of online dating when... when... what? Images come to me in a blur, a man with his mouth on mine, his mouth between my legs while I kissed someone else? God, I need to lay off the midweek bar trips.

I stink of sweat and sex and someone else's apartment, and I'm meeting a couple at eight-thirty. I don't usually go for such early meetings, but they asked for special accommodations since the wife has to go out of town for work. I try to be flexible; these are usually trying times for couples when they're divorcing and I find it helps set everyone in a better mood if I bend over backwards to meet their schedules.

I turn my head and see a mess of short, dark curls facing away from me. He's similarly lying on his stomach, and hopefully that will make for an easy getaway. I want to pull the sheet with me, to cover up the indignity of last night, the indignity of not remembering. I make the sacrifice so I can avoid facing him... and whoever else I was kissing last night.

I slide out from under the arm, earning an undignified grunt from the man as he folds his arm under his head, settling back in. I straighten up and turn my back to him, focused on finding my clothes before he realizes I've slipped away. The dress I borrowed from Vivian is in a heap on the floor and I bend over to grab it, pausing when I see a photo resting on the dresser.

A dark-haired man with light brown eyes stares at me from the frame. Beside him is a woman in a white dress. They are a striking couple. She also has dark hair and pale blue eyes that create a vivid contrast. They look gorgeous together in their wedding finery, and holy fuck, I suck. I've slept with plenty of guys since calling off my engagement, but this is a new low. Way to go, Ainsley. Sleeping with a married man is the ultimate rock bottom.

I turn to face him where he sleeps. The sheet I wanted to pull with me is wrapped around his bottom, but I go still when I realize that there is a woman he is spooning. That explains the decidedly female lips I remember. Swingers, great. At least I'm not a cheater? Does that count as cheating? I've entered a decidedly moral gray area, and I'm not thrilled with it. I can debate the finer moral implications with my friends over brunch.

I wish I had more than a hazy recollection of last night. I pull my dress over my head and look for my underwear. I try to be as quiet as I can, but when I move his jeans, his keys drop to the ground with a clink. I wince and look up, hoping that I've escaped notice.

"Five more minutes!" the woman cries, her voice muddled as she burrows into the pillows. When I look up, I'm met with those same brown eyes from the photograph, and I go totally still. He's more handsome in person. His hair is on the longer side. It curls around his neck and the bottom of his ears, but it's sticking up seven ways to Sunday. He has a trimmed beard that's not quite a full Tony Stark with the mustache-goatee combination. It's a shame; it looks like it hides a sharp jawline.

He looks confused by my presence for a moment, until the night comes back to him and he smiles.

"This is all just a dream. Go back to sleep or the Easter Bunny won't leave you any presents," I whisper, giving up on the search for my underwear. Maybe I wasn't even wearing any to begin with. I wouldn't be surprised by that.

"I'm agnostic," he whispers back, and I don't have a moment to feel bad about it because I've started to back away from the door.

"Where are we?" I ask, fumbling with my phone. In my drunken, sex-fueled haze, I never plugged it in to charge, so getting a PickMeUp! is out of the question. I'll call a taxi. Or, hopefully, I'm close enough to my apartment that I can just walk. Either way, this awkward moment is over.

"One-hundred-second and Fifth."

I nearly sag with relief. "Great, well, have a nice life," I say, turning my back on the sleeping couple. I need to pee like a pregnant woman, but I'm not sticking around any longer than necessary. I close the bedroom door gently as I step into the living room. Here I have more memories, the night slowly coming back. The three of us lounging on the couch with drinks when the man kisses my neck. His wife, I assume, taking the glass from my hand and setting it down so she can kiss my lips, pulling back enough to give me a chance to say no.

I didn't say no. In fact, I can vividly recall begging for more.

I shake my foggy head, grabbing my coat and purse, which are thankfully together at the kitchen table. I would take longer to appreciate their apartment, but I'm eager to get out of here. It's spacious, nothing like my ex's penthouse, but sizable for New York City. I slip on my ballet flats and step into the hall.

Never in my life have I been more excited to see the familiar hallway. The cream-colored carpets don't lend themselves to cleanliness, but the common charges for this condominium are astronomical enough to maintain the weekly shampooing. I slip into the elevator and press up instead of down. I won't have time to get to my apartment and my small clutch doesn't have my usual stuff in it, but it's going to have to do.

When the elevator lets me out onto the top floor, I don't hesitate to knock on the door at the end of the hall. I've walked these same steps so many times in the last year, and I'm glad that it's here now. As I knock again, I admire the cheesy wreath that's on the door. It's covered in pastel-colored eggs, no doubt homemade.

The door swings open, revealing my six-foot-tall ex. He's buttoning up his shirt, giving me a full flash of his abs.

"Ainsley?" Charlie asks, his brow furrowed. I never looked at myself in the mirror, and for a moment I'm sure I look like exactly what I am, a woman doing the walk of shame. Except, I'm not ashamed, so it's not that. I just really need to shower before I go to work and this was the best option.

"Hey, Chuck." I greet, throwing bravado behind my words.

"Who is it at this hour?" his wife, Elia, calls as she emerges from their bedroom in just his shirt. It's long enough to reach her knees, and a smile spreads across her face when she sees me.

"So, I have a meeting in, like, an hour and I desperately need to shower, so can I borrow a dress and also your shower?" The dress means I'll be commando all day, but I can't ask to borrow underwear. Maybe I'll have my paralegal run out and get me a pair. It's the least offensive line I'll cross all day.

"Of course," Elia says, giving Charlie a look. He steps back, letting me in. A tiny blurr rushes the door and I lean down to scoop up one of the not-so-little cats they adopted.

It would be weird coming to them for help, but Charlie and I have come so far from when we were together, and Elia helped make that happen.

"Charge this," I order, thrusting my phone into Charlie's hands.

I know my way around the apartment and kick off my shoes, dropping the cat on the kitchen counter before going to the guest room. I have to be quick about my shower, using the little travel-sized containers collected from their extensive travels that they have set up in there for guests.

When I emerge, I see Elia has laid out three dresses for me to choose from. I grab a simple black dress with a square neckline. Under the clothes, I see she's also left me the chicken cutlet boobs that she uses for strapless dresses. We're not the same cup size, but this offers flexibility so I can have some support. Going braless last night was bold when the dress had some sort of support and it was for a few hours, but I cannot go to work without a bra. How she knew I didn't have one on, I'm not going to ask.

I slide the dress on. She's taller than me by almost four inches, so whereas the dress would be short on Elia, it lands just above my knee. I have heels at my office, and my hair should dry while I take the subway.

When I emerge, Charlie is gone and my phone is charging on their kitchen island. Elia is sitting at the table, her computer open in front of her. She glances at me, no judgment in her grey eyes.

"Do you need anything else?" she asks, stroking one of the cats, trying to push it away from her keyboard.

"A time machine or a teleporter?"

"Sorry, ours are out for repair." She gives a dramatic shrug.

I grab my phone and seeing the time, I blanch. I shoot off a text to my paralegal, asking her to pick up a coffee for me. I hate asking her for such petty favors, but I won't have time to get it myself.

"I have to run. I'll fill you in when we get drinks with Viv and Taryn, promise."

"Go, good luck!" she calls as I pull the door shut behind me. Then I literally sprint to the subway.

There are, of course, delays. I'm going to have barely enough time to read over the intake notes from when my clients called in before I meet with them. I bounce on the balls of my feet, not caring that I was among the last to arrive when I push myself into the subway car. Sometimes it's helpful to just barely scrape five feet; it means I can weasel into spots that might be too small otherwise.

I power walk as fast as my little legs will carry me from Grand Central to my office on 40th and Madison. When I emerge from the elevator on my office floor, Eloise is waiting with the file and my coffee. She's chatting amiably with the receptionist until I walk in.

My hair is still damp, and I have no makeup on. Whatever I have in my desk is just going to have to cut it today.

"You look like you're having a morning," Eloise says, thrusting my coffee into my hand. My paralegal looks spectacular in a 1950s-style halter dress with a sweetheart neckline. She's got on a jacket to cover her bare shoulders, though she doesn't need it today. Most of the men in the office are off-site doing team building, AKA golfing. They're getting an early start to the male-only summer Fridays...on a March Wednesday.

"And if you want to keep your job, I highly suggest that you keep any questions to yourself." I take the coffee and squint against the painful fluorescent lights.

Eloise snorts. "If you fired me, who would be ready with your file and your coffee when you drag your hungover ass into the office?"

I glare at her, wishing I had my purse, wishing I had my sunglasses that I could put on to shield my eyes. Was it this bright out earlier?

"Angela would do that, I'm sure. Right, Angela?" I ask, turning to the receptionist.

Angela blinks up at me. Her unruly curls are pulled back in a clip that's still barely containing them. She's a good kid, working hard through night classes and this job. The partners don't love that she does classwork when it's slow, but I always turn a blind eye to it.

"You are way too high maintenance for me," she says, shaking her head. She's early; the firm doesn't open for another forty-five minutes, but she's here because I have an early meeting. I make a note that I have to treat her to breakfast or lunch.

"You are both such babies," I whine, pushing back to my office. It's not the highly sought-after corner office with dual exposure lighting like the partners have, but it's an office, one I earned on my own, without my father's interference.

We've never talked about it, but I'm sure going into family law is a disappointment to my father. I went to Dartmouth for my undergrad and then Harvard for law school. He pulled strings to ensure that I got the best internships, but I didn't even tell him I applied for this job. Perhaps this is what I get for that: a sad excuse for a frat house of an office run by misogynistic men that peaked in high school.

Sometimes, I think they keep me at the firm so when they inevitably get divorced, I'll be on hand to mediate for them, or, if the case calls for it, litigate the end of their marriage.

"Is this dress new?" Eloise asks, following me into my office. It's become something of a little ritual. Every morning we get the bullshit out of the way first thing while we're still having our coffees and our computers are waking up alongside us. I made the right call leaving my laptop here overnight, something I seldom do, but I had a date.

"It's actually Elia's," I say as I smooth out the creases before sitting. I lean over, digging around in my bottom drawer for a pair of sky-high heels. The sleeves on the dress are thick but still show my bare shoulders. I keep a spare suit jacket here for when I have to dress up for a client, and a quick glance at the back of my door reveals it's covered in the telltale dry-cleaning plastic.

I really need to talk to the partners about a raise or a promotion for Eloise. Her talents are wasted as an assistant.

"Like, your ex's new wife?" Eloise sounds skeptical and I don't blame her.

Eloise never understood how I was able to not only repair my broken friendship with Charlie but also befriend his wife. The truth is, Charlie's been in my life so long that he's family to me, and while I love him dearly, I fell out of love with him long before we even got engaged. I thought I could muscle through it and marry him, but I realized with each and every divorce I mediated that I didn't want that life for myself.

Eloise flips her pale blonde hair over her shoulder as she settles into the chair on the other side of my desk. My office is a mess, and there is no way I can have clients in here. Eloise to the rescue again with booking me a conference room. I glance at my watch and see that I have all of ten minutes to prepare. I can spend five of those telling her about last night. The couple, the Bakers, are going to have to do some leg work in the room with me. I'm part mediator, part therapist. Many of my first visits are spent listening to the couples vent about the reasons their marriage is ending, slinging blame across the table.

"Right, so my Sleepless Nights date totally stood me up."

"Prick," she mutters, gesturing for me to continue.

"But I guess I still went home with someone else because I decidedly did not wake up in my own bed."

"Oh, scandal." She sips her coffee, eyes bright over her drink.

"I woke up in bed with this guy and his wife."

"Shut the front door!" Eloise sits up abruptly, nearly splashing her coffee all over herself.

"Yeah, they happened to live in Charlie's building and I was already running late and there was no way I was getting from the Upper East Side to the Columbus Circle and then down here in time, so I improvised."

"That was bold improvisation, going to your ex-fiancé's apartment and borrowing his wife's clothes."

"It's so not like that anymore," I say before finally sipping my coffee. The minute the java hits my lips, I start to transcend into the world of wakefulness and caffeine. She's not wrong. Only last

New Year's, the one before Charlie and Elia were married, I was giving him a lap dance in front of her.

God. I am a trainwreck sometimes. But did I try to pull those breaks? Nope. I am riding that train straight into the middle of crazy town. There is something about having all your hopes and dreams ripped out from under you to make you really go with the bad decisions. Good news is, I'm on the verge of making some changes.

This past fall, I decided I'm going to start a family with or without a partner. My big hang-up has been biting the bullet and deciding how I want to go about it. A part of me keeps putting off the appointment with my doctor because I'm terrified of the next steps. I let myself get drowned in work so I have a convenient excuse.

The buzzer in my office goes off. "Can Eloise cover the front desk for me?" Angela asks over the intercom. "My gran keeps calling and I have to call her back to see what's going on."

"Of course!" Eloise responds, jumping to her feet. "Besides, Ainsley needs to review this file before her clients get here."

I stick my tongue out. Dartmouth College, Harvard Law School, and I still stick my tongue out at people like a petulant child. My Ivy League education is working wonders for me.

With Eloise gone, I'm able to focus on the information in front of me. Kenneth and Leslie Baker, married for five years, together for ten. He owns a bar and she does set design on Broadway. They met right after college at an art show at the MoMA. Assets include artwork, vacation homes, and instruments. No children and no pets. As far as divorces go, it looks pretty straightforward. For a mediator to be involved, things must be getting ugly.

"Ainsley? Your eight-thirty is here," Eloise chirps.

They're early; not a great start.

"Thanks, Wheezy. I'll be right there. Keep them at the front."

I glance in the mirror at my desk, running my fingers through my straight blonde hair, tugging at any knots. Regardless of what

10

my night looked like, I am damn good at my job, and I'm not going to let my hangover get the best of me. I pull on the suit jacket and slide into the pumps that I retrieved from my desk. Legal pad and coffee in hand, I can conquer the world.

I walk out of my office and toward reception, where I see the Bakers waiting. They're facing away from me as I hear Eloise offering them beverages. They both decline.

"Kenneth and Leslie?" I ask. I've learned not to address clients by their last name when there is a divorce involved. It was a lesson I only had to learn once.

The couple turns to me, and I feel all the blood drain from my face. I nearly drop my coffee, but I grip it tightly as I'm faced with the couple that was in the photo on the dresser and in the apartment I woke up in this morning. Now, they're not dressed in their wedding finery or naked in bed. They're dressed normally, and they're equally surprised to see me again.

Two

"OH, FUCK," I say, my filter dissipating without having finished my coffee. I clear my throat, gesturing them to the conference room quickly. The woman looks at me like she can't quite place my face, but recognition lights on Kenneth's face. He remembers me, and from the way his eyes travel my body, he remembers more than just my face.

"I'll be just a minute," I promise, ushering them into the conference room, my voice cracking at the end as I close the door behind them. I walk over to Eloise and put my coffee on the front desk, not trusting myself to not drop it.

"That's them," I whisper, torn between my fight or flight instinct. Can I run?

"Them who?" Eloise asks.

"The couple I slept with last night." My voice sounds strangled, even to my ears.

"Oh, fiddlesticks," Eloise whispers, ducking her head as if they don't know this is happening out here.

"I admire your dedication to not cursing during Lent, but I think if any situation calls for it, it's this one." My whisper is harsh, but I straighten up, pulling on the bottom of my suit jacket.

Eloise covers her mouth with her hand, hiding a giggle now that the awkwardness of the situation has sunk in. I scoop my coffee back up and move toward the conference room.

"Apologies. I'm Ainsley Seaborn. I understand you have requested the services of a divorce mediator." I take a seat opposite them and pretend like Kenneth isn't looking at me like he knows what I look like with my clothes off, even though I know he does. No, I need to focus my attention on what I'm dealing with. Most couples would sit on opposite sides of the table from one another, but these two have opted to sit side by side.

"Are we just going to ignore the big naked elephant in the room?" Kenneth asks. His voice is clear now that it's not coated with sleep. I'm doing my best to just look past him or between them. I can't bring myself to meet their eyes. I'm not ashamed that I slept with them, but I am frustrated that my professional credibility is now in question.

"I would understand if you would like to hire a different attorney based on what transpired last night. I believe I can still provide my impartial opinion, but I leave the decision in your hands." I finally meet Kenneth's eyes and my entire body goes molten. I might still be trying to piece together the exact events of the nights, but I remember his demand to open my eyes as I came on his cock. My hands are shaking when I reach for my coffee in a sad attempt to hide my blush.

"Do you know how hard it is to get an appointment with a divorce mediator in this city?" Leslie asks. I'm jarred by her quiet voice. She has one of those voices that's subtle and soft, but I have no doubt that when she yells, the world shakes.

I do know how hard it is; the only reason I had an opening was because one of my few litigious clients decided it was too expensive to divorce his wife based on the prenup.

"I do," I confirm, waiting for them to voice their agreement to proceed.

"Well, let's get this over with." Kenneth slouches in his seat, gesturing for me to go on.

"Right, well, to start, I want you to tell me a little bit about you two as a couple." I always start small, trying to see what really matters to the couples based on their relationship. It's gotten easy to pinpoint the wives starved for attention or the philandering husbands who just want to make up for their mistakes.

"Here's the thing, as you may have surmised last night, Ken and I actually still love each other a lot." Leslie reaches out and takes Kenneth's hand, giving it a squeeze. He frowns, pulling it out of her grip to reach for a water bottle on the table. "We've just reached an impasse and think it's better for the other if we move forward with someone else."

I stay silent, waiting for them to go on. Not all of my divorces are spurned lovers and people who want to salt the earth with their exes. Sometimes, they're people who truly love one another and they just can't make it work. It actually makes my life so much more difficult because they're so busy bending over backwards to make the other happy that next to nothing gets accomplished.

"We've been together for seven years and suddenly she doesn't want a baby." Kenneth might have less love for Leslie than she thinks, if his tone is any indication. He can barely stand to look at his soon-to-be ex, but when he does, I can see the hurt etched in the lines around his eyes.

"Do you regularly make it a habit to pick people up at a bar together?" The snark slips out of me before I can apply my filter. I reach for my coffee and take another sip. Kenneth's eyes slide to me, and I get the feeling he's seeing a dangerous amount of myself. He's not mad or annoyed, but interested.

"Just the good-looking ones," he says.

A flash of hurt crosses Leslie's face at his words. I wonder if he's acting out because the terms of their agreement changed. Does he even realize it? Does Leslie?

I close the folio in front of me. This is a monumentally bad idea. "I think maybe it would be better if I find you a different attorney," I say, reaching for my phone. "I'm sure I can call in a favor or two and get you in with a different mediator."

"We want you," Leslie insists, her hand reaching out and stopping me. "I think you have what it takes to help get us through this. We need *you*. You handled us both so easily last night; it's hard to find that sort of comfort with someone. I think it will be easier for us both if you say yes."

Kenneth clears his throat. "At least on this, Leslie and I agree."

I'm pretty sure something like this could get me sanctioned at the least, disbarred at the worst. This could definitely get me fired. I'm nothing if not consistent with living my life on the crazy train.

"I need to be perfectly clear that nothing can happen between us again. That what happened was done in the past. It will not influence any decisions made here. I will draft an acknowledgement for all three of us to sign, indicating that what occurred was a onetime consensual occurrence."

"Is that really necessary?" Kenneth asks, sitting up.

I hold my ground. "Absolutely. We haven't even discussed the terms of your divorce. Say one of you is unhappy with the outcome and decides that I played favorites. I could get fired, sanctioned, and disbarred. I am *only* proceeding with this at your behest. Either you sign the form or that's the end of the meeting."

"We'll sign it," Leslie agrees immediately. "Thank you."

"I'll have it drafted by the end of the day. Should you find the verbiage agreeable, you can come to my office to sign before a notary at your leisure." I reopen my folio, grabbing my pen to go back to my notes. "Now, you're divorcing because a difference in opinion regarding future children?"

"Yes. Children were something I thought I wanted, but the older I get, the less I feel inclined. I want Ken to have everything in the world that he wants."

"I wanted a life with you." Kenneth's words are emphatic, but he doesn't reach for Leslie the way she reaches for him. He's careful to keep his hands folded in his lap.

"You can say you would be fine not having children, but I see you in the park. I see you with your sister's kids. You want that, and I can't bear to be the reason you don't have it."

"Okay. Do you have anything else you want to say on the matter of children, Kenneth?" I've been scribbling away on my notepad how I've interpreted their verbal and nonverbal clues.

"No, Leslie has already had the final word."

I glance at Leslie, who looks crestfallen. How many times have they had this conversation about not having children? I can't imagine the pain and agony that rehashing this must feel like.

I've been waffling on how to go about having kids on my own for the last six months. I can't imagine the kind of torture it must be to be ready to grow your family when your partner isn't for eight *years.*

"Okay. You were asked to bring a list of your material assets that have significant worth. Are there any things on the list that you haven't already determined between yourselves how to divide?"

Kenneth snorts at my question as Leslie pulls this list from her purse and slides it to me. I'm thankful that the multiple pages are organized by section. It's detailed down to the size of their paintings and estimated values as well as the square footage of their homes and their realtor assessed value. I'm used to people coming in with scraps of paper and I have to draw details out, like how many designer handbags a wife has or if the husband has a watch collection.

"Wow, I can appreciate a detailed client," I remark, turning the stapled page, studying its contents.

"I'll make it even easier," Kenneth says. "She can have everything but the New York apartment and my instruments. Otherwise, she can have it all: the art, the stupid thousand-dollar shoes, the chalet in Switzerland, the apartment in Paris, the flat in London. I don't care." Kenneth crosses his arms.

"But you love those places. You wanted the apartment in Paris and the chalet," Leslie points out.

"And you wanted children and now don't. I think we can both agree that people can change their minds." Kenneth frowns then checks his watch. "I have to get back to the bar for a delivery. Are we done here?"

"Right. Well, I think this was a promising start," I say, ignoring Kenneth's abrupt dismissal. "Maybe think about exactly which items you would want in the divorce. I want you both to look at the list separate of the other. I'll email it to you, along with a draft of the agreement. Eloise will schedule you for your next appointment in a week. Please coordinate payment of the retainer with her."

Kenneth pushes up out of his seat. "Sure. I'll email her my availability." He clears his throat. "Thank you for agreeing to still work with us." His tone loses the gruffness, and I nod, walking to the conference room door.

I hold my hand out to shake his. "I want to make this as painless and as quick as possible. Once we can get somewhere real with the assets, I can start to draft documents. You need to actually do the assignment and look at what you want. No more grandstanding and throwing a temper tantrum."

Kenneth slides his hand into mine, shaking it, and I remember the feel of his hands all over my body. I have to bury the tremor of arousal that zings up my spine. I really should have turned this down. And yet...

And yet, I didn't, despite how bad this could be for me. I can pretend like it's all because I know how hard it can be to get an appointment, but I can't lie to myself.

I want an excuse to see him again, even if it's just to give me the inspiration to reach for my vibrator.

Leslie comes next, shaking my hand as well. "Really, thank you so much. I promise to keep it all professional and to work on the list. I look forward to your email."

Once they leave, I walk to my office and close the door, wishing I had a pillow to scream into.

I sit at my desk with my head in my hands. I have gotten myself into a unique type of situation and I don't know what to do about it. There isn't a form waiver I can use for having slept with clients. Eloise slips into my office, hip-checking the door closed.

"Do you want to..." She trails off. I've been a mess plenty in the two years that we've worked together, but this takes things to a whole different level.

"Wheezy, I think I'm making a mistake."

"I think that that ship sailed last night when you slept with them."

I glare at her. "I shouldn't have taken this job. I should have stood my ground."

"Okay, well, you clearly recognized them this morning. What do you remember from last night?" Eloise asks. It's an innocent and necessary question, but one I can't answer.

"I remember my Sleepless Nights date standing me up. I remember Leslie approaching me and chatting with me before Kenneth came over. We had a few more drinks and we went back to their apartment. Sex was not on the menu initially. I have vague recollections of kisses and clothes being taken off. Then I woke up in bed with them. I think the rest is self-explanatory." I don't tell her how it felt to feel his body on mine while her mouth was on my neck, a hand on my breast. I wouldn't tell her the torrid details of the night, anyway, like how it felt to be impaled on Kenneth's cock while Leslie sucked my clit.

"I mean, I babysit this file if you feel like you're being swayed?

Keep me in the meetings, and then you can have a witness to your impartiality."

"I think I would literally sink without you in my life. Honestly, Wheezy, you're worth your weight in gold."

"All the best paralegals are. Do you think your friend Taryn can get me a reservation at Claudia Jean's this weekend for brunch?"

"Consider it done. Draft this sex waiver and send it to me for my review."

"On it, Ains!" Eloise pops out of the room to her own desk across from mine. Of all the divorce mediators in this city, why did it have to be me they brought home last night? I want to ask more questions, like if this is something that they regularly do, pick up women or men at bars and take them home. I was so glad that I didn't take them to my own apartment, but god, what hobby to have.

My phone dings and I see it's the guy I was supposed to meet last night. I frown at the message. It's simple, pleading for forgiveness by way of emojis followed by an eggplant and a squirting. Diego stood me up once, but from the pictures he's sent, he has a rocking body and I could use the distraction, especially after last night. I frown, clicking to the 'Behind Closed Doors' part of the app, where consenting adults can share illicit pictures if they want. There is a security protocol there that doesn't allow screenshots, but there are other ways around that, of course. The lawyer in me hates it, but it's a convenient way to hide unwanted dick pics that are inevitably sent. Outside of emojis, no pictures can be shared in the messages part of the app.

This dick pic was not unwanted and, honestly, was part of the reason I agreed to go on the date. He's a minor league baseball player, swearing up and down that he's about to be called into the majors to play for the Yankees. I blow out a frustrated breath, looking at the picture he just sent, his hand is wrapped around himself, the tip brimming with cum.

I agree to meet with him, his last chance, but I won't go back to that bar and risk running into my clients again. I choose a different part of town and ask for his availability. It's springtime, so I know baseball has started.

If the man is that ready to blow his load, maybe I play roulette with having sex with him tonight. He's athletic and built, but I can make the final determination when I meet him in person. For a woman who's thinking about getting pregnant, I've been terrible at tracking my cycle and even remembering to take my birth control. I keep telling myself that if I want to get pregnant badly enough, I'll just stop taking my pill, but that feels too much like possibly baby-trapping a man, and I won't do that to another person. Maybe part of me hopes that carelessness will take the decision out of my hands.

My date doesn't hesitate to say tomorrow night, which is a relief. Tonight, I need to go home and take a nice, long shower. The day feels sluggish and slow as I wait for Eloise to send the draft. I have several more meetings with couples who are much more complicated, trying to divide kids and assets and pets.

I want my day to be over and consider cutting out early, until an email requesting a time to sign the sex waiver pings in my inbox. It only serves as a reminder that I'm still not wearing underwear.

I swing side to side in my chair, contemplating meeting with Kenneth again today. The night feels too fresh, the memory of his tousled hair and bedroom voice as he told me where he lived makes my skin burn.

I told myself I would be a professional. I am not going to think about his hands between my legs and the feel of her soft skin under mine and...I stop my movement to respond to the email, scheduling a time for next week before their next session. I need some time and space from the Bakers and work should be the perfect cure for that.

Three

THE BAR that Diego picked for our do-over is this annoyingly trendy spot on the Lower East Side. The name is familiar, but I assume it's because I must have heard someone talking about it. It has this rustic look to it, like it's more dive-bar than Top Bars to Hit in NYC Tonight, and it is definitely not the type of place I would pick myself.

I have brunch scheduled for tomorrow with Taryn, Vivian, and Elia, a nice mixture of old friends and new friends, and I'm hoping I get to regale with tales of Diego's home-run cock. Maybe if I talk about that, Elia won't have a chance to ask why I showed up in her apartment before eight a.m. doing the walk of shame.

I spent hours picking out the right lingerie for tonight. I started on Sleepless Nights because it seemed like the easiest way I could get a feel for what I was definitely not looking for in a husband and baby daddy. It seemed easier to set myself up to fail there than to try for something real on Happily Ever Afters.

Really, my date with Diego is a stalling tactic. If I want a baby, I need to get serious about it. This weekend, I'm going to work on really looking into it. Fertility doctors and different types of treatments and what exactly I can expect from being a mom. In the six months since I decided to go down this path, Mr. Right has failed to make himself known.

I settle in at the bar, ordering a dry vodka martini with three olives while I wait for Diego. Being stood up once means that I'm not going to waste my time waiting for him to show without something to drink. The bartender places my nearly twenty-dollar drink down in front of me in a mini mason jar, and I hate this place all the more.

When I hit the twenty-minutes-late mark, I start to flirt with the bartender, flipping the hair that it took me forty-five minutes to curl over my shoulder. He looks on the younger side, but he's been winking at me with each flip of the bottle, giving me an extra olive with each drink. At thirty minutes late, I slip into the stock room with him.

My red dress is hiked up around my waist and my panties are on the floor. I make sure to note where he drops them. I've already lost one pair this week; I'm not in the mood to set any records. There is no foreplay, there is just raw need as he slides a condom over the length of his cock and plunges into me. I stifle the urge to cry out by biting my lip, gripping the metal storage racks on either side of me. Our hips move in unison until we're both satisfied, which is a lot more than I expected. He winks at me as he withdraws.

"Next round is on the house," he says, like he's given me the best gift in the world.

I scoff at him as I pull up my panties. "Try I drink free for the rest of the night." I tug down my dress, smoothing it out. I touch at the corners of my lips and he gives me a nod, confirming that my makeup is still right where I put it.

"I can do something like that if you promise to come back." He winks again, leading me out.

"I can promise I'll come again for sure." My double entendre carries no weight. There is no way I am coming back to this god-forsaken hipster hideout. As I leave the back room with the bartender, I walk right into another patron, and I want the world to swallow me whole.

"Miss Ainsley Seaborn. Fancy meeting you here." Kenneth's smooth voice catches me off guard and my flight instinct wants to send me back into that storeroom, but the bartender has already locked the door behind me.

"Mr. Baker. Of all the gin joints." I give a nervous laugh. "I don't want to hold you back from your evening." I hurry away from him, my heart slamming in my chest, back to the bar where a fresh drink is being placed right where I was sitting. I slam it back, signaling for another when Kenneth takes the seat beside me, where a beer and some chips are waiting for him. A lot happened in the five minutes since I left.

"Care to join me?" Kenneth offers and I balk.

"We should keep things professional," I say, grabbing my drink and my purse. A quick glance at my phone tells me that Diego hasn't responded to any of my messages and I'm done waiting. All the free drinks in the world are not worth staying and talking to Kenneth.

Each time our eyes meet, I'm reminded of the comfortable feeling of his arm banded around my middle in sleep. Just thinking about that night sets my heart racing and my skin ablaze. This needs to stay professional, because look in his eyes makes me think I should let him drag me into that storeroom to have his way with me.

"I think you already had your needs met for the night. Besides, it seems like I'm destined to be your knight in shining armor again. I'm guessing you got stood up...*again*." Kenneth's voice isn't unkind, so I drop back onto the stool.

"Is it that obvious?" I ask, setting my drink back on the bar.

"That you were waiting for someone who clearly didn't make it? Yes. That you just fucked the bartender? Only because I caught you and Lyle sneaking out of the back room."

"You know the bartender's name?" I ask, realizing I didn't even know that.

"Only because I hired him."

This bar, the name–I realize now why it sounded familiar. It was in Kenneth's file.

"Then you really need to work on getting real drinkware," I say, lifting my mason jar in his direction.

An easy smile engulfs his face and I want that smile directed at me again and again and again.

"I'll take it up with management."

I take a sip from my drink, wildly uncomfortable with the fact that not only have I had sex with my client, but I've also had sex in his bar. Really killing it at the professionalism thing. Why he wants to stay my client, I have no idea.

"I'm sorry. You shouldn't fire him or anything," I say trying to feign coolness.

"I won't, but he will have a talking to about having sex with patrons *again*." Kenneth's tone is pointed as he locks eyes with Lyle, who immediately looks away.

"I should settle up." I reach for my purse to drop some cash on the bar.

"Don't leave on my account, Miss Seaborn." His hand rests on mine and my skin burns where we touch. My brain is screaming at me to move my fucking arm, but I can't. I'm enjoying how it feels to have his hands on me.

"Ainsley, please," I tell him reflexively. "I really should go, anyway. I think this is the universe's way of telling me to call it a night, Mr. Baker."

"If you're Ainsley then you should call me Ken."

I roll the nickname over in my mind. Ken always brings to mind Barbie's ex-boyfriend, with his plastic body and missing junk. But this Ken is nothing like the plastic counterpart. I can vividly remember that he is not lacking in the junk department. I don't even realize I've bit my lower lip as my eyes dropped to his lips, pink and full, until his hand reaches out, his thumb grazing my skin. It's enough to jolt me back to myself. Finally, I pull back my arm, reaching for my hips as if I'm not wearing a skin-tight dress and my phone might be in a non-existent pocket.

"I really should go," I repeat, looking into my wallet and dropping cash on the bar to pay for my last drinks.

He seems to realize that things have gone a step too far because he lets me go. "I'm sorry if I've crossed any boundaries and made you uncomfortable. I'll admit to being in unfamiliar territory," Ken confesses.

I soften, nodding. "Divorce is hard. It's clear you still love your wife, which is why you hired me."

"No, it's not that. It's more the opposite of that."

Something in his tone makes me sit down. It's clear that he has something on his mind from the faraway look in his eyes. "You don't still love her?

"No, I don't. I mean, I love her the same way I love my sister, with deep affection and respect. It's not just that; we've lived an unconventional lifestyle. I've forgotten what normal boundaries look like."

"Normal boundaries? You mean you don't expect you and your next wife will be picking people up in bars together?"

He laughs, and it's a deep rumble. I want to surround myself with the sound. I think I need a spray bottle on hand so I can be sprayed like a cat on bad behavior anytime I have impure thoughts about this man.

"I mean, when I married Leslie, I wanted different things from my life. I was clear when things changed for me. I told her when I wanted to have children and that I wanted a more exclusive life-style. She told me that she just needed another year, another year, and then another year to get it out of her system before wanting kids and then she finally said, 'You know what? I don't want kids. I don't want to get pregnant. I like my life and I don't want to change a thing.' And I respect the hell out of her for knowing what she wants and being uncompromising. She gets a thrill from having multiple partners, and I won't begrudge her what makes her happy, but I'm also entitled to my own happiness."

I'm going to regret it, but I reach out and touch his hand anyway. "It's natural for couples to grow apart, and it's not an easy decision to make. It sounds like you tried to make it work."

Ken takes a sip of his beer, turning my words over in his head. "The writing was on the wall for too long. A child isn't a puppy. You can't half-ass it, with someone else doing the minding. I mean, sure, nannies are an option, but I know Leslie. She would want to be a mother, more than just an egg donor. It's not fair to her. The Broadway sets she creates are her babies. It's been harder to let go of all aspects of the life we shared." There is an insinuation in his tone that I don't miss.

"Like taking home young divorce attorneys?" My tone is flirty, and I need to shut this back down, but I don't.

"You looked sad, and honestly, at first it wasn't about ravishing you with my wife. What's your story? Liquor usually makes people's lips looser, but you're locked up tight."

Another insinuation I don't miss. I am tightly wound, choosing liquor and sex as my way to unwind, but even then. His hand rests on my shoulder, waiting to see if I push him away. When I don't, he rises and digs his fingertips into my skin, massaging my aching muscles. I make a sinful noise in response.

"To be fair, my ex-fiancé got married a few months ago."

Ken winces at my words, his hand continuing to work the knot in my neck. He's close, too close, but by now I've had too many vodka martinis and I'm not turning him away.

"What kind of idiot would let you slip through his fingers?"

"Charlie. He's really not a bad guy, and I really love his wife. I actually went to their wedding, but he's different with her than he was with me. He was a finance bro who was always, always working. Sure, we could have a penthouse facing Central Park on his salary, but I don't want that life for me or my children."

"I'm guessing you want kids?" It's a natural question, and I think about how to answer it for a minute. My eyes drift closed as I focus on the feel of his hand. His hand, Ken's hand, Kenneth Baker's hand, my client's hand. My eyes shoot open and I roll my shoulder, a stop-touching-me gesture. He releases me but waits for an answer.

"I do. I always thought that I needed to be married for that to happen, but now I'm thinking I forgo the husband and try a turkey-baster baby."

"Well, you can find a better gene pool than my bartender."

I laugh and sip my drink. "I really should be going now that I have told you, my client, something I haven't even told my best friends." Taryn said she thought I would make a great mom someday, but I haven't admitted how soon I want someday to be. I hop off the stool to stand beside Ken and I'm startled by the height difference. I'm looking up at him, realizing that I could climb him like a jungle-gym with the excuse of not hurting my neck to look up at him. A flash of memory from our night together reminds me that I did just that.

"I'm sorry if I pushed boundaries by asking you that. My therapist wants me to work on it," he tells me sheepishly.

"Your therapist?" I question. It's not every day that a man admits to seeing someone for his mental health. As much as I wish it were the norm, it's simply not.

"Yeah, I've been seeing one for a few years, probably when Leslie and I started to have problems. I wanted to talk it out with someone. Eventually, he correctly pointed out that since becoming a bartender, I'm used to getting involved in people's lives when sometimes I shouldn't. Not that I'm doing anything wrong, but sometimes people want to come and not talk about their problems. Hence, the need to establish boundaries."

"I am happy to let you practice boundaries with me. If I'm honest, I'm not the best with them, either."

"Do you need me to call you a cab?" He looks hopeful, not

ready to end our interaction. I'm honestly not ready either, but I have to leave if I want to keep my job and my sanity.

"I'll just order a car from PickMeUp! No ride sharing; just a black car for me," I reassure him.

Ken leans down, pressing a kiss to the corner of my mouth. "I'll start practicing boundaries tomorrow."

I just need to get through the next few weeks of wanting this man, and then after his divorce is finalized, I won't have to be faced with the idea of seeing him constantly. It's like Lent on steroids.

"Get home safe."

I nod, ambling toward the front door. I can feel his eyes on me the whole way.

Claudia Jean's is packed, which doesn't surprise me. It's prime brunch time in springtime New York City and we're thankfully seated on the street due to some excellent connections. I'm lucky to have built friendships with these women: Elia, Charlie's new wife, Taryn, my friend from college, and Vivian, my old roommate. Before Elia's bachelorette party, Vivian wanted us all to bond, so we decided to make this a monthly get-together. Some months are harder than others, but this time, everything worked out smoothly.

"Are you still boning my brother-in-law?" Elia asks Taryn before the mimosas are even served.

Taryn snorts. "No, we actually stopped before the wedding." The final nail in that coffin had been during Elia's bachelorette party when Taryn was already pulling away from Brad.

"Believable, except that I caught you two fucking in the pool," Vivian retorts.

"Okay, but that was all the romance in the air. It's actually over, for real. I'm starting my big girl job after this semester and he's taking another semester off to do legal aid in Haiti or something, which is super admirable, but I went to Columbia to find a rich dick to marry, and I do mean that both ways," Taryn says with a laugh.

I try not to draw attention to myself. Maybe Elia will forget, but for a woman who had amnesia, she doesn't forget anything. She waits for the waiter to leave with our brunch order to ask her questions.

"So, tell us more about your early shower at my apartment on Wednesday morning," Elia leads.

Vivian and Taryn both sip their drinks expectantly. It would seem a little birdy already prepped them for this conversation.

"You're an asshole," I say with a laugh, tearing off a chunk of bread.

"You promised," she reminds me, grabbing her own drink. Her engagement ring and wedding band sparkle in the light, and I feel a surge of love, not jealousy, for the circumstances that brought this resilient woman into my life.

"Fine, fine. I was stood up by my Sleepless Nights date on Tuesday night and got to chatting with this couple by the bar, and I sort of went home with them." I take a sip of my drink, watching my friends' faces.

"Like, with both of them?" Vivian asks, her eyebrows high, curious but not judgmental. Her auburn hair glints as she tosses it over her shoulder.

"Achievement unlocked," Taryn says with a grin. She and I had unofficially competed in college to see who could have sex in the most public spaces. I feel like for her, this is a side quest that just got unlocked in her nerdy little brain.

"Yes, with both of them, and they are also now my clients in their divorce mediation." I drain my drink and raise the empty glass at the waitress as she walks by. She sees how my friends' glasses are equally as empty and takes off to get refills.

"That's complicated," is Taryn's understatement of the year.

"I mean, are you still taking them on?" Vivian asks, chewing her lower lip.

Elia has remained suspiciously quiet and when I glance at her, I see she has a thoughtful look on her face.

"Yes, they're signing a waiver and I am clearly not going to be doing that again, but I am on very shaky ground," I admit.

"That sounds, like, not good enough. You should do what you can to get this one done as quickly as possible," Vivian warns as the next round of drinks are served.

"Thank you, Captain Obvious. I would love to do that, but they refuse to use a different attorney," I say with a frown.

"Why not?" Vivian pushes.

"Because it's impossible to get a quick appointment with someone who is as good as I am. No one has availability, and I'm quick enough that I am available more often."

"Listen, you and I both know that an affidavit like that isn't worth the paper it's written on. You need to CYA and end this." Vivian's voice is almost shaking, and I can see the way my situation is making her anxiety rise. She's giving me a look that tells me that she knows I'm full of shit. I could have had someone else in the practice take this one case; we do have another family law attorney, but I don't share well.

"Of course, I'm going to cover my ass. I will not be interacting with them outside the office ever again. Their divorce seems cut and dried with the division of assets, so all I have to do is get this signed and over with. The hardest part is going to be getting them to be selfish about their property. Then I will never have to see them again." I try to keep the edge out of my voice, but I don't appreciate being made to feel like the asshole or the idiot in this situation.

"Of course," Elia cuts in soothingly. I don't miss the look she shoots Vivian, who promptly takes a deep breath and leans back in her seat.

"Sorry, I know you're not an idiot This just...you could be

disbarred. It's at the very least a conflict of interest and the number one thing on our ethics test before we're sworn in," Vivian pushes.

"I am *well* aware of that, but I had no idea they were going to be my clients at the time. They also had not signed a retainer letter or paid any money at the time of the coupling. It was a prior sexual relationship that ended before I was hired, so as long as I don't sleep with them now, which I won't, I'm in the clear."

Taryn bangs her knife on the table. "I demand order in my court. Enough fighting. Ainsley is going to do what Ainsley does best, toe the line of appropriate and inappropriate and look like a boss bitch while doing it. She got the same law school education, so trust her to know what she's doing."

It's a big claim from Taryn, and I appreciate her support, but like in most things in my life, I have no idea what I'm doing.

"I appreciate your concern, but I'm fine. Really, at the most they're going to be my clients for a month. What could go wrong?"

"You realize that literally any time someone says that it gets so, so much worse," Taryn points out.

I can only hope she's wrong.

Eloise deals with getting the sex waiver signed, since I'm not willing to face Ken or Leslie. I will have to eventually, but I would rather put it off as long as possible. Our next scheduled meeting isn't for another week, and I could use some space from them. Instead, I'll focus on trying to achieve my own goals. I have to admire Ken's decision to go for what he wants. But the thought of Ken, of how it felt even just to have his hands massaging my neck, makes me bite my lip.

I click over into the computer browser I was looking at. A couple I'm working with now is divorcing with a lot of bad feelings between them. They involved me only after their lawyers were struggling with getting them to come to an agreement regarding their prior IVF treatments.

She's arguing that the funds used for the treatment were paid exclusively from her savings account after years of being unable to conceive a child. It turned out later that the husband was manipulating the entire situation after he had gotten a vasectomy years before the treatments began. They spent years and countless tests for her to go through more tests and treatments to figure out why they were unable to get pregnant. The wife wants her husband to pay her back those monies uselessly spent on specialists.

I'm reading about the processes and the pain that this poor woman endured, and at some point the research becomes less about this couple and more about what it would entail for me to undergo. Eloise taps on my door and I quickly close my tab, aware of how guilty I must look.

"Can I help you with something?" I ask, spinning to face her.

"Why do you have that 'I've been caught looking at porn on my computer at work?' look on your face?" Eloise asks, plopping into her chair. She props her feet up on my desk like it's her own.

"I have not been, but thanks for your concern."

She purses her lips, disbelievingly. "Both your lovers signed the sex waiver. I have had them signed, witnessed, and notarized."

"Well, aren't you helpful." I give her a fake smile and she gives me a wicked grin in response. She's only made these teasing jabs behind my office door. She knows I want to make the case for partner this year, and this situation would hardly help me get it.

"It's not every day that your boss walks into the office saying that she *thinks* she had a threesome and then that's the couple she's representing. I have to say, I'm here for the comedic antics."

"There will be no more comedic antics. Strictly professional," I say, taking one of the signed forms and filing it in my drawer. Not exactly something I would hang up next to my law degree, but right now I would argue it is of equal value.

I haven't confided in Eloise or my friends about running into Ken at his bar after being stood up again. It was fluke, and I'm content to leave it at that. Manhattan is a large island. What are the chances I run into him again?

"I just don't understand why you ladies get such big salaries if all you do is *gossip*."

Eloise scowls at me when Kyle Stonewall sticks his head into my office. It doesn't matter that my door was mostly closed. He just bulldozes his way into every situation he can.

As a second-year associate, he gets more face time with the partners than I do. I would be concerned, but he's still a baby lawyer, which means there is no way that he will get promoted to partner before me. When the time comes to try for partner, there isn't anyone else at the firm who could be competition.

"We actually are working, Kyle. I know that seems foreign to you since you just flit from one partner's office to another."

Unfortunately, he takes my rebuke as an invitation into my office. He strolls in and stands behind Eloise, resting his hands on her shoulders. She goes tense immediately as he digs his thumbs into her shoulders.

"Hands off, Stonewall," I demand, glancing from Eloise to Kyle.

"If Eloise doesn't like it, she can tell me to stop herself. She's a big girl." He doesn't fucking stop.

I remember those early days at a job when it felt like there was no option but to laugh at the sexist jokes and realize that you held no power as an intern or a first-year associate. You had to just accept when you saw an email that called you and other female associates "bitches" or when a male in the office made an uncomfortable remark about how many women he banged. To get by, you needed to prove you were cool enough to hang with the guys, which meant letting go of comments like that.

I know Eloise and other women in the office have expressed their concerns to me about it. We don't have a human resources department to complain to; most small firms don't. There is no one Eloise can turn to about how Kyle touching her made her feel, and how she doesn't want him to do it again.

There is no one who will do anything about it, because going to the partners is pointless. There will be comments about how he doesn't mean anything by it, or that it's all in good fun, or that she should be flattered that he would show her that sort of attention. As if there is something defective about her for not wanting to be touched without invitation.

I should get out of this firm. If I'm being honest with myself, I should have left the firm a long ass time ago. There are moments when my job here feels like a bad long-term relationship– there is comfort in the familiar, even if I've recognized that I've outgrown it. It's that same comfort with the status quo, the devil you know, that's holding me back from actually jumping on having a baby.

"I actually remember now that I have paperwork to do on the Jefferson divorce," Eloise announces, rising. The Jefferson divorce was finalized last year, not that I'm going to call her out on it. No sooner is she out of the seat then Kyle is sliding into it.

"Did you hear that we just hired someone that handles employment law? His name is literally Eddie Vedder. I heard they're hiring him as a partner."

I should win a motherfucking Oscar for not reacting.

Of course, my bosses are hiring another man. *Of course*, they're not only hiring him, but making him a partner ahead of me, someone who has been with the firm since I graduated law school. *Of course*, Kyle knows this before me since his uncle is one of the partners and Kyle is one of their little lapdogs. It simply wouldn't do to have as blatant a case of nepotism as hiring him as a partner fresh out of law school so they have to make it look like he's having to earn the title.

"Good for the firm. I know they want to expand there." My voice sounds like a serial killer's. So maybe no Oscar for me.

"I'm also hearing they're talking about adding another partner.

I'm thinking it could have your name all over it." He's watching me as he divulges this information, like a cat stalking a mouse. Kyle is giving me a false sense of security, waiting for me to think I have the upper hand to maybe reveal to him that I'm looking for jobs elsewhere.

As if I was born yesterday.

"Thanks for the heads-up." I keep my tone dismissive and then look back at the papers I have on my desk. I take this information with a grain of salt. It's constantly being discussed that there could be a new partner. A lowly associate raised above their station to all new heights.

"I see how when it's gossip about getting plowed last night, you have time to chat, but when it's actually work, you don't have the time of day." Kyle gets up abruptly and plants his hands on my desk, leaning close to me.

I meet his stare, refusing to lean back. "I have a lunch meeting I need to get to, if you don't mind."

Kyle eases back with a fake smile. "Of course, Ainsley, I wouldn't want to keep you from a midday rendezvous with your flavor of the week."

I get out of my chair and step around my desk to be toe-to-toe with him. Moments like this make me hate that I took after my mother's stature and not my father's, but it doesn't matter. If my father taught me anything, it was how to carry big dick energy.

"You might be able to get away with speaking to other women in this office like that, but don't for one second think that I won't get a restraining order for harassment and make sure it's papered all over the law journals."

I don't break eye contact first. Kyle is the one to look away and move toward my door with a laugh.

"Don't take everything so seriously, Seaborn. I'll catch you at the meeting this afternoon after your 'lunch meeting.'" With a wink, he saunters out of my office.

It's slimebags like him that make me wonder if I even want to go for partner here. But I tell myself the same thing I've been telling myself for months now: if I make partner, I can get a new job out of here that much easier.

It just means I have a few more things to look forward to this year.

Four

I'M SECRETLY DREADING my next meeting with the Bakers. It's more than just the flirtation with Ken; it's the attraction I feel to him. On Friday afternoon, I check my calendar and see I'm scheduled to meet with them again the following Thursday. Their homework is to make a list of their property and who gets what. I also asked them separately via email to detail what they would give the other. I asked them to stop with the selfless crap and to be honest. If my first meeting was any indication, they're going to be a huge pain in my ass with regard to division of assets. Some things should be straightforward, like his bar, but their homes won't be.

Eloise is sitting at her desk when I grab my jacket and bag.

"Exciting plans this weekend?" I ask, leaning over the edge of her cubicle.

"I'm actually going to a By the Edge concert tonight, and I'm already running late to meet my friends." Eloise slips out of her heels and into a pair of sneakers, meant for speed-walking to the train.

"I won't hold you then. Have a good weekend." I follow her out to the elevators.

"Was there something you needed?" Eloise presses the call button for the elevator.

"Not at all. Just checking to see what you had going on."

A few hours earlier, two of the partners took all the male associates and our spring interns out for drinks, just the men. They're not going to make my bid for partner easy. After all, I'm missing one key piece of anatomy to fit into their club. I've seen younger men brought on as partners ahead of me.

"Do you have anything special planned?" she asks with a mischievous grin, no doubt expecting me to talk about going out for dates and drinks.

"Nope. I have a quiet night at home planned. I'll hopefully read a book or catch up on Streamz shows."

Eloise hides her shock well. I can't blame her. We've done almost daily postmortems on various dates I've been on, but none of them have felt good enough for me to want to make a child with.

Until Ken.

I don't know where that thought comes from, but it hits me with a ferocity that spills color onto my cheeks. Quickly, I mentally check myself. It's just because I know he wants to have children that is sending my ovaries into overdrive. Though, I can imagine a kid with his cleft chin and stunning eyes, with my smile and hair. The kid would be set in the looks department for sure.

"That sounds riveting," Eloise teases and I clue myself back in to our conversation after that wild train of thought derailment.

"You disapprove?" I ask as we get onto the elevator. "Not at all. I think I'm a little envious."

"You could always stay in, maybe come have a movie marathon with me?"

Eloise has always been more friend than subordinate, and this wouldn't be the first time we've gone back to my place and bitched about work over takeout.

"And miss my chance to make a move on Leo Edge? Not a

chance." Eloise gives me a big grin when the elevator stops on the ground floor.

"Isn't he the only one of them that's married?" I point out.

"Good thing I know a *really* good divorce attorney." Eloise gives me a suggestive wink as we step into the cool spring air.

"Happy to help. Anything for my favorite paralegal."

"Yeah, yeah. Remember that when it comes time for raises or the next time you're at Nordstrom." She checks her phone again.

"Run. Go!" I waver her off, and she runs.

I'm not ready to start my weekend of solitude, so I stop by Nordstrom to get Eloise a purse, and then I turn off my cell phone to completely disconnect.

I meander out on Saturday morning for a coffee and to check out a street fair that's shut down a few blocks of the city. For the most part, there are a lot of food booths set up, helping to overwhelm the trash scent.

I'm looking at a booth with jewelry, shopping from afar while I walk, when I hear my name called. For a moment, I think it's my imagination, until the crowd parts and I see Ken Baker, and...

Fuck.

Why does he have to look so damn fine in a white t-shirt that stretches over his muscles? They seem to go on and on, with his pecs and down his abs. Those are what they mean when they describe washboard abs. I feel like I could scrub a stain out on them, but really all I want to do is touch and touch them.

"Well, if it isn't Ainsley Seaborn."

I look up into his face and grimace. It's the best I can do after being caught ogling my client.

"Kenneth Baker. Lovely running into you." It is a lie. It is not lovely. It is a temptation that I do not want and do not need, not when we're meeting on Thursday to go over his divorce papers.

I wonder if it will be too conspicuous to just walk past him, but he's looking at me like he wants to spread me out on his table and eat me for lunch. My hussy of a vagina wants him to.

"What brings you out here?" he presses.

I glance at his friend, a good-looking, polished man. He's distinguished and seems vaguely familiar. There is a streak of silver along his temples that only makes him more tempting. He's white with dark brown eyes and brown hair, and I know I would remember if I had tapped that. The ring on his finger confirms I haven't, but I can't muse on it any longer because I have to actually answer Ken's question.

"I was just in the neighborhood, doing some light meandering."

"No date?" Ken asks.

His friend glances at him and raises an eyebrow. Sensing the shift of Ken pressing for more than I might be willing to share, his friend steps forward and offers me his hand.

"I'm Howie. It's nice to meet you. I think Ken said your name was Ainsley?"

We shake, but I can see that Ken is nearly bothered by this as he runs his hands through his hair.

"Sorry, I forgot myself. This is my brother-in-law, Howie. He's in town for work, and I promised I would show him around. You should join us," Ken offers, but I'm already shaking my head and taking a step back.

"I should let you two be." I have to force myself to continue to step away from them because I want to see Ken again. But I know that I have to do this right and by the book and at the very least I have to wait until I finish with the paperwork. I was able to get the initial filing done, and given the lack of hiccups, I'm hoping this will be on the faster end of my cases.

"You don't have to," Ken offers again, and I can see something in his face too. He enjoyed my company just as much as I enjoyed his and in more than the carnal way.

No, if I'm going to do this, I'm doing it right.

"Let the poor girl have her weekend back without you harassing her," Howie teases, nudging Ken's shoulder. "Besides, I need to find something for Apple, and if I want to avoid spending thousands of dollars, I need to find her something unique here."

"My suggestion is that there are gorgeous acorn gem necklaces back the way I came. Hopefully you can find something there."

Ken shoves his hands in his pockets, and I can feel his gaze as clearly as I felt his hands that night as his eyes travel from my ankles up to my face. The amount of effort it takes to keep from going to him is considerable enough that I want to just go home and crawl into bed with a dirty book and my favorite vibrator.

"Of course," Ken agrees, nodding his head so vigorously, I'm afraid he's going to give himself whiplash. "I'll see you on Thursday."

Ken and Howie walk past me, with Ken intentionally brushing against me. There is a moment as he does it when I look up into his eyes and I know that I'm totally sunk for this man.

"Earth to Ainsley?"

I glance up into my father's eyes, noting from his brusque tone that I must have missed him saying my name several times.

"Yes, Daddy, sorry. You were saying?"

"I was saying, you need to decide if you're going to stay at that firm and go for partner or let me make a few phone calls for my favorite girl."

My lips twist into a frown. "I told you I don't want you meddling."

Leaning back in his chair, my father smooths his tie so the

waiter can clear his appetizer plate. "Is it so bad that I want the best for you?"

Ever since my parents divorced and my mother left the two of us, we've been close, but it's meant that my dad isn't the best at staying out of my business. Like when I was fundraising for my sorority, my father would swoop in with a check for the full amount or the time he took it upon himself to have a meeting with the dean of Harvard Law when I was applying. Nothing like having a giant of a man with a bank account more than 300 times the endowment of your school knocking on your door to tell you his daughter is applying.

"Of course, it's not. But I like to do things on my own merits."

"I let Charlie walk away with both kneecaps after your engagement ended. I think that was rather big of me."

I'm sipping my drink when he says this, and I have to fight not to aspirate the wine. "I know we've talked about this. *I* ended the relationship. You had no reason to cut him off at the knees."

"Your tears said otherwise."

It was the first time since graduating college that I moved back in with my dad, even if it was only for a few months until I found my own place. There was a certain comfort of going home to our apartment and knowing he was there when I needed him.

"Can we not revisit the past? I'm going to try for partner. I think I can get it. I want to get it, but I'm worried about the timing."

My father sips his gin and tonic, patiently waiting for me to continue.

"I've been thinking that I want to have a baby."

This is the type of conversation that I would think occurs between a couple or, if not a couple, with friends, but I know that I'll need my father's support. If I'm setting out to be a single mother, I know that I'll need people in my corner. Money can buy a lot of things, but I'm sure it's not enough where a child is concerned.

"Are you already pregnant or should I keep the date I have scheduled for you next Friday with Parker Worthington?"

My lips twist into a scowl, but I don't give him a "no." I know Parker Worthington by reputation but not personally. From what I've seen of him at various events over the years, I know he's a stud. He's well-educated and smart beyond belief. I know he started his company with money from his grandfather, but he's grown it into a billion-dollar company.

Maybe he could be my stud.

"I'll entertain this date, if only because I'm sure this is really a favor to someone."

"It's a favor to my daughter, who I want to see settled down in my old age."

"You're fifty-three."

He pauses as his filet mignon is placed in front of him and I'm served my order of lamb chops. "You say that like I'm Benjamin Button and aging in reverse. I want to take these grandchildren you're talking about on the yacht and be able to do a cannonball with them without needing a doctor on call."

"Considering you've never done a cannonball in my lifetime, I might have to speed up that timeline just to witness it."

"You do that, but you have my full support for whatever you need."

I can't answer him because suddenly, I have too many emotions fighting their way out of me. When he and my mother divorced, he took time off work to be with me so we could figure it out. He wanted to make sure I never felt the absence of both parents. Rather than leave me to a nanny full-time, he made himself available to me and we took a trip to Europe just us.

It's why when he sets me up on dates, I go. It's why when he asks me to attend galas or go out of town, I go. He gave me the world, even though he was practically a kid himself.

"I'll let you know what I plan on doing. I'm sort of just testing the waters."

"Like when you were testing the waters about eloping during law school?"

I choke on my glass of wine. "What are you, an elephant? How the hell do you remember that?"

My father looks smug. "It's not every day that your only child calls you and tells you that she's catching a flight to Vegas to wed some guy named Sam."

"His name was Sean and you know that." Twenty-two was too old to pull such teenage antics just in a bid to get my dad's attention. It worked, too. He had been in Russia working on securing an exclusive contract to distribute a brand of vodka, and he turned around and flew home. I never did elope with Sean like I threatened, but it got my dad to visit me for the first time in three months.

"I do. He's a good kid, Sean. How is he doing lately?"

"This conversation isn't about Sean or my youthful temper tantrums. Wanting to be a mom isn't some phase."

My dad reaches his hand across the table to take mine. "I know that, jellyfish. I wasn't trying to trivialize what you want in life. I only wanted to poke fun. I see I've gone too far, and for that I'm sorry."

When our plates are cleared, he refocuses on me. "What is the tentative plan for this? I know a few names in the industry that I could reach out to for you."

"I'm thinking that I'll need to go to a sperm bank. I was hoping that I could hit it off with one of my many dates, but..."

Since breaking up with Charlie, I haven't tried very hard to find something serious. Even after deciding that I wanted to have a baby, the thought terrified me so much that I continued to pick fuckboys to sleep around with–men who were good looking, but no one that I felt confident enough to want to follow up with, confident enough to want to have them father my child.

Except maybe Ken.

Ugh.

Stupid, stupid brain. I need to stop thinking about him.

"That look on your face tells me that you have someone on your mind."

I lift my gaze to my father, and in keeping with my attitude trend of the evening, I stick my tongue out. "Get out of my head."

He shrugs as the waiter places a crème brûlée between us to share. This table, this meal, this restaurant, we have a standing reservation every two weeks to come. It forces us to have a meaningful conversation and not just fill our talks with idle chitchat.

"It's not my fault you wear your emotions on your face, or maybe it is. I can't decide. You do have half my genes, after all." He smugly leans back in his seat, pushing the rest of the crème brûlée toward me after his perfunctory two bites.

"And now he fashions himself a comedian too."

"I don't fashion myself as anything, I just dress in whatever is in my closet." He says this with a straight face.

"The dad jokes are not cute," I scold, pointing my spoon at him before scooping up the last of the deliciousness.

"Well, I have to practice again for when they become granddad jokes."

My father is laughing on that one all the way out the door.

Five

I WEAR my dowdiest outfit for my meeting with the Bakers on Thursday. My palazzo pants are a dark grey, and I have a deep red blouse tucked into them. The top is light and breezy, with long sleeves and an attached necktie styled in a bow.

"Leslie, Ken, so nice to see you again," I say, pushing open the door to the main conference room.

They did exactly what I expected them to do when it came to their assets. I had them email me earlier this week, and they both tried to give each other most of their things. A few items, they did say they wanted to themselves. Ken claimed his bar Leslie put dibs on some artwork, but otherwise, they're making my life harder.

I sent an email in response to them both, asking them to please look again. The second time around, they got a little closer to fair. Today, we will actually be going down the list, marking items to sell if they can't make a decision.

"Ainsley, you absolutely have to come to our divorce reception!" Leslie says as I take my seat.

Eloise, who is opening a document on her laptop, actually guffaws at the statement.

"I'm sorry, divorce reception?" I ask, casting a look at Eloise.

Her face immediately schools itself back to that of a consummate professional.

"Yes! They're all the rage. With your experience, I'm surprised you haven't been invited to one before. We just have one more meeting after this, right? We're planning to have the party around Memorial Day."

"That could work. Once you sign the documents, they still need to be submitted and signed off by a judge. This can take up to six months, but I know a few people, and if you two stop playing the martyr, then I can make this happen."

"So, Labor Day instead? I can put off moving…" Leslie lets the question trail off as she looks to her husband for guidance. Her husband. It's a good reminder that I need to get my head out of my ass and focus on my job, not Ken. Not the things I know he can do with his tongue.

"You can have your party whenever you want and start your post married life at any point. I just wanted to let you know that the ink won't necessarily be dry until the judge signs the divorce judgment."

Ken swivels to look at me, the want naked on his face. I have to force myself to keep him in my peripheral, otherwise I might find out exactly how my bosses feel about sex with clients on a conference table during work hours.

"So, you're still our attorney until then." It's not a question. Ken's stating for clarity, for us.

"Yes. Once the paperwork is drafted and submitted, it's just going to be a matter of waiting for it to come back. I've already started the filing with the courts, so once we get your final agreement signed by you, it's just a matter of the judge." I'm being repetitive, but it's because I'm envisioning running into Ken on the street when the divorce is done and I no longer have to think about the fact that he'll be my client.

I have to stop that line of thinking, because envisioning Ken's face between my thighs is counterproductive, and besides, maybe he doesn't even want back in my pants. He wouldn't be the first guy to be one and done.

"Right, should we get started?" I say, quickly changing the subject, hoping that I can hide my desire. When I look up at Ken, I realize that maybe this isn't all in my head.

I start to list the assets that they thought should go to the other versus the ones they wanted, and unsurprising things lined up as far as what was sentimental to the other. They're so attuned to the other that it gives me pause. What am I thinking to consider getting involved with a married man? With a man who still has a deep love for his soon to be ex-wife?

I must be out of my fucking mind.

"There is one last thing that I think you both overlooked as far as assets," I say, resting my pen down. Eloise can keep taking notes on what I'm about to say.

"What would that be?" Leslie asks, folding her hands on the table.

"Your engagement ring and wedding band. I know it can be a sensitive subject, but they tend to be of high value, and from the looks of it, yours are no different."

Leslie looks at her hand, where the comically large sapphire rests in a bed of smaller diamonds.

Ken looks at it for a long time, and I see his body nearly deflate. "I want it back." It's the first declarative statement he's made right out of the gate.

Leslie similarly folds into herself. I hate to see both of them going through this, but it's necessary. The rings are usually among the most sensitive items to discuss.

"Of course, you can have it back. It's a family heirloom." Leslie reaches for the ring, to tug it off, but Ken stops her.

"It doesn't need to be right this minute." His voice is pitched low, and I have to look away and study my notes. I always feel like an intruder in these moments.

"Was there anything else?" There is a hitch in Leslie's voice when she asks.

I shake my head. "No, you both confirmed no alimony to the other, you have no children or pets, and you're agreed on the distribution of marital assets. I'll send over a draft for your review. It is encouraged that you each hire your own attorney to review the documents separately to ensure that it's a fair split. An affidavit from the attorneys will help speed the process along. If you need names, I'm happy to provide them, though one attorney you could use is your trusts and estates attorney. They will be best suited and it will also serve as a reminder to update your wills."

Leslie and Ken look at each other, at the reminder that they're getting closer to cutting each other out of their lives so completely. I can see the pain on Ken's face, but he looks away from her first, to me. I school my face into perfect indifference.

"I'll take those recommendations," Ken says, rising.

"I'll email them to you both." I shake their hands. Ken holds my hand a moment longer than necessary before releasing me and following Leslie out.

My hair is curled and my pussy is waxed and I look fucking edible tonight. Only, my date hasn't gotten the memo. Parker Worthington and I met at the bar as agreed, and I thought things were going well enough to continue to actually sit down, only he hasn't looked up from his phone since we sat at the table.

"I'm so sorry," he says, slipping his phone into the interior pocket of his suit jacket.

I'm fighting the urge to really watch him. He's gorgeous with a textured crop of hair that sweeps to the right and a close buzz all around the rest of his head. The thought of grabbing it while bouncing on his cock should appeal to me, but it doesn't.

"Business, right?" I say, not looking up at him, choosing instead to stare into the depths of my wine glass as if the red liquid holds an answer to questions I've yet to ask.

"Put down the wine glass, Ainsley."

My head snaps up at the demanding tone in his voice, and I lock gazes with his ice blue eyes.

"I've been rude, and I'll pay for my mistakes gladly, but you're no stranger to the demands of someone running a billion-dollar company. I've turned my phone off and told my team to handle it."

"Is that how you do things? You have someone else handle them for you?"

"If you're asking if I'll make you finish the job for yourself when we're together, the answer to that is a resounding no. I deserve the ire, but when it comes to satisfying my partner, I get the job done."

I set down my wine glass and finally engage. "Big talk."

"I'll let my dick do the talking."

"I slept with a guy who called his dick Hotrod," I tell him, as if this is meant to scandalize.

"And was it?" Parker asks, leaning forward.

"Was it what?" I feel like I've lost the thread of the conversation.

"Was it a hotrod or was he all talk and no action?"

I scoff. "Chad had the moves." I can't believe I'm talking so candidly about another guy I've slept with.

"I don't know what I want to focus on more, that you slept with a guy named Chad or that he had a cock named Hotrod and that this is the most Chad thing I've ever heard."

I want there to be more chemistry with Parker. He's funny, and something tells me that he can back up his claims, but I know he's been with enough super models that it's not uncommon to joke that he has a flavor of the week.

"Why did you agree when my father asked you to go on this date with me?" We're splitting an appetizer when I bring this up.

"Well, he promised me six cows and enough vodka to sink a ship."

When I fail to look amused, he pushes the rest of the food toward me. The dish is paltry; there's only enough food for two bites. That's the problem with these high-end places. The food might be otherworldly, but we're paying out the ass for two bites only to still be hungry later. Post date, baby's going to need a *burger* with extra fries.

"And the reason that's grounded in reality?" I unapologetically scoop the rest of the food onto my fork and eat it, not missing how Parker's gaze lingers on my mouth. It stays there even as I slowly pull the fork between my lips.

"You dad asked, and has been a good enough associate that I agreed to it. You know that you've got a body made to be worshiped, and I'd like very much to be the one to do so."

The confidence in his tone should make my toes curl, but I can only think of Ken worshiping my body, even if it's only in my dreams.

"Ainsley?"

I turn and meet Ken Baker's eyes, as if I conjured him into being just by thinking of him.

"Ken." I wince at the strangled sound of my voice. I glance at my date, then back at the man I was just thinking of. Ken is alone and I look around to see if maybe he's meeting someone.

"I'm Parker," my date says, rising and holding out his hand.

The effect that I had hoped to have on my date has stopped Ken in his tracks. The man looks like he wants to haul me onto this table and fuck me in front of everyone, claiming me as his. The worst part is, I want him to.

"Ken Baker." At least someone has their wits about them, because it sure as fuck isn't me. "Ainsley is my attorney. I didn't mean to interrupt your date." There is a harshness to his voice when he says "date," and it gets my blood pumping.

Parker is glancing between the two of us, no doubt picking up on the fact that I've chosen to stand on the other side of my chair, forcing the piece of furniture to act like a barrier between Ken and me.

"Appreciate it. It was nice meeting you." Parker leaves no room for argument as he smooths down his suit jacket before sitting again.

Ken's gaze lingers on me before he nods. "Of course. I'd like to get the signing on the books for next week, if possible."

I burn all over my body at the idea of his paperwork being signed sooner.

"I'll work on your papers first thing Monday. I believe Eloise sent you the names of attorneys to independently review the paperwork?"

Parker clears his throat, signaling me to wrap this up, and I glare at him. Ken doesn't acknowledge him, which is the better move, but I would have to answer to my father if I did that.

"Yes, and I already called one of those names on the list and he said he would review it as soon as you got it from your hot little hands into his."

I might internally combust because all I can think about is wrapping my hot little hands around his cock and making him beg to stick it in me.

Ken steps closer to me, and Parker rises, but I wave him off. "Ainsley. I may have fucked Leslie when all three of us were together, but she and I have been separated for two years. She spends most of her time with her boyfriend in London. I'm ready to move on with my life, and I need you." Ken's voice is lowered so he's only talking to me, not that Parker isn't trying to eavesdrop. Ken almost ends his sentence there, but he looks at the man who I'm supposed to be on a date with, the man I got my pussy waxed for, and he continues. "I need you to help me settle this so I can build my future."

Ken's hand covers mine for a second and his thumb brushes back and forth over the back of my hand, and I want to feel that touch all over me. The intent look in his eyes makes me hope he's trying to communicate something else to me, but damn him. He is *still* my client.

"I'll do what I can, but it's Friday night, and I will not be going back to the office to finish your paperwork. I'll reach out on Monday."

Ken drops his hand from mine. "Have a good weekend."

I drop into my chair, watching him walk away.

"So, are you still sleeping with him or do you just want to fuck each other's brains out?"

My attention snaps to Parker, who is smugly watching me from behind his glass.

"It's none of your fucking business."

This only makes him laugh. "So, the latter. I'm not judging. I've had my fair share of, shall we call them, ethical grey area affairs. I'm guessing you're trying to play good lawyer and not lust after your client as you help him through this difficult time."

"What would you know about it?" I challenge.

"Did you miss what I just said? I know plenty about wanting someone when they're off limits. I know what it does to a person, being unable to get another out of your head that you'll scratch any itch that passes." Parker looks away from me, back in Ken's direction. He's seated now with a group of other people, and I notice Leslie is among them, though they're sitting far apart.

"Tell me more?"

Parker grunts before flagging down the server for another round. He's silent until he has a fresh drink in his hands.

"She was my subordinate at work. We hooked up once, and I found out a few weeks later that she had gotten engaged. As far as I know, they're very married now with a couple of kids."

I'm quiet a moment before pressing for more. "Did you know she was in a relationship?"

"No, Ainsley, I don't fashion myself a homewrecker, though that didn't stop me from trying to convince her otherwise once I heard she was engaged. When we talked about it, she admitted to me that they had just broken up, and being with me confirmed that she did love and miss him, so they got back together." Parker finishes his drink.

"Why are you being so candid with me? As far as I've heard, you're the untouchable Parker Worthington, who has slept with more Angels than I think exist in the heavenly army they are based on."

This earns me a real, deep laugh. One that I don't think he shares with anyone.

"And the last I heard, you're Ainsley Seaborn, enjoying yourself as you sleep around Manhattan. Hardly seems like now is the time you're looking to settle down."

"Are you slut-shaming me?" I demand, sitting up. Our conversation has felt easy until this point. It's gotten personal in a way I didn't expect on a first date.

"Not at all. If I was, I wouldn't have a leg to stand on. I sleep around just as much, if not more, and I haven't been in a serious committed relationship since just after college." His gaze darkens for a minute, then refocuses, shaking away that particular bad memory. It makes me want to question him more about it, but it's clear he doesn't want to discuss it.

"So, what makes you think I'm here for a long-term relationship now?"

Parker runs his thumb over his bottom lip, and if it isn't one of the sexiest things a man can do. And yet, my panties stay bone dry. I realize then that since running into Ken at his bar, I can't think of anyone but him. When I pull out my vibrator at night, it's him on my mind, and I just can't go there. My libido needs a hard reset, clearly.

"I'll level with you, Ainsley. I'm not exactly looking for anything serious right now, either. I agreed to come tonight as a courtesy to your father. Stop, don't look offended. I would take you back to my apartment and fuck you in my car and again against the window as you look out with Manhattan at your feet. Then again, the last time I fucked a woman who was thinking about someone else, it worked out very well for her."

"Did it ever occur to you, Parker, that I wouldn't want to fuck *you*?"

Again, he flashes that dazzling smile, and I have to wonder if he's putting on a show for me or if he actually is this joyful.

"Not possible, but I appreciate the effort of resisting me."

Parker surprises me again by scooping up food on his fork and holding it out to me. Just on principle, I want to knock it out of his hand.

"What are you doing?"

"Is he watching?

"What?"

"Don't play dumb. It's not attractive. Is Ken watching us?"

My gaze flicks to Ken, who is indeed watching. I nod and open my mouth for the fork, closing my lips over it. Ken's hand, which is on the table, clenches into a fist before he moves it under the table, trying to look back at the conversation in front of him.

"Why did you do that?" I ask, grabbing my own fork and feeding myself.

"Because he's going to hate that level of intimacy." Parker rises abruptly and counts out enough cash to cover our meal and drops it onto the table. "Let's go," he orders.

"Why?" I ask, still confused.

"Stop asking questions and do as you're told. Another reason this would never work. I'm tired of eating this bird food, I'm still hungry, and I would rather let your boyfriend think that I'm taking you home to bend you over my couch than risk him overhearing us wax poetic about past heartbreak. Now, get that fine ass out of that chair so I can help you into your coat, so he can imagine all the ways he wants to be with you and assumes I'm the one in his place."

When I rise, Parker does help me into my coat, stepping closer to me to fix the collar. I look up at him, like I have to most people, unable to stop a smirk from spreading on my lips. Parker choses that moment to cover my mouth with his.

I probably would have hit him if I knew he was going to do this, but as it is, I'm struck dumb, going along with it mechanically. There is no spark, no flame. My body is as cold and inert as usual. There will be no internal combustion in need of dousing with my vibrator when I go home the way I needed it after the brush of Ken's lips at the bar.

When Parker pulls away, he guides me out the door with one hand on the small of my back and one simple order.

"Don't look back."

"You are scarily good at that," I tell Parker before taking a huge bite of my burger. It feels a little like I have to unhinge my jaw to do it. The Kobe beef has a layer of cheese that's topped off with thick-cut bacon, crunchy onions, and a "secret sauce" that I'm positive is escaping both the other side of the burger and the side I'm eating.

Yup. I can feel the secret sauce sliding down my face. Parker, to his credit, doesn't make a comment or a joke.

"What? Fitting this burger in my mouth?"

"That too. I meant the way you, I don't know, teased Ken when you ushered us out?"

"Oh." Parker puts his burger down and wipes his hands on a napkin. The restaurant we're in is quiet. We moved to a midtown location that caters more to the working lunch crowd in the area. "I know the look of a man who will sell his soul to be with a woman, and that man looked like he was ready to sell the soul of everyone he ever met just to touch you again."

"He's probably just looking for a good rebound," I hedge, focusing on the wedges of fries on my plate.

"Or he's the marrying type and looking for more that you're just not ready for."

I grab one of his fries and throw it at him, unwilling to forfeit one of mine for the gesture. "Would you stop it? I never said I didn't want more. I want a lot more." I pause, feeling shitty about how open I want to be with Parker right now. "I haven't had, like, a formal conversation about it with my friends, but I've been toying with the idea of having a kid."

"To go on playdates with?" He's joking, but his face is serious.

"No, jackass. I want to have a baby, and I'm not getting any younger and sure, I can freeze my eggs and wait till I make partner, but work isn't going to get easier. It's not a now or never thing, but it does get harder for me to move someone into a college dorm at 60 versus doing it when I'm younger. I'm never going to find Mr. Right, so I really just need Mr. Fast Swimmers."

"So, is this date really just an audition to see if my swimmers will make cute babies with you? Because while I think they would make insanely attractive children, I'm not sure I want kids at all."

I set my own debate aside and lean forward to grab my wine. "No?"

"No, I have my own fucked-up family drama, and I don't want to think about a child on top of all that. I have a kid sister who I love but, like most people in our circle, there's divorce and affairs. Money changes people. It's why I can't and won't do serious."

"Unless you're getting a good deal on cows and pigs and vodka."

"They're goats, not pigs," Parker corrects. "For all the two cents my opinion is worth, go for it. Do what you have to do to be a mom. Time is the only thing money can't buy. Your career will always be there, work will always need to get done, but having a child and watching them grow up, that's not something you can do over. You're a good person, Ainsley. From the few interactions we've shared, I feel confident telling you that."

"And where do you get off making that assumption?"

"Because you could have gone into the bathroom at our last restaurant and let Ken fuck you senseless and you didn't because 'ethics' and because you were on a date with me. I've seen it happen plenty of times."

"To you?"

"Never to me. I *very* rarely get turned down."

"Never and rarely are two different things," I point out. The waiter comes and clears our plates after dropping off a fresh round of drinks.

"Okay. How about this: once I get to a date, if I want things to happen, they usually happen. I prefer my partners be excited about the idea of me taking them to bed. It's fine, this gets your father off my back about taking you on a date, we can say we're incompatible romantically but will continue to be friends."

Parker is again pulling out his wallet and I wave him off. "This isn't a real date. You covered the first meal. The least I can do is cover this portion."

"Ainsley, I'm going to do something that I'm sure you won't appreciate right now." Parker grabs my wallet from my hand before handing off his credit card to the server. My scowl deepens.

"Think of the goats I'm losing because you won't marry me." He hands me back my wallet once the threat of me paying has passed.

"And that is why I should pay. You're taking a loss on the evening."

"Spending time with a beautiful woman is never a loss. Think about what you want. I know of a well-respected, exclusive, high-end sperm bank if you need a referral."

My heart warms at the offer. "Do I want to know how you know this? Will I see your face in the book?"

"Not a chance. You're not the only woman with a high net worth who wants to have a child alone or, in some cases, their spouse can't contribute for one reason or another. In our social circle, discretion is valued." Parker signs the receipt before getting out of his chair to help me from the booth I'm sitting in.

"I'll let you know. I think it's time to stop pussyfooting around and take the plunge."

"You should. Remember, once you decide, you still have to wait before you actually *get* pregnant."

It's an excellent reminder.

We walk through the streets of the city that never sleeps, practically alone for a city teeming with over a million people just on the island of Manhattan.

"Really, I took this date because my sister's girlfriend just proposed and I know my sister, she's going to want me to settle down. She's still got that post engagement glow, but once she has a date, I'm sure it's only going to be a matter of time before she starts setting me up."

"Well, if you need a date for the wedding, call me."

We stop at my subway station. "Sure I can't get my driver to take you home?"

"No, I do try to make environmental decisions when I can."

"Your funeral. Go for what you want, Ainsley. Don't let expectations hold you back."

After a final kiss on the cheek, I watch Parker walk to a black car that's been trailing us, and I wonder how I can make my dream work.

Six

UNTIL NOW, the only people I've told about wanting to have a baby have been inconsequential–Ken, Parker, and my dad. Maybe that's why I decide to ask my friends out for drinks the following night so I can tell them. If they know, then maybe someone will hold me to my word.

It's my own masochism that makes me choose Ken's bar to tell them. I want to see Ken, even if it is from afar, knowing that he's something I can't have. It makes for a fitting setting as I tell my friends the one thing I do want and can act on. It's Saturday night, so I doubt he's even here. He probably has his own life, with friends or maybe some fresh rebound pussy.

I'm the first to arrive, sliding into a booth with a view of the door. I order a dirty martini and grimace when it's served in a mason jar.

I'd forgotten about that somehow.

"That's three days in a row."

My gaze locks with Ken's as he leans on the table, eyes sparkling.

My tongue flicks out to wet my lips, and I can't miss how he grips the table while watching. "You are correct."

"How was your date?" he asks, not keeping the disdain from his voice.

"He's not exactly baby daddy material." I glance at my phone to see a text come in from Elia saying she's running late. It's followed up by both Taryn and Vivian indicating that they're about to leave their offices. It's Saturday night and I shouldn't be surprised, but it's not right the hours that they have to work.

"Still planning on that?"

"On having a baby? If you must know, yes. I was going to tell my girlfriends about it tonight."

Ken is quiet for a moment, seeming like he's considering something before he slides into the booth next to me. Around us, people are starting to gather as friends and dates arrive at the bar. This place seems successful, if the crowd is any indication. The booths are some of the last to fill up, and I'm glad I got here when I did.

I open my mouth to ask what he's thinking when his mouth crashes over mine. My body comes alive immediately and I lean into him, nearly moaning as he threads his hand in my hair. His finger slips into my hair tie, pulling it free so my blonde hair spills over my shoulders.

It feels like the room falls silent and there is only us and the way we fit together with my hands on his chest. I manage to remember myself and pull back, feeling just as dazed as he looks.

"I'm sorry," Ken says immediately. He carefully places my hair tie on the table. "I shouldn't have done that, not when you made it clear that you won't do anything while I'm your client, but the idea of that guy being the last one to kiss you didn't sit well with me." I can't come up with a witty response because I'm still seeing stars. "I'm sorry," he repeats.

"No, it's...it's not fine, but, forget it." I need to think about yoga and deep breathing and clearing my mind of the one thought that is rattling in my head—that I need to slip my hands into his pants and get him to make a mess of himself, right here, in front of everyone. I want him to walk around his bar with his boxers hardening with his cum because I made him need me that badly.

It's not even so much that he's offering me pleasure. It's that he makes me feel wanted for the first time in what feels like a long time. All his talk about wanting to get me on my back is great, but it seems like more than that. His need to be around *me* and not just a warm body is infectious. I haven't felt this kind of draw in a *long* time. And maybe that's why it's been so hard to quit wanting him. I can believe that Ken wants me for me and not just as a tight place to get his dick wet.

"That's the problem, Ainsley. I can't get your smart mouth and sense of humor out of my head. I have been trying. I have been trying so hard to get you out of my head, but every time I tell myself to put you out of my mind, my cock has other ideas and I'm stuck with blue balls until I get myself off thinking that it's your mouth or your hand or your tight, perfect cunt."

Why didn't I also get water? I need something that's going to cool me down because now I want to get under this table and do exactly that. Fuck.

"We can't." It's a weak objection and damn if it doesn't make me the worst person ever.

"I know. It's why I want you to get the papers signed and the legal stuff over with so I can take you on a date and show you just how much I've been missing you. How much I've been thinking about you. And yes, it probably makes me an asshole to put this on you. To make you responsible for the need you inspire. But that kiss? That kiss told me that you feel the same, and I bet even if Mr. Bad Haircut took you home last night, I have no doubt that you left feeling unsatisfied. If I wasn't respecting your professional boundary, I would have my hand up your skirt right now until you came so hard you saw stars. So please, Ainsley, put me out of my misery and finish this."

I feel like all the words I would say have shriveled up somewhere between my brain and mouth. In a few hours when I'm lying in bed alone, I'm sure I'll come up with the perfect response to his declaration of lust, but right now, I can barely so much as stammer his name.

"Ken…"

He silences me with a kiss with the heat turned on low. It's a good thing too, because I would have straddled him and dry humped him until we both came like teenagers in the backseat of a car.

"I want to take you on a date. After this is all said and done. I have a proposition for you."

I wait for him to elaborate, but he doesn't.

"Well, what is it?" A sixth sense draws my attention up, and I see Elia walking into the bar.

Ken follows my gaze then starts to slide out of the booth. "You're going to have to get my divorce finalized if you want to know. Your tab is on the house tonight, so enjoy."

I turn as Elia approaches the table. She casts a wary look at Ken before sliding into the other side of the booth.

"This is Ken, the owner of the bar. He was just making sure everything was satisfactory," I say quickly, probably too quickly.

"Right, well, it looks very cool." She gestures absently at the exposed beams in the ceiling. It's the first time I've taken a moment to really look around the space. Last time I was here, I focused on being stood up and was seated at the bar, away from the rest of the space. The wall our booth is against is all exposed brick with several large booths pressed against it so parties of eight or more can gather.

"Thanks, it's been my baby for a few years. I'll leave you ladies to it. Enjoy your evening."

At the word 'baby' I look back up at him and bite my lip, thinking about what it would be like to grow round with his child, and then I immediately shake my head. Even if a baby was one of the reasons his marriage was ending, I doubt he's going to want to jump into having one right away.

63

"He seems nice," Elia says as she shoots off a text, no doubt letting her husband know that she got to the bar alright.

"Very," I concur, but I'm not focused on her. I'm watching Ken walk away through the throngs of people, admiring his glorious ass in well-worn jeans.

We have a short catch-up while waiting on Taryn and Vivian, mostly discussing if she and Charlie are planning to travel anytime soon and how work has been. I tell her a little about a new couple I'm dealing with who are trying mediation in hopes of avoiding more contentious proceedings that involve their six-year-old.

Vivian and Taryn walk in at the same time with their laptop cases weighing them down.

"You both were working?" Elia asks.

I'm lucky. There are nights when I have to work late, and my usual day runs from eight to six or seven, but I never have to work weekends or as late as these two do.

"Duh," Taryn says, opening the drink menu to peruse it before closing it just as quickly.

"I had a meeting yesterday where I learned they're putting me on the partner track," Vivian explains, but she doesn't sound happy about it.

Elia cheers for her anyway. "That's awesome!"

I can't say it doesn't sting just a little. We might be at different firms, so office politics aren't the same, but Vivian is a few years younger than me, and partner hasn't even been mentioned with my name, despite Kyle trying to dangle the idea in my face. Still, she's my friend and I'll cheer for her.

"Yeah, it is, but it also comes with a whole new set of expectations, like working at five on a Saturday."

A waitress with dark red curls makes us hit pause in our conversation as we all order something. Vivian and Taryn add shots to their order, and I get that in the worst way.

"So, what's the big news?" Taryn asks after a waitress leaves.

It feels like we've only just ordered when our round is delivered by Ken himself. When we lock eyes, he winks at me before slipping away.

"Oh, well, yeah. I wanted to talk to you guys about something I want to do." All three remain silent, waiting for me to elaborate. "Right, I want to be a mom, and I want to start doing treatments this year. And I thought finally telling you guys about it would make you hold me accountable. I've been thinking about it for a while, probably since Elia's bachelorette."

"Just think, you could be having Brad's baby now if you had wanted," Taryn teases. I'm glad she and I are able to joke about the disaster that was both of us sleeping with him.

"Don't forget Chad!" Vivian pipes up, reminding me of another one of our friends I slept with that weekend.

"So, sperm bank?" Elia asks, keeping us remotely on task.

With a straight face, I turn to look at her. "You don't think Charlie would mind providing a sample, do you?"

Elia spits out her drink, the distance it gets almost reaching Taryn and me. I'm unable to contain it, and I laugh.

"That was a bad fucking joke," Elia scolds, trying to get over the shock.

"Yes, but you should have seen your face. I know someone who apparently knows someone and can get me an appointment with some fancy sperm bank. By this time next year, I'll have Keanu Reeves's baby and you'll all be jealous."

"More like I will be the happy aunt who will give your child any and all of the toys that make noise," Elia threatens.

"What can we do?" Vivian asks, reaching across the table for my hand.

"Be my friends. I'll be doing this alone, so maybe come with me to appointments? I don't know what I need yet."

"I shall endeavor to throw you the best baby shower seen this side of the Mississippi," Taryn adds, squeezing my knee under the table.

"Only this side of the Mississippi? What, you don't want to compete with the West Coast girls?"

"Bitch, of course I don't. I've seen the bananas shit those California girls can do, and lest we forget the forest fires that have been started by gender reveal parties gone wrong." Taryn laughs.

The server swings by with another round and some bar food, like potato wedges and nachos. I look around the room for Ken but don't see him anywhere. Vivian starts to send them back but I shake my head.

"It's fine. I ordered them before everyone got here and just asked that they hold them till you showed up. Anyway, I do not want a gender reveal party. Who cares what it is? I'm shooting for ten fingers and ten toes. The rest is gravy."

No one commits to not having a gender reveal, leaving me to scowl.

"We'll take turns with appointments and babysitting. You never have to do this alone," Elia vows and all of my friends agree that I will never be alone in this.

I am true to my word, mostly because curiosity is burning away at me. I want to get the Baker divorce finalized, so I unfairly use my influence. I've never in my entire career called in a favor, but I know my dad happens to golf with the one of the judges who could sign off on these papers, and I grease the wheels a little, letting him know that as soon as the ink is dry, I'll be sending the finished documents to his clerk.

It takes two weeks from when Ken told me he had a proposition for me to when I finally get them in my office to sign the papers. Even for me, I got their agreement done quickly.

"You've had a change in your schedule," Eloise announces, plopping in her chair.

"What?" I ask, my mind muddled from the bank statements I was reviewing..

"I said you've had a change in your schedule. The Coyles had to cancel because of a death in the family so the Bakers are coming in at three-thirty."

I look at the clock, and I swear. It's three p.m.

"They're coming in to sign their paperwork?"

"That's what I said, didn't I?"

I reach up and touch my scalp. I skipped a shower this morning because I was going to hit the gym after work, and my dress, fuck, the dress I'm wearing shows a little too much cleavage. I bought this dress a size down because I always told myself that I would lose weight to fit in it perfectly because it was just a hair too tight. That was three years ago, and it still shows off my bra a little. The only reason I'm wearing it is because I haven't done laundry, and I'm fucking commando because I haven't done *laundry*.

Of all the fucking days.

"Have you heard a word I've said?" Eloise asks.

"No, no I haven't. I'm not wearing any underwear and the last time I saw Ken Baker he told me he wanted to do some of the dirtiest things to me," I whisper-yell, leaning across my desk, very cognizant of the open door.

Eloise barks out a laugh. "People can say what they want about you, but working for you is truly a treat."

"You're fired, effective tomorrow, after you help me figure this out." I fold my hands together to beg.

"Unfire me and I'll consider it." She turns away from me, feigning annoyance over being fired.

"I'll buy you that pair of Jimmy Choos that you've been panting over for a year."

"Sold. What do you want?"

"I need to be presentable, I need the papers to be printed, and I need a time machine to take me back to before I slept with both of them."

It's a tall order, but I know Eloise must have a time machine somewhere.

"Their papers are printed and tabbed for signature as well as the locations with what their attorneys requested to be changed, and you really just need a brush to start." Eloise hops up and heads to her desk, returning with a lip stain in a neutral shade and a brush.

I pull out my desk mirror and quickly primp, getting myself ready for this meeting.

"How does my breath smell?" I ask, remembering the garlic cheese fries I got for lunch. I quickly look down at my cleavage and glimpse melted cheese on my boob. Quickly, I scrub at it, sticking my finger in my mouth. I might be falling apart, but I'm not wasting good cheese.

"Does it matter? You're not going to be kissing them."

"I still don't like to go in with garlic breath. Okay, it's okay. Can you, uh, can you call Jeremy at Judge Linden's office? Let him know that I'll be sending paperwork to him by messenger. That Judge Linden knows to expect the paperwork. By messenger, I do mean I'll be sending you."

"VIP treatment, huh?" Eloise asks as I gather part of my hair back into a ponytail while leaving some down.

"I think everyone involved is ready to move on."

I can't think or focus when I know that Ken is going to be here in thirty minutes. The sound of my intercom makes my heart stop.

"Ainsley? The Bakers are here for you. Want me to send them to your office?" Angela offers.

"NO!" I scream so loud I hear myself out in the office through her headset. Much calmer, I repeat, "No. Offer them coffee or tea or whatever and I'll be out in five minutes."

"Sure thing, boss." She's laughing; I can hear it in her voice.

Eloise stands back up. "Oh, I'm sorry, did I say they were coming at three-thirty? I meant they were coming at three. I'll go greet them and get them settled in while you get your shit together."

"Oh, you know me, Wheezy. I never have my shit together."

Eloise walks out of my office and I can hear her cheery voice as she greets the Bakers.

It's good because I need the time to get my head on straight. It's probably for the best that they showed up now. It gave me less time to freak out about them coming. Having someone like Eloise in my corner makes my life and my job so much easier.

After a few deep breaths, I finally step out of my office.

When I make it to the conference room, things are much chillier between Ken and Leslie than they have been before, and even Eloise is picking up on it as she glances between the two of them.

As cold as things are between them, it heats up exponentially when Ken looks at me. He brings his hand up to his mouth as he rubs the stubble on his chin, looking at me like I'm a prime cut of meat.

No, no, none of that when I'm not wearing underwear. I rub my thighs together when I sit, aware of the slickness that just seeing him caused.

"Leslie, Ken, lovely to see you both. Your attorneys turned around their comments pretty quickly and we were able to hammer out some very fine details. I'll review the document now, with the specific callouts to the changes proposed."

"We've already read the document," Leslie says softly. I notice for the first time that her rings aren't on her finger.

I glance at Ken, who looks away, down at the papers that Eloise already gave them. "Right, then. Let's get started."

We take almost an hour going through each line item. I keep checking on them as I go, glancing at Eloise, who brought her laptop into the meeting so she could keep working.

"Can we take a minute?" Leslie asks when we're halfway through the document.

"Absolutely. We'll be right outside," I tell them, rising from my chair.

Leslie is looking at Ken, but he's looking at me. I want to scold him to stop, that somehow she will know the way we seem to yearn for each other, but I rationalize with myself instead. I'm his lawyer. I just stood up and I'm going to be leaving him with his very-soon-to-be ex-wife. Of course, he's looking at me, wondering why I'm abandoning them.

Eloise offers to get drinks when we step out of the room and they both nod gratefully.

"Do we have to do this?" I hear Leslie ask from the other side of the door. I'm much more invested in Ken's answer than I want to be.

"Les," he sighs. "I love you. We have spent ten amazing years with each other, but I think we've both outgrown this relationship. You've been spending more and more of your time with Vance in London, anyway."

"But you're my Kenny. You're my hot sauce to this bland world."

Do I feel a little guilty eavesdropping? Sure. But I did tell them we would be right outside. It's not my fault that I can hear them while Eloise and I congregate around Angela's desk.

"Leslie." The silence is so long I wonder if they're whispering. "Unless your feelings about having a baby have changed, my answer will remain the same. You've gotten to spread your wings during our entire marriage, and I won't ask you to change for me. But now I need you to let me go. I need you to let me have my dreams."

"You knew who you married."

"Leslie," he gives a sad laugh. "I did know, and I never *once* asked you to stop doing what you wanted. You wanted an open relationship? Done. You wanted to be shared with other partners? Done. You wanted to have a life in New York and a separate life in London? I did it. And maybe that's the crux of the issue."

"What?"

Ken is silent before pushing ahead. "I want to start seeing someone else. Exclusively."

My heart stills in my chest and I strain toward the door, desperately hoping no one else makes a sound. In fact, I glare at the phone so hard when it rings, Angela just sends it to voicemail.

"I'm not telling you this to hurt you, Leslie, but the few times I've seen her, I've felt so light being around her. It's a different experience, and the hot rage of jealousy that burns through me seeing another guy check her out or buy her a drink is enough to level a city block. I love you, Leslie, but I never knew that feeling until now."

I don't realize I'm clicking the pen in my hand incessantly until Eloise covers my hand with hers. Our gazes lock and I wonder if she suspects that he's possibly talking about me. No, he can't be talking about me. Even I'm not that conceited to think so. Maybe he's talking about someone else.

Then I remember that kiss and I bring my fingers up to my lips. No, he is totally talking about me.

"But you're my home."

"If we're both being honest, I never was. I was your safe zone. I was where you could feel safe to be yourself, but we both know better, and we both know it's time to move forward."

"You really feel that way about someone?"

"Maybe in a year I'll tell you about it, but I think we need to work on putting us in the rearview."

"After the party?"

He chuckles. "Yes, Leslie, after the party."

Ken emerges from the room, looking for Eloise and I. When his eyes land on me, they soften imperceptibly and I wonder if he knows I heard his declaration.

We proceed into the conference room. The rest of the meeting moves along quickly without Leslie stopping every few paragraphs for clarification. There is only a moment of hesitation before Leslie scrawls her signature on the paperwork and pushes it toward Ken, who does the same.

"My last act as Leslie Baker," she announces sadly, capping her pen and dropping it into her bag.

"At this point you can consider your marriage over. I'll let you know when I have the sign-off from the judge. Please feel free to reach out to me if you have any questions or concerns."

I shake hands with both of them before showing them out the door. Once I hear their elevator, I thrust the papers at Eloise, who has already changed into her sneakers so she can get to the courts before they close.

Maybe it means I'm going to hell, but next week, once the dust settles, I'm going to email Ken.

Seven

I'M CURLED on my couch, staring at my phone like it's going to bite me. I'm fighting the urge to text Ken on the number I pulled from his file. Then there's the matter of the email I got yesterday from the sperm bank letting me know that I'm being granted the honor of making an appointment if I want.

And I do want.

Still, I'm swirling my wine around in my glass, wondering what my next year looks like. I could be pregnant by this time next year, or, if all goes according to plan, I could have a baby. My apartment, which is grandiose by New York City standards, wouldn't be enough for me and a child. At first, sure. They don't need much, but I'll want to give them their own space as they get older.

A knock on the door startles me out of the spiral my thoughts were going down. I'm not expecting anyone. I peer through the peephole and go still and think maybe if I don't move again, he'll go away.

Because it's Ken on the other side of the door. Slowly, I do a pit check and am glad that I at least put some deodorant on. I wasn't planning on leaving the house. It's a dreary Saturday and the last thing I wanted to do was play 'guess how deep that puddle is' on the corners of New York City streets.

"Ainsley?" Ken calls, and my heart nearly leaps from my chest.

Panic is settling in. "She's not home at the moment, dear." I try my hand at a British accent, and I sound like Mrs. Doubtfire. Ohhh. A nanny is something else I need to consider. Maybe I can hire Mary Poppins, though if I'm honest, she seems rather flighty.

Ken's laugher echoes in the hall. "What the hell sort of accent is that supposed to be?"

I whip open the door. "My accent was perfectly fine." Realizing what I've done, I cross my arms over my chest. "What are you doing here, Ken?"

My nipples pucker at the assault of the cool air from the hallway. When Ken's gaze drifts to where I'm emphasizing my chest, I realize I'm wearing a threadbare tank. My shirt is all but see-through, and my nipples are demanding his attention, which he gladly lavishes on them.

"Are you going to invite me in?" He braces his hands on the doorframe, caging me in against my own open apartment. There is all this space behind me for me to flee into after slamming the door in his face. Droplets of water are still sluicing down his face from his wet hair. Who is this beast in me that wants to lick the water off him?

"Why should I?" There is a waiver in my voice that seems to only show up when he's around. Being with him makes me feel so vulnerable, and I want to feel that way. I want to feel his body against mine. I want to open up to him about my life and my goals, and I have no idea why he makes me want to do this. I don't know what it is about him that draws these thoughts from me.

That's an utter lie. I know what it is about him that makes me want to. It's because he's listened to me when we've talked and shown me just how much that matters. It's because he's been wanting this moment just as badly, if his speech in my office was any indication. It's because he's making me feel things with more than just the organ between my legs; he's made me hope in my heart of hearts for more.

"Because I've been waiting weeks for this."

He doesn't hesitate to cup my face with both hands the way he did in the bar, before slamming his mouth into mine, claiming me for his.

And, fuck, I let him have this piece of my soul that he seems to have taken for his own, and it feels like since having him in my life he's slowly infected me with the need to be near him and talk to him.

I step back into my apartment, and he hesitates, pulling away with the question in his eyes. He's thinking all the things I've been thinking.

Is this in his head? Is this attraction real or made up?

With one hand still holding the door, I reach the other toward him. I fist my hand in his shirt and tug him toward me. Ken falls over my threshold, and both of us push my door closed behind him.

We are crushing teeth and frantic tongues as I push his leather jacket over his shoulders, not caring when it lands with a wet thud on my floor. He toes his shoes off and I want to laugh at the consideration, but then his hands are on his pants and I realize that it was more about expediency than being mindful of my floors.

We pause as I reach to twine my hands in his hair. Everything about this feels so right from the way our bodies crush together.

"I haven't stopped thinking about you," Ken murmurs against my lips. We take a moment, breathing heavily.

"I haven't either," I confess.

My hands rest on his hips as he traces one finger idly down my cheek to my tank top strap. I lick my lips, just staring at him as he watches his hand as it drags the strap down my arm, freeing my breast. It's a scorching touch that burns me all the way through.

Ken's finger slowly trails toward my nipple but never touches it, just winding me up tighter and tighter until I feel like I'm going to burst. I've never been one of those women who can get soaked from a caress, but this man does it for me. I am achy and needy for him in the worst way. His gaze flicks up to me to watch how I'm responding to these caresses. I know my desire is written on my face, but part of me doesn't want to give him the satisfaction.

"You're making a puddle on the floor," I point out, trying to keep my voice level, but I hear the hitch in it.

Ken lazily looks from my erect nipple to my eyes. "Fuck the water," he growls, scooping me up.

I yelp with surprise and wrap my legs around his hips. One of his hands braces my back while the other holds my ass.

"Where is your bedroom?" he breathes before kissing me. To call this a kiss is an insult to all kisses everywhere. This is a claiming, an unequivocal marking of me down to my soul as he coaxes my mouth open so his tongue can brush against mine. I'm not content to be a passive participant, so I dig my hands into his hair, pressing down into him, until there is no clear sign where he starts and I end. If we could stay like this, fused together everywhere, I would be happy, but we haven't even gotten to the best part yet.

I point him toward my bedroom, where I know the bed is unmade and my room is a mess. Hot Saturday night booty call was not on the calendar, but here we are and I'm not going to hide who I am. There are too many things I'm thinking of, like that my tank top has a stain on it and that these are my period sweats.

Ken doesn't seem to notice as he throws me back on the bed. With one easy hand he reaches behind him and strips off his shirt, giving me a chance to admire his bare chest. We don't take our eyes off each other as he finishes slowly sliding his pants from when he started in the hallway. It's not a strip tease, but I can feel in every crevice of my body that if he ever *did* give me a strip tease, I would expire on the spot just based on how his hands graze his powerful thighs before shucking off his pants.

I should use the time to take off my sweats, but I have one breast free and am afraid any sudden movements will break the spell over this moment. His erection is thick and needy, and I want to wrap my lips around it until all he can think about is spilling himself in my mouth.

When he settles one knee on the bed, I realize that at some point over the last month with our professional emails and less than professional run-ins, I started to like this man. Not just like or lust, but I've started to fall, and that means letting him see every dark corner of who I am. In for a penny, in for a pound.

Ken doesn't hesitate to climb over the bed to me before I can second-guess this decision to welcome him into my bed and between my legs. He helps pull my sweats off, only quirking an eyebrow when he finds me commando. Sometimes a girl has to just let the goods breathe. I don't think Ken particularly cares about this theory, because he keeps touching me. He presses a kiss to the inside of my knee, slowly moving up. The kisses are so brief, so bare, I would wonder if he's even touching me if I wasn't watching him. Each caress of his lips sends my heart beating faster and makes me twist my hands in my sheets. I might come just from the anticipation of his mouth, his cock on me.

"I remember how amazing you taste," he says, his breath hot between my legs. One swipe of his tongue causes me to suck in a sharp inhalation of air. "I've been chasing that taste since that night. Damn it, Ainsley. You're so fucking wet, it's unbelievable." He continues his journey up to my mouth, pausing at my breasts. Only one is still exposed, but when I reach to pull my tank off, Ken stops me.

I would say something, but the way he's being bossy has me practically panting. I've been wanting this, wanting the completely sober experience with him since I saw him again in my office. If this is how he wants to run the show, I'm inclined to let him.

His eyes come to my still-covered nipple just before his mouth closes over the fabric, causing friction on the sensitive skin. I arch my back into the sensation, wanting more. He sucks on my left breast while his hand comes up to pull the strap from my right shoulder down to expose my other breast, leaving my tank twisted around my middle. If this is the attention he gives my nipples, I hate to imagine the soaking wet puddle he will leave me if he ever eats me out.

No, I don't hate it, I fucking love it, and the thought alone has my needy pussy clenching in anticipation of being filled, and a strangled moan claws free.

"I've been dreaming of being inside you again since the first time. You've been haunting my dreams. I can't stop thinking of you," he murmurs, finally releasing my nipple with a wet pop.

Ken's lips find mine, and the weight of his body over mine brings back memories of our first night together, but this is going to be so different. There isn't going to be a drunken haze coating the memory, making me wonder how much of it is real or imagined. His body is settled between my legs, his erection pressing at my entrance.

Ken kisses my neck. "Tell me you want me," he demands, teasing me. His blue eyes are focused on mine as he reaches between our legs to his cock. He uses it to tease me, sliding it up to my clit and rubbing the head of it against me. His repeated motion makes every thought eddy from my mind. I have had a lot of sex, but never like this. It's never driven me to mindless animal need to be joined with another person. My skin feels hot and tight all over and if he doesn't fill me soon, I might cry.

"I want you," I manage to choke out. It's torture, pure and simple, but I can't help but give in. I can't even vocalize to him that this has been on my mind too.

He lowers his cock to where he can slide inside me. "I want you to tell me how you need it."

"I need it," I beg through clenched teeth.

He tips his cock back up against my clit and I actually fucking whimper. A sound like that has never come out of me while having sex, or in this case, being touched by a penis, because this motherfucker will not put his cock in me, goddamnit.

"What do you need?" he asks, teasing just inside me.

I was amused by this, but now I'm full of the urgent need for him. Ken has to see it on my face as he teases me. My hands fist in my sheets as I writhe below him. My thoughts are incoherent; there is just his body touching mine, my heart reaching for his.

"I need you inside me."

He thrusts hard inside me, and I cry out, unable to help it. The feel of him is almost too much, but at the same time, it's not enough. I bring my hips up to meet him.

"What else do you need?" he asks, pulling back before slamming home again.

"I need you," I cry out before I even realize it.

"What do you need from me?"

"I need you to love me." And the minute the words are out of my mouth, I know they're true. I want to be embarrassed and ashamed that the words have run away from me without my permission, but Ken slows his movements as his eyes bore into mine.

"You have me, buttercup. You have all of me," he promises, lowering his body over mine. He braces himself on my pillows, fingers threading through my hair.

A tear wants to slip free from the sweetness of him, of feeling so completely treasured, but I've already broken all the rules by begging to be loved in bed.

At some point the movement of our bodies stops being fucking. It stops being animalistic rutting for release and instead it slows down as we savor each other. His eyes mark every time my body tenses in pleasure. Ken keeps me grounded, here in this moment, and there is nowhere else I would rather be as he slowly pistons inside me, trying to draw out every whimper and moan as he tries to change what angle he enters me at until I'm a mess shaking with the need for release.

My orgasm builds as slowly as we make love. I arch into him as I scream his name, letting the whole of Manhattan know that this man, who fell into my life by purse happenstance, has taken everything from me.

He takes care coaxing the pleasure from my body. Ken's body slows after my orgasm subsides, and he rolls over, pulling me with him.

"If I recall, this was your favored position." There is a gleam in his eye as he says this, his hands urging my hips forward, sending a spike of pleasure through me. I let my body guide me, watching him suck on his lower lip as he watches my breasts. I pause to discard my tank top before I proceed riding him.

I feel the tide of another orgasm take hold, and I let it take me away. Every thought I have eddies from my mind and there is only how wonderfully we're connected. I grind against him, my body clenching around him before I lean forward, utterly spent. Our bodies slicked with sweat, his arms fold around me, holding me to him.

He's still inside me, and while we've had sex before, this feels more intimate. I want to hide my face in his chest and duck the scrutiny from my outburst, but Ken deserves better than my cowardice.

"You didn't come," I remark, starting to push off him.

He presses a kiss to my shoulder. "There will be time for it later." His blatant expectation for this to happen again gives me pause.

"There is time for it now," I insist, rocking against him. I push on his chest, feeling his muscles as I start to move over him. He releases me, watching, before thrusting up, causing me to cry out.

"I won't object."

As much as I want to watch the pleasure on his face, I slide off him, turning my back to him. I face his feet and slide back down on him. I lean slightly forward so he has a great view of my ass before I start to move over him. He slaps my ass before grabbing my hips. I let his hands guide me and set the speed that he wants and needs.

"Oh fuck, you feel so good," he groans.

I keep going until he speaks again.

"Stop. Get on your back," he orders.

I do, rolling on to my back. He moves quickly, following me. He lifts my legs up, setting them over his shoulders. Ken is more forceful this time, slamming his way home. His thumb presses against my clit as he urges us both toward orgasm. This one is a slower, bone-deep release that hollows me out, not just from the energetic sex, but from that feeling of being right where I'm supposed to be, with the man I'm supposed to be with.

"Fuck, fuck, *fuck. Ainsley*," he screams my name and it lights me up like a tree at Christmas knowing that I did this to him.

We collapse together into the sheets, sated and exhausted. Ken stays where he is, not yet pulling out of me, until he presses a sweet kiss to my lips. When he does roll off me onto his side, he drags me against him so he can keep kissing me lazily. It's been forever since I've had this post-coital cuddle that I almost forgot how good it feels to come down from an orgasm with someone there to hold you.

"Where's your bathroom?" Ken asks, his voice a little gravelly from how he screamed my name when he came.

I point toward my bathroom door, which is open. With a kiss on the tip of my nose he slides out of bed and I get to watch the ripe globes of his ass as he walks away.

Damn.

I wrap my sheets around myself, suddenly worried that he fucked me out of his system and that he might just leave. I don't think he will hold me to what I said at the height of passion, no matter how true, and even if it would hurt, I won't hold him to it either.

He returns from my ensuite bathroom with a wet cloth in his hands. "No need to hide," he murmurs, pulling the sheet from my hands, baring me to him again.

Ken trails kisses down my body, hitting each love bite that I hardly remember him leaving until he takes care to clean me, pausing when I wince.

"I'm sorry, was I too rough?" Ken presses a kiss to the apex of my thighs.

"Not at all. It's just cold," I tell him honestly, even as he wipes the sticky cum from my legs. Then I sit up abruptly. "Oh shit, we didn't use a condom. I'm clean and I'm on the pill."

Ken tosses the cloth toward the bathroom, where it lands on the tile. He presses me back down onto the bed, gently kissing me as we fall back.

"I'm also clean. It's fine. I forgot too." Ken molds his naked body around mine.

Silence settles around us, and I feel so comfortable where I am with him.

"Was this the best idea?" I ask, worry and doubt creeping into my mind.

Ken is idly tracing circles around my chest and stomach. "Hey, look at me." I turn to look him in the eye. "We're two consenting adults. And if what we just did was any indication, you wanted this as much as I did."

"You just got divorced," I point out.

He gives me a half-smile. "Yeah, and I have been separated for a long time. It just means I have a better idea of what I want right now, and that's you. When I said you had all of me, that wasn't a heat-of-the-moment thing. I meant it. I don't know if you fully appreciate how hard it was to track you down. I got lucky that you bought this place in your name and not some LLC. It made it easy to find."

"Well, that's a little terrifying."

"Public record, buttercup. My point is, I've had you on my mind nonstop. This isn't some teenage infatuation. We may have gotten together quickly, but I'm not interested in playing head games. I have feelings for you beyond lust. You're clever, unafraid to stand up for yourself, and you're the sexiest woman I've ever had the pleasure to lay eyes on. Every meeting with you was terrible. You'd be in these clothes, and all I would do is imagine taking you out of them."

"Sounds like you just really wanted to sleep with me," I point out, blatantly ignoring how he's proclaimed feelings for me. I can't lie and say I'm unaffected. It makes my head a little woozy with the idea that all these emotions rattling in my chest could be reciprocated. Because if I can't be honest with anyone else, I need to at least try to be honest with myself, and there are feelings.

He's drawing lazy circles on my skin, working his way up to my breast. He nips my shoulder. "I actually had a proposal of a different kind, but we can talk over food. Later," he demands, kissing my neck. His mouth latches onto me, making my body tense and loose all at the same time.

"You don't want to tell me now?" I hope my voice doesn't sound as breathy as it feels, but his chuckle tells me that it is. My curiosity burns bright, but his mouth on me is honestly so distracting.

"Over dinner." His hand slides down my side to cup my ass. "First, I need to eat this pussy and make you come all over my face."

"Dinner sounds good," I agree, pressing my lips to his.

Ken leaves to get food, even though it's raining and I think we're better off ordering in. Every time we would try to start to make a plan to eat, we would get distracted by something simple, like my inability to keep my hands off his cock. The decision was finally made when my stomach growled loudly as he went down on me. We both dissolved into a fit of laughter, putting a hold on all play until Ken returned with food.

"They really meant April showers," Ken says with a laugh when he returns. He has his hands full with shopping bags.

"Still raining?" I ask conversationally even though I can see very well out my window where the storm clouds end, a perk of having a high floor. Too much of this afternoon with him has been weighed down with feeling. I need to get out of my head, get us to a safer ground. Talking about the weather seems perfectly logical.

"It's a deluge out there. I think I'll have to spend the night." He winks at me, and I should be bothered by the presumption that he's going to spend the night but I'm not. I love that he's feeling comfortable enough to poke around my kitchen, pulling out pots and pans. There is something to being able to fall into step with someone so easily. After the fraught relationship Charlie and I had with being on and off, I'll welcome the ease of having someone step into my life with limited complications.

"What was that big proposal you've spoken so highly about?" I ask after pointing him toward the drawer filled with miscellaneous cooking utensils that fit nowhere.

"We can talk over dinner. Tell me why you picked family law." He points me back toward my table when I get up to help.

I scowl at him. "Now you're just leading me on," I protest, but I oblige him. "My parents got together when they were in their early twenties, and if I'm being honest, I was definitely an oops baby. To start, their relationship wasn't the strongest, but my dad knocked my mom up, and did the right thing for the time.

"They had a really ugly divorce when I was a kid. My mom tried to use me as a pawn to get more money from my father, going as far as accusing him of assaulting me and sharing me with his friends. It was only when the court-appointed supervisor saw her manhandle me that the truth came out." I notice Ken's stirring slows as he listens to me. I'm rather flippant about the whole thing, thanks to years of therapy as a teen, and I deliver the story matter-of-factly. The truth is, it's just part of my story. And while it crafted the type of attorney and person I would become, it's made me tougher. "He *never* touched me. My father was the best. My mom just wanted to get as much as she could from him in the divorce and figured alimony and child support would go a long way. He paid her some sort of settlement, though I never knew how much."

My past is not something I'm ashamed of, and that's one of the important things my father taught me. The tension in Ken's body is still pulled tight like a bow ready to snap. Even over the sizzle of the pan I can hear each deep breath he releases before speaking.

"So, you chose divorce?" Ken is dropping batter in a pan. He keeps trying to twist to talk to me, but the stove is against the wall, so he's facing away from me. I can appreciate that he doesn't offer me platitudes or try to tell me that it wasn't my fault. What happened between my parents made me who I am today, but it's not going to scare me away from love.

"Well, originally, I was supposed to work for this great big corporate law firm to take from the poor and give to the rich, but that hardly appealed to me. So instead, I switched to something more worthwhile in the hopes that maybe it would give me a pass for being a lawyer in the afterlife. I had a summer internship that left me feeling all sorts of icky, and I decided to change my focus then."

"Sounds noble."

I swirl the mimosa Ken delivers to my hand. "Noble would be actually doing good and not negotiating who Mr. Mittens goes with in the divorce. Noble would be helping people in truly awful situations into better ones. I'm not noble. I want to do more pro bono work, but my firm keeps shooting me down."

"You should push harder. You don't strike me as the type of woman to roll over for anyone."

"Says the man who two hours ago told me to do exactly that, and I *obeyed*," I point out.

"That's different and you know it."

He's right, and I'm a little mad about that because who is he to come into my home and start to make me think and feel? This *is* going fast. It was one thing when I couldn't get him out of my head for the last few weeks. But now, he's this tangible man, standing in my apartment and making me dinner.

And my stupid foolish heart wants to see what more he has to offer. How many times can one man make your heart race to bursting? With Ken, the limit doesn't exist. It has me wondering if this is what falling in love feels like, and maybe I didn't understand the feeling until now.

This thought scares the shit out of me immediately because if I wasn't actually in love during any of my previous relationships, then losing this man will break me. If I thought that I experienced heartbreak before...But maybe this is what I need, to let myself fall because there might be part of him that is falling too, and maybe we could fall together, knowing the other is there to catch us.

Ken is quiet as he finishes cooking. He delivers a steaming pile of pancakes, eggs, and bacon. Before he takes his seat, he gives me a gentle kiss on the lips.

It's a terrifying glimpse of domesticity with this man, and I want it all. I want to have him look at me like this food is just the appetizer and I'm the main course, even when I'm wearing slouchy sweats and a tank. I feel very not cute, but the way Ken keeps glancing at me, you would think I was dressed in lingerie, trussed up like a model.

"Breakfast for dinner?" I tease, helping myself to the bacon.

"And why not?"

Having no good answer to that, I eat. I'm not going to ask

again about whatever proposal he has since he's made it clear he's only going to share it when he's ready.

"I think I disappointed my mom," Ken starts after he's finished his first helping. He's not looking at me as he heaps food onto his plate. "She and my dad had this amazing love story. They were in love right up until he had a heart attack after my wedding to Leslie. I don't think it's that my mom believes divorce is a sin so much as she thinks that when you take a vow of marriage, you need to honor it and push through the hard parts."

I'm familiar with having to help clients grapple with the other ramifications of their divorce. So many families disapprove for any number of reasons, including religious or moral. There have been more times than I can count that I've had to talk someone off the ledge. I wait for Ken to see if he's going to push on.

"I obviously didn't tell her that I was tired of having an open marriage and that I was the one who wanted kids. My mom doesn't know that Leslie and I had an open marriage. I don't want to destroy their relationship, so I'll let her be disappointed in me."

Ken turns his chair, letting it scrape on the floor so he can face me completely. He maneuvers my chair the same way, pulling me closer to him so our seats touch.

"My family matters a lot to me. My sister and her boys mean the world to me, and seeing her with them really cemented that I want my own family and kids. That's why I have this insane idea, and I want you to really consider it and not just answer me flat out. I'll actually be mad if you answer now."

I sit up straight, worried now that I have no idea where he is going with this.

"Are you listening?"

"Of course." I want to be glib or say something obnoxious, but I hold my tongue.

"I want to make a baby with you."

I'm stunned silent. I don't know what I expected, but it wasn't that. "A baby?"

"Yes. You could lawyer the shit out of the situation, and it's going to take some finessing. I want to take you out and have more conversations about it, but I think this is something that could work for both of us."

"A baby?" I repeat, trying to force the idea into my brain. It takes a few minutes, but eventually, it takes hold. We've spent a total of less than one day together, but in that time I've seen him be accepting, forgiving, and loving. Even as his marriage was ending, he showed Leslie grace, and he wasn't afraid to stand up for what he wanted when he wasn't getting it out of the relationship he was in. I could list every positive attribute about this man, but it's not going to change what my gut reaction to him is.

I'm studying the slope of his nose and the curve of his smile, imagining these features with my blonde hair and cheekbones. It's a huge fucking step with someone I'm sleeping with, but if I'm honest with myself, this has been more than just that for a while. He's been on my mind since I met him.

But a baby, with a man who is practically a stranger to me? I mean, I know he has the net worth to pay childcare, and it's nice to know that he has nephews so my child would have cousins to play with. Perhaps, up there in importance, is that he wants a child as much as I do, if not more if he's asking me, a woman he picked up in a bar, to be the mother of his child.

"What is your health history?" I ask.

"My father died of a heart attack. My mother is in perfect health and ran a marathon last year. My sister had gestational diabetes and I have an uncle who has asthma. My maternal grandmother died of breast cancer when she was young, before they had made all the advancements in treatment, and my paternal grandmother has a history of chronic kidney stones. I'll subject myself to whatever genetic testing you want. Next question."

He smiles like he wanted me to ask these questions. Ken's openness to my interrogation only serves to ingratiate him further. Would it be absolutely insane to consider this? Yes. Would I jump in with both feet if I found out tomorrow I was pregnant with his baby? Also yes.

"What is the worst thing you've ever done?"

"I lied about how my sister got hurt once. It wasn't anything like I did something to hurt her, but we were playing on a playground and I didn't want her to leave me behind, so I held on to her two hands and she was leaning away from me because she didn't want to play with her little brother. I was maybe five or six when this happened. I wasn't strong enough to hold on to her, so I just let her go. Since I was holding her arms behind her back, she wasn't prepared to break her fall. She *just* got her hand in front of her enough to break it but she hit her head on the railing and got a concussion. My dad would have beat my ass if he knew the real reason she got hurt, so I lied. So did my sister."

My heart clenches when he talks about her fall, and it makes me wonder if my heart is strong enough to be a parent. Raising a child is more than just all the good times and taking them to school and wiping their tears when they're heartbroken. There are the scary times too, which I logically know, but hearing Ken spell it out like that reminds me that having a partner to share the burden with could make a huge difference.

I thought because I was raised in a single parent household that I could do it alone, but maybe I should give more weight to what Ken is offering me. It's more than just him fucking me to fill me. It could be a partnership. Or, dare I hope for more?

Ken is absently rubbing his hands together as he slips into the memory.

"Did you ever come clean?"

Ken scoffs. "No, but she has lorded it over me at every turn. She wanted the last cookie at dessert? It got mentioned. Sometimes she *still* does it for sweets now. When I wanted to take a girl out and use my parents' car? She would bring it up and say she wanted to go out with her friends instead. She would remind me that I owed her. Never to my parents, just between us, of course, because if she ever told them then she would lose all of her leverage."

"What was it like having a sister?"

If I surprised Ken with my question, he's good enough not to show it. "It was really great. I have someone to forever commiserate with over what it's like to have our parents. It meant having someone to keep my secrets and give me advice. She helped me navigate teachers and crushes and helped make me a better man." Ken pauses. "I want three kids. Maybe four."

"With the same mother?" I ask, raising an eyebrow.

Ken grabs my hips and pulls me onto his lap, so I'm straddling him and he can thrust up against my core. I have to bite back a moan. I slide my hands around his neck, threading my fingers into his hair. This feels like a definite yes. "If she's willing and if it's safe for her. How many kids do you want?"

I could see this getting out of control fast. If having him shower me with care the way he has today is even close to what it would be like when I'm pregnant with his child, I think I would spend the next decade swollen everywhere.

"You say that like it's a done deal and I'm going to agree to have your baby."

He grips my hips, tugging me toward him so I grind against his hardening cock. "I thought I was just being conversational."

I shift my hips, not holding back a moan this time. "What kind of education do you believe in for your children?"

Ken leans back, letting me rub against him like a cat in heat. "I'd like them to get a quality education but also remember to be kids. I'm not going to ship them off to boarding school the first chance I get, if that's what you're asking. I want to give my children a sturdy, loving home. I want to be there to read them stories at bedtime, and I want to know that I can't work late because my family is home waiting for me."

Slowly, Ken moves his hand forward to grip my breast, kneading it roughly. I arch into his grip, wanting him to keep going, but it seems he's tired of these games and he's ready for dessert. He rises to his feet, kicking my chair out of the way so he can carry me off to bed.

I've always been one to follow my heart when making decisions, and going forward with this wouldn't be rational in the least. I might still be debating it in my mind, but my heart is already made up. My heart made its decision the moment the words were out of his mouth, and I just have to hope that it won't break me to give all of myself to him.

Eight

THE REST of the dreary weekend is spent fucking. I don't think there is a surface in my house that we don't do it on. Ken had me riding his cock as we watched a movie. He was seated perfectly in my favorite chair. My mistake, or good fortune, was to challenge him that there was no way it would be a good place to do it, but we made it work.

I'm quiet on Monday, going straight to my office and closing the door so I can look up examples of custody paperwork. It takes one call to another attorney I work with at a different firm to get a sample.

Custody isn't my forte, so really, I'll need to call in a favor if we decide to go through with it, but for now, I play with the document, taking note of the different things that you wouldn't even think of right off the bat. There are considerations like medical decisions and holidays and steps to introduce a new partner to the child.

I hate how my heart trips over itself at the idea of Ken with someone else. He said that he would give me all of himself, but I can't trust that this relationship will work, not right away. I've been burned too many times by men in my life who said they wanted me, wanted us, to work, only for them to give up when it got hard. Ken and I have been dancing around whatever this thing is for several weeks now, and it would be a lie to say that I haven't imagined what a future with him could look like, but he just got out of a marriage. There's no way he's looking to settle down again.

Except, that's exactly what he told me. He's looking for a family. He wants something sturdy and comfortable that he can come home to. I want to be that home. But I have to ask myself, is it me he wants? Or am I just a convenient womb that is similarly looking to be filled? It feels almost like fate that two people who want to be parents stumble into each other's paths.

I want to be more than just a vessel for a baby, but when I wanted to go this alone, that's exactly what I was signing up for. So then why does this feel different?

It's because I like *like* him, and I know it. There would be nine months of birth classes and planning that we would be doing together, and I'm already addicted to his touch. I could stomach doing those classes with Taryn or Vivian at my back, but having someone there who I want to love me but who maybe doesn't feel the same way would be like death by a thousand cuts. What would hormones do to this yearning?

I'm not able to ponder this longer because Kyle strolls into my office without knocking.

"Ains, I'm going to need you to cover some files for me this week. There's an urgent client meeting I need to take in California, so you'll need to cover the rest of my workload."

I bristle at so many things that he just said that I don't know if I want to start with him barging into my office without knocking, calling me Ains, or expecting that he can dump all of his work on me so he can go bang some porn star in California. Because that's what he's doing. The client meeting he's taking is for his porn star actress who keeps him on retainer so he can pretend like he's an entertainment lawyer when he does copyright law.

"Kyle, I don't really have the capacity this week." I don't tell him it's because I'm wondering about making a baby with a former client, and I don't tell him it's because I have actually jammed my schedule trying to see if I can fit in a few extra clients. It's not that I believe that the firm is going to really put me on the partner track this year, but it doesn't hurt to make myself look good and earn extra incentives from these clients.

"You're a dream. Thank you so much. I'll be sure to mention it to Uncle Robby that you were a real team player this week. I'm sure he'll make note of it when you make your pitch for partner."

The jackass blows out of my office just as quickly as he came in, leaving my door open, despite me having had it closed. My phone vibrates on my desk with emails from Kyle's assistant, who is actually his paralegal but he refuses to treat her as such. She's sending me his schedule as well as documents I need to review this week.

It's fine.

This is fine. I'm used to having to step in for Kyle and do his job in addition to my own. In fact, I've done it often enough that sometimes his client's email *me*. Not that I get the incentive bonus in my paycheck for doing work for his clients.

If I want to be partner, it means having to roll over and play nice, but just because I know some cute tricks doesn't mean I'm not afraid to bite. Especially once I'm partner and Kyle is the one who has to lick my shoe. I'll be able to roll out my pro bono program and make sure that Kyle has to do intake because I don't actually trust him to do any legal work.

I'll just see if I know anyone who can take out a hit. I'm sure Charlie knows someone. He almost killed Elia's ex last year, and I know for a fact he's keeping tabs on the dirtbag just so he has a warning if he ever tries anything again. Charlie will definitely know who I can hire to kill Kyle.

I shoot off a text to Ken, letting him know that any plans for this week will need to be put on hold so I can salvage this shit show that Kyle left me.

I'm not going to squander my hard-to-get appointment at the sperm donation center while I come to terms with the fact that I already decided in my heart to make a baby with Ken. At the least, I owe it to Parker and myself to go to this appointment he got me and try to avoid the heartbreak that could be looming.

There is a little voice, the angel on my shoulder, telling me that maybe, just maybe, I should take Ken at his word, that he wants to be a father and he wants to be with me. To hell with it being too fast. I was with Charlie for *years* for all the good it did me. Sometimes when you know you've found your person, you just know.

I might be incredibly adjusted over what happened with my mother, but there are still emotional scars that lurk in the corners, especially knowing that my parents were madly in love and she did what she did to him, to us. I don't think that Ken is capable of those things, but there is always that fear that maybe I won't be good enough. Maybe I'm not worth loving, the way my mom chose money over me, the way Charlie picked his work over me. I'm always left wondering if I'm a little bit deficient.

My appointment turns out to be super informative, and they loan me a tablet while I'm sitting there to review the sperm donors, but in every generic white box where a photo should be, I'm picturing Ken. They have everything I would want to know about the donors, facts about their family histories, their SAT scores, and how bad their morning breath is.

They're not telling me what the donors dream about or if they bite their lips when they come. Facts like, if they're a good lover or if they rub their jaw when they think, are details I didn't realize I wanted. The size of their cock is a detail I never needed but now have.

All these little nuances are things that I know about Ken, and spending more time together is only going to make me love him more. It's his easygoing nature, how he spent years willing to let his ex-wife be who she was even if it meant his own unhappiness. It makes me want to protect him from any future hurt and show him that a partnership is more than just one party bending to the will of another.

This appointment did one thing for me, and it was the most important thing. It convinced me that I have to say yes to Ken.

It's nine on Thursday night and I'm the only one left in the office. The cleaning people have come and gone and I have my music blasting from my computer. During work hours, I use headphones when I need to focus, but I won't put myself at risk by not being able to hear if someone shows up when I'm alone.

That's how I hear the banging on the office door. I grab my phone, leaving 911 dialed in case I need to call it quickly, and I grab a letter opener from Eloise's desk. It's designed to look like a knife and I hope it works in a pinch.

I walk toward the front doors of the office and call out to the possible intruder, "We're having a late team meeting. Who is it?" My thumb is anxiously hovering over the call button as I wait.

"Ainsley?"

"Ken?" I ask, surprised. I open the office door and he scowls at me.

"Why did you just open this door?"

"Because it's you."

He pushes inside, pressing a kiss to my forehead like we've been lovers for years instead of days. "You still shouldn't have answered the door without actually verifying that it was me. You could have called me to make sure. Maybe I wasn't alone. You didn't know that it wasn't actually me."

He's making very good points, and that only makes me angrier. "I heard your voice. I heard you moan my name enough times this past weekend that I know the sound of it. You wouldn't have said my name if you didn't think I was here."

"That's not the point, Ainsley. The point is that it could have been dangerous. You didn't know for certain it was me. You could have been hurt or worse."

We're at a stalemate verbally, but he's still following me back to my office, which I take as a good sign. He's not wrong. I should have been more careful. It's why I was listening to my music through my speakers. But still, it's the principle of the thing, and I'm a lawyer. I'm not built to back down from a fight.

"You can't show up at my place of work and order me around. You're not my father."

Ken places the bag he's holding on my desk and crowds close to me. "I may not be your father, but I could be your daddy. And I'm telling you that this wasn't safe. If you have to work late, go home."

It feels like the room is on fire. I've never been one for playing dom/sub games, but the idea of him bossing me around sends a spike of lust right between my legs. My mouth is suddenly dry and I can't remember why we were arguing. Ken's fingers dig into my hips and he lifts me, setting me on my desk. My heart hammers in my chest as my imagination runs wild while all he's doing is looking at me. If he touches me, if he does any of the things I'm thinking, like pushing up the hem of my dress, I might expire on the spot.

"Why are you here?" I whisper, but it sounds more like a pant.

"You know your pupils are the size of saucers. My dear, you look like if I don't fuck you right this minute, you might die."

And here I was thinking the opposite, but honestly, both are true. Either he touches me, and I come apart right here and right now, or he doesn't, and I'm left as a puddle of desire. Either way, there is a wet spot on my desk right now.

"Why are you here, Ken?" I ask, trying to put strength into my voice.

He gives me a knowing smirk, and fuck if I don't want to do something wild to wipe it off his mouth. "I assumed you worked through dinner, so I picked up some sushi. You mentioned you like it, and if you're going to let me get you pregnant, then I figured you should enjoy the things you won't be able to while you can."

My imagination takes this and *runs*. It's the visual of him pumping me full of his seed until it takes, Ken standing over me, making me eat when I'm swollen with his child or rubbing my belly, trying to elicit kicks. It's all too much.

My hands glide up his chest and he watches me, his hands coming up to grip my wrists, and I pull him down to my mouth so I can kiss him. Ken presses into me, easily stepping between my legs so I can feel the length of his erection.

I've always wanted to get fucked on my desk, and it seems tonight is the night.

With shockingly nimble fingers, I'm pulling on his belt and dragging his zipper down slowly to tease him just a little, because I know that this is going to be fast and fierce and that's the way I want it.

Ken hauls me to the edge of my desk before batting my hands out of his way. Daddy indeed.

His cock springs free of his pants and he slides my panties to the side so he can notch himself at my entrance. Ken teases my slit with the head of his cock, sliding it up and down, spreading my arousal.

"You've always wanted this, haven't you? Someone to come in here and bend you over this desk. You might be the boss in here during the day, but you want someone to take the control away from you. You want to come in to work tomorrow knowing that you let me do this. That you let me see the dirty little slut you hide away, trying to be proper."

It's like he's able to see my darkest desires. I'm full on panting as he says this because, holy shit, no one has ever spoken to me like that, and I've had *a lot* of sex. Just the way his words make me feel so dirty has me moaning into the empty office.

"Tell me what you want, Ainsley," Ken demands, still toying with me. I'm not sure I can think straight, and he must see that because he stops with the head of his cock pressing against my clit.

"What?" I ask, looking at him.

"I want you to tell me what it is you want." His voice is quiet now, waiting. He will wait all fucking night with his cock against me until I tell him.

"I want you to fuck me. I want you to make me scream so loud I'll still hear echoes of it when I come back into the office." I lock eyes with him so my intent is clear. "I want you to fill me with come until it's leaking down my thighs and you've put a baby in me."

There is a stillness to Ken as my words register. The smile on his face is slow, turning my whole body molten. If I wasn't already ready to fuck him, that grin on his face would be enough to make my clothes melt off from its brilliance. I know, as I look at him, that this might not be a rational decision, but it's right.

He pulls back enough for his cock to line up with my entrance and then he slams himself home. He's in me to the hilt, and I scream at the sudden intrusion. I have to grab his shoulders as my body adjusts. Then I'm whimpering, begging him to move again.

Ken complies, pulling back and thrusting into me. "I'm going to fuck you on this desk, and after we eat, we're going back to your apartment and I'm going to fuck you senseless until your alarm goes off and you're begging me to fuck you again. And we're going to do this as often as it takes until you're pregnant."

Who knew a breeding kink would be my thing? His words

send me spiraling into my orgasm and I can feel my body clenching around him as he moans his own release. His face is buried into my neck as he delivers short, punishing thrusts into me while holding me in place. I'm going to have bruises on my hips and I'm not even sorry about it. I know he won't be either.

Ken stays inside me, kissing along my neck and up to my mouth, murmuring sweet nothings. "You're so perfect and strong. You're going to be an amazing mom."

Only when he's sure he's through coming does he pull out and shove himself back into his pants. Looking at my face, which I'm sure is flushed, coming straight off the orgasm, his lips land on mine in a plundering kiss. I give myself over to him, leaning against him and all the strength he has to share.

I'm convinced now that this is the right decision.

Ken lets himself fall back into Eloise's usual chair, pulling me with him. I settle on his lap, aware of the stickiness between my thighs and what this all means.

I had planned to go through with this, so when I realized I forgot my birth control pills at home after my reminder went off, I decided I would just roll the dice with remembering when I got back.

"Are you alright?" Ken asks, nudging me with his nose so I have to look at him.

I honestly do feel a little dazed. "Yeah, I'm good. That was just..." I pause, trying to come up with the word. "Yeah, mind-blowing is the only thing that I can think."

"Be careful there; you're going to overinflate my ego," he scolds, kissing my neck. Gently, he nudges me off him so he can pull out the food he brought. He pulls out three trays full of rolls.

"Did you buy one of each?" I tease.

I go to walk around to my side of the desk, but Ken grabs my middle and slingshots me toward the other chair in my office. Taking the hint, I sit in it. Ken grabs my legs and hauls my feet onto his lap so I can lean back and enjoy the meal.

"I wasn't sure what you liked." We eat in silence for a few minutes before he goes on. "I won't hold you to a declaration you made in a haze of lust." There is something tentative about his voice.

"I'm not sure what you're talking about." That's a lie, and not a convincing one.

"If you're still considering if you want to be the mother of my child, I won't hold you to that agreement. I would rather explore us than bury you under the pressure of maybe becoming parents, if that changes anything for you."

I chew the inside of my cheek, wondering if not taking my pill a few hours ago was a mistake. It's only been a few hours, so it's easy enough to rectify in case this is the other shoe dropping. "Have you changed your mind?"

He lifts his head, almost looking startled. "Not even a little bit. I meant what I said, Ainsley. I think you're going to be an amazing mom. You're dedicated to your work, your clients, and your friends. I'm not sure how many women out there would have gone to the bachelorette party for their ex."

"I finally told them, you know, that I was thinking about getting pregnant," I say. "Obviously that was before your *proposition*." Ken waits patiently for me to go on. "They said all the right things about how they will be there for me and help me and be the cool aunts."

"Then I look forward to meeting them. Does that mean what I think it means?"

I slide my foot further up his lap, and Ken leans forward to put his empty tray on my desk. I stop my movement only when I find his cock already pressing against his jeans. I'm not sure if it's that I'm stroking him with my foot or the idea of making a baby with me that has him hard again already.

"Yes."

"Yes, what, Ainsley?" he grits out. Ken lets me keep touching him as he white-knuckles the armrests of the seat.

"Yes, I want to make a baby with you. Yes, I want you to fuck me and fill me. Yes, I want to have *your* baby."

I expect him to shoot out of the chair and use his already-hard dick to plow me right into next week. He doesn't. Instead, he leans back in the chair and grabs my foot, digging his thumb right into the arch.

Okay, I can live with this being the reason I'm moaning. Because I do moan. My head falls back as he works a knot in my foot from constantly trying to modify my height by way of sky-high heels.

"So tell me, why are you working so late?"

The whole situation feels so normal as I tell him about my week. He listens as I explain about Kyle dumping his clients on me abruptly before going to California and how frustrating it is.

To his credit, Ken stays until I finish gathering materials with me to take home. Working this late all week has me feeling all sorts of rundown.

Much as I don't want to, we go our separate ways at the subway with a lingering kiss and a promise to hammer out details soon. Tonight was unexpected, but if we're going to do this for real, we need to have a plan in place.

It's not until I get home and see my birth control packet on my nightstand do I realize I'm not even positive when the last time I took it was. Since I've committed to Ken that we're making a baby, I drop them back onto my nightstand to deal with later.

I give myself a summer Friday in May and leave work at two. If the rat Kyle was there, he would tell me that I wasn't behaving the way a partner should, and I would absolutely tell him he could shove being a partner up his ass.

It's not like I'm going to a hookah bar or day drinking or to the golf course. I'm going to go home and work more. I just want to do it in sweatpants and not a pencil skirt. Last night, I worked from home until two a.m. and then overslept my alarm, so by the time I call it a day, my hair is dirty, and I feel dirty. It doesn't help that the building doesn't turn the AC on until June, and it's an unseasonably warm day, so my office is like an inferno. But not like the night before, when Ken made me feel like I was burning alive in the best way.

I work until two a.m. again on Friday and shoot off a text to my friends that I won't be able to make brunch on Sunday because I just need the weekend to lie on my couch and watch my comfort show. I should be making plans to see Ken, but even that feels like almost too much. My brain has done all the thinking it can do.

No more.

I'm bundled in a blanket on Saturday afternoon when there is a knock at my door. Usually, my front desk will call up if there is someone here, but that's only if they stop. If someone just walks past, they won't really do anything to stop them. So glad my monthly common charges are being put to good use with security.

I'm surprised when I see Ken standing on the other side with bags in his hands. Pulling open the door, I study how good he looks. He's got a faded band t-shirt stretched over his muscles, and the urge to cover him in whipped cream just to lick every delicious hill and valley of his chest almost brings me to my knees.

"I could have been anyone," Ken scolds, stepping over the threshold.

"Are you tired of the same old song and dance? I have a peephole," I point out, letting the door close behind him. "But by all means, please come inside."

"I thought you would never ask." He gives me a kiss on the cheek before he steps into the kitchen and sets his bags on the counter.

"What's all this?" I ask, poking my head into the bags.

"Brunch. I called Eloise yesterday to check on the divorce

filing, and she told me you left early. Since I assumed you had work to do, I decided to come today to check on you. As much as I wanted to come over yesterday to spend time with you and watch you work, I figured you wouldn't appreciate the distraction, so…" He gestures at himself as if to say, *Here I am.*

"It's a little late for brunch," I point out, sour for no reason. All work and no play makes Ainsley a bitchy girl.

Ken lifts his head from unpacking the bags and really looks at me. My tank is stained with something from lunch, and my sweatpants are two sizes too big. They hang low on my hips and are comfortable as fuck. My hair is piled on my head in a loose scrunchie that has slowly slipped to the side all day. My lack of movement meant that it stayed just there. I am not dressed to be eye candy and that only makes me more annoyed. Ken and I might have agreed to make a baby together, but we're still a very long way from me being comfortable with him watching me shit myself when I give birth. I would have rather maintained the illusion that I am sexy at all times for just a little longer.

"Someone is in a mood," he comments, walking over to me. He doesn't seem bothered by my current status.

Some days, you just need to lie on the couch and veg out. Today was that day for me, and I don't want to be distracted from my mood. Ken places his hands on my hips, tugging me toward him. I don't move my feet, but I let my body lean toward him. I let myself sink into his kiss and his embrace and the feel of his firm chest against mine.

One of his hands slips up, grazing my cheek, then pulling my scrunchie out. My hair falls back and he slides his fingers through it.

"You know I enjoy your company," he says, looking at me.

"I do."

"And you know I'm invested in you and invested in us, not just as you being the mother of my child, but hopefully as something more." I blush a little at this, but nod. He's made that clear. "Then don't take offense to this."

"To what?" The words are barely out of my mouth before he's scooping me up and throwing me over his shoulder in a fireman's carry.

"You need a shower, because I plan on spending the rest of the night dirtying you up." He slaps my ass as he hauls me into my bedroom and then my bathroom.

When he sets me on the counter, I scowl at him and cross my arms defensively.

"What do you think you're doing?" I ask haughtily.

"Well, first I'm going to start the shower and then I plan on fucking you in it. I'm going to take extra care to clean your pussy after. Then once we're out, I'm going to lay you on the table and eat you out like you're my own personal feast. Once you're satisfied, I'm going to make you dinner because I plan on keeping this fuckfest going until at least midnight, so you will need your energy." While Ken is making this proclamation, he turns on the shower, waiting for it to get to a comfortable temperature.

"Is that all this is? Sex until I'm pregnant and barefoot in your kitchen?" I ask, annoyed.

Ken only laughs, approaching me slowly like an animal stalking its prey. His hands grip the bottom of my shirt, slowly lifting it, giving me my chance to object. I don't. Instead, I raise my hands over my head.

"I tell you I have feelings for you and *that's* what you ask? If this is just sex? Just because I love being inside you and I love hearing you swear under your breath when you come doesn't mean that there aren't feelings there too. Don't try to make this something that it's not because you're in a piss-poor mood. Let me have my feelings for this incredible, sexy, smart woman who swept me off my feet. Who, for the record, I don't expect to be barefoot in my kitchen."

I lean forward and kiss him. I tug his shirt off and then his pants, sliding myself off the counter. His hand threads into my hair, tugging gently, but I sink to my knees before him, taking him into my mouth.

"Ainsley." He moans my name and it sounds so sweet as I cup his balls, licking his tip. When he tries to thrust into my mouth, I cup his balls tighter, a warning to stop, but I think he enjoys the shot of pain with his pleasure because he does it again. Ken's hand is fisted in my hair, guiding my head in tandem with his thrusts, until he pulls his dick out of my mouth.

Around us, the steam of the shower has created a hazy fog, and Ken is clenching the counter. I bat my lashes, looking up at him. Once his hand is untangled from my hair, he grips my shoulders and pulls me up.

His kiss is hard and consuming, his tongue diving into my mouth. I can't even react before he pulls away abruptly. I look at him, surprised, but he doesn't tell me what to do. He moves my body, bending me over the counter. I make eye contact with him in the mirror and watch his fierce determination as he pulls down my sweats, exposing my ass to him. I gasp in shock at the hard spank he gives me and then the eager grin on his face before he uses his feet to nudge my legs apart. He thrusts inside me slowly, making sure I feel every delicious inch.

"Oh God," I moan, gripping the counter and dropping my head forward. Ken thrusts harder and harder, slapping my ass until he grips my hair, tugging my head up. I meet his eyes again, and I see him bite his lip in concentration. There is something deeply erotic about watching his face as he takes me from behind.

"I want to see your face when you come," he demands, focusing on his task.

I keep my head up even after he releases my hair so he can reach forward between my legs to my clit. My legs nearly give out at the feel of him touching me and inside me, and I want to move. I want to squirm against him, but he has me pinned so I have to take what he gives me, and he gives it to me so good. This is going to leave the best sort of bruise, even as my hip makes contact with the hard marble.

My nails dig into the counter as I feel my orgasm grow until it crashes over me. My head drops forward instinctively, but Ken grabs my hair again, lifting my head, so he can watch the flush spread on my skin. Watch the way my mouth drops open as a moan makes its way out of my throat. He explodes into me then, with my body clenching around him, both of us weak from our simultaneous orgasms.

Our knees give out and he eases us to the ground, my body cradled against his. He kisses my cheek, my jaw, the shell of my ear.

"And that was just the appetizer, ma chérie."

I'm dragging my French toast through cinnamony syrup when Ken reaches forward and tucks my hair behind my ear. He made good on his promise, nearly burning the first round of French toast when I sat on the counter and spread my legs, touching myself while he watched. He dropped the spatula before putting his mouth on me and making me scream just before we set off the fire alarm.

"Let's take a trip," Ken proposes before lifting a fork to his mouth.

"Where would you like to go?" I ask. It would be fun to play around with the idea of traveling. Outside of Charlie and Elia's wedding, I haven't taken more than two days off at a time in an embarrassingly long amount of time.

"I have a place on the Amalfi Coast. We can hole up there, drinking fine wine and eating fresh seafood."

My fork freezes halfway to my mouth and I lower it to look at him. "You never mentioned a place in Italy."

"I wouldn't. It's a family residence. My mother still owns it.

Not marital property. Don't worry, I'm not trying to pull a fast one on anybody." There is a flatness in his voice when he says this.

"Can you blame me for my concern? You mention this place, right as your divorce is finalized?"

"No, but I expected you to have a little more faith in me." He refills my glass of Prosecco.

"You're right. I'm sorry. Call me jaded. How do you expect this trip to fit in with trying to get me pregnant?"

Ken swirls the wine in his glass. "I expect it would be a good time for us to start trying in earnest. Or we can practice while we're there and hammer out all the details you want. I should have offered to use a condom since you should be getting off birth control to reset your cycle."

I push my empty plate away and pull my knees up to my chest, stretching out my shirt and tugging it over my knees. Ken, meanwhile, adds another helping to his plate.

"Yeah. I had that thought already." I pull my wine glass toward me, but Ken holds my wrist back gently.

When I woke up this morning, I counted out the days on my pill pack and saw I was only four days behind. The last time I was with someone who wasn't Ken was that ill-conceived hookup with the bartender at Ken's bar. Not one of my better moments, but I needed something to get my married client out of my head. If I could do it again, I wouldn't.

After counting my pills, I tossed the pack into my purse so maybe the next time I would remember it when the alarm went off. It was all fun and breeding games in my office, but we have no plan in place if I actually do get pregnant. Being responsible would mean taking my pills until we have an agreement signed and in place.

"What sort of thoughts?" Ken asks.

"Just thinking about when I should stop it."

"Today. Stop it today. We have time to figure out the logistics of custody and education. Run a background check on me, and you'll see that there are no skeletons in my closet. My sister is married to a senator. Having an open relationship with my wife was just about as controversial as it got. Well, that and I think my brother-in-law might be the only man in government who has sex with just his wife." Ken grabs the leg of my chair, pulling me closer to him. "If you're ready, I mean. Fuck, this isn't something I should be pressuring you into, but I'm ready and I want this. I want you, and I want a baby with *you*. But if you need more time, it's your body, and we can go at your pace."

"No radical views I should be aware of?"

His fingers stroke along the inside of my thigh, working higher and higher, until he finds me wet and wanting. He smirks then kisses me.

"Just that I think modesty is overrated. If you're not ready to take that step, then keep taking the pill. We can discuss it all as we sit on my balcony with your perfect tits out while I go down on you." He slips a finger inside me and I gasp.

He takes the opening, his mouth descending on mine while he brings me to the brink with his finger sliding in and out of me. The heel of his hand presses against my clit and I grind against him, glad I opted to not put on panties in favor of this ludicrously long shirt.

Ken pulls away so he can watch me, so he can listen to me beg him for my release. I grip his arm, my fingers digging into his skin until he hisses when I draw blood.

"Fuck, Ken, I'm so close," I whine, my hips moving harder. His other hand grips the nape of my neck, turning my head so he can kiss my throat. He brings his mouth up to my ear, kissing before tugging with his teeth. I cry out as the orgasm wracks my body, and he keeps moving until my breathing and hips have steadied.

When I open my eyes, I see he's removed his hand from my hair and he's touching himself. I bite my lip, glimpsing the bead of liquid on the tip of his cock before I get up and lower myself over him. I'm facing him, lifting my body slowly before bringing myself down over him, over and over again, until I can't do it anymore and I just have to move my hips back and forth, chasing a second release in as many minutes. When my head tips back, he sucks and nips at my neck, no doubt giving me a hickey like we're teenagers.

"That's right, baby, ride me."

I'm screaming my release before biting down on the fleshy part of his shoulder in an effort to keep myself even somewhat together, but I can't because I'm whimpering as I hear his own grunts when he thrusts up into me, coming inside me again.

His eyes are hazy with lust and satisfaction when he leans forward with a quick kiss.

"I think this calls for ordering in some Sleepless Cookies and watching some movies," he says before easing me off him so he can start the cleanup. I cross my legs, holding him inside me as I watch him walk away, and I know that any objectivity or hope I had to not catch feelings disappeared long before this moment.

Nine

SUNDAY MORNING, we're entwined on the couch.

Since I've decided to hell with doing things the way they should be done, I agree to go to Italy. If Kyle can dump a steaming pile of shit on my desk to fuck a porn star, I can take two weeks off to spread my legs and see what it takes to make a baby. Once I mentioned to Ken that it was my birthday this month, he wasted no time booking flights so we could celebrate the day properly—with lots of dick and Prosecco.

We've been trying to come up with a plan for our trip to Italy and I'm torn about wanting to go out and do things and just screw the entire trip. I do mean literally fuck for two weeks straight. Ken is lazily stroking me while I eat pizza when I hear the sound of keys in my door.

I drop the pizza, my body tensing at the sound. It causes me to clench around his fingers, and I can't help the moan I release.

"Does someone have keys to your apartment?" Ken asks, annoyingly calm as he thrusts his fingers deeper in me, moving from lazy to a punishing tempo.

"Plenty of someones," I hiss, batting his hand away. The most concerning someone is my father. I wouldn't put it past him to drop by, though usually he has the decency to text first.

"Who is it?" I call, glad I engaged the security lock, until the door pushes open, revealing Taryn. Apparently, I *forgot* to re-engage the lock after the pizza was delivered. I grab a throw pillow and toss it at Ken, who drops it on his lap, his boxers around his ankles.

"Hi," Taryn says, brow furrowed as she takes in the sight. "You skipped brunch."

I did skip brunch, but in my defense I told them so on Friday night when I knew I wasn't going to be in the mood to see anyone after the week I had at work, cleaning up Kyle's mess.

"You didn't answer our texts!" Elia exclaims as she and Vivian burst through the door behind Taryn. I'm confused how they managed to get separated, but I'm more focused on my friends standing in front of me while I'm only wearing the band shirt that Ken had on when he came over yesterday.

"Hi, I'm Ken," he says, standing, holding the pillow in front of him. There really is no clean way around this.

Elia and Vivian both come up short, looking at Ken from head to toe. I step around Ken to block his body so we can awkwardly shuffle toward the hallway to my bedroom, where the rest of his clothes are.

"If this is why you blew off brunch, I get it," Vivian says appreciatively before breaking into giggles.

I spin to face Ken, who is fighting a smirk. "Why don't you shower or something?" I ask as if we aren't fresh from a shower.

"Or something," he mutters before looking away from me to my friends. The searing look in his eyes makes me wonder if he's going to go in there and finish what I had started. "Nice to meet you."

"Yeah, you too!" they chorus at him. All three of them tilt their heads to catch his ass in the brief moment between him moving the pillow from his front to his back.

"What are you doing here?" I whisper-hiss at them.

"Wellness check," Taryn says defensively, sitting down at one of the chairs at my kitchen table. "Though it seems you are puh-lenty well here. Endowed, that is."

Elia giggles, grabbing a slice of pizza and eating it cold.

"Someone was over-served," I observe with a smirk.

Vivian is already journeying into the kitchen to get glasses of water. "Charlie's dad showed back up at the apartment," Vivian explains, and I blanch.

"What?" I demand.

Elia waves her pizza at me. "Don't worry. I mean, it's not like he called me a low-class whore out for his son's money and threatened to forcibly remove me from my home since I'm not on the deed. Something about membership of the owning LLC or something." She swipes at the corner of her eye to stop a tear, suddenly so much more sober.

"Well, where the hell is Charlie in all this?" I nearly shout.

"He was literally in the air flying to London for work. It's like Charlie's dad knew and was waiting for Charlie to be out of reach."

"Why didn't you call?"

I feel Vivian's hand on my shoulder as she eases into the seat beside me. "She called me. I happened to be with an adversary at the time, and he jumped in to help. Nothing like having two lawyers show up to get you to shut up."

"I told Charlie to finish his trip, and that I was okay. I just, I'm still rattled by it. He's flying home today."

"Is there anything I can do?" I offer, feeling so helpless to see my friend this way.

"Pour me another drink."

I glance at my bedroom door but get to my feet to head toward the fridge to pour drinks for all of us.

"We should go," Taryn says, testing the water. "You have a

literal hot piece of ass in that bedroom waiting to devour you whole."

"It's fine. This, *you guys,* are more important than bouncing on a dick for a few hours." I pass out a glass of Prosecco to everyone.

"Is it just bouncing on it, or is there more involvement from the other party?" Vivian asks shamelessly.

"There is a whole lot more than just bouncing on his dick, I promise," I tell her with a laugh.

"But what about having a baby? I mean, obviously no pressure, but like, I won't admit that I haven't been buying onesies," Elia says, though I think she gets lost in her own sentence.

"What?" Taryn sounds as confused as I feel.

"I've been buying cute onesies I see online, like 'I love my auntie' and 'milk drunk' and other really adorable things for future nieces or nephews. Could be multiples if you're doing IVF."

"I'm actually going on vacation and will have an update after that about getting pregnant."

The girls all *ohhh* and *ahh* over this news. They're asking questions I don't have the answers to, and when they ask about being able to go over the sperm donor books with me, I wave them off.

I'm still trying to figure out exactly what this is with Ken before I dive into explaining it to my friends. I would love to tell them that I'm actually trying to make a baby with the gorgeous man hiding in my bedroom, but telling them that while he's still here feels a little odd. Besides, we could get to the end of this two-week trip and decide we're both unbearable to live with, and then I might have a baby but no man.

When the door closes behind my friends, I turn and find Ken leaning against the hallway toward my bedroom.

"Sounds like a group of eager aunties I would hate to disappoint. We should get to work on giving them that nibling."

Ken rushes me, scooping me into his arms before hauling me into the bedroom so we can do exactly as promised.

Ken stays with me most nights unless he's working late at the bar. Sometimes in the early morning hours, he wakes me with kisses and a quick, dirty fuck during which we're both half asleep but full of need. I'm not complaining.

On nights when he meets me after work, he takes care of me, cooking dinner and taking care of my laundry before popping out to check on the bar. It's a glimpse of the domesticity that we could share.

Even though he's at my apartment most nights, thoughts of him are distracting as I try to wrap up work the week leading up to our trip. It has been a whirlwind, but sometimes you don't need a long courtship to prove you have something worthwhile. Honestly, though, traveling together might be the best way to really see if we're compatible long term. There is nothing like having to occupy a small space and be the only source of company to really get your priorities in order.

"You're really going away?" Eloise asks the Friday of my flight.

Ken and I have a red-eye from JFK to Rome and from there we're taking a train to Pompei and a car from there on. My suitcase is calling to me from the corner of my office.

"I'm *really* going away," I say, looking over my calendar. I took off to go to Charlie's wedding, but I otherwise haven't taken much time off since...ever. Part of that was because getting Charlie to take a vacation was like telling a kid they need to go to the dentist. It was painful for all involved parties.

"It's weird," she says, picking at her nails.

I lift my eyes to look at her. "I promise to bring you back some good wine and olive oil."

She sighs dramatically. "I guess you deserve it. I just don't know what I'm going to do. You're going to be gone for two weeks."

"You're going to support Jeff and make sure that my clients are taken care of if they have any questions. You're going to have a life for two weeks because you won't have to work until eight at night."

"Sure, sure, but I'm still going to miss you." Eloise shifts in her chair, tossing her notepad onto my desk. We've just spent the last forty-five minutes going over everything that could possibly come up. Kyle might be willing to dump all his clients on someone else, but I don't trust anyone else to handle my files.

My phone chirps, and I glance at it, not surprised to find a text from Ken.

> Were you aware that cunniligus could increase my sperm count? Sounds like I get to feast from you and then fill you to the brim with my come.

I shiver at the text then flip my phone over. He's been sending me fun little facts about sex and getting pregnant. When he brings groceries over, the bags are packed with food meant to increase our chances. I'm almost worried he doesn't see me as more than just a vessel. He's said that he wants more, but I need to really *see* that from him.

Maybe I should pump the breaks and take my birth control. Ken said he would be fine with it if I waited until I was ready. I haven't taken it, not since before we agreed to try for a baby, but as a lawyer I know I should do more to get an agreement in place first.

"I might miss you, but I'm not going to miss this place." I glance behind her. "Close the door."

Eloise leans back on the hind legs of her chair before pushing it closed. "What's the big secret?" she whispers conspiratorially.

"I'm going to shop my resume around when I'm away and see if I can get anyone to bite, but I need to know if we're a packaged deal." Switching jobs while trying to get pregnant isn't the best course of action, but the lack of support from the partners when

Kyle decided to go away really rubbed me the wrong way. Regularly, I'm asked to pick up slack even from different departments. They seem to think my Harvard law degree makes me an expert in all things.

"As long as you're not going to drag me into corporate law hell, then absolutely. I'm wasting my life away when there are no cute attorneys here for me to hook up with." She's teasing, but I hear a hint of concern in her voice.

"You've proven yourself way too valuable to me for me to not make sure you're taken care of."

"I appreciate that, but honestly, I just want to get out. I've been considering leaving, anyway."

My head snaps to Eloise. She never expressed an interest in leaving before now. I wonder what's changed.

My phone rings, stopping me from delving into the issue. I wave Eloise out before picking up my cell.

"Hey, Dad," I greet after checking the caller ID.

"Any chance I can take my favorite girl to lunch today?"

"I have a lot of work to get done. I'm actually going away tonight."

"Some bachelorette party or something?" I can hear the creak of his office chair as he leans back. I can picture him, propping his feet up on his desk, looking down Fifth Avenue with New York City at his feet.

"No, I'm actually going to Italy for two weeks."

He's silent for a beat. "You're going to miss your birthday."

"I know, Daddy."

"Well, who are you going away with? Or are you doing some of that Snacky Holy Happiness?"

I chuckle at his very wrong name. "No, Dad, I'm not going to *Eat Pray Love*. I'm actually going with a guy I met. His family owns a home in Positano."

"And when do I get to meet this young man who is whisking my daughter away to another country?"

"I don't know, maybe never?"

He laughs from his side of the phone. "Come to lunch with me. If you're leaving your old man alone on your birthday, it's the least you can do."

I lean back in my chair, wanting to rub my eyes, and glance at the clock.

"I can meet you at our usual spot," I relent. To be honest, I do miss my father and it will be good to see him.

"I'll call ahead. See you in an hour." He doesn't even give me a chance to respond before hanging up, but the hour is good. It gives me time to wrap up what I'm working on before meeting him.

Just as I'm packing up to go, there is a knock at my door. I glance up, about to power down my laptop, but in walks one of the partners of the firm.

"Eugene," I greet, looking around my desk to make sure everything is in place.

"I was going to call you to my office, but I heard from my secretary that you were headed out the door." He glances at my suitcase disdainfully before stepping totally into my space.

"Is there something I can do for you?" I rise, careful to slip myself back into my heels that are under my desk. Most days I work barefoot until I have to walk around and then it's sky high heels and long legs.

"I wanted to have a chat with you about your future in the firm."

I'm almost certain that he can hear my heart hammering. "What about it?"

"We're looking at some mid-year raises this year, possibly elevating someone to partner." He glances again at my suitcase. "I know that you have some time off scheduled, but I would be lying if I said that we weren't considering what your future at the firm could look like."

"I'm going to need you to be very clear about what you're trying to say, Eugene."

"I'm saying that if you buckle down, you could see partner after your name by the end of summer."

I fight the urge to bring my hands up to my mouth so I can gnaw on my nail. It goes against everything I *just* told Eloise, but if I make partner this summer, maybe one more year wouldn't be so bad. Only one more year, and I can easily translate that into a new job, even if it doesn't necessarily mean partner there.

It could mean the difference between finding a place where I can make my own rules for Eloise and I and having to land somewhere else that I need to spend another five to ten years working my way up to partner.

"Would becoming partner make it easier for me to get my pro bono work started?"

The only thing more distasteful to Eugene than his staff taking vacation is them doing free work. "We can discuss the possibility."

Not exactly a yes, but not a no, either. "Is this a guarantee?"

Eugene laughs. "Nothing is a guarantee, sweetheart, but you have shown promise, even if you're doing something like taking two weeks off right on the heels of another vacation."

Two weeks off, as if I take vacation time constantly.

"Just something to think about," he continues. "We want to see you take a more active role in the other departments in the firm. You need to be well-rounded. It means long hours, but I'm sure you can do it. It's not like you have a family to go home to."

My father is standing outside the Italian restaurant, shouting into his phone. His entire demeanor changes when I approach him, and he quickly ends the call to embrace me.

"How is my daughter?"

"Just fine, Daddy. Who were you yelling at?" I ask as he holds the door open for me.

"Charles Breckenridge crying for more money."

I slow my steps as we approach the hostess stand. "Charlie?"

"No, his lout of a father keeps trying to get me to invest, as if I liked the guy. I only invested with him in the past because of Charlie, and he doesn't seem to accept that. Just wait till he hears that I gave Charlie some seed money to invest in a new startup he was telling me about. But enough about them. I want to hear about the man that is whisking you away to Italy. Full name, date of birth, social security number, just the basics."

"His name is Ken, he owns a bar, and that's all you're getting out of me right now. It's still new."

We're led to our table and we take a few minutes to get situated. For years, my father and I have met here for lunch, to the point that we are no longer provided with menus because they know our usual. We have a usual table tucked in the corner with a server we have come to know well over the years. It certainly helps that my father was an angel investor that got this place on its feet.

"As long as he doesn't expect you to be his airheaded Barbie with no ambitions of your own. You didn't get two ivy league degrees to sit at home and be some trophy wife. It's bad enough you're playing around with this divorce law."

"I enjoy what I do."

"Breaking up marriages?"

That one hits a little too close to home for me. Ken and his wife were already ending their marriage when we met, but it doesn't make me feel any less icky when I think about lusting after him after the first time we met.

"No, I help guide people through a really difficult time in their lives. I wish that you could accept this. I wish that you could see the good I'm doing and not just focus on how much my salary is."

My father leans back in his seat, chastened. It's an argument we've had countless times. It's an argument we're going to have unless I switch to corporate law. "You're right. How could I forget?"

We're silent while we wait for the waiter to bring over our meals. I wave away the glass of wine that is offered and my father's eyebrows shoot up.

"What? I'm making some changes in my life."

He leans toward me, abruptly pressing his hand to my forehead. The truth is, I want to take down my wine intake before really trying to get pregnant. Just having that thought makes me think of my birth control sitting in my purse–judging me for playing it both ways. I haven't taken them, but having them with me feels like a safety net...like if Ken changes his mind, I can just start them again like nothing happened.

"You don't feel sick. Are you a doppelganger of my daughter?"

I scowl. "You're *so* funny."

He chuckles to himself. "I am. Are you ready to at least get out of that dead-end firm you've been stuck at?"

"I don't know what you're talking about," I huff. I still have to think about Eugene's offer about possibly becoming partner. Not that it's a genuine offer yet, but it's still something to consider, especially when weighed with having a baby. It's a total dick move to negotiate for a new job and then spring that I'm pregnant on them. I know it's fine to do, but I'd feel bad. I want to have a real future at my next firm and whether I agree with them or not, there are serious judgments about starting a new job when you're knocked up.

"Darling, don't play dumb with me. You're too smart for that. I know that you're not happy. Let me make some phone calls for you."

I'm twirling my squid ink noodles around my fork then put it down. "Stop meddling. If I wanted your help, I would ask for it, but the more you push me, the less I actually want it, so please, Dad, stop."

He holds up his hands defensively. "Okay, I'm sorry. But you are leaving that firm, right? You've always been smarter than those schmucks that run that place."

"Your opinion is noted. Yes, I am going to start looking for a new job, but probably not until after I get back from Italy."

"Right, right."

We spend the rest of lunch discussing what I'm going to do while I'm away and what sort of jobs I'm going to be looking for. I'm not ready to confess how real my feelings for Ken are, not yet. My father can be a little intense, and he knew Charlie for years before I finally admitted to him that we were a couple. I can't imagine what throwing Ken at him with no preparation on any of our parts would do. No, I can't do that to Ken.

I promise to let my dad know when I get to Italy and when I get back so we can have an appropriate birthday celebration. I even agree to talk it over with Ken to see if he can be coerced into coming. Knowing Ken? He'll say yes. But I know my father and what he will do to any man coming into my life.

When I get to the airport, Ken has already checked my bag. We had the foresight to know that I was going to cut it close with leaving work late and the traffic getting to Queens. I spent the hour-long drive biting my nails and checking my watch. Thank God for TSA Precheck.

"Sorry I'm late," I huff, running to meet him at the entrance to the security line.

"It's not like you missed anything." He kisses my temple and we flash our passports at the agent making sure we have Precheck to get in.

It feels natural leaning into Ken when his arm is slung over my shoulders. I'm exhausted and we haven't even gotten on the flight yet. I wish we had splurged for business class or first class, but the thought didn't even cross my mind when I booked the tickets. I've never been one to pay extra for the things that we deserve as humans. I might have the money, but it makes me mad to incentivize the assholes at the airlines to treat us like cattle.

A red-eye transatlantic flight probably would have been the time to bury my principles.

"Have a good last day?" Ken asks after we slip through the metal detectors.

"I had a day. Dad and I got lunch. He wanted to grill me on my new beau who was stealing me away to Italy like you were Hades riding off with me into the Underworld." I don't mention my conversation with Eugene, because I still haven't figured out what I think about it.

"I would corrupt you in the most beautiful of ways, my fair Goddess of Spring."

"You only wish you could do the corrupting," I tease once we're away from the TSA agents. Ken gives me a twisted grin, grabbing my carry-on without a word.

I'm still trying to fire off some emails to anxious clients while we walk to our gate. We skip the lounge in favor of sitting at our gate because our boarding begins soon.

"Is everything set up at the bar?" I ask, slipping my phone into my pocket.

"Yeah, I have a buddy of mine checking in on it and Leslie agreed to pop in when I told her I was going out of town. And before you say anything, I'm trying to break the habit. She was the one person I told everything to. It's going to be a minute before I remember I don't have to tell her my comings and goings."

"You can't expect these things to happen overnight and it's okay if you still talk," I hedge, digging into my bag. I'm glad I changed at the office into my flight-ready gear: a pair of comfortable leggings with pockets, of course, and a light sweater.

"Really? My girlfriend is okay if I keep talking to my ex-wife?" He sounds dubious.

"You make it sound like you're booty-calling her in the middle of the night. I believe you when you say you're no longer looking for that open relationship that you had with her, so of course, I'm not worried you're going to go back and fuck her. Am I jealous? Yes. Do I love that you're still talking to her? Not really? Am I in any position to tell you who you can and cannot talk to after we've been together for a month? No. I mean, look at Charlie and me. It took some time before we were back to speaking terms again, and he's not exactly my in-case-of-emergency, but he's someone I know is reliable and I can count on if I'm in trouble. I have no leg to stand on. Don't make me the villain in your story."

"I wouldn't dream of it. I just... you're being insanely calm about this whole situation."

I laugh in his face. "What would you like me to do? Go off the rails every time you mention Leslie? Would you like me to forbid you from ever talking to her or about her? You had a life together. You were a family. It's not going to endear me to you or your family if I get all huffy every time you mention her."

"You don't have to worry about meeting my family anytime soon. My sister and her kids live in DC, and my mom moved closer to my sister so she can be there with the kids."

"Won't I meet them at your divorce reception?"

Ken chuckles and stands when first class is called for boarding. "Come on. Let's go." He offers me his hand. "You weren't seriously going to come to that, were you?"

"Aren't we in economy?" I ask.

He grins and passes me the boarding pass, which shows first class. "Let's go, buttercup. We're flying in style. Happy Birthday." He gives me a devilish wink, taking my bag again.

It's a welcome surprise as we move down the gangway and are led to the honeymoon seating chairs in the middle of first class.

"Thank you," I say, rewarding him with a kiss on the cheek.

He grins at me, proud to have pulled this off. "Anything for my girl. But seriously, are you coming to the party?"

We settle into our seats with a glass of champagne each.

"Of course, I was considering going. I've never been invited to a divorce reception in all the years I've been doing this. You don't think it's a good idea?"

"Buttercup, you can do whatever you want. If you want to come, we just have to decide if you're coming as my divorce attorney or my girlfriend. I figured the latter would have complications."

Girlfriend sends a little thrill of delight through me. I want to be his girlfriend. I want to have his baby, and all of those things are big feeling things outside of just an agreement to have a baby together. Maybe because I've started to want a baby *together*.

"Let's see if we even survive this two-week vacation before we decide how you're going to introduce me."

We clink our glasses in agreement.

The honeymoon seating means we can comfortably talk to each other during the flight, though I plan to try to sleep after they serve dinner. The pod we're in lets us get close, but not close enough to snuggle while we sleep. After the dessert is cleared away, I pull my blanket up around me.

"This is extravagant," I say as the separator door slides shut behind the flight attendant.

"It's all in good fun. Besides," Ken's fingers graze my cheek before he lets his hand slip lower, "it gives us more privacy than in coach."

"What, sir, do you think you are doing?" I ask with a smirk. I know where this is headed, and I have no objection.

"I think an orgasm should be considered for the mile high club," Ken whispers as his hand slips into the waistband of my pants.

I can't contain the harsh breath I release as he slides his fingers against my clit. I whine at the first contact with my sensitive nerve endings.

My mind eddies of all thoughts as his fingers circle me. I don't think about the man snoring already across the aisle or the flight attendant who can walk by at any moment and scold us, even if it could be possible Ken's just touching my hip. The whimper that escapes through my clenched teeth is a dead giveaway as he dips his fingers inside me.

I close my eyes and let myself relax into his touch, like I can forget that we're on a plane, thirty thousand feet in the air.

"When we get to Italy, I'm going to make sure that you know every which way I want you. I'm going to fuck you in the shower, in the pool, on the train."

I can't form a witty response as he brings me closer to the brink. I grip his arm, my nails digging into his skin.

"Ken," I cry, trying to keep my voice low.

"Just fall. Just let go and fall," he pushes, and I obey.

My body clenches around him as his movements continue. I bite my lip so hard that I taste blood.

He waits until I open my eyes again, until I can see straight again and my heart rate calms. He pulls his hand from my pants so he can prop on his elbow. I meet him halfway for a kiss.

The kiss is so soft I think I might have missed it before he pulls back to lie comfortably in his pod. I catch how he has to roll his wrist to adjust from the strain.

"Now, get some rest. We still have a few more hours of the flight." His eyes skirt over me, even under this comfortable blanket.

Contentment and exhaustion wrap me in a warm cocoon, and I let myself sleep.

Ten

ROME IS POSSIBLY one of my favorite cities to visit. I have been here several times before, thanks to my father's insistence that I be worldly as I grew up. He wanted to make sure that I was aware that there was more to the planet than the shores of the United States.

"We should get a cappuccino and wander for a little," Ken suggests after we drop off our bags.

A coffee sounds like exactly what I need, so I readily agree. We wander until we find a small coffee shop on a piazza where we can sit and people-watch.

"I've always been jealous of people who were able to make travel their jobs."

Ken's eyes slide away from a couple who are very clearly on their honeymoon. They're nestled so close that they're practically on top of each other. It's disgustingly adorable. "From what I understand, you're wealthy enough to make that a reality. Why not do it?"

I look away from his steady gaze and swirl my cup around the plate it sits on. "Instead, I did all the things I was supposed to do—

college, law school, boyfriend, fiancé, good job. Things sort of broke down at the get married part."

"I'm glad it did, but why not do some of that now?" Ken's words touch something inside me, the options that I wanted, that I wished I had.

"Haven't you heard? We're trying to have a baby. Besides, I like to have roots. My apartment is amazing and getting brunch with my friends is often the highlight of my week. I just want to travel more. You know, before Charlie and Elia's wedding, I can't remember the last time I took more than two consecutive days off?"

"I hate to break it to you, buttercup, but babies put a cramp on traveling."

"For a few years, sure, but my dad introduced me to traveling young, and I want to do that for my kids, kid, whatever the case may be."

"My family having a place in Italy will be convenient then. My sister used to bring the boys to the house once a year to make them cultured. Not sure how much it's working because they spend most of the time on their tablets."

"How old are they?" I grab the cream pastry on the table and take a bite.

"There's three of them, all boys, much to my sister's disappointment. Eleven, eight, and five. I think she mentioned that she and her husband were thinking about adopting a little girl. They're devils, but they're a great time. And don't think my sister is disappointed in her kids. She loves them to pieces, but she's a girly girl, all frilly things and nonsense."

"Frilly things are not nonsense," I correct petulantly.

"Perhaps you should never meet my sister. I'm afraid what would happen if you did."

"Probably infect you with our frilly girliness."

"Do you know what you want?"

"I mean, I want another chocolate croissant, if that's what you mean."

Ken chuckles and sips his coffee. "I meant do you want a boy or a girl, wiseass."

"I don't really care. A happy and healthy baby would be enough. I feel like there can be so much pressure in wanting one or the other. Like those crazy gender reveal parties where one of the parents is so disappointed that it's clear on their face and then the kid will see that when they get older. It's like naming a child after their parent; it's so pretentious, and sure, it's nice to pass down a family name, but kids already have to worry about so much as they grow up. Having to deal with living up to their parent, never mind if their parent passes or is a terrible person."

"You say that with such authority."

"Well, I hate that this keeps coming back to my ex, but Charlie has the same name as his father. He hates being called Charles because of that, and I think he was more cognizant of not becoming his father."

"It's not like you can ignore that you were engaged. It would be like pretending that I was never married. It's no secret we've been with other people, but those relationships helped to get us to each other. They helped to make us who we are, and they got us to this moment."

"This moment?"

"Yes, this very moment, sitting in Rome, eating pastries and drinking expensive Italian coffee. This moment, of course, proceeds several moments that are going to be spent absolutely and completely naked."

"I'm looking forward to those moments," I say with a blush.

"I'm looking forward to those moments too, but I'm thoroughly enjoying *this* moment. I'm enjoying all of my moments with you." He reaches out and snags the last bite of my cream puff.

"You might have a lot fewer moments if you keep that type of behavior up."

"Can I make it up to you by plying you with gelato and baked goods?"

"I think you're going to need to figure out a way to get me a vegetable at some point on this trip, otherwise I'm going to die of sugar overload."

"What a way to go though, am I right?"

His words are teasing, but I lean into him. Ken's right. Every moment in our lives led us here and I can't be mad about a single one.

The drive to the house in Positano took longer than usual. The picturesque cliffside roads were gorgeous as we drove, and they were gorgeous every time I had to ask the driver to stop because of my nausea. I've always had mild car sickness, but in New York City, it's not enough of a problem to worry about. The roads of Italy are a whole other ballgame. It felt like too much, as if the pressure to get pregnant and the possibility of making partner at work looming over my head was weighing on me when mixed with all the gluttonous foods we've been eating.

There was so much curving and winding that every time there was a lookout, I would squeeze Ken's knee in a silent plea to stop. The driver started getting antsy after the third stop, but there was clearly an amount of money that soothed that aggravation.

I had planned to thoroughly explore the villa we're staying in, but by the time we get to the house, all I want is to lie down with a ginger ale and some crackers.

Ken takes care to pay the driver before heralding me into the house and setting me up in the bedroom we'll be using.

"I'm so sorry," I whisper, apologizing for the thousandth time.

"You have nothing to apologize for," Ken tells me, pressing a damp compress to my forehead.

"We should have been here hours ago. I should have gotten Dramamine or something."

"You asked to sit in the front seat to alleviate any carsickness, and the driver said no. Buttercup, it's okay, we're still here for nearly two weeks. There will be plenty of time for everything we want to get up to. I'm going to run out to get us some groceries and some Dramamine for the drive home."

"Stop talking about this trip ending already. It's barely begun," I whine.

Ken takes care to tuck a blanket up around me before heading to the store, opting to leave me alone in the house while he gets groceries. I'm not sure I can even call this place a house or a villa. It's enormous, the kind of place that you see in movies pretending normal people live like this. Normal people do not live in places that are actually small hotels.

This villa has at least ten bedrooms and enough bathrooms to match. I want to explore and be nosey, but I let my body rest instead. I want to be able to enjoy the decadent food, amazing views, and sinful sex.

I wish I had paid more attention to the foyer when we walked through because the bedroom alone is spectacular. A king size bed is pressed against what looks like an original fresco. I would be impressed, if I could see straight. I must doze off because the brush of Ken's lips across my forehead wakes me.

"How are you feeling?" he asks, pushing my hair back.

"A lot better. I think that I still haven't recovered from the jet lag. It's hitting me harder than I thought." It's a different level of bone-weary exhaustion, and I wonder if it's my body's way of adjusting to the complete lack of pressure.

"Getting old has its disadvantages."

"I think you're teasing me and it is not at all funny."

"Buttercup, I am older than you, I get it. Let me make you some delicious dinner and we can sit on the balcony and watch the sunset."

"You have a balcony?" I ask, throwing the blankets back. My interest is piqued, but my focus on food matters more.

"Why don't you start feeling human and then I can give you the whole tour? Because yes, there are more than five balconies, and we have our own brand of limoncello."

"Sounds like this is a lot more than a five-cent tour."

"More like a five-dollar tour."

I slip into the bathroom, which features a beautiful blue mosaic in the freestanding shower stall. I can't wait to let the shower heads bear down on me. I can't wait to enjoy the space. I needed a break from New York City more than I care to admit. The trips for Elia's bachelorette and Charlie's wedding were great, but there was a level of needing to be "on" that I don't need to be for Ken. With him, I'm allowed to be me.

When I emerge, I catch Ken dumping to-go containers into beautiful hand-painted pasta bowls.

"I promise, I will cook, but tonight is about relaxing. I stopped at the hotel across the street and asked them for takeout. The hostess almost balked at the request, but she knows my family."

"I get it. This is your vacation too. You don't have to cook for me the whole time. I'm just glad we're getting to do this."

I take my time now, really looking at the space. We're on the main floor of the villa. I know that there is a second floor as well as another level below, but I don't think the downstairs is a basement.

The front door opens to a large living area. A pool table is set out, along with four couches that circle around a fireplace. The-floor-to-ceiling windows are more modern than the rest of the space. Oddly, it fits. The large windows let in ample amounts of sunlight so even if the weather isn't conducive to sitting outside, you still get a beautiful view of the Italian coast.

Outside the windows is a beautiful outdoor sitting area with lounge chairs and an infinity pool. This place has all the hallmarks of being a hotel more than a private residence.

"Should we sit outside?" Ken offers, carrying over the two bowls.

I don't have to open the door to know that it's chilly outside. Early May and being on the coast means that while the view might be great, the temperature won't be.

"How about a fire instead?" I propose.

"Your wish is my command."

I settle onto a couch, pulling the bowl up with me. The seafood risotto is bathed in Pecorino Romano–the only real way to eat pasta is with a mountain of grated cheese on top. The fresher the grate, the better. At first sniff, my stomach churns. The seafood may not be the best idea, but I want to soldier on because it's going to taste amazing. I know it will.

I moan at the first taste, my head dropping back. The initial sound is for pleasure, the second little moan is me trying to force myself to swallow. Thankfully, Ken doesn't seem to notice.

"If you keep making sounds like that, your dinner is going to go cold." Ken glances up as he turns on the gas fireplace. The fire roars, filling the space with warmth. He grabs his plate from the table and nestles beside me. His plate of gnocchi in a red sauce calls to me, but I'm not sure I'm at the point where I can ask him to switch with me.

"We can play later. Now, we need to fill my tummy with the yummy." I play with my food, moving the seafood off to the side while I grab a big scoop of just the rice so I can take a big bite.

"It's very sexy, you know, how much pasta you can fit in your mouth at once."

"If you want to get laid ever again, you will not discuss how much I eat and how much I can fit in my mouth at once."

"I've got something that you can fit in your mouth." Ken leans over and kisses my neck.

I laugh and take another bite of my food. Each bite is getting easier than the last. "Food first, blow jobs later."

"You're right. We do have plenty of time for all the sex in the world." Ken's eyes flick to my plate, taking note of how I'm moving the food around. "Stomach still unsettled?"

"Just a little," I admit.

Ken takes my plate and switches it with his. "Try that. Otherwise, I did get some bread in case you were still feeling like this."

I take a bite of the gnocchi and moan again. This seems to please my stomach and I'm able to eat this at least. "Sorry for stealing your meal."

"Enough with the apologies. I'll eat whatever. I don't want you feeling sick or eating something just to please me."

It's a glimpse of the treatment I'm sure to get if we ever get pregnant together.

"How long has your family owned this place?"

Ken talks me through the ownership, how his great-grandparents converted their large home to a hotel during World War II for the British who were based there. It makes sense now, the number of bathrooms and bedrooms that fill the space. It was a big house before, but they purchased the house next door to spread out even further.

The family fights to keep it with direct descendants, with ownership being held in a trust with very specific ownership requirements. The law nerd in me would love to get my hands on the ironclad document to see how both the trust and the ownership really work together.

I love the romanticism behind the story. How the family has been so devoted to the maintenance and keeping it in the family.

"It's an amazing story," I say, gathering our plates and walking them into the kitchenette.

"There was even a rumor that my great-aunt was from an affair with a British soldier because she is so much younger than my grandparents."

"Could be she was actually your aunt," I propose, drifting back into the living room. I plop beside him on the couch, exhausted.

"I don't know if I like what you're proposing but for the 1940s, it checks out. Nothing like an illicit love child, either way. Certainly makes for an interesting story."

"Someone in your family really needs to write a book about it."

Ken maneuvers my legs so they lie over his lap. He takes my foot gently and starts to rub it, digging his thumb into my arch. I have to fight a moan, otherwise this man will jump on me. Not that I'm complaining, but I'm enjoying getting to know him outside the bedroom.

"I think my sister might want to, but I don't particularly want to discuss my sister or my grandmother having sex in this house. Right now, I want to know what you want. Do you want to fuck in here, in the kitchen, in the shower, or in our room?"

"Can you give the tour and we pass on the sex for tonight? I'm still off from the drive." As if the meal swap wasn't evidence enough.

"You don't need to ever give me a reason. A pass is a pass; a no is a no."

"Then how about a tour?" I propose.

Ken lowers my feet back to the floor and helps me up.

We start on this floor. Ken guides me back to the entrance and we walk through the space from there. He guides me through the kitchenette and the living room and into four of the bedrooms on this floor. There are freestanding showers and tubs in each room.

Each room is nicer than the last. In addition, there is a second den with a poker table and a large flat-screen TV. This is more my speed when it comes to what I expect from a living room. This room faces the street to afford the bedrooms ultimate privacy.

He takes me down a thin hardwood stairway to the second floor. There is another balcony that looks out on cliffs of the Amalfi Coast.

This patio has an infinity pool. The one above us has a hot tub. There is no shortage of luxury.

"It's a little too dark now, but if we went outside, you could see the gardens and the lemon trees that we make our limoncello with."

"You have enough trees to make your own limoncello?"

"We have a small operation. It's a rather exclusive blend. It's not our bread and butter, but it is something special. Even during the war my family kept making it."

"It's nice to have that kind of legacy. Does that mean even if the relationship doesn't work out, I can get a bottle as a consolation prize?"

"Play your cards right and maybe I will get you two bottles. There is another floor that operates as our cellar."

"Sounds sexy."

"If you find cold, dank spaces a turn on, then I will make sure that I show you that space once or twice a day."

I chuckle, slipping my arm into his. I lead him outside onto the patio. I'm instantly hit with a burst of cold wind. It's enough that Ken shivers too.

"I'm not sure it does it for me, but I'm not saying that it doesn't do it for me."

"Does this freezing cold air do it for you? I think it's at best thirty out right now." His arms fold around me, giving me a little of his warmth.

"Definitely not. I just wanted to see out here."

We scurry back inside and Ken finishes the tour of this floor, including an additional five bedrooms and seven bathrooms. This place is palatial compared to other houses in the area.

We find our way back to our room, and I can feel the nervous energy from Ken. Just because I'm not interested in having sex doesn't mean I'm not interested in doing something for him. When we're settled into the bed, I turn on my side to face him. He turns on his side to face me. When he opens his mouth to say something, I kiss him instead.

Ken leans back, pulling me with him and I follow, letting my hand slide along his naked chest down to where he is at half-mast.

He groans into my mouth when my fingers graze him. I stroke along him, feeling him harden in response. Each movement makes him come more alive in my hand and I love the feeling. He pulls back to look me in the face, his brow furrowed.

"I thought you didn't want to tonight."

I kiss him, grateful for this man who respects my boundaries. "Just because I don't want to have sex doesn't mean there isn't more in store for you." I kiss down along his jaw, which is sporting the new beard he is growing out. I kiss down his neck, nipping when he grabs my breast and tweaks my nipple.

I don't stop kissing him until I get to his cock, and then I lick up the length of him, letting my tongue swirl around the head. He groans and his hand twists in my hair as he guides me down along his length.

I suck on him, taking him as deep as I can. I suck hard enough to put some vacuum brands out of business. I pull up, not coming off him entirely before I lower down again. My speed is too slow for Ken because he starts to pump into my mouth, fucking it as we find our tempo. I let go of the base of him to grab his balls and he twitches under me, surprised by the grab.

I don't want to stop. I want to keep feeling this power of him needing me so badly that he can't be still under me. My teeth graze him and he hisses. For a moment, I worry that it was one of pain, but when he thrusts into mouth again, I know that the hiss was one of pleasure.

"Fuck, god, oh fuck," Ken swears when my tongue slides along the slit at the tip of his cock. There is a small amount of moisture there and I don't hesitate to keep going.

"Ains, I'm going to fucking come. Oh, god."

But I don't stop. I keep going until I feel him spill against the back of my throat.

When he's done, I pull back and run my thumb along my lower lip. His eyes track the movement, his pupils blown. Ken's hand snakes out and he grabs the back of my head, pulling me to him.

The kiss is deep and consuming. I want to combust right then and there.

"You are the sexiest woman alive, but that's the last time I come in your mouth on this trip." Ken's eyes are heated with something else, and I wish I hadn't begged off sex because now I want him.

He pulls me close to his chest and we snuggle there, wrapped around each other, content in our little nest.

Eleven

OUR FIRST FEW days in Positano were lazy. We spent them eating and fucking until we were too tired to do either. I can't imagine there was a surface we didn't fuck on.

On my birthday, Ken surprises me by taking me out on his family's sailboat. We really lucked out with the weather. The day before, it poured all day, which just meant being spread out in front of the fireplace, slowly exploring new facets of each other.

"We can head back?" Ken offers as I grip the railing at the front of the boat. For a moment I feel like Rose and I wonder if he's concerned I'm going to make a jump for it.

"No! I am just fine," I promise, but I'm still feeling green around the gills.

"It's probably because of the storms. I'm turning around," Ken decides. We're only about halfway down the coast toward Capri, which is only supposed to be, max, a forty-minute trip, but I keep stalling us the same way I did when we came down to Positano.

"I thought we had clear weather?" I shove a cracker into my mouth.

"We do, but the rain yesterday probably left the sea all churned up." Ken moves to where I'm sitting to gather me into his arms and onto his lap.

This persistent nausea has been ruining my trip, and I'm tired of it. I was finally feeling better yesterday too. If I wasn't so prone to motion sickness, I would be worried that I was pregnant, but there haven't been any of the other telltale signs, like breast tenderness or sensitivity to smell. The idea has crossed my mind, but if I was pregnant, these moments wouldn't be centered around being on a boat or in a car or during the aftermath.

"I hate this, for the record." I relent and gesture him back toward the controls so he can steer us safely back to shore.

"What sort of names were you thinking?" Ken asks in a clear attempt to distract me. It works because my head snaps up to him.

"What?"

"For the hypothetical child we're supposed to be talking about. What names were you thinking? Clearly Kenneth Junior is out."

"Oh, Atticus for a boy. And for a girl? I don't know. I like Luna or Ava."

"Is Atticus because of the book?"

"Maybe a little. He was a great lawyer. What about you? Have you given any thoughts to names?"

"Ayala if it's a little girl. Eli for a boy. But I also like Atticus. It's a strong name."

"Yeah, but I don't know if Atticus Seaborn has the right cache."

I'll be damned if his distraction isn't working. I settle myself at the bow, watching as the boat cuts through the water.

"But Atticus Baker sounds pretty good. So does Luna Baker or Ava Baker." There is a glint in Ken's eye as he watches me and I realize that this might be one of the bigger conversations we have.

"Looks like we'll have to figure out whose last name the kid gets."

"Easy, mine. This way, when I propose to you, the only last name paperwork is your own."

My heart catches and I stare at him, wondering if he's going to crack a joke or something, but he's dead serious.

"*When* you propose?" My voice sounds faint, barely audible over the rushing wind.

"That's right, when. I realized something, Ainsley, sometime around when you recklessly let me into your office when no one else was there, and when I heard you fired up to help your friend. I realized that there is no world in which I won't fall in love with you. And watching you grow swollen with our child, watching you be a boss bitch eight months pregnant and not slowing down, I know I'll be hopeless for you, because I already am. But this is new, and we're trying to figure a lot of shit out right now. So yes, *when* I propose to you."

I'm frozen dumb by this declaration that I don't even realize we're back to shore until Ken is helping me up and holding me steady while I get my land legs back.

He sounds so sure of his ability to love me, but he barely knows me. He doesn't know that my feet can smell awful or that the only reason my apartment is clean is because when Vivian was living with me, she got tired of the chaos so she hired a cleaning woman.

"You're awfully confident I'm going to say yes." I lean into him, looking deep into his eyes. I might tease Vivian about how sometimes she gets that anime anger flare, but I'm positive I'm looking at Ken with hearts in my eyes.

"I've got nothing but time to convince you."

Ken makes me pasta with a butter sauce and fresh bread from the restaurant down the block. As far as birthday dinners go, it might be the best one I've ever had. The rain that was supposed to stay away returns, so we wind up sitting on the floor in front of the fireplace, watching the rain lash against the windowpanes.

"I want to be up front," I tell him. "I plan on working until my doctor says I can't or I give birth. Whichever happens first. I was planning to go on maternity leave until the baby is three months old and work from home until a year if I can, or at least six months. I was going to have a nanny available during this whole time, but since I was going to do this alone, I clearly needed to keep my job. Even if I didn't need to, I would want to go back to work. I like my job. I like helping people."

"I won't object to a nanny because it will be good to have an extra set of hands, but I'll be there when you're ready to or want to go back to work. I do think daycare is necessary even if we do have a nanny. I would like our child to socialize with other children from a young age."

"You said once you were agnostic?" I leave the question there.

Ken chuckles, refilling both of our wine glasses. "Wherever my mother is, she just did the sign of the cross. I was raised Catholic, but religion feels too big for me to say either way."

"Do you object to raising our child Catholic?"

"I'm guessing you are?"

"I am, lapsed, of course, but I think I'd like for my child to be baptized and raised with some faith."

"How about a compromise? That's what you lawyers love to do. We can do a baptism, and when they're old enough, all three of us will get an education on whatever religions they want to explore."

"So, I take it if our child came out as gay or trans or nonbinary, you would be alright with it?" There is only one answer to this question and somewhere in my heart, I'm holding my breath, waiting for his answer.

He reaches out to cup my cheek, a soft sort of smile on his face.

"Ainsley, I'm bi. I wasn't just with other men because that's what Leslie wanted. It would be hypocritical of me to not be accepting. Even if I wasn't, they will be my child, and I will love them with every fiber of my being."

Whatever I was expecting him to say, that wasn't it. I'm touched that he feels comfortable enough with me to tell me he's bi. Gently, I pull his hand away from my cheek, and I kiss his palm. "Thank you for sharing that with me."

The corner of Ken's mouth lifts in a half smile. "You're not bothered by it?"

"What's there to be bothered by?" I kiss his palm again, nuzzling into his touch. "How do you see custody working?"

Ken presses me back and down into the plush carpet before his hand travels south. There is a moment of hesitation before he slides his hand into the pair of his boxers that I've been wearing around the villa. He doesn't touch my pussy right away. He lets his fingers stroke along my thigh until I'm desperate for friction.

"Assuming you don't want me to live with you, and assuming I don't convince you to marry me, then I think a fifty-fifty split would be best, but I'll work with you, not against you. If you need a day just for you, then you should take it. I'll, of course, take the baby when you have brunch with your friends."

That's the moment he chooses to end this conversation by brushing his blunt fingertips over my clit, sending me bowing off the floor.

"Fuck me," I cry, and he chuckles darkly.

"That's the idea," he whispers before kissing me.

It's soft and sweet as he works me into a frenzy of need. My hips are bucking, chasing the pressure of having him against me and when he finally, *finally* decides to finger me properly, I cry out when his digits slide into my hot, sensitive heat.

He works me just to the edge of orgasm before he stops. My eyes pop open and I don't even remember having closed them. I'm fisting the carpet and my breast, and Ken is leaning over me, watching.

"Are you done?" I ask incredulous.

"Buttercup, I'm just getting started." He peels the boxers down my legs, exposing my pussy to the warm night air.

"Does this mean our negotiations are done?" I ask, propping myself up on my elbows to watch him as he reaches behind his back to pull off his t-shirt. My breath catches as if I haven't seen him execute this move countless times before, but each time it's like the first time all over again.

"What it means," he pushes my shirt up so my breasts are bared to him, "is that I'm going to give you something for your birthday." He puts his fingers in his mouth, only to pull them out again. "Something that I am the only person," he pinches my nipple on my left breast, nearly snapping my back in half as I bow under the sensation, "eligible to give you."

The desire to tease him that he's the only person who can give me a baby dies on my lips as he shoves his boxers down, exposing the rigid length of his cock.

Fuck.

Yes.

I would be stupid to dismiss this man out of hand because I already know what he can do with that dick and I fucking like it. That's a lie. I fucking love it. And yes, maybe I am being a coward, choosing to focus on how good the sex is between us instead of the feelings because feelings are where I can get hurt, but sex is easy. Sex is about fitting part A into part B and making the other person feel good as long as you're doing it right.

And Ken does it right.

"You know, meeting you in that bar was probably one of the best things to happen to me."

I swallow thickly, watching him as he moves over me, guiding his cock to my entrance. He doesn't penetrate me; instead, he guides the tip through my slick arousal, up and down, working me back into a frenzy as he brushes it against my clit.

"Why's that?" I pant. What is it about this man that reduces me to a blithering idiot?

"Because I would have said I wanted to be a father, but I probably would have never done anything about it. I would have buried myself instead of burying myself inside you."

That's when he eases inside me, leaning forward to feather kisses down my neck as he sinks into me, inch by glorious inch. Each movement, each kiss is unhurried, like we have all night to lie here with each other, skin-to-skin, after he rolls me so I'm on top and he removes my shirt.

We're a tangle of limbs and there is nowhere on earth I would rather be. When tears leak from my eyes after my orgasm, he kisses each one, bundling me in his arms. At some point as I'm held close in his arms, I realize that this moment wasn't sex for the sake of making a baby or for fucking. This was pure, unadulterated making love, and that's the scariest part of all, because in Ken, I have something to lose. And I desperately want to hold onto him.

My whole life, I thought I knew what it was to be loved and treasured, and not a moment of that compares to this. Not a moment compares to him.

We're lying out by the pool on an unseasonably warm afternoon five days into the trip when Ken stops reading to look at me.

I glance up, feeling his eyes on me. Since we're in Italy and people don't look twice at boobs, I've decided to start sunbathing naked. It hasn't been the most productive since every fifteen minutes like clockwork, Ken reminds me that I need to reapply sunscreen to the sensitive skin on my chest in an attempt to either touch my boobs or get me to touch my boobs.

"Can I help you, sir?" I ask, watching as he rises from his seat.

He comes over to my lounge chair and blocks my sun. "No, you just keep lying right there."

My rebuttal about him blocking the sun dies on my lips when he leans over and kisses me. I prop myself up on my elbows, but he pushes me back down, letting his kisses cover my breasts and my neck and all the way down my torso. I like where this is headed, so I lie back, watching as he nuzzles my navel with his nose.

Ken's teeth scrape against the spot on my hip that's torture when tickled, but right now, how he touches me there has my back arching. A soft sigh escapes my lips and I close my eyes, letting him continue.

I feel the ties of my swim bottoms loosen as he tugs on them until they slide off completely.

"Have I told you how much I love having you here, so slick," he drags a finger down my folds, "so ready for me?"

Ken is on his knees now and he hauls me to the end of the chair. I don't care about the friction of the nylon chair. I just want to tug him closer to me. He takes care, letting his hot breath blow over my pussy.

My own breath is coming in quick, shallow pants.

"I've barely touched you and you're fucking dripping wet for me."

At the first lash of his tongue against my skin, I cry out. This is a familiar song and dance and Ken has promised me that there is no one around to hear our lovemaking when we're outside. It doesn't change the fact that I do try to keep my volume down because sometimes I feel like I scream loud enough to rattle the mountains.

His tongue on my lower lips has my back bent in the need to be full of him. I need him inside me, and as my thoughts cry out for that, he slips two fingers inside me. Maybe I made that plea out loud.

He pumps his fingers inside me while sucking and licking at my core until my body clenches around him as I come.

When I think my body is too spent, too tired, I hear his shorts hit the ground. I open my eyes and he is kneeling at the end of the chair. I scoot back to look at him, at the golden tan he's already sporting after a mere three days in the sun. Some people really get all the luck.

He's stroking himself, waiting to see when I'm going to lose my patience.

"I just need you inside me, and I need you inside me before I explode."

"Your wish is my command." He's kneeling again when he says it, lifting my hips up and on his powerful thighs for a different angle. I don't have time to respond because suddenly he is inside me, his cock undoing me.

He's thrusting me all along the chair, our hips moving together. He reaches out, capturing one of my breasts in his large hand as they bounce with the movement of our bodies. I want to grab him, grab onto something, anything, but I can only clutch the arms of the chair for support. My hands slip almost immediately as the force of my orgasm rips through me.

I grip his arm, my nails digging into the soft flesh on the underside of his wrist, and the other grabs my free breast. The pinch of pain from my nails is soothed with the crescendo of pleasure that shudders through my body.

"Holy fucking shit!" Ken roars as his orgasm tears through him. His breathing is ragged as he leans down toward me to kiss me. I can taste myself on him, and it's intoxicating and I want more of it. My tongue slips into his mouth, and he kisses me back harder.

"Wow, I am glad I told Mom I would come ahead to check on you without the kids," a dull female voice says from behind us.

With a yelp, Ken flattens himself over me to cover me up. I

can't crane my neck to see who it is, but judging by her words and Ken's reaction I can only assume it's his sister.

"Apple!" he shouts, keeping us both covered. He's still inside me and this is really not how I imagined meeting his family.

"I came here to see how you were doing. Les told me you came to Italy to lick your wounds. I just didn't realize that you brought someone to lick them for you."

"Can you just turn around, for, like, a minute?" Ken sounds pained at shouting at his sister. I have to assume she complies because he gets off me quickly, grabbing the towel off the ground beside me.

I pull it around me while he pulls on his shorts.

"Are you decent?" she asks, turning around anyway. I'm tightening the towel around me when she turns her assessing gaze on me.

Ken's sister couldn't look less like him. Her hair is a light blonde, closer to mine. She raises one dark eyebrow into an exaggerated arch.

"Apple. What are you doing here?" Ken asks again while tying his bottoms.

She shifts her attention to her brother. She's taller than Ken and looks like she just stepped off the runway in Paris, not off a plane from DC. She's in a sleek, wrinkle-free dress and a light linen jacket. Behind her in the entrance are two large suitcases.

"I already explained myself. I'm waiting for your explanation." She actually crosses her arms and taps her foot at him.

"I told you and the family that I was going to be here. I told you all I was going to need the space. So *why* are you here?"

I try not to be annoyed that Ken still hasn't introduced me, but I'll wait. It's not like I'm standing here completely naked under this towel. One strong wind, and I'll be baring everything to her.

"Right, you told us you were going to be here right after you filed for divorce from your wife of eight years. Sorry we were worried about you so we decided to come keep you company."

"Don't your children have school?" Ken deflects.

"Kenneth. You're my brother. This is more important. So, who is your friend?"

"This is Ainsley Seaborn. She and I are seeing each other."

I appreciate Ken's respect of not throwing a title on us, but at this moment, I sort of wish he would give us something more firm in the face of his sister's criticism.

"Is this the reason your marriage blew up? Some blonde bimbo?"

"I would like to point out that you're blonde and would hate it if someone assumed you were a bimbo because of your hair color," Ken says in a rebuttal. It feels like familiar sibling banter.

"I would also love it if you both would stop talking about me like I'm not here," I snap.

"Oh, I'm sorry, homewrecker, did you have something to say?" She's finally turned her attention to back me.

I draw myself up to my full height, as if all five feet of me amounts to anything next to this five-foot-ten amazon in six-inch heels.

"Hey, enough, Apple. She has nothing to do with why Leslie and I broke up. Ainsley and I are going to go get changed. You can cool your jets until you decide to behave like my sister instead of the fire-breathing bitch you're acting like." Ken grabs my upper arm roughly and leads me past her and into our room.

I toss the towel onto the bed and beeline for my suitcase. I pull out a pair of leggings and a sweater that I wore on the flight over. It's probably a little warmer than I would have wanted, but I'm not interested in showing any more skin around his sister after she caught us having sex. I feel like a teenager all over again.

"I'm so sorry for Apple," Ken says, grabbing a shirt and pulling it on over his head. It's backward at first until I point it out to him and he fixes it. I would be endeared to how flustered he is right now, but I'm too anxious about the presence of his sister.

"You have nothing to apologize for. She's the one who owes me an apology." I can only hope that meeting the rest of the family goes over better.

"I can't disagree. This is not really how I imagined you meeting the family, but I guess my mom and the kids are coming down soon."

"Only way we can find out is if we go out and talk to her." I have colorful words I want to call her right now but decide better of it, knowing that it's not going to make me look like the better one in this fight, so I reserve the name-calling for in my head.

When we emerge, she's sitting on the couch in the living room, sipping a glass of wine like it isn't eleven in the morning.

"Apple, I want to do this the right way," Ken starts off, sliding his fingers in with mine.

"Fine, go ahead." She stands up and smooths her dress. That perfect arched eyebrow is still raised as she appraises me with her dark brown eyes.

"Apple, this is Ainsley, my," he hesitates, but it's only a fraction of a second. It's enough time for Apple to catch it and narrow her eyes, "girlfriend. Ainsley, this is Apple, my overprotective and sometimes a bitch older sister." He already made a sort of introduction, but now she can actually look me in the eye since I'm clothed.

I have to fight the urge to look at him with hearts in my eyes at being called his girlfriend, regardless of the hesitation. We've talked about how fast this is going, but while "girlfriend" feels young for us and what we're doing, 'partner' feels much more serious and long-term than what we are as we try to figure out where we stand. I'm not sure "future mother of my child" would go over much better.

"I resent that statement. I am just looking out for you. I don't get why you and Leslie broke up." Her attention is back on her brother, her expression somewhat softer.

"Nice to meet you," I say, trying to keep my tone even, despite her frigidity toward me.

"I would really rather have this conversation with my brother, alone."

"That's all fine and good, but she's not going anywhere." Ken's voice is rough, and while I appreciate him trying to defend me, I'm not interested in getting caught in the middle of this family drama.

"Talk to your sister. I'm going to shower."

Ken eyes me, trying to confirm that I'm actually okay. I nod and slip out of the room, but I still catch his sister's words before I close the door.

"Are you out of your fucking mind?" Apple hisses, but it's the last I hear from them.

I try to let the relaxing stream of water distract me from the faint screaming I can hear from the living area.

This is not at all how I imagined meeting his family. We haven't decided how to really define ourselves, so this is not the stress either of us needs.

I take my time, trying to find a way to relax. It's a waste of water, but I don't care. I let my hands probe along my freshly-lathered body. I need to release some of the tension that's built in my body since getting caught. What's worse is there is a strange sort of desire that's gripped me. The idea that now someone could walk in on us at any moment when we have sex here makes me needy.

There is a bench along the wall that I drop onto. I let my thoughts drift to Ken, to the feeling of him being inside me. My breaths come faster, envisioning that it's his hands rubbing my clit as I touch myself. I can't tell if it's the heat of the shower or the reaction of my body but I feel the flush in my cheeks.

I dip one, then two slender fingers into myself, gasping at the intrusion. It's not the same as when Ken touches me, and it makes me yearn for him all the more. I grind the heel of my hand against my clit as I pump my fingers. My eyes are closed so I can see the moment playing out in my mind. In my mind it's Ken's fingers inside me, his that pinch my nipples. He's kissing my neck, sucking and nipping, leaving love bites as he moves down my body.

The fire inside me catches, burning through my body. I try to hold back, but I can't stop the moan that I release. I ride through my orgasm, the tensing of my muscles, and the inevitable looseness that follows.

I finish rinsing in the shower and emerge to find Ken leaning against the counter, my towel folded over his arm. The grin that splits his face is one of the cat that caught the canary.

"Have a nice shower?" he asks innocently.

"It was extremely relaxing," I respond primly.

His grin broadens, unfolding the towel and enveloping me in it. I let myself loosen, leaning into his touch.

"I'm sorry for Apple."

"Stop apologizing for something out of your control. You don't tell her what to say."

"My mother and the children will be arriving tomorrow, so that marks the end of our sexcation," Ken tells me, kissing my neck. He sucks and bites his way down to my collarbone.

"God, you really know the way to get a girl in the mood: talk about your mother."

"Right, because it's a hot shot to my libido too," he says through a laugh.

"You're the one feeling me up," I point out, and he grins sheepishly as his hand slips under my towel to my breast.

"I'm sorry, but watching you touch yourself made me wish I was in there with you, but I didn't want to interrupt." He brushes another kiss along my pulse point. "Was it me you were thinking of when you entered yourself? Was it my cock or my fingers you imagined yourself coming around? Did you imagine that this was going to be the time I put a baby in you?"

I reach for him, finding him straining against his bottoms. My hand moves up his body, under his shirt so flesh meets flesh. Gently, I tweak his nipple, which earns me a growl of pleasure.

My hand drops lower and into his pants, where I continue the exploration of his skin. I've come to know his body so well. I don't waste any time, knowing that his sister is outside. In fact, just like how I thought in the shower, the idea that his sister could hear us together makes me needy. I want him to fuck me until I have to fight not to scream.

I drop to my knees before him, pulling his cock free of his pants.

"Ainsley," he warns, but it's half-hearted. He has no real objection as I lick him from base to tip. "Fuck," he grinds out.

My mouth closes over him and I moan around the fullness. His hips flex forward, his hand threading into my hair. He's chasing the same release I was and instead of me setting the pace, his hips buck into my mouth with desperate need. I let my teeth skim against him. The sound that comes from him when my teeth glide against the sensitive skin of his cock sends a fresh wave of wanton desire between my legs.

Ken's hand fists into my wet hair, holding me so he can thrust harder. This moment is all about his pleasure and his needs. He's done more than an adequate job of taking care of me.

I let him fuck my mouth while I do my best to channel my inner vacuum. He said that the only place he was coming was between my legs, but I'm not going to let up because I wholeheartedly doubt my ability to be quiet if he's inside me. Instead, I slide my fingers between my legs so I can chase my own release while he comes.

"I'm going to fucking come," he groans, easing back, but I grab his ass with my free hand and hold him to me. His hips keep moving until I feel the hot liquid against the back of my throat. I don't think about it; I just keep swallowing until he's spent. I'm so distracted by finishing his pleasure that I forget about my own, and I think that might be a first.

When he's done, Ken doesn't pull me up to him. He gets to his knees before me, tucking himself back into his pants. His hands come to my face, and the look I see on his face I attribute to the post orgasm bliss, but part of me hopes that the adoration on his face isn't just over my blow job skills.

His mouth slants over mine in a consuming kiss. Ken sucks my lower lip into his mouth, his teeth biting into my skin.

"Let me finish," he whispers against my lips before sliding his fingers into my sensitive heat. Tears spring to my eyes again, and I don't know where this torrent of emotions is coming from. I bury my head in his shoulder, and he stills his hand. I can feel him withdrawing, but I clamp a hand on his wrist. My eyes meet his as I lean away.

"Don't...stop." The choked plea manages to emerge amidst more tears. I rock my hips into his hand as he holds me to him.

My orgasm is a soft, quiet thing, not the screaming pleasure of earlier in the morning. It's the feeling of souls being forged together over this shared intimate experience. Ken pulls me against him and I press my lips to his. This is the type of kiss that locked lips was created for because we're there, holding each other up, unable, no, *unwilling* to break this connection. Ken's hands cup my cheeks and I can feel his thumbs stroking away the tears that are still sliding down my cheeks.

I do *not* understand what has gotten into me. What I do know is that this feeling is something I don't want to lose. This fledgling feeling needs to be protected and kept safe because what scares me most now is the idea that I could lose what Ken and I have started to build.

I want to keep this going; I want to go back to our sexcation where Ken was relentlessly fucking me on ever surface. I want to go back to where I was safe from the feelings I refused to admit were growing. But his sister is outside and his nephews are on their way. His mother.

Oh god. I have to meet my boyfriends' mother. My mind catches on that word– boyfriend. When he called me his girlfriend earlier, it felt like the safest way to describe what we have, and I won't lie, I like it.

I break off the kiss and shake my head at him. "Your mother is coming here with your sister's children."

"Yes, they are. Looks like I'll finally get you out to the lemon tree grove. It might be the only place I can have you where you can scream."

"Kenneth. I'm enjoying this time with you, but you are out of your mind if you think I'm going to have sex with your mother in the house."

"I think that's exactly what you're going to do, and I think they're going to enjoy it when I fuck you against the wall outside her room."

I choose not to debate him on that point, but instead push forward on another. "You called me your girlfriend," I point out.

"Would you rather I went with another title? I could call you my sperm bank, although I'm not planning to make any withdrawals, only deposits."

I can't stop the loud laugh at escapes my mouth. "You are gross, and no, that is *not* what you should be calling me."

"It's not gross if it's true." He steps into my space again, rocking his hips into me.

"You *cannot* be ready to go again," I say, outraged.

"I'm highly motivated. All I have to do is think about that first moment you hold *our* baby and..." Ken thrusts against my bare bottom, and I have to bite back a moan. This noise is all the invitation Ken needs to bend me over onto the bed and slide into me until I'm grabbing a pillow to muffle my scream as I clench around Ken, milking him as he comes.

My poor pussy is going to need a vacation from this sexcation.

Ken pushes the hair off my shoulder, pressing a chaste kiss along the curve of my neck.

I can't help the shiver that rolls through my spine. He smiles against my skin before planting one more kiss. I step away from him, trying to put some distance between us before I let him fuck me against the wall like he promised.

Only, Ken pulls my towel away, leaving me bare to him. His eyes take a lazy perusal of my skin. I scowl at him but it quickly becomes a smile because sex is something familiar and definable. It's easier than the no-man's land I've entered with both of us catching feelings.

Twelve

≈

I SLIP on a billowy yellow dress that skirts just above my knees. When I reach for panties to put on, all of mine seem to have been misplaced, including my swim bottoms. Ken doesn't seem bothered by the fact that I'll have to go outside knowing he made a mess of me between my legs. In fact, I think the jerk gets off a little on it.

Ken doesn't have the faintest idea where my panties are when I ask him about it. I don't need a lie detector to know that is a lie. Not even knowing I have to go outside and make nice with his sister will make a pair appear. His dirty, teasing playfulness only endears me further to him. Without the stress of his sister outside, if he asked me to marry him right now, I'd be inclined to say yes.

His sister is waiting on the patio with a full glass of wine and a bottle on the table before her.

"I'm going to need to finish this entire bottle to scrub the image of you two from my mind. If you want a drink, get your own." Apple waves her full glass at us.

Ken snorts and kisses the back of my head before he turns back inside to get us a bottle.

"So, Apple," I start, sitting down beside her. She's facing the beach but she turns her head toward me. She has on giant sunglasses that dwarf her face.

"So, homewrecker." She takes another long sip of her wine.

"I tend to prefer Ainsley, if it makes any sort of difference to you."

"Can I be frank with you?" Apple asks, peering down her nose at me.

"Seems a little weird, but Frank is a better name than Apple, so sure."

Apple rolls her eyes, frustration seeping out of her pores. "They were married for eight years, dated for two before that. They were great together. Leslie was perfect for him. She loved my kids and my brother. What do you have to offer? Great tits and spread legs?"

"Wow, you're a real bitch. It's no wonder your brother stayed in his marriage as long as he did. Leslie was already immune to your charm; any other woman would have run screaming."

"And you're not running?"

"Contrary to what you might think, I'm not a homewrecker, so no, your petty eighth-grade jabs are hardly going to bring me to my knees. I know five-year-olds meaner than you. So if you have more, bring it on, but I'm here to stay."

I reach over and take her glass and drain it before putting it back in her hand. She tilts her chin down so she can look at me over the top of her glasses and I can't tell if she's irritated or impressed.

The words were out of my mouth before I could really examine them. I effectively staked my claim to her brother, telling her that I'm here to stay. My heart knows what it wants before my mind can make itself up.

"Sorry, I couldn't pick which wine I wanted to start next," Ken announces as he re-emerges with two glasses in hand.

He plops down a bottle of white, which has already been

corked. Apple is still glaring at me over her glasses as her brother refills her glass.

"What time is Mom getting here with the boys?" Ken asks, leaning back in his seat. He looks so at ease with the top three buttons on his shirt undone while he gently caresses the back of my neck.

"I convinced her to come tomorrow with the kids. I didn't want you to expose them to whatever you've been doing."

Ken snorts. "Your eleven-year-old caught you and Howie screwing in your kitchen. I know because he called me and asked if his dick will be that big. So really, sis, you don't have a leg to stand on here."

"It's different when it's your own child. You can scar them all you want. But you can't scar someone else's kid. It's just uncouth."

"Glad you can be so blasé about it, but we wouldn't have been just screwing outside if I knew that you were going to come." Ken sips his wine, narrowing his eyes at his sister.

"That would defeat the purpose of a surprise. Like I said, had I known you were bringing your mistress, I wouldn't have pulled the kids from school."

I don't interject into the sibling bickering. They squabble back and forth with the practiced ease of two people who love and respect each other. I worry for a moment my involvement with Ken might have damaged that respect.

"So, Ainsley," Apple puts emphasis on my name, "what is it that you do?" She shoots her brother a look as if to say, *See? I can play nice.*

I have to fight the urge to snort into my wine glass. "I'm a lawyer."

Ken is fighting his own laugh and Apple eyes us both suspiciously.

"What's the big joke?" Apple pushes.

I look at Ken, leaving this in his hands. She's his sister. I'm not going to butt in and share anything he doesn't want to.

"Ainsley was our divorce lawyer, well, mediator."

Apple looks between us, disbelieving. "Mediation implies that you were trying to save your marriage."

I hate the hope in her voice. Like I'm a passing fad, and there is still hope for Ken and Leslie.

"Applesauce, do I need to blast Taylor Swift? Leslie and I are never getting back together. She's more interested in fucking other people than starting a family with me, and that's fine. I respect her for knowing what she wants in her life, but I deserve more respect. I deserve to be happy too. I want what you and Howie have. I want a big family. Leslie doesn't want children, and I'm not going to force that on her. Honestly? It's been a long time coming. I'm finally out of a situation I felt stuck in. So, please, let me be happy. Let me enjoy being with Ainsley."

Apple frowns. "You didn't tell me that Leslie was cheating."

Ken sighs. "The things about my marriage that you didn't know could fill a book that rivals the Bible in length. Leslie wasn't cheating on me because we had an open relationship. I met Ainsley before she was my lawyer because my ex-wife thought she was hot and looked lonely so we brought her home with us...together. I'm aware that's an overshare, but I think it's the only way I can get you to drop this. Please stop sticking your nose into what you don't understand."

Quietly, I sip my drink before squeezing Ken's hand. He lifts my fingers to his mouth and presses a kiss to my knuckles, in support or apology for letting his sister know I had a threesome with them, I'm not sure. Mentally, I make a note to ask him about his Taylor Swift reference.

"Well, it sounds like dinner is on me tonight," Apple offers, apology in her eyes. I accept that this is the closest I'll get to an apology from her.

"Try the rest of this week," Ken admonishes.

Apple rolls her eyes, but before this can continue, I interject. "So, Ken tells me you have three boys?"

She brightens at the idea of being asked about her sons. "Yes. Timothy, Tyson, and Tobias. Tobias is the baby. Well, he's not a baby anymore. He's five and is being absolutely run ragged by his older brothers. We keep contemplating if we want another, but the idea of gambling with having a fourth boy makes me hesitate. They all love their Uncle Ken, who lets them run roughshod over him."

Ken grumbles, taking a sip from his glass. "The little monsters actually broke my nose last year. Tyson, the eight-year-old, hit a growth spurt what felt like mid-air as he launched himself at me off the stair landing. He smashed his head into my face. The kid was also in pain, so of course, I couldn't react because he was crying."

"It didn't help that Tim was calling him a big baby for crying and proceeded to tell his little brother to nut up or shut up," Apple continues with a chuckle.

"Which prompted the baby, who was three at the time, to run around the house screaming, 'NUTS!' while your husband was on a conference call with the whip, if I recall correctly?"

"Senate majority leader, but same difference. Of course, the old sea crustacean was not amused, but Howie was, even if he had to come out and bring down the hammer."

I smile at the wistful way these two banter when telling the story. "Sounds like you have a loving family full of chaos."

"I do. I wouldn't trade the boys for anything, but damn, sometimes I wish they understood why the door was closed." She sighs heavily. "I should warn you, Tobias is obsessed with his penis."

"I would tell you he'll outgrow it, but I'm thirty-seven and I'm still obsessed with my dick," Ken adds with a chuckle.

"Ew. Honestly, I shouldn't have left Mom with all three of them, but she was crying that she never gets to see them and I just couldn't handle it, so I left."

"You birthed the monsters," Ken points out.

"I did, you're not wrong, and I wouldn't have it any other way."

We sit in companionable silence as Ken strokes my knee, inching his way further up. The sun is starting to set, and I'll never get tired of how it sets the world ablaze as it dips below the peninsula. Ken talks a big game about taking me to the other side to watch the sunset over the water, but we still haven't made it there yet.

When Ken's hand inches a little too far of my thigh, I grab his hand and cross my legs. We can play behind closed doors. It's bad enough his sister has already caught us screwing once.

"What have you two done since coming to Positano? I mean, besides fuck."

I am not one to be shamed for my sexuality, but I also do not want this to be the first impression that his family has of me. "We did some wandering in Rome. Tried to take the sailboat out but haven't left the villa much since getting here," I admit.

"Well, we'll fix that. We can leave the boys to their uncle and you, my mother, and I can go shopping. Have you gotten sandals yet? They custom make them, and besides our limoncello, they're the best thing you can get here."

I raise my eyebrow at Ken as if saying, *See? I knew there was more to do around here than fuck.* Ken tries to cover his smirk with a pout but can't help himself.

"It sounds like a great time, so long as you don't call me homewrecker or that 'blonde bimbo,' we're cool."

Apple grumbles, "I said I was sorry."

"Actually, Applesauce, you did not," Ken points out with a grin.

When I wake the next morning, the other half of the bed is cold, and I want to whine in annoyance.

We were up late into the night seeing how far we could go

without the other making a noise. I won, of course. Months of having sex in quiet corners of bathrooms or stock rooms made me practiced at keeping my cool.

After going through my morning wake-up routine, I stumble into the living area, where Apple and Ken are making breakfast. They're adorable, dancing around the space, each managing a different part of the meal. There is a small radio softly playing music that they're signing along with.

Ken looks up when I step into the room. I can feel his eyes trace my legs up to the hem of my short shorts and over my breasts in my tank top just as surely as if they were his hands. The rush of desire has me sucking on my lower lip so I can bite on it. Anything to diffuse the need running through me.

"Good morning, buttercup. Glad you've decided to join the world of the living."

I slip onto the stool at the island, resting my chin on my hand so I can watch them move in dance. Ken abandons his pan on a trivet so he can safely lean over and plant a soft kiss on my lips.

"Why didn't you wake me?"

"Thought it best you faced our mother well-rested." Ken and his sister share a look and I'm starting to think I should be worried about meeting the matriarch of the family.

"That fearsome?" I ask, breaking off a piece of cheese that Ken put on my plate. At some point after my birthday, my stomach started to settle.

"No, she's just..." Ken pauses, unsure of how to describe his mother, and I can't help but smile.

"Our mother is a lot. Ken is her favorite, by a long shot."

"I am not!" Ken objects, flicking some egg off his pan at her. With unbelievable skill, Apple drops to her knees just in time to catch it in her mouth. When Ken looks at her, shocked, she shrugs.

"I have three boys. One of their favorite pastimes is throwing cheese balls and seeing who can catch them in their mouths. It's why I'm excited to have some girl-time today." Apple places fresh cornetti on our plates.

I can't wait, tearing open the warm, flaky Italian version of a croissant.

"I still think you're wrong about Mom favoring me," Ken grumbles, placing scrambled eggs on three plates.

"How? You're the golden boy. You wanted to try guitar, she bought you a brand new amp, three types of guitars, and daily lessons. I wanted to try ballet, and I got three months of lessons and wasn't allowed to go to the dance recital because you had practice. So yeah, you were the favorite. I'm only salty about the dance recital thing, but otherwise, whatever. Mom loves my kids more than you and that's all I care about now. But you would have thought you shit gold bricks the way Mom doted on you. No one is ever good enough for you."

Ken opts not to dignify that with a response by shoving a full cornetto in his mouth, much to his sister's consternation.

"I'm guessing she was tough on his high school girlfriends?" I say.

"Oh god, yes. She actually made one cry the first time she came over for a family dinner. Mom basically told her that being a teacher wasn't a good enough job. Last I heard, she's working at the strip club in our hometown."

"No, she's not, and yes, Mom did make her cry, but only because Lisa told Mom that she was a vegetarian after Mom cooked a meat-heavy meal. Her ire was aimed more at me, but she was just shouting in general."

"Oh, Lisa Park. But it's still true. I heard she's a stripper. She does have one older kid from what I heard, looks an awful lot like you..." Apple grins when Ken levels her with a glare.

"What do you plan on doing with my girlfriend today?" Ken asks, winding a loose hair behind my ear. There's no hesitation this time.

"You two really need to get your story straight about what

exactly you are before Mom shows up. I heard your hesitation to call her 'girlfriend' yesterday. Mom is going to tear you both apart. She is a damned bloodhound when it comes to lies. Caught Ken sneaking out with his car in the middle of the night to fuck around in his back seat more than he'll ever admit. Made him cry for sure once when she caught him."

At some point last night, Apple warmed up to me considerably, and I'm glad to finally have her on my side. She's right about us being consistent in our label. I understand why he panicked when Apple showed up yesterday, but I agree with Ken that girlfriend doesn't seem like the right word when we're actively trying to make more of what we are. I could possibly mentally separate our relationship from the family we're trying to make, but they're too entwined, too interwoven for me to do that. We're getting to a point emotionally where I'm not sure if I can have one without the other, and if I look past my fears, I'm not sure I want them separated again.

The more time I spend with Ken, the more I see what a great dad he will be, and I'm positive that watching him interact with his nephews is going to make my ovaries explode. It's like each time we talk, I find a new reason to fall in love with him, from his sense of humor to how accepting he is, and, never last, what a dominant lover he can be.

"Is fuck buddy not good enough?" I ask, offering another title while sipping my coffee.

Apple snorts. "Only if you want her to think you're just a rebound."

"To be fair, Apple, I brought her here so we didn't have to make any declarations about our relationship. You're all crashing the party."

Apple takes a big bite of her eggs, pondering this before she pushes her plate away. "Whatever. I'm going to go sit outside on a totally different level so I don't have to pretend like I'm not hearing you both have morning sex like the disgusting creatures you are."

"Not feeling the love from Howie?" Ken asks, but grimaces like the words are rotten in his mouth. Clearly teasing his sister about her sex life is a line too far.

"Try having three kids and see how often you get it in," she snaps, putting her plate in the sink. When she realizes what she's said in connection with the reasons his marriage failed, Apple slouches. "That was insensitive. I'm sorry. I had no idea that you wanted a family and she didn't. I always thought that you two were just happy with your lives and didn't want that. It never occurred to me–"

"It's really fine, Applesauce." Ken pushes his eggs around for a moment before looking at his sister. This feels like another moment I shouldn't be a part of. I want to leave them to have their sibling moment and bond without my interference. I go to slide out of the chair, but Ken stops me with a hand on my thigh. "I started to realize after Titus was born that not having kids was going to be a dealbreaker for me. Les kept putting the conversation off and off and off, saying we could talk about it, but every year I felt like I wasn't getting any younger. When you had Tobias, I pushed the issue more, and she told me that under no circumstances did she want to have children. It was just harder to end things than I thought it would be. Every time I tried, we would just fall back in bed together, and I..."

Ken glances at me, and I wonder if he's uncertain about going on. Does it suck to hear about him and Leslie? Absolutely. But our past relationships made us who we are today. Without those hard conversations that he and Leslie had about making a family and trying to make it work, he and I wouldn't have come together. I offer him an encouraging nod. It's like we discussed in Rome, we can't completely pretend that Charlie and Leslie didn't exist.

"I just got more and more unhappy," Ken finishes, turning his attention back to Apple.

His sister throws her arms around him before giving him a big wet kiss on the temple. "When Mom asks why you and Leslie ended, tell her that. She'll understand this."

"It's none of her business," he tells her through gritted teeth.

My job means that I'm in the middle of the end of a relationship. I see the impact that it can have on the spouses, but I never see the emotional impact that it can have on the extended families.

"If I may?" I interject, and Ken turns to me, giving me a nod. He squeezes my thigh again. "You were with Leslie for a long time, and yes, you don't owe anyone an explanation for why your marriage ended. But, you were together for years. I'm making some assumptions here, but the boys lost their aunt, and your mom lost a daughter. I think whatever explanation you're willing to give will go a long way to soothe those hurt feelings."

Ken's eyes narrow at me. "It's not my job to make other people feel better about my divorce. I thought you, of all people, would understand that."

I glare at Ken, getting off the chair. For a second, a flicker of surprise crosses his face, but then he shuts it down just as quickly. Not eager to leave him hurting, I grip his face. "Ken, trust me. Boiling this down to a simple understandable reason will encourage them to leave you alone. This is ultimately what you want, right? To not have to answer the hard questions for your mom that you met your fuck buddy after your now ex-wife picked her up at a bar?"

There is silence in the room, until a small voice with a lisp asks, "What's a fuck buddy?"

My skin feels hot all over as I realize what has happened. There is no way that my luck is that bad, but honestly, Apple caught Ken and me while he was balls-deep in me, so naturally, his mother would walk in as I try to explain to Ken why a baseline of honesty is the best policy.

"Toby!" Apple greets, pushing past me and Ken. I'm only comforted by Ken looking equally as stricken and unsure of how to get out of this situation. "She said 'puck' buddy. Like a hockey puck. Ainsley helps make sure Uncle Ken can score with his puck! Isn't that right, guys?"

Ken and I turn to face the entrance, which is now crowded by Apple, a little boy who is wrapped in her arms, a young boy who is starting that awkward transition into pre-teen with long limbs and pimples on his face, an older woman who looks regal with perfectly-styled hair, and one more boy who has a mess of dark curls on his head. The pre-teen looks like he would find it more believable if a giant purple dinosaur danced in the room with a song about cleaning up, and Ken's mother looks livid to have to be part of a conversation trying to explain away fuck buddies.

The three boys share the same unruly curls at varying lengths. Their eyes are all the same shade of blue that I think must come from their father.

"But Uncle Ken doesn't play hockey," Tyson points out, making his older brother snort.

"Your Uncle Ken did play hockey when he was a boy and then he hit his head and didn't want to play anymore," Apple says, eyeing me.

Timothy looks like he has something more to say as he gazes at my bare legs, but decides against it, his cheeks turning red. I want to tug my shorts down and my tank top up. I'm not ashamed of my body by any stretch of the imagination. I'm just very aware of how cold it is in here and how visible my nipples are.

"I didn't realize you had a guest," his mom says in an unconvincing tone.

"That is patently false. We were talking last night about which shops to go to, but it was a nice try, Mom. We weren't expecting you until ten," Apple says, straightening. She hoists her youngest son onto her hip, giving a whole new meaning to the phrase mom strong.

"Right, well, I was expecting you to have still been asleep, although that was a miscalculation on my part. You didn't exactly clue me in on what type of friend your brother brought with him."

I bite so hard on my tongue that I can taste blood in my mouth. I would snark at her, I want to snark at her which is so much worse, but this is Ken's mom, and damn it, I want to make a good impression.

"Mom, this is Ainsley. You can stop talking about her like she's not in the room. Like we're both not standing right here." Ken's words lack the annoyance I would have used, but the sentiment is all the same.

"As in Ainsley, your attorney?" There is censure in his mother's words. Both Ken and I mirror surprise.

"I didn't tell her," Apple says. "Boys, go say hi to your uncle and then let's see what I can whip up for breakfast," she orders.

Our conversation is put on hold as Tobias wriggles out of his mom's grip and launches himself at his uncle. I give them all space to embrace, grabbing a shirt of Ken's that was discarded at some point during our trip. I pull it on as all three boys start to hang from Ken in one way or another.

When they're done, they eye me curiously but understand that they're waiting on their grandmother's approval of the situation.

"I still talk to Leslie. All she's done is laud me with tales of how professional your attorney has been and how seamless the process was." For a moment, her dark eyes flick to me, then to her son. "And how much she misses you."

"My marriage with Leslie is over. You can still be friendly with her, but don't include me in it and don't make it out to her like I'm trying to reconcile with her. I'm not. I've been divorced for five minutes and you're already trying to get me back together with Leslie." He lets out a humorless laugh. He turns to me, pressing a kiss to my temple before pulling me to his side. A grand gesture of sorts that I'm here to stay.

His mother looks at the two of us, studying the protective stance that her son has taken to shield me from her. I'm not sure what it is she sees on his face, but she finally steps out of the front vestibule and offers her hand to me.

"I'm Roberta, and I'm glad to make your acquaintance."

It would be bitchy to not take her hand, so I do, giving it a firm shake. "I've heard wonderful things about you and your family. This is not how I imagined meeting you, but I guess it's a good thing we got it out of the way quickly."

"Planning on sticking around for the long haul? As my son put it, he's only been divorced for five minutes." She's watching me with shrewd eyes, and for a brief moment, I put myself in her shoes, and I get it. I would want to protect my child after heartbreak. I wonder if she's looking at me and thinking gold-digger, since I had access to their financial records. It's not like she knows I'm sitting on a trust fund that would make Ken's net worth look like lunch money.

"Mom!" Ken warns, but I hold my hand out to him, silencing him.

"I'm around as long as Ken wants me, regardless of how the other people in his life feel. I would like for us to be on the same page, but don't think that my relationship with your son is predicated on your approval."

The room is silent as Roberta studies me closely, I think with a hint of approval in her eyes, but maybe it's my imagination. "I see."

I don't know what to make of her words, so I turn to Ken, turning my back on her to show her I'm not afraid of her. "I'm going to go get changed. You talk to your mother and sister and we can work out a plan for the rest of our time together later."

Apple raises her eyebrow, familiar with my disappearing act after I pulled the same stunt yesterday. But their closeness, their hovering, is unfamiliar to me. I'm close with my father, but I've never had family like this, in each other's business, rallying around one another when things are bad. It's part of why I think that Charlie and I got on so well. We could disappear and have our own holidays with friends away from the chaos that was family, if he even got away from work. When I broke up with Charlie for good, my dad sent me a case of Prosecco and told me he loved me.

Ken worriedly nods his head, rubbing the back of his neck before turning to his family. I can only hope that someday, I'll be included in that title.

Thirteen

WHEN I EMERGE AN HOUR LATER, showered and dressed for the day, Ken is talking animatedly with his mom and sister. The boys are outside, sitting on the deck, though the oldest, Timothy, looks like he's just sleeping on one of the chairs in the shade.

"Why didn't you tell us you were unhappy?" Ken's mother asks. Her brow is creased in concern, and there are wrinkles around her eyes and mouth. She doesn't strike me as a woman trying to forever seek the fountain of youth, and I find I like her for it.

"Why would I? My marriage was *my* marriage. That's what you always said when we asked why you were unhappy. I'm an adult. I can manage my own life."

"You're right, you can, but that doesn't mean you can't lean on your mother for support. You could have sought guidance from me. I have years more experience with relationships."

Ken scoffs. "Do you have experience with having an open relationship?"

Roberta lifts her chin. "What you don't know about me could fill a book, my son. I had a life before your father and before you and your sister. I've loved and been hurt. I've been in relationships that were bad for me and not known when to walk away. You children always forget that parents exist separate from their children."

"I think I could have lived the rest of my life without knowing my mother was with a fuck boy." Apple cringes at her own words.

"Several fuck boys. I lost my virginity at fourteen. I once did a line of coke off a man's Johnson and then proceeded to suck on it like it was a thick milkshake and that was the only way to get to the creamy goodness."

I laugh loudly, padding into the room. While Apple and Ken writhe on the floor from the imagery, Roberta looks up at me.

"I could have done without that visual, Mom," Ken cries, rubbing his temple.

"Do you think I need liquid soap to scrub that from my mind or will bar soap be best?" Apple asks her brother.

Roberta waves them off. "Such babies. Don't hurl accusations if you're not ready to hear the truth." She turns her attention on me and pushes a fresh cup of coffee in my direction.

"So, I'm guessing you got the full story from your son?" I ask, gripping the warm mug.

"I suspect I'll never get the full story, but he gave me the key details. It wouldn't have mattered to me either way, but it does explain why you're here. My son wants babies and why not have babies with a woman who wants them?"

I turn and gape at Ken, wondering what exactly he told her. He has the decency to look chagrined. When he meets my eye, he shrugs. "I only told her that I wanted a family and that during the divorce we connected because we wanted the same thing."

"Why wouldn't you two come here in hopes of making a baby? Though I do caution against jumping into something so hastily. I wouldn't be your mother if I didn't warn you. Make sure you know your bedfellows well." Roberta meets my eye as she says this, as if extending the same warning to me. It's unlikely that I'm pregnant already. We always could wait this out a month and really get to know each other. I wonder what Ken is thinking in all this.

"Mom, I'm a thirty-seven-year-old man. I don't need you to wipe my ass anymore."

"Excuse my saying so, but you do, otherwise you wouldn't have stayed in a loveless marriage for as long as you did."

Ken turns red, and not from embarrassment this time. I lean into his side, wrapping one arm around his shoulder. His mother marks every movement I make.

"Leslie and I loved each other."

The look on his mother's face is nothing short of pity. She cups his cheek with one hand. "Loving each other and being in love with each other is so different. You loved each other, I don't doubt that, but you were in lust with each other. I told you: I adore Leslie, she's sweet, but if you think I didn't hear how you originally met, you're out of your mind."

Apple bursts out laughing, and I think I must have missed something. Roberta catches on that I have no idea what we're talking about, but Apple looks at her brother.

"I certainly didn't tell her," Apple swears, holding her hands up defensively.

Ken's arm snakes around my waist and he pulls me to him. He buries his face in my neck, and his face is so hot, I can feel it against my skin. The embarrassment must be real. As much as I'm enjoying watching him squirm, his open affection with me in front of his mother and sister makes my heart grow three sizes. Just when I thought that my feelings for him couldn't get any bigger, he does something like this.

"Well, if he's not going to tell me, I would love it if one of you would."

Roberta and Apple both watch Ken, waiting to see if he will admit to it.

"She was one of the bridesmaids in a wedding I was in. They had a joint bachelor and bachelorette party because they couldn't handle being apart." Ken finally lifts his head and looks at me sheepishly. "We rented a limo to take us from the airport, and

Leslie's flight got in first. I was the second one there and caught her having sex with the driver in the backseat."

He presses his lips in a tight line, clearly not willing to carry on with the conversation.

"What my son is leaving out is that Leslie then invited him to watch. She said something to the tune of not baking out in the Las Vegas heat when it was air conditioned inside." Roberta sips from her coffee, thoroughly amused by this. Apple also can't stop cackling from her side of the kitchen island.

"Something like that," Ken mumbles, unwilling to make eye contact with any of us.

"I could have told you that monogamy was never going to be enough for Leslie. She's the type of woman who loves to be loved. She enjoys having eyes on her, enjoys knowing that you're there watching her. I don't doubt that she loved you in her own way, but she didn't love you the way you deserved."

"No one was ever going to love me the way you think I deserve. Besides, who even told you that story, Mom?"

"Your groomsmen were the most indiscrete bunch of degenerates I've ever met, and I had to meet all of Howie's fraternity brothers at his wedding to Apple. I'm fairly certain even Nana heard about how you jerked off watching Leslie get pounded by the limo driver."

Apple bursts into another round of laughter. "Since when do you know terms like jerked off and pounded?"

"I'm sixty-seven, not dead. I hear your son doing his Click-Clacks or whatever and posting to Pictogram. I know all the cool kid slang. But those particular terms I heard from the groomsmen."

"Enough of this talk about my now ex-wife in front of Ainsley, please."

"No, it's an interesting look at your life." My eyebrows quirk up, and I consider if he was a voyeur, watching Leslie and the driver, or if he was an active participant.

"Ken is right. The last thing I want is for one of the boys to overhear this and then blab to someone about how their uncle likes to watch other people have sex. Howie would have a fit."

"Good thing I'm not married to Howie," Ken jokes, kissing my temple. He excuses himself to get dressed for the day. I watch him, the movement of his body as he walks away. As Ken turns the corner, he catches my eye and winks.

"So, Miss Seaborn, what are your intentions with my son?"

I cough into my coffee and turn to face Roberta. "I'm sorry?" I ask. Clearly, there is no way I heard her right.

"She's grilling you," Apple clarifies before starting to clean up.

Slowly, I get off the chair, and try to pull myself up to the tallest height my frame will allow. I'm just level with her sitting on the stool.

"Mrs. Baker," I start. If she wants to call me Miss Seaborn, then she can expect the same level of formality. "My intentions with Ken are his business and his business alone. When there is something he wants to share, he will share it, but I have no intention of spilling the beans on his personal life."

"Attorney-client privilege?" she asks, not as haughty as her facial expression says she is. She's more amused than anything else. If Ken didn't tell her we came here to *actually* make a baby, I'm certainly not.

"Something like that, but also, it's none of your damn business. He's an adult. If he wants to tell you what's going on, he will. Just like he didn't tell you how he and Leslie really met. He respects your opinion of him, he doesn't want it tarnished, and he cares enough about your opinion about Leslie and me to not want to color it."

"You seem to have some sort of insight into keeping things from parents. What of your own?"

"First impressions matter. What about my parents? You can look up my dad and find out all you need to know of him, and my mother is and has been out of the picture long enough."

Roberta regards me for a moment then looks back at her daughter. They share a silent conversation, I can only assume about me, before they both smile.

"I already talked to Ken," Apple says. "He's going to watch my boys today. The three of us are going to go shopping and get to know each other a little better."

The back sliding door opens and in walks little Tobias, his finger in his mouth. All three of us wrinkle our brows, curious about why he's not saying anything. He approaches me and grins.

"I have a looth tooth," he announces, grinning and pointing to it.

"Very awesome. It looks like you've already lost a few," I point out, squatting so I'm at his height.

Tobias nods enthusiastically. "Wiggle it," he demands, pointing to the tooth in question.

I glance at his mother for confirmation before I do anything of the sort. Apple gives a halfhearted shrug, letting it be my decision.

I reach my finger forward to very gently touch the tooth in question. The second I touch it, it falls out, and Tobias starts screaming like I've ripped out.

Ken comes running from our room, his shirt totally open while Tobias wails.

"I barely touched it!" I exclaim, stepping back, and looking to his mother, grandmother, and uncle.

Apple is around the counter before I can even speak, gripping Tobias' face to get a better look at him.

The jig is up quickly from there because he starts to giggle, holding the tooth out to his mother.

Her eyes narrow at her youngest. "Explain," she orders, collapsing onto the floor in front of him in relief.

"God, Toby, you're so bad at this," Tyson laments.

We all look up to where Timothy and Tyson are standing in the doorway, disappointment on their faces. Their mother rises and places her hands on her hips with a practiced grace.

"Toby lost his tooth outside and we thought it could be fun to see how Ainsley would react," Timothy elaborates. He glances at me, then his mother, hanging his head in defeat.

"And what on earth made you three think that was a good idea? You know the tooth fairy does not appreciate being the butt of a joke," their mother admonishes.

The eldest boy gives their mother a look.

"We thought it would be funny, but Toby doesn't know how to keep up the joke." Tyson sounds extraordinarily put out by this whole situation.

"This was not a joke, this was hazing. You are not hazing your uncle's new girlfriend. I won't allow it. Apologize, all three of you."

I want to tell her that it's not necessary, but Ken catches me opening my mouth and he gives a little shake of his head.

Tobias is the first to relent, throwing his arms around my neck, knocking me off my feet. He puts his lips right to my ear to whisper, "It was all Tython's idea." The child's breath is hot on my neck and I hug him close.

"That didn't sound like an apology," Apple admonishes. One look at her and I can see that she's fighting a grin, but she needs to stay strong for her parenting.

"I'm thorry," Toby says sheepishly.

Before I can accept it, she turns to her older two sons. "Timothy? Tyson? What do you have to say?"

"Sorry you can't take a joke?" Tyson says, all attitude.

I think it takes everything Apple has to not stomp her foot at her middle son. Her foot actually twitches from the effort.

"That's not an actual apology," Ken scolds.

Tyson looks at his uncle, whom he so clearly adores, before really looking at me. "I'm sorry that we tried to play a prank on you. We meant it in good fun and did not intend any harm." Tyson finally sounds a little bit sorry, even if it is just sorry he got in trouble.

"Yeah, it seemed funny at the time. I'm sorry that the actual pull-off wasn't funny at all, and that we thought to trick you." Timothy's apology seems the most to hedge on an apology that's not actually an apology.

Apple turns to me, leaving it to me if I'm going to accept or not. There is no way that I can't accept their apology. I'm dating their favorite uncle, if you can even call it dating. It honestly was a harmless prank, and I can see it being all in good fun.

"Apology accepted, *but* if you want to really prove how sorry you are, you'll have to come with me to pick out that best gelato flavor there is at the place down the street."

"That's not really much of a punishment," Toby tells me earnestly, and I just want to gobble him and his sweetness up.

"Shut up, Toby!" Tyson tells him, glaring at the baby of the family.

"Don't tell your brother to shut up." Apple says, turning her attention away from the issue at hand now that everything seems to be resolved.

"*Momma!*" Toby cries in earnest now that he's been yelled at by Tyson. Given that his mother has turned away from him, he throws himself into my lap again, his crocodile tears flowing freely.

"That's enough, boys," Roberta warns, and they all seem to take notice now that grandma has gotten involved.

Toby keeps his arms around my neck, his little legs tangling around my waist. I lift him easily, resting him against my hip. When I look back at Ken, there is something in his gaze that I can't quite place. If pressed for a name, I would say desire, but not in the sexual way.

Fourteen

~❧~

I DON MY CUTEST ROMPER, something that hasn't had much wear since we got here, given most outings were spent wearing whatever I could get my hands on before we ventured out for gelato. The black and blue floral print has a tie around the middle that Ken won't stop playing with.

"You'll miss me?" he asks, nuzzling in my neck.

"Don't act like you're going to miss me while you're doing cannonballs or whatever else it is that boys do all day."

"Don't let my mother bully you, because she will if given half a chance."

"It won't be hard. I think your mother already likes me, so whatever drama you think is going to happen, you're just manufacturing that on your own."

We kiss and I suck his upper lip into my mouth while he nibbles on my lower lip. This moment, these feelings of contentment and the feeling of home, is what I've been chasing. Even at my best moments with Charlie, I never had this. I never had that absolute certainty that this is my person.

And that scares me. That scares me in such a big way because there is this constant feeling of waiting for the other shoe to drop.

I stop myself and my train of thought as it devolves more and more. We've both been up front and honest about what our goals are. If he was questioning my desire to be a mother, I would be pissed. There is no way that I can question if he really wants to be a father and if it's me that he really wants.

I slip out with a sun hat on my head and a small cross-body over my shoulder. Once Ken and the boys are set up for some time in the pool and the tub, Roberta, Apple, and I start to venture to the waterfront. The map of Positano looks more like the game board for Shoots and Ladders than a map of a coastal town. Between buildings are narrow stairways guiding travelers and locals either up or down the cliffside.

Roberta and Apple's conversation is not intentionally excluding me, but Roberta is trying to get more information out of Apple about Howie and if they're really planning to sell their house that I'm just naturally excluded.

For now, that suits me just fine. I'm enjoying wandering the stairs, falling behind so I can snap some pictures and send them off to my friends or post to my Pictogram. Also? Even if they're a million steps down, it's still a million steps. By the time we make it to the first shop, I'm soaking in sweat.

Apple takes pity on me and suggests we stop for a cappuccino. When Roberta looks back at me, she seems to pick up on what Apple is getting at and agrees. We sit down at a table outside and I let Apple order for the table, including some pastries.

"I'm sorry. Our legs are honed from years and years of doing this very walk. Sometimes we forget that stairs are actually pretty fucking difficult." Apple flips her hair over her shoulder, watching my every inhale.

With as much nonchalance as I can muster, I sip from my drink.

"If I had known, I would have just suggested the bus," Roberta says with a lift of her shoulder.

"There's a bus?" I ask, trying not to light these women on fire with my eyes.

"There is, but where's the fun in that? Walking builds character and gives a good workout," Apple teases, sipping her drink.

"Your brother and I have gotten plenty of cardio in before you showed up. There was little to no need for this." My words mean exactly what I intended them to mean, but then I realize that I am drinking coffee with his mother and sister and maybe I should check my temper, even if it is deserved. "Swimming. We've been swimming a lot," I amend.

"Right, well, there's that too." Apple laughs, relaxing in her chair.

"What made you get into divorce mediating? I imagine that's not an easy profession," Roberta says, ignoring my innuendo. I'm a little glad for it. I'm not sure I could stomach hearing more about how she did drugs off a man's dick, even if it was before she had Ken and Apple.

"I went to law school, realized during my last year that I didn't really want to be a lawyer, but by then I was in too deep. I wanted to do something that actually helped people, and what is better than trying to make sure that some of the hardest times of their lives are actually easier?"

"How noble," Apple praises me, but I'm not sure how much of it is sarcasm.

"I'm not sure how much of it is noble and how much of it is just not wanting three years of law school to go to waste. I have the means to do more, but I just haven't found that niche yet."

Apple taps her fingers to her lower lip. "Can I make a suggestion?"

I wave her on. "I'm all ears."

"I bet that there are low-income families that could benefit from having a lawyer help them through the process. Especially in New York City, you could easily set yourself up to really help people who are truly needy."

"I want to, please, believe you me, but every time I try to float the idea of setting up some sort of pro bono clinic at my firm, I get shot down."

The burn of anger rises in me so swiftly, I'm surprised. I've thrown around the idea of trying to offer rates for low-income families or trying to do something to extend our community outreach. As awful as the firm was that I worked for in law school, they still had a volunteer day where we would all go out and do something as a firm, even if it was to go into the poorer communities around Boston and provide legal services. We would answer questions about landlord-tenant work, structure basic wills for families that needed it, or advise on other legal issues. It was the benefit of working at a firm that had a finger in all the pots. Even if I was working in their corporate litigation department, my knowledge as a law student was put to the test by some of the partners on those days.

"Maybe it's time to find a place that will let you spread your wings a little. It's not easy. Howie is a Democratic senator from Virginia, so I understand feeling like you're backed into a corner. He wants to support social programs while also ensuring that when he's up for re-election, he'll get elected again. He's had to face decisions that were hard, not the best for him personally but the best way to serve his constituents."

"Did you always live in Virginia?" I ask, taking the opportunity to move the conversation off me. As much as this is a chance for them to get to know me, it's my chance to get to know them as well.

"Howie was. He played football at UVA, went to law school at Vandy. I'm sure the two of you would have some cute legal nerd-offs. When I told him about this place and how it was a protected asset before we got married, he begged me to look at the legal paperwork. Not because he wanted to find a loophole, but because of how interesting it was to him that our family had structured the ownership in the best way possible to protect us."

I chuckle. "I said the same thing to Ken."

"Legal nerds," Apple gripes with a smile and an eye roll.

"What do you do?" I ask her, realizing I haven't heard anything about what she does.

"Officially? I'm a stay at home mom to three wonderful boys, who have full schedules for me to manage. Unofficially, I'm an assistant to Howie. I dropped out of law school after I got pregnant with Timothy. I was a marketing manager before they became all about the forty-seven different types of social media. I went to law school so much later, and I was older than all my classmates. Honestly, having Timmy was a blessing in disguise. I never would have made it."

"I doubt that. You're smart, compassionate, and what I've seen between you and your brother and your children, you have a big heart. I think if you really wanted to go back to law school, you absolutely could."

"Well, I don't want to. I would much rather try and figure out this social media nonsense. I made one of those stupid short videos with Howie, introducing him to try to keep him hip and young. We both hated the whole thing. It was tedious and like pulling teeth. But Timothy? Forget about it. He watched us struggle and then was like, 'This is how you do it.' And then did in fifteen minutes what had taken me over an hour."

"Naturally. Children's minds are so much more pliable than ours. When they say children are the future it's not just because you have children to figuratively take the place of their grandparents on a population level, it's because they're able to become something more than what we are," Roberta chimes in.

"Mom, that is such a depressing way to look at it. I didn't have the boys to replace you and Dad." Apple shivers.

"Of course not. You would have needed to have four children to replace the four grandparents." Roberta is so matter-of-fact that I laugh.

"That is both mathematically wrong and wrong on so many

other levels that I can't even begin to correct you, so I just won't. How about instead we get some new sandals, as is tradition, and then we can really grill Ainsley?"

The shopping and the grilling really aren't as bad as I thought they would be. While our custom sandals are being made, the three of us walk around, trying on new things until we pass a lingerie store. Apple winks at me and then discreetly whisks her mother away so I can look around at the gorgeous lace underthings.

I've only known them a short while, but I've come to really like his mother and sister. Their version of grilling isn't at all what I expected. It's genuine get-to-know-you questions. Not like what my favorite color is or what was my childhood trauma, but they asked about college and law school. Apple wanted to hear all about living in Boston and even went as far as inviting me to visit her and Howie and the boys in DC.

A huge part of my heart starts to envision a future that I could have with them as my family. Am I just getting attached to Ken because he already has a built-in family for any kids we might have? I stop myself, my hand reaching out for a red garter.

My heart already has me married off to Ken, barefoot and pregnant with his kids in the villa here. Regardless of how we're both feeling, I want to be smart about this. This feels so, so right. Should I bother fighting it? Should I give in and let myself fall and fall and fall for this man?

I'm on autopilot, checking out, handing over my credit card as I think about this future. The future with those kids and with this family, and I decide that yes, I should let myself do this. For too long, I've been fighting my heart, trying to drown myself in prosecco and free dates. Why should I fight something that feels so right? Is it because of the timing?

Stepping out of the store, I tell myself that I'll have to leave the psychoanalyzing for later. Today, this week, it's about feeling the connection with Ken that I've craved my whole life, even if it leads to heartbreak again. Shielding my heart and my life will mean leading a life half-lived.

Toby winds up glued to my side for the next few days, nestled firmly against my chest, often falling asleep while trying to stay up with the big kids. Apple keeps trying to apologize, but I won't let her. It's good practice for something that will be in my near future. Ken's eyes always turn molten when I say it, probably thinking the same thing–how soon that future could come.

It feels unkind, but I'm glad Apple and Roberta choose to leave Positano early. They stay with us for three days, and while it's been fun playing board games with the boys, I'm eager for me and Ken to go back to our sexcation.

Ken lets out a sigh of relief once their taxi disappears.

"I thought they were never going to leave," he cries. He drops his shoulders so he can run at me, grabbing me around my middle. I yelp as he secures his arms around the backs of my knees, carefully tossing me over his shoulder. All of my blood rushes to my head, but I'm not sad about this view.

"What are you doing?" I exclaim, knowing exactly where this is headed, and I'm not at all sorry for it.

I'm so wrong about where he is taking me because instead of going into the bedroom, he carries me outside in the direction of the lemon trees. He had promised me a night of making love under the stars in the lemon tree grove, and it seems he's finally ready to follow through on that.

I slap his ass as we walk, pleading with him to just put me down, but he knows I don't mean it and refuses. My hand slips into his shorts and I pinch his bare ass, which earns me a slap on my own bottom. Ken chuckles darkly when it makes me moan.

When he does set me down, I spin to see that he set up a blanket and a picnic basket with a bottle of wine on ice.

"Is this where you disappeared to with the boys?" I ask, looking at the plates that are set out. My heart wants to leap out of its chest to be one with this man. My whole body twists toward him, and I lean against him, knowing that if I look him in the eye, my heart will be on my sleeve.

My feelings for him have not changed. With each passing day they only grow stronger, but I don't want to put any undue pressure here. He says that he's trying to avoid it as well, but this is a moment of change for us both.

"Yes, Toby wanted to make sure you knew that he was the one who packed the gummy bears."

"Ah, of course, the necessary gummy bears. No picnic would be complete without them."

Ken kisses the top of my head. "I'm the one who packed the rest of the dessert, if you must know."

"And what does that include?" I ask, teasing. I shimmy out of his arms and sit down beside the picnic basket.

"You mean besides carrying your fine pussy over here, there's also whipped cream."

I want to giggle and roll my eyes, but I can feel my body react to the idea of him touching and licking me all over.

We set up our picnic in silence, setting the meats and cheeses out on their separate plates, along with a fresh loaf of bread. This easy companionship makes me want to take him to Paris, where we can walk along the boulevards with a baguette between us so we can sit in a park and drink wine.

Ken takes a bite of his approximation of a sandwich and washes it down with a sip of wine before looking at me. "My mom said she likes you."

My head snaps to him in surprise. "From just the three days? The bar must have been low."

"No, but she told me she saw something in you that she didn't see in Leslie. I asked her what and she told me only time will tell, but Apple agreed that she likes you too."

His face is so open and earnest that I move with my instinct and cup his face. "Oh, hon, it's probably just because she didn't hear about how you watched me fuck another guy in front of you. I have been meaning to ask, were you watcher or participant?"

Ken pushes the wine glass out of my hand. It lands in the grass with a dull thunk. His mouth is against mine in an instant, guiding me back onto the blanket. I'm hungrier for him than the sandwich, so I push back against him, letting my legs fall open so there is space for him between them.

Ken's body falls into that gap, his erection straining against his shorts. I can feel him against the softest parts of me. Sometimes, it feels like we're magnets, always drawn to fit together the way we're supposed to.

"Oh, Ainsley," he moans, thrusting against me. That sweet friction just between our clothes drives me mad, my back arching and pressing my taut breasts against him. Ken's mouth is in my hair and on my neck as he pulls on my dress, not caring as the buttons pop off one by one, leaving me bare to the world.

He captures my nipple in his mouth and I cry out, pressing my nails into his shoulders. I'm wearing the new underwear I bought in town, but I don't think he notices. As Ken's tongue and teeth work against my breast, his hand kneads the other, making me pant.

Keeping one hand in his hair, I slide the other between my body and the new silk and right into the slick warmth of my pussy. I cry out again, rocking my hips into my own touch. Ken's eyes bore into me when he realizes what I'm doing and he nips at my hardened peak, moving his mouth just over it to bite and suck, leaving me with a hickey on my breast.

"Make yourself come," he orders, moving his hand off my breast. Ken hovers over me, undoing his shorts. His mouth is the only point of contact with my body. I rock my hips again, whimpering at the need that has gripped me. My thumb circles my clit while my fingers pump in and out of my pussy, and I want him and need him.

"I want you," I plead, not realizing the words are out of my mouth. It's a desperation that goes beyond primal desire. He leaves a trail of kisses down my body before he captures the silk of my panties in his teeth, biting at the back of my hand before he guides them down my legs, tossing them to the side. I watch his strong arms as he strokes himself, my eyes drawn to his erection.

"I want you to come on your hand before you come on my mouth, so when I fuck you, it's going to take one thrust before you come on my cock. So come for me, buttercup."

The types of women who could come on command were always a mystery to me, but his words hit differently this time, and I feel my back arch as my body clenches around my fingers, my orgasm gripping me. And when I think I'm done and truly spent, Ken thrusts his cock deep inside me, and I scream. I'm surprised by how my fingers and his dick fit as I stretch to accommodate both.

My fingers slide out of me, and I grip his ass, urging him into me again and again. I let go of his ass and push him back with his shoulders. Ken keeps thrusting, and I push him back harder, until he stops, the frantic animalistic part of him watching my face.

Ken lets me guide him out of me, so I can turn over, my ass lifted in the air. He nips at one cheek then the other before he hovers over me.

"Is this what you want, buttercup?" he asks, his cock sliding against my soaking folds.

"Fuck, yes," I grind out, needing him in me again. For a moment, I wonder what the fuck I was thinking when I pushed him out of me, but then he thrusts in and hits me at a different angle. My eyes roll into the back of my head, and I remind myself that this is what I was thinking.

He pushes my body down so his chest is against my back, my tits rubbing against the coarse fabric of the blanket as he hammers into me. One hand circles around my throat, exerting just a touch of pressure as a reminder of who is in charge.

"Is this something you like?" he grinds out, pumping harder. His other hand is braced on the ground beside me, twisting in the blanket.

"Yes." The answer comes out choked even as my body clenches around him in response to the roughness. My hands are digging into the grass, and I know as it happens, as my second orgasm tears through me, that I'm ripping up the ground in front of me.

"Oh, go, oh, yes, fuck, Ainsley!" he cries before his movements become jerkier as he empties himself inside me while my body milks him.

When his movements stop, he rolls off me, staying on his side to look me in the eye. I roll so I can turn to look at him as well.

"What happened to me coming on your mouth?" I tease, biting my lower lip.

Ken leans toward me, kissing me deeply, drawing me closer to him.

"Later. I couldn't wait to have you again." His fingers brush along my bare skin, from hickey to nipple to pussy. He dips a finger inside me, watching for the telltale soreness. I surprise him by thrusting against his hand. "Greedy."

"Always have been."

We lie there like that in the fading afternoon sun, feeding each other, getting drunk on wine and kisses and the feel of the other. I nearly doze in his arms as he plays with my hair with one hand, the other tracing symbols on my skin.

"I was a participant, but I think you knew that."

"Mmhmm?" I fight to open my eyes, confused about what he's talking about.

"You asked me earlier, about Leslie. I was a participant. I think I fell in love with the excitement that Leslie brought. She was unconventional and seemed to always have love for everyone. It was also my first time with another man. It wasn't something I thought I would like, but I did. Not nearly as much as I love being inside you." I feel the brush of his hardening cock against my hand where it rests on his thigh.

"I made out with women before, and I've always been drawn to boobs, but I never really explored my feelings toward women before because I know I love dick."

Ken thrusts into my hand, and I drag my nails against him gently. "If you want to try again with another woman, I would support you."

I stop my movement, withdrawing my hand so I can prop up on my elbow, totally awake now. "With or without your participation?" I ask, curious.

"Either would be fine. I think there's too much pressure by society and parents that relationships need to fit in a tidy little box. Relationships are messy. Sex is messy. I don't want you to feel restrained by me."

"So, you're telling me you left an open relationship because you're tired of being in an open relationship, only to offer the same thing to me? You must be off your rocker, old man," I joke, my teeth snagging his nipple.

"But that's why I feel okay telling you that. I've been with men and women. I know what I like. I know the taste I've acquired. It's you. You're the only one I need in my bed, but if you wanted to explore that side of yourself, you could."

"Enough." My voice comes out harder than I intended, but there is no judgment on Ken's face. "Thank you," I say clearing my throat. "I appreciate that. But you," I tell him, leaning up to kiss him as I throw my leg over him so I'm straddling him, "this," I gasp as I slide down onto him, "is all I need."

Fifteen

"CAN you grab my work phone? I think it's in my purse," I call to Ken. I haven't checked in with my office, which probably isn't the sign of a good partner. But seriously, they can fuck right off. I'm on *vacation.*

I'm curled on the couch with a glass of wine in one hand and the first book I've read in about a year in the other. Ken, who was already up, digs through my purse. When it takes him a while, I try to help. "Maybe in a side pocket on the inside?"

"Yeah, I got it." Ken sounds subdued as he walks over to me to hand me my phone. I set my book aside and pour over my emails. I have almost a thousand emails. Any with Eloise copied on them, I ignore, marking them as a low priority. Too many are from Kyle and Eugene; at least one has the subject line of partner.

Annoyed, I finish my glass of wine and turn my work phone back off. "Do you want more wine?" I ask, realizing that the bottle of wine on the table is also empty.

"If you're going to possibly get pregnant on this trip, maybe you should stop drinking."

I'm already halfway to the kitchen when he says this. I turn around very slowly. "When I'm pregnant or even think I might be pregnant, I'll stop, but until then, it's still my body and I get to decide that I can drink. Besides, I'm so tired of my fucking bosses. They give me the shit end of the stick and say, 'But partner!' As if that's supposed to change that they're fucking me over."

I study Ken's face. There's something off about it, and I don't know what.

"Of course, but you could already be pregnant, and if we're going to do this, we need to communicate how we're feeling as we go along."

"Right, well, I'm feeling like I hate my bosses and I need a drink. Is that enough communication for you?" I don't know where this sudden attitude is coming from.

"Then quit. Ainsley, you're well-off enough that you were considering being a single mother. Quit."

I take my time uncorking the wine, not looking at him. "I told you I want to keep my job. But aside from that, they actually mentioned possibly promoting me to partner this year. Which could make it easier to land somewhere else, but who even knows?"

I told Eugene I would give some thought to what he said about becoming partner, but outside of my conversation with my dad and mentioning work with Apple, I haven't thought much about it at all. My focus this whole time has been on Ken and the life we could be starting, both inside me and together. For me, it's a huge red flag that maybe being partner isn't something I'm really looking for right now. And that's okay, but it's a concept that I haven't done any deep introspection about yet.

Being partner was my dream for so long because we're told in law school that it's what we should strive for, like getting married and having babies is what women are told to want. And I did want it, when I spent most days, nights, and weekends alone because my fiancé was working all the time. Wanting to be partner is what kept me warm on the nights I went to bed alone. Since being with Ken, it's started to occur to me that maybe I don't need to be partner to be happy and feel successful.

But Ken's started a fight about it now, and I won't back down from it because it feels too much like he just wants a happy little wife who will spread her legs and walk around in a perpetual state of knocked-up.

I hear Ken's footsteps as he crosses to me. "So, you want out of this?" he demands, much closer than he was before.

"What? No." I look up at him, surprised. I don't know what would make him think that. I've been all-in this entire trip. Ever since I told him I wanted to give this a real try as he made me scream on my desk, I've been all-in.

"Are you considering becoming partner?" his voice is low.

"I mean, of course, I'll consider it, but I've barely thought about it. It's like I said, it could make it easier for me to find a job at a different firm, but I haven't thought beyond that. Eugene literally mentioned it to me before I got on the plane."

"Why didn't you mention it before now?"

I hate how crowded in I feel, so I step away from him, moving to the other side of the island. "Because I don't know what I want. I also told Eloise that I was going to get us both out when I got back and now I'm trying to make a baby with you. So excuse the fuck out of me if I don't know what to make of what could be an imaginary job offer."

"Then why the fuck do you have these?" There is a lethal calm to Ken's voice as he throws my birth control pack on the island.

Fuck.

I had completely forgotten they were in my purse, tossed in weeks ago just as we were starting this in case one of us changed our minds. It shouldn't make a difference, only I can see how it looks. The blister pack is half-broken because I was in the middle of one when we decided to try for a baby.

"They were just in my purse, Ken. I haven't been taking them. You were the one who said that we could go at *my* pace!"

"What am I supposed to think, Ainsley? You never mentioned any sort of hesitation. I thought we were in this together. I thought that you were just as invested in having a baby with me as I am.

"But now, you just admitted that you're considering becoming partner. That means long nights and hours when you could be pregnant. Or from the looks of it, maybe you were just planning to let me think we were having trouble conceiving unless it fit in with your schedule. You know how badly I want this, and now you're thinking about reneging on the deal."

His accusations just confirm my fears, that all his flowery words about wanting me mean nothing, and he only sees me as an incubator for his child. My anger is a living boulder and it's crushing me. And, yes, maybe I should have had a conversation with him about it, but any guilt I had about unintentionally with-holding information went out the window when he started to throw blame at me like I was doing something wrong.

I'm done trying to dignify his accusations with a response. "Go fuck yourself, Ken." I put the wine bottle on the table, even though I want to smash it, and walk around the island toward the bedroom.

"Where are you going?" he demands, following me. "We're not done with this conversation."

"Au contraire, I think we are. You clearly can't trust me if you think that I would go behind your back like that." And that's what hurts, that he can so quickly assume that I would lie to him.

I slam the bedroom door in his face and engage the lock. It's only once he's out of my physical space and I can hear him banging on the door do the tears start. I can't fucking believe he doesn't believe me, especially when I haven't given him a reason not to trust me.

And I think that's why it cuts to the quick so badly. I have been nothing short of an active participant, gladly spreading my legs for him so we can do this together. It might have been his idea, but it's grown into something of my daydreams, the day we could be parents.

It doesn't take long for my thoughts to spiral into the possibility that he's the one deflecting blame. That he might actually be the one with doubts of his own. Finding that old blister pack was just the excuse he needed to pump the breaks himself.

So what if I'm justifying this with my own concerns, my own fear that he's jumping in too soon? I listened to him, I believed him, and having him not believe me is a betrayal of its own.

Quickly, I shove my stuff into my suitcase. Anything I can live without, I'll leave, but otherwise I'm grabbing everything I can as quickly as I can.

"Ainsley, open the door so we can talk about this like adults," he shouts, still banging on the door.

"No!" As quietly as I can, I open the balcony door and step outside with my bag. When I cross back through the living room, I'll grab my purse and my phone. I don't know where I'm going, but I'm going to get the fuck out of here so I can think about what this means.

"Ainsley!" I hear him say again.

When I step into the living room, I know I'll only have a minute or two before he registers I'm out there. Quickly, I grab my stuff and race for the door, ignoring his pleas as he calls after me.

My hands are shaking as I open my phone and call the only person I can think of that won't put Ken six feet under for this argument.

"Charlie?" I ask, my voice wavering when I hear him on the other end. Our romantic relationship might have been a mistake, but the friendship that grew out of it never was. He's always been reliable, and I need that right now.

"Ainsley? What's wrong?"

"Do you still have that place in Florence?"

Without asking a single question, he helps get me to somewhere safe.

I sulk in Charlie's villa in Florence for the rest of my vacation and fly back a few days earlier than I planned. I'm tired from being up all night crying while video chatting with my friends until the early morning hours. Nothing can soothe the jagged edges of my broken heart. I've ignored every text and call from Ken, not even reading them when they came in. I can't make myself block his number, though.

I'm restless on my return flight, only adding to my exhaustion. So when I see Taryn, Elia, and Vivian sitting outside my apartment door, I break down again. They don't ask questions as we all enter my apartment, and I'm grateful when they order pizza and help me get my life back together.

After a shower, I'm lying on the couch with my head in Vivian's lap. She's running her fingers through my hair like I'm a small child. When I called them, it was mostly for a distraction so I didn't talk about what happened between Ken and I, and while I lie there, listening to Taryn talk about work, I realize that I never gave them the full story.

"We were going to try to have a baby," I tell them when there is a lull in the conversation. The only indication that they heard me is a hesitation in Vivian's hands after my proclamation.

"You and Ken?" Elia asks.

I glance at the chair she's sitting in and fight a frown. "Yeah. He wanted a baby. I wanted a baby. It made sense. It seemed like the right thing to do, and so I said, 'Sure.' It didn't hurt that I was, I am, unspeakably attracted to him, and I think I'm falling in love with him."

"Babes, there is no thinking about it. You're totally in love with him." Taryn doesn't say it with any malice; it's a statement of fact.

The truth is, I'm terrified of that feeling. I'm terrified of that all-consuming feeling of being in love and needing to have this one person in my life. I'm terrified because the times I thought I had just that, I lost it and it was devastating.

But I'm devastated anyway. A sob chokes its way from my chest as I realize I've lost this amazing man and I thought I was safe, but I wasn't. Love is like a cancer that works its way into your every system, only instead of death, there is uplifting love that lends strength and bolsters you.

When I calm down, I hug one of my stuffed animals to my chest.

"Have you heard from him?" Vivian asks quietly. She resumes idly brushing my hair back. There have been text messages from Ken, asking where I am, if I'm alright. I've ignored them all. He hasn't stopped reaching out but I don't think I can reciprocate. Not yet.

"He's called, and I'm just not ready to talk to him. He found my birth control pill in my purse and it was right on the heels of me mentioning that they approached me for partner."

"They did?" Vivian would, of course, catch on this tidbit.

"Not directly. It's not like Eugene walked into my office and was like, 'You're going to be a partner.' No, it was more like, 'If you keep jumping through our arbitrary hoops, then maybe you will maybe possibly be promoted mid-year.' But I know this place. I know it's full of empty promises, but on the off chance this was really going to be a thing, I thought it would be easier to transfer jobs if I had that title."

"For starters, you're a bad bitch. I don't know why you underestimate that," Taryn scolds. "You've got two Ivy League degrees. You should be able to walk into whatever firm you want, hand them a post-it with your salary requirement on it, and they'll bend over backwards to make it happen. What about Sean?"

I sit up so fast I make myself dizzy. That could also be my lack of eating. The first night in Florence, I cried so hard, I threw up. It's been such an emotional few days that the thought of food nauseates me. The pizza the girls bought was some of the first food I've had outside of crackers or bread.

"Sean, like my law school ex, Sean?" I reach forward and snag a garlic knot. More carby goodness.

"Yeah, you said that he was constantly offering you jobs and such. Why not reach out to him and take him up on it?"

I did have reasons, once upon a time, for not reaching out or accepting that offer. Chief among them was that I was with Charlie, and though he would never admit it, there was a level of discomfort with the idea of me working closely with an ex. During law school, if I wasn't dating Charlie, I was dating Sean. It was a brutal yo-yo between the boys, which, as an adult, I can realize was cruel. Rather than have my partner be in an uncomfortable situation, I just declined to join Sean's firm.

After so many rejections, he stopped asking.

"I'll call him, but can I lick my wounds first? I'm pretty sure I've made enough life-altering decisions in the past month."

It occurs to me that it's really only been a month since Ken came to me with the proposal that maybe we should try to co-parent. It's been a month since I agreed to this insane idea that I could make a baby with Ken. A month of kisses and text messages and finally opening my heart to someone.

I thought motherhood was going to be a journey I embarked on alone, but then Ken came to me with the possibility that I could have a partner. Someone who said he wanted to marry me down the road.

"We can do whatever you want."

That's how the four of us wind up snuggled in my bed for the night, watching an old season of Mr. Eligible until we're all snoring, tangled up together.

Sixteen

"WHERE IS MY OLIVE OIL?" Eloise asks before I can even put my bag down.

"Can I take my coat off?" I ask, deliberately waiting for an answer.

"If it's going to get me my olive oil faster, then yes." Her saccharine smile has an edge to it.

"What's wrong?" I ask, reading her face for some hint of what happened while I was gone. Honestly, I would rather focus on that instead of my drama with Ken.

"Kyle made a pass at me, and I was told to quote, 'Suck it up, but not his cock, honey' end quote." Her eyes fill with tears. I set my bags down and move to the other side of my desk, pushing my door closed, not caring if I get reprimanded for slamming the door before I hug her.

Eloise doesn't cry. Her body melts against mine, thankful to have someone else here to help carry her burden. Everything I hate about this job boils down to their unwillingness to listen to or believe their female employees. We're treated like a commodity, easily replaced by another nameless, faceless woman for ten percent cheaper until they're hiring twenty-year-olds, promising to pay them their age as a salary.

When she's done with the hug, she pushes away from me. Her eyes are narrowed as she takes in my tan.

"Why don't you pay me enough to go holiday in Italy for two weeks?"

"Because I don't write your checks. Did I miss anything else noteworthy?" Not that I don't consider what happened to her noteworthy, but it makes my next steps more urgent.

We resume our usual positions, me behind my desk, tracking emails and work while she rests her feet on the corner of my desk, pushing her chair back precariously far until she comes back on all four feet. The truth is, I spent all day yesterday looking over emails and working, but to her, I only landed yesterday afternoon.

"No, you missed nothing. Your schedule is a little more packed this week with new clients and returning ones, but for having been away in Italy, you were shockingly responsive to emails and getting me drafts of settlements at the end. I would have assumed you would use those days for all the last yummy travel days."

"Yes, well, Ken's family showed up."

Eloise rocks back then forward forcefully so she can rest her elbows on the chair. "Do tell."

I fill her in as I get my desk cleared, going over the better high-lights of the trip. I skip the juicy bits about quiet orgasms and exactly what position we were caught in, but I tell her about the boys, their attempts at pranks, and everything in-between. I skip over the fight, over how we're not even speaking right now. It's been almost a week since I last saw Ken and it's killing me a little.

"I need to find someone to date reliably." Eloise says when I'm done.

"What about Kevin? Or Smithy? Or Wrenchy?" I ask, trying genuinely to remember the names of her last few boyfriends.

"None of those, you cow. His name was Cale, and I mean, we

still hook up every so often, but we're both so busy, and also, his name is Cale, like kale, like the salad. That's not exactly husband material."

A knock on my door startles both of us.

"Yeah?" I ask, not bothering to screen because like most people back from vacation, my coworkers will want all the dirty details.

Kyle sticks his head in the door, and I want Eloise to slam it on his head. "Look who's back! I almost forgot you worked here. Your paralegal was extra attentive to my needs while you were out. You're lucky."

"Get out, Kyle," I warn, getting to my feet. I plant my hands on either side of my desk, not wanting to look at Eloise. Her usual brightness has shuttered in his presence. No, this settles it. Partner at this firm is not worth the amount that I would have to put up with this asshole to get it. I don't know what I was thinking to even consider it.

I never liked Kyle. He's weaselly and looks like it too, all slicked back hair and hard edges. His auburn hair is long, tied at the nape with a strip of leather like this is some medieval world and not New York City law. The longer I have to look at his narrow face, the more I want to box his ears. I'm no stranger to getting around based on my father's merits, but Kyle has never earned a thing in his life.

"Where is all this hostility coming from? Did Eloise tell you those rumors she's been starting?" He pushes my door all the way open, so the whole office can hear every word we're saying.

I stand to my full height before walking around my desk in my four-inch red-bottomed heels. My movements seem effortless as I glide in his direction. I'm careful not to touch him, but just having me prowl toward him has Kyle on edge and he takes a few steps back to keep space between us. He knows who my father is, what my father can and will do. He might fuck around with my paralegal, but he's not stupid enough to fuck with me.

"This hostility is coming from you thinking that I'm afraid of your pencil dick energy. Stay away from Eloise and stay away from me, or you'll be looking at a class action lawsuit for the firm. Eloise is off limits."

"She's a firm asset. She doesn't belong to you." He's trying to muster courage and I want to coo at him for thinking that it will accomplish anything.

"Let's you and I run that past the partners, see who they value more: you or me. I've kept in touch with all of the twenty-eight women who have come and gone through these doors. I've held their confidence all this time. I bet they would all love to come down on you with the whole force of the law."

Kyle sneers at me. "If you actually had something actionable, you would have already done something about it."

I grab his tie and tug it down so I can whisper in his ear. "Believe it or not, it's not every woman's wet dream to talk about how you dry humped them while they changed the paper in the copier. How else would I know how little you're packing? You're overcompensating for something. Actually, a lot of somethings." I let him go and level him with a firm glare. "Leave the women of this office alone."

I stalk back into my space and slam the door in his face. The glass pane rattles satisfyingly. When I look at my faithful paralegal, she's grinning behind a folder.

"I have never been more turned on by a woman in my life than I was while watching you put that asshole in his place."

"I'm pretty turned on by myself, if I do say so. Call Sean McGinty at Catania Maida Rinaldi and tell him there is thunder and lightning in the forecast. See when I can get him for lunch."

I start to shuffle the envelopes that Eloise didn't address. For the most part, she opens my mail and handles it, unless it looks like it's something personal. I often get thank you cards or, in this case, birthday cards.

One envelope stands out, as it's thicker and feels more like a wedding invitation. My name is embossed on the cover in gold. Eloise, who was getting up to make that call, sits back down to see what I have.

"Nosey," I chastise, grabbing a letter opener from my drawer and opening the letter with a satisfying rip.

I wasn't far off with thinking it was a wedding invitation. Instead, it's an invitation to a divorce party hosted by Leslie and Ken. My heart flip-flops seeing his name on the invitation, and I wonder why he wouldn't tell me.

Eloise wisely doesn't say anything as she slips out of my office, closing the door behind her.

I'm not sure what the safe dosage is, but I shove three chewable Pepto pills into my mouth and grind them in my teeth as I walk into the restaurant. My nerves have made my stomach roil since I told Eloise to call Sean, and I'm not sure that these pink pills are up to the task of keeping my nausea at bay. It took a week to finally get this lunch on the books, and since making the call, I've been stressed to a whole new level.

All my issues that I was having in Italy have carried over, only so much worse. I was weak enough this weekend to actually read through all of the texts Ken has been sending me. What has to happen is I need to pull on my big girl panties and actually talk to him, but I want to be able to go to him with at least this work situation settled first.

"Well, if it isn't Ainsley Seaborn, the Queen of Obscene, in the flesh." Sean McGinty rises from his seat, smoothing his tie over his chest so he can embrace me. It was a desperate call, reaching out to my ex-boyfriend from law school, but I trust him.

"Sean McGinty, the least Irish Irishman in all of Manhattan. Still willing to drop everything to aid a damsel in distress." I kiss his cheek before sitting down in an exhausted huff. It seems like no amount of sleep I get is enough. I'm anxious and restless all night long.

Sean's still got that gorgeous face that I used to love to sit on, and his suit can't hide that he has muscles forever under all those clean lines. His straight, dark hair is on the longer side, with a few strands adding character as they drape across his forehead. The key difference about him is while his green eyes used to dance with mischief and fun, they're now shadowed by the grief of losing his wife two years ago.

"You told me that there was thunder and lightning in the forecast. Of course, I did what I could for my schedule to meet you. Addison is many things, but even she is limited to the hours in a day. Do you want to tell me what is so urgent?"

There is a glass of water and wine on the table, and as much as the wine will be horrible for my heartburn, I grab it and take a gulp before I barrel forward.

"Yes, I need a job for me and my paralegal. We've been at the breaking point with my firm for a while now and their recent handling of a problem means we need out sooner rather than later."

Sean leans back in his chair, studying me as he smooths his tie again. It's an old nervous quirk that I watched him do a hundred times on his wedding day alone. He's thinking, but he's already made his decision; he just wants me to think he hasn't.

"Package deal?"

"Yes."

The server interrupts us by dropping off food. I shouldn't be surprised that Sean ordered for me before I even got here. We've been doing this lunch off and on for years with varying levels of frequency, but we have it down to a science. He orders a burger with all the fixings while I get a Mediterranean panini and an order of truffle fries to share. I get a glass of white wine and he gets a beer to round out our meal.

The smell of the truffle fries kick-starts my nausea again. I sniffle and rub my nose, but grab an offending fry and take a bite anyway. Nope. Nope. Nope.

Sean doesn't miss a thing. "Are you alright?"

"Yeah. I was in Italy and must have caught a cold on the flight or I'm just getting older. I feel like shit putting in seventy to eighty hours for this firm and I haven't had a solid meal in a week, so I'm just running myself further into the ground." More like two weeks but I'm not going to tell him that.

"We're not getting any younger, are we?" he jokes.

"No, we are not." I can practically feel my biological clock tick again. It causes something to nudge in the back of my mind. My biological clock has been running off schedule, but that's not unusual given how abruptly I stopped taking the pill. Maybe I should make an appointment with my doctor to make sure everything is running as it should be. Regardless of where Ken and I are at personally, a baby is still something I want.

"Well, no formal interview needed. You know you have me by the balls. I've been trying to get you to come to Catania Maida Rinaldi forever. I'm just sorry it took something happening to finally get you in my snare."

"Me too." The most regrettable part of this is that it's not even something that happened to me. I could handle the male aggression and the come-ons at my office. I've been writing them and their behavior off for years. It's that Eloise got caught in the crosshairs is what makes it truly unforgivable.

Sean and I fall into our easy banter, catching up on firm life and what other law school friends have been up to.

"Have you finally started dating again?" I've been gently prodding him about this for months now.

Absently, Sean spins his wedding ring around his finger. "No.

Addison downloaded a couple of apps, Tumble and Sleepless Nights, trying to find me something to do with my nights, but I have fun going out for drinks with my guy friends or just staying in and watching games."

His wife, Olive, passed away during what should have been a routine surgery, but the doctor that came in to do her surgery was drunk and nicked an artery. She bled out in minutes while Sean sat in the waiting room, looking at houses. That was two years ago.

"There are some real losers on Sleepless Nights. I would know. I was on it."

Sean laughs into his beer, leaning back. "Is that an invitation to rekindle our old flame, Ainsley Seaborn?"

I laugh along with him, draining my wine glass. Noticing I can't stomach the truffle fries, Sean gladly shares his potato wedges with me. My issue is not with the fries themselves but more with the decadent topping. I smother a potato wedge in mustard, not my usual condiment, but sometimes life can use a shake-up.

"That is anything but an invitation. I got stood up twice by the same guy, and it worked out. I met someone really great instead." My voice breaks by the end and I'm starting to wonder if I've royally fucked this up. Once I start down that line, the tears begin to flow more freely until I'm sobbing into my napkin.

Sean is silent as he moves from the seat across from me to the one beside me so he can slide an arm around my shoulders. The more I try to calm myself down, the worse it gets, until Sean starts to rub my ears. It's enough of a shock to jolt me back to myself.

"What?" he asks defensively.

"What was that? Why were you rubbing my ears?"

Sean flushes red. "When Olive would get upset, it would help calm her down. I didn't know what to do. I haven't had to deal with a crying female since the funeral."

"That is weird, but also sweet." I rub under my eyes, knowing that all the concealer I put on is probably a waste.

"Want to talk about it?"

"I think I royally fucked up with this guy."

Sean nods his head, like he agrees with me. "Is he alive?"

"What?" I ask, aghast.

"I asked: Is he alive? If this guy is still on this earth and is breathing, then you can fix it. I'm never going to get to apologize to Olive for forgetting to run the dishwasher all the time or for leaving clothes in the dryer. Those are little things, and I have to assume if you're crying it must be a big thing, because I'll be honest, I don't think you cried any of the times you and Chuck broke up, and I know you never cried when we broke up. So, go apologize, even if you didn't fuck up. Start the communication. If I could do it again with Olive, I would. I would say I'm sorry. I would throw myself at her feet for absolution for all the times she almost fell in the toilet because I left the seat up. Humble yourself, and fix it."

"How?"

"Grand gestures go a long way, or so I've been told. You know your man better than I do."

I wipe my eyes again, trying to stop the tears. "Getting a new job might be a step in the right direction."

"I'll increase Eloise's salary by twenty grand if you walk into your boss' office right now and take a shit on their desks and leave."

"Tempting as that may be, I know you don't have that sort of authority."

"You're right, but that doesn't mean I'm not going to fight for you both. You're honestly an asset. We've been needing to expand our family law branch. We have someone handling Trusts and Estates, but we want to be a one-stop shop."

I sit up abruptly and lean toward him, remembering Apple's words. "I need some free reign to do some pro bono work."

Sean leans toward me intrigued. "Anything I can help with?"

I want to kiss the man for being so willing to jump in with both feet. "Not yet, but I will call on you once I know."

"Great. I'm going to go to my office, change some numbers on your offer letters, and hit send on an email I've had sitting in my drafts folder for two years." He thumbs out enough money for the whole check and a generous tip before rising.

Sean McGinty never fails to bail me out of my messes, no matter what kind they are.

Seventeen

SEAN WASN'T SHITTING me when he said he would send the email once he was back in the office. I've been at my desk for no more than fifteen minutes before I see his email come through on my phone. I give it a quick perusal, surprised by the salary offering for Eloise. Her pay alone is at least a twenty-five percent increase, plus the benefits are much better.

Happy workers make work happy. Sean has told me their unofficial firm tagline and I never believed it before now. They're an old firm that managed to stay relevant with the passing years by being competitive. Where other firms failed to change or keep up with the younger workforce, Catania Maida Rinaldi has made sure to keep their employees happy as their way of ensuring they keep good talent.

Honestly, I can't come up with a damn good reason why I've been so resistant to the switch. I know that they have a low rate of attrition, and Sean's been feeding me details of their outings and offerings since he started.

At some point, I started to believe that Catania Maida Rinaldi was too good to be true. I managed to convince myself that the grass is not always greener. I've suffered for it and Eloise has suffered for it. There hasn't been anything keeping her at this job other than me and that same mentality. It's still a boy's club at most firms.

I buzz Eloise and ask her to join me in my office. When she enters I gesture that she close the door. Always prepared, she has her notepad in hand and her pen sticking out of her thick, curly bun. Once she sits, she pulls it out, ready to write.

"I need you to look over this paperwork for me," I say, pushing her offer letter in front of her. It's not an unusual task, so she relaxes into the seat, ready to review it and give me her feedback.

What she wasn't expecting was to see a six-figure salary outlined with a signing bonus. The papers shake in her hands as she flips through them, reading every word of the letter once and then again before she looks at me.

"Is this a joke?" she whispers, and I grin.

"Nope. Sean's made the official offer with the partners copied on it. That's where I was for lunch."

"And they don't want to interview me?" Eloise sounds close to tears as she grabs for the benefit packet. I let her sit and digest the information.

"We would have an informal sit-down as a get-to-know-you, but they've been wanting to start their family law arm, and I would be spearheading it."

"Are you sure?" she asks me, her brow furrowed.

I can't help but deflate a little. I expected more excitement from her, not this uncertain reaction.

"I am totally sure. It's beyond time to switch firms, and I trust Sean. He knows what I've had to say about this place. I know that this is somewhere we could really be happy."

She bites on her lips, studying the papers again before looking at me. "When do we start?"

"We can go give our notice today."

Eloise grins at me and gets to her feet. She smooths out her skirt around her generous curves. "Then what the fuck are we waiting for?"

"I wasn't sure if you would want to meet the partners first. You haven't even met Sean."

"I trust you, and I know you've met them before."

Her faith in me is not something I take lightly. I squeeze her hand. "Then let's go."

I know that the partners are in their weekly meeting, where they review everything that is going on. It's not so much a meeting as it is them hidden away in one of the corner offices, drinking whiskey and complaining about the little women of the office.

With my shoulders pulled back, I knock on their door.

"Oh, for fuck's sake," I hear muttered. "Who is it?"

I don't wait for an invitation. Instead, I push the door open so seven heads swivel toward me. "Gentlemen."

Eloise is right on my heels, and I scowl when I see Kyle sitting beside the decanter. When he spots us, he freezes like a deer caught in headlights. I push further into the room, closing the door behind me.

"Ainsley, Eloise, what can we do for you? We're in the middle of a meeting."

I frown in the direction of Eugene, the partner behind his desk. He's one of the ones who pushed to bring me on, or so he told me. There had been comments from him about how I should be grateful to him for my job, but he never went as far as a blatant come-on. I was acquainted with his wife enough to know that he wasn't as restrained around other women.

"I know. I've come to give you my notice," I announce triumphantly. There was no caveat to bringing my client book, but people know me. They know how to find me. It's not that they like what my firm has to offer. People like to work with this firm so they can work with me.

"What? You're leaving? What happened to our conversation about your future? With more commitment from you, we were going to put you on the partner track." Eugene jumps up, splashing his drink over the papers on his desk.

The lawyer in me wants to wince, hoping that they weren't original signatures. The bitchy part of me wants to hope that they were. It's not beyond me that this wording about the partnership has changed. Now it's that I *would* be on the partner track with more commitment? Fuck right off.

"Yes," Eloise adds forcefully. "We both are. Your recent conduct has proven that you do not value me as an employee, and I will not stand for that."

"Over a simple misunderstanding?" This comes from Matthias. He's on the couch, nearly swallowed by it, he's so relaxed into it. I want to knock his drink into his face. Of course, he doesn't see anything wrong with this. Matthias is Kyle's uncle, so he's got more on the line to defend his little shit of a nephew.

Their attitude about this is making me sick, and I actually grip my stomach, hoping to keep the nausea at bay. Maybe this is one time I shouldn't fight it and should vomit on them so they see how disgusted they make me.

"I would hardly call groping a paralegal a misunderstanding." Eloise sounds frantic, and I grab her hand, squeezing it.

"Slapping your ass is a compliment!" Kyle shouts, mounting his defense and digging his own grave.

Eloise didn't tell me the specifics, but even if other women don't want to sue the firm for sexual harassment, I'm sure as shit going to talk Eloise into it now that there is a room of lawyers who can be deposed as hearing firsthand from the aggressor that he admitted his actions.

At least four of the attorneys in the room seem to realize this because they start to squirm in their seats. Their department is separate, so I could find it believable that they hadn't heard about this until now, but at this point, they're stuck in it. This is their firm too.

"No, it's not a compliment. And telling me you're surprised a fat chick has a nice ass isn't either." Eloise has blown past the tears and is finally tapping into her anger over the situation.

"I said you had a nice ass, didn't I?" Kyle is on his feet, his drink sloshing onto his shirt.

Eugene sees this getting away from him, and he turns to look at me. "You might as well just pack your things now, because you're not taking a single client with you. I'll make sure you take your things and go. It's clear that your presence in the firm is doing more harm than good, and we don't need that sort of toxicity."

"Go fuck yourself, Eugene." *Because your wife certainly won't*, I mentally add. I refuse to say it out loud so I can hold onto the high horse in this situation as much as I can.

Eugene and Matthias follow Eloise and I to our desks, where we pack up our things. I want to be able to send farewell emails and let people know where I'm going, but the first thing Eugene does is take my laptop.

The asshat doesn't realize I have my work emails on my phone and all of our documents are uploaded to the Cloud. Since I wasn't expecting this turn of events, I'll have to rush home to get the templates that I've built over the years.

As I walk past Eugene, he grabs my upper arm, stopping me. I look at where he's touching me then meet his eyes with a raised eyebrow.

"You could have been great. *We* could have been great. Instead, you're just going to be another divorce attorney slutting her way through New York City." His voice is low so no one else can hear him.

Eloise glances up, shoving the last of her shoes into a paper box one of the other paralegals gave her.

"I can't wait to sue you for everything you've got. You really should be better about checking the recipients of your emails and how you address people in them. Calling your female associates bitches and sharing our Pictogram photos on the company server was not the best call. Don't try to delete them now, Eugene. The internet is forever." I push past him, with an old gym bag from under my desk full of everything I can fit. One of the other paralegals grabs my diplomas and art off the walls and helps me carry them downstairs. With every step away from this place, I feel more and more free.

When we're down on the street, I look over at Eloise. "Want to come to my place and get day drunk?"

"Abso-fucking-lutely," she agrees.

When we get to the apartment, I pour us both drinks before I try to grab as many of my forms as I can before I'm locked out. When I'm done, I glance over at Eloise, who looks practically catatonic.

"You okay over there?" I poke her shoulder.

"I have rent to pay and I just quit my job with no notice. I have student loans and utilities. What if they shut off my streaming access?"

"No one is taking away your streaming services and you're not going to be homeless and you're not going to get put into debtors' prison for being late on your student loans."

Eloise grabs my wrist. "Was that an option!?"

I chuckle. "I'll text Sean now, see if they're flexible on a start date. They probably need to get some paperwork and time to get laptops for us, but otherwise, take a week off. Since I got you into this mess, I'll get you out."

"I can't take your money."

For a moment, I want to admire her gumption, but really, I'm just annoyed by it. "Shut up and accept my generosity. None of this rejecting it because you feel like it's too much or you should or whatever other reason you can come up with. This is about the fact that you are a good, loyal paralegal who should have quit long, long ago and didn't. So literally, as the meme says, shut up and take my money. And while you're at it, just take a fucking vacation. You've been squeezing as much life out of the ten days you had. It's time to do more with it."

"And where *exactly* do you propose I go?"

"Where do you want to go? Pick a city and I'm sure I know someone with a house there."

"Scotland?" she throws out, sipping from her wine.

"Done."

I ponder what *I'm* going to do with all this time off. Part of me wants to go to Ken and grovel. The idea of my grand gesture is still out there, but for sure on the list is going to the doctor. Ken and I discussed being clean, but I'm due for my annual visit anyway. While Eloise excuses herself to tell her mother, I shoot off a text to Charlie to see if his stepfather still owns that castle in Scotland.

The web portal for my doctor shows that she has an opening at two the next day. Quickly, I snag it and relax. When Eloise is off the phone with her mom, she frowns at me.

"She said that she's proud of me but wonders why I couldn't have quit this job before I signed a new lease so I could have moved home with them. It's like she doesn't realize that I've built a life here."

"You're her baby. Of course, she's going to want you to move back home." My hand falls to my stomach, thinking what my life could have looked like thirty years in the future.

No, fuck that. It still can look like that. I just need to grow up and talk to Ken.

Eloise catches the movement, and her eyebrows shoot into her hairline. "Is there something you need to tell me?"

Startled, I look up at her with big eyes. "What? No. Nothing to tell." Eloise stays silent, staring at me with an intensity that makes me squirm. "Still nothing to tell. You can stare at me all you want, but I'm not going to cave."

"Fine. I'll ask the question that is banned among all persons with a uterus–are you pregnant?"

I get to my feet and walk to the kitchen to get another bottle of wine. "You ask as we day drink? That's a no."

"Okay, stop me when I'm wrong. Nausea."

"My stomach has been unsettled from all the stress."

"Exhaustion?" Eloise ticks off each item on her fingers.

"It's called jet lag."

"You complained this morning about the hard boiled egg that Angela was eating for breakfast."

"Because eggs smell rancid no matter what. All these symptoms are also PMS symptoms, not to mention I had some spotting this weekend. What is it about the assumption that women in their thirties must be pregnant if they feel off?"

Eloise looks repentant. "You're right. I was out of line. My most sincere apologies. How would you like us to celebrate the rest of today?"

Her words rattle around in my head, but I immediately dismiss them. There's no way she's right. Still, I choose not to refill my wine glass.

"I think I might just try to enjoy the last of my vacation feel goods. And I have to set up a vacation for the best paralegal in the world."

Eloise gets to her feet. "I'll take the hint. Text me if you need anything."

Once Eloise is gone, I wonder if I've made a mistake leaving myself to my thoughts for the day. My first plan of action is to let Sean know about this turn of events and see about having Eloise stay in a castle in Scotland. I fill the remaining time with cleaning my apartment and self-care, like getting a manicure and a wax.

It's only when I'm bundled in bed do I look at my phone and

reread the text messages that Ken left. It hurts to think about opening my heart to him, but I have to take the first step.

> Lunch, maybe?

I stare at my phone for an unhealthy amount of time, willing him to answer the text. It never comes. It's not until I get up to go to get a glass of water that I hear the tapping on my door.

Eighteen

"I WASN'T sure if you were still awake," Ken whispers, stepping into my apartment. He is the walking embodiment of how I feel. His shirt is wrinkled and I'm not sure if he's shaved since the last time I saw him. Him showing up is something I never could have imagined. I expected a text back, but having him here is the response I need.

"You never answered me," I say. There is a pull for me to step into him and feel him comfort me in the way I need most. I need physical reassurance that we can get past this.

"I got into a cab and came straight here. I didn't want to risk you changing your mind. Ainsley, I'm so sorry. I jumped to a conclusion that I never should have drawn. I thought you were going to do what Leslie did. I thought you were going to keep pushing it off and pushing it off, and then we were never going to do it."

"I'm not Leslie. I know what it is to compare someone to their ex over and over again. And honestly, maybe that's the problem. You want this to be more than just a rebound, but you can't tell me you want to marry me someday and in the same week treat me like your ex-wife."

"Can I touch you? Please, Ainsley. I've been out of my mind not knowing if you were okay."

It tears at my heart, seeing the effect my absence has had on him, and I nod, letting him pull me against him. My hands fist in his shirt and for the first time since I walked out of the villa in Positano, the world seems to be the way it should. His lips move against mine softly. It's full of the sweet reverence of our lovemaking and not the desperate need of our fucking.

But that need is still there, still under the surface. His hands come around my waist, and I don't resist him as he lifts me into his arms. My body acts of its own accord, my legs locking around him, and I grind against him, moaning at the wicked trill of pleasure that reverberates through me.

This is more than I expected, and I'm glad we're home for this. If our reunion had been at a restaurant, I would have gotten on my knees for him under the table to remind him of why we're good together.

Ken doesn't hesitate to toe off his shoes as he holds me, walking us into my bedroom. I'm glad part of my day was manic cleaning. My sheets are clean and my bed is made, and the only thing I want is to have Ken inside me.

He doesn't throw me on the bed like I expect him to. He follows me down onto the mattress, his large body covering my own. I lead us up to my headboard and he follows me with sweet, soft kisses.

Ken moves like we have our entire lives ahead of us to have moments like this. His hand slowly moves up under my shirt, choosing to tease his fingers along my waist instead of going straight to my breasts or between my legs.

I'm desperate to have him touch me, and feel me, but I can't stop the soft sigh that leaves my mouth as I turn my head to give him better access to my neck. The scruff of his beard rubs my neck raw with each kiss and suck and bite.

I'm normally impatient, but the truth is, I don't want tonight to end. I want to keep Ken with me and forget all our problems. All the problems we still have to talk about.

I lose myself to the feeling of him against me again. He tugs me up so I can take my shirt off, and I hate how it makes me want to cry like this might be goodbye.

Tears must be falling because Ken grips my face and thumbs away my tears, gently shushing me.

"Why are you crying, buttercup?"

I hate the sniffle as I wipe away my tears. "I don't want this to be goodbye." It's a plea more than anything else.

The corner of Ken's mouth tugs up. "It's going to take a hell of a lot more to get rid of me. This isn't goodbye, unless..."

"No! I don't want this to be goodbye."

"Then let this be I'm sorry."

Ken proceeds to take his shirt off and I love watching it come off. It's been nearly two weeks since I saw him last, but it's like the first time all over again. I don't hesitate to lean forward and drag my tongue up his abs and to his mouth, relishing the slightly salty taste of him, and fuck if that doesn't make me want to suck him off.

Ken hovers over me as he urges me back onto the mattress. He's cradled between my legs and I roll up to meet his hardness, which makes me moan.

"I missed the feel of you inside me," I whine as he starts to move down my body. When he gets to my nipples, I hiss, drawing his attention.

"Sore?" he asks, envy tinging his voice.

"Just PMS, I think. There's only ever been you," I promise, knowing that he's used to having to share the woman he loves.

Ken rubs his scruff in the valley between my breasts before pressing a reverent kiss to my sternum.

"Then I'll take extra care of your pussy tonight."

He's methodical as he kisses down my body, slowly pulling my pants down as he goes.

"We still need to talk," I remind him, not wanting to lose the thread of want is important, but he only snickers.

"We can talk when your throat is sore after screaming my name. Until then, be a good girl and open your legs wider for me."

I comply with his demand immediately.

He looks down at my bare pussy, which is still red and swollen from my waxing earlier. Ken only raises an eyebrow, his fingers gently stroking the raw flesh.

"What?" I ask.

"Such a pretty pussy, dripping and ready for me. I think someone missed me."

I don't even get to respond because his mouth touches my clit, and I cry out from the assault of sensitivity.

"Please, no, I need you inside me," I demand. Truthfully, his beard is wrecking my poor skin, but I don't want him to stop altogether.

Thankfully, it doesn't take much more than that plea for him to stop and shuck off his pants. My gaze is glued to his crotch as I watch his erection finally come free. When it does, I almost hate how my mouth waters as the sight of it.

"When I'm not about to make love to you, I'll ask if it was me or my dick that you missed," Ken says with a chuckle. He's holding himself at the base of of his cock before he strokes along himself. "Should I get a condom?"

There is so much in his question. "Do you think you need a condom?"

"Getting pregnant when you're trying to become partner isn't the best time. If that's still what you want, I can wrap up now and talk about it after," he points out, still stroking himself.

I suck my bottom lip into my mouth, watching him. I'm so distracted by my desire that I lose the train of conversation. It takes me a second to catch back up and realize that I haven't even told him about quitting.

"If you don't get inside me in the next three seconds, I'm going to have to take matters into my own hands, or fingers, and you're just going to have to watch me climax with what should have been your orgasm."

Ken takes the threat for what it is, and he moves, grabbing my wrist, which was headed between my legs, and holds it over my head.

"I'm glad you know that it's meant to be *my* orgasm."

Using his free hand, he guides his cock directly to my core and slides in just the tip. My back arches at the feeling. He's barely done anything, but it's the anticipation of the impending fullness. When he pulls back to slide himself through my slick folds, I nearly growl. It's been almost two weeks since I've shared a bed with him, and I need to fix this immediately.

"Ken!" I cry. It's equal part plea, whine, and demand.

After that sound, he doesn't deny me. He drives home into me, and I cry out from the sudden intrusion. We stay like that for just a moment, still and breathless until he leans down to rest on his elbows to kiss me. I grip his face and move my hands to thread into his hair.

"I need to move, buttercup," he tells me, his voice strained, before he does. He shifts back before thrusting back into me, slowly.

I never want us to leave this bed or lose this feeling between us. My body rocks to meet his unrelenting strokes. They're slow but no less powerful as he moves with my body until I feel my climax spike.

"That's right, give me your orgasm, because it's mine. You're mine" he chants, like it is everything to him. I feel tears start again, and I'll be angry about it later because right now he's everything to *me*.

My whole body goes tense as a soul-shattering orgasm grips me. I can feel my body clenching around him as he shouts his own release. His hands are fisted in the sheets, and my nails drag down his back as I try to find something, anything, to hold onto.

Ken stills as aftershocks wrack my body. His lips brush along my sweaty scalp until he falls onto the bed beside me, tugging me close into his chest.

I want to open my mouth to tell him all the things we need to talk about, but I feel sleep grabbing me and pulling me under now that I'm back in the safety of Ken's arms.

"Gorgeous, you need to wake up." Ken is kissing my neck, drawing me from sleep.

"Why?" I grumble, rolling away from him. It's not an effective move because now my ass is pressing against his morning wood and I am suddenly *very* awake. I wiggle my hips, grinding into him. Ken growls and nips at my ear before folding his arm around my middle and tugging me closer to him.

"Because you have to go to work if you want to be partner. I'm not going to get in the way of that."

It's a reminder that for all of my stressing that we needed to talk, we spent most of the night luxuriating in the sensation of one another. I open my mouth to tell him the truth, that I've quit my job, but his phone rings loudly from his jeans on the ground.

"Who's that?"

Ken rolls away from me to grab his phone and I *hate* how bereft I feel at his absence. "I have my mother, sister, and Howie able to bypass my do not disturb so they can reach me if it's an emergency. I can't trust Timothy with that honor yet because he's prone to texting me updates about his video games at two a.m. when he should be asleep."

Ken grabs the phone and lifts it to his ear. I expect him to leave the room, but instead he lies down beside me, wrapping an arm around my shoulder.

"It is too early, Mom."

I can't hear what his mother is saying on the other end, but I use his distraction to trail my hands down to his cock.

Truthfully, we didn't stay asleep for long. We managed to get sleep in forty-five-minute increments. Otherwise, we were tangled up in each other. Somewhere around two we showered, and Ken took the time to comb my hair until I fell asleep, leaning back against him.

I'm not paying attention to what he's saying. I'm just focused on kissing my way down his body, slowly enough that it's more like I'm just dragging my lips on his skin. One glance at Ken and I see that most of his attention is on me and my mouth and not the call he's on.

Good.

When I reach his cock, it's already thick and heavy, waiting for me. While maintaining eye contact, I lick him from base to tip while fondling his balls. When I finally slip my lips over the head of his cock, he thrusts into my mouth.

"I gotta go," he blurts, hanging up the phone and dropping it onto the floor.

I moan around him and take him as deep as I can, but from this potion, I'm the one in charge and he can only take what I give, no matter how much he tries to make it otherwise. In an attempt to change the power dynamic, he fists his hands in my hair, surging his hips up into my mouth.

"Fuck me, Ains. I'm going to come, and if I'm going to do it, I want it to be in that tight little pussy of yours."

I stay right where I am until I can feel the hot liquid spilling down my throat. When he's done, I make an exaggerated show of licking him clean before moving to lie beside him.

"What did your mom want?" I ask, tugging on his nipple with my teeth before looking into his molten gaze with innocent doe eyes.

"I have no idea." Ken is reaching his hand between my legs but I grab his wrist to stop him.

"No, I'm just—"

"Ainsley, I told you that you never have to explain."

"Well, I'm sore is the reason." Really, I'm sore all over my body, but marathon sex will have that effect.

"It's probably for the best. My mom got her flights mixed up, so she's flying here today. I need to go back to my apartment and make it habitable before she and then my sister and Howie get here. And by today, I mean she's already boarded and wanted to see if she needed to get a PickMeUp! or if I was going to pick her up."

"I thought you said you didn't know why she called?" I laugh.

"You ever have that moment where your brain and your mouth and your ears are just not in sync? Yeah. It's like that. She said her flight was wrong, and then I hung up on her."

"She's what, in DC? How long of a flight is that?"

"It's just about an hour, which means I need to run. We really need to talk about us, though, and I don't want to leave us in this weird limbo."

I sit up, pulling my sheet with me as I watch him find his clothes. Every few seconds he glances at me, worry in his eyes at how I'm shying away from him. Really, I'm not though. I'm just cold.

"We're not in a weird limbo," I say defensively.

"We are, buttercup, even if you don't want to admit it."

"You know what I want?" I demand, shedding the sheet to move to the edge of the bed, closer to him. Ken waits expectantly, letting me say my piece. "I want us to work. With or without a baby. I'm not saying no to a baby, and I'm not even saying not right now, but I want to know that even if that doesn't happen, you'll still want me. Getting pregnant isn't a guarantee, and I don't want you to think that just because I'm young and should be fertile that it means everything will work out. You were ready to walk away when you thought I was still on birth control, and I can't live my life wondering if a baby is the only reason you want me."

"Stop it," Ken demands fiercely, cupping my face. "Baby or no baby, *you* are the one that I want. Thinking about you has made life bearable. I couldn't sleep after you left. I want a child. I want that child to be shared by us. We're going a hundred miles a minute, and honestly, we don't know how to communicate together."

"What are you saying?" I ask, unsure.

"I'm saying, I want you to come to the divorce party Friday night. I want you there in whatever capacity you're comfortable with. But I'm thinking that we take this slow. Go back on birth control, and we'll take it one day at a time. Make partner, and we can make a baby next year."

I nearly tackle him as I spring off the bed into his arms. He catches me easily and hugs me to his chest. Maybe slow is the right call, but I don't want to wait. I left my old job for a partner gig and now I don't have to worry about busting my ass to become one. Will it be extra effort while I work up my book? Maybe. But Ken said he wanted to put my career first and it's all I needed to hear.

The decision doesn't need to be made now. "I actually wanted to talk to you about that. Maybe we can do dinner this week?"

"Next week? I've honestly got to get the apartment in order. My mom and sister are helping me sort things out so I don't have to see Leslie and do it. It didn't feel right."

"Will I get to see you this week at all?" It's already Tuesday, so I doubt we'll have time before Friday.

"How about we get brunch on Saturday with my family? I want to do this right."

"And how are you going to introduce me?" I tease.

"As my girlfriend. But I do have to go. My apartment is a mess." He kisses my forehead. "Let me know how you want to come to the party, and I'll take care of it. I'll take care of you."

"I'll see you Friday," I promise him. Plopping back on my bed, I watch Ken slip out the door with my heart in his hand.

It's only when I'm waiting for my doctor that I realize I never told Ken that I quit my job. It's fine. I can tell him when I am able to have an actual sit-down conversation with him. As long as it's not dropped on him in front of his family, I'm sure it's not a big deal. We do have to work on communication, but this isn't the worst infraction in the world.

Between texting Sean about a start date for me and Eloise and helping Eloise connect with Charlie about the castle in Scotland, my thumbs are getting exhausted.

"Ainsley?" the nurse calls, and I pop up, looking away from the other visibly pregnant women in the office.

"We're going to have you pee in a cup, and then I'll take you back to your room."

I do my business and then the nurse takes my vitals and asks the usual questions, including when my last period was. That question trips me up for just a second, and I have to place when I last had it.

The nurse is watching me expectantly.

"I'm sorry. It's usually so light that I don't even need a panty-liner, so I always forget to think about it. Maybe in January? I had some spotting..." I pause, thinking about when I was in Florence. It feels like it was a year ago. "Last-ish week?"

For a second, my heart rate kicks up. It's been five months since I last remember getting my period, but I have nothing to worry about because I double protect. I have the pill and I always make my partners wrap it up. Except for screwing Ken without a condom for the last month. But that was intentional.

Except.

Except for the first time Ken and I slept together. The memory slips through, and it's fuzzy around the edges, thanks to booze and exhaustion. Ken had already come in a condom, and I figured I was safe from him coming again and I asked if he would be okay fucking me bare because I was craving that physical connection. But he pulled out before he came in me, so I should be fine.

"It's alright. That's why Molli always runs the test. Better safe than sorry."

"Yeah, safe," I murmur to myself.

The nurse leaves the room so I can get changed into the paper gown, and I sit there and wait, wondering if I should have called Ken. The knock at the door stops me from spiraling too badly before my doctor walks in.

"Ainsley, only three months late for your annual this year. I'm surprised."

"Well, when you see me monthly for STD testing, how important is the annual, really?"

Molli narrows her eyes at me and sits on the wheely stool. "So, talk to me. I see your period was last in January, but I know you're prone to lighter periods since we started this new birth control. Are you sexually active?" She's just doing her due diligence, but we both know the answer to that question.

I snort. "Yes, I am."

"With multiple partners? Are you using a condom or any other form of birth control?"

"Yes to multiple partners, but I've been seeing the same guy for about two and a half months. We stopped using birth control last month because we wanted to try to get pregnant."

Molli brightens when I say this. "So, it shouldn't be a surprise to find out you are?"

"Are what?" I ask. It's just like Ken said this morning, my hearing and my brain and my mouth aren't lining up with the information being presented. Everything is a half-second behind.

"You're pregnant, Ainsley."

"Pregnant?" I echo before I black out.

When I come to, Molli and two nurses are around me, taking my vitals.

Molli looks down on me with a sympathetic smile. "I take it this is a surprise?"

That's when I burst into laughter. I wipe my eyes as my laughter slowly subsides. "I mean, how much of a surprise can a pregnancy be after you've spent the last month and a half having sex with a guy to try to get pregnant?"

"Well, we'll still do an exam and then I'll hook up the ultrasound. We'll start with a transvaginal in case this is still new."

I want to text Ken. I feel like this is a moment he should be here for, but if this is real, then there will be plenty more ultrasounds he can be there for.

My phone is the only thing in my hands that I can fidget with as Molli positions the wand before sliding it into me.

It's no time before I can hear the gentle *womp womp womp* from the monitor. I nearly jackknife up to get a better look at the screen.

Molli laughs and nudges me back. "Easy, killer. Lay back and try to relax."

I try to do what she says, but I'm so surprised by the little blob on the screen that I try to sit up again. I can barely digest everything she's saying. I'm only five weeks along, which means that while I haven't been taking birth control, I've been eating things like sushi and drinking like it was my only sustenance.

She gives me assurances that everything will be fine, and I need to take her at her word for it because somehow our plan worked and I got pregnant, even if it worked a little too well. So much for taking it slow now and taking time to get to know each other.

When she goes over the risks for the first trimester, my heartrate amps up, and she assures me that she'll monitor me and that I should come back in a few weeks.

All sarcasm leaves me, and I'm unable to think of anything witty to say. I leave with a script for prenatals and other information about what to do and foods to avoid. I nearly walk into traffic three times while staring at the blob in the sonogram photo.

I try to text Ken to see if maybe we can get together, but when he responds hours later, he sends me a picture of Apple sitting on a pile of boxes with a bottle of wine in each hand, accompanied by a text: "The inmates are running the asylum."

That's fine because it gives me more time to figure out how I'm going to tell him the news.

Nineteen

MY MOOD SOURS the morning of the divorce party when Ken texts that it will be best if I'm just introduced as the lawyer. When he explains that it's because his former mother-in-law is coming, I soften a little.

It's almost like finding out I'm pregnant flipped a switch in me, and now I'm seeing all the signs that I wrote off as just normal life. The exhaustion, the queasiness–things I tried to explain away are so obvious now.

Our agreement to try to take this slow has been running through my mind, and all I want to do is tell Ken the good news and say to hell with slow, move in. While I'm surveying my apartment, considering how it would work with two of us here, I realize I haven't even told him I love him. Because as I touch my lower belly, and my heart swells for this little pea, I realize I do. I want all-in with him. I want dinner for breakfast and days making love in the lemon tree grove. I want to see him with his family during the holidays, and I want to see him take care of our child when they're sick.

I want it all, and it only makes me more anxious to talk to him about it, because what if he prefers to go slow? It's a little late for that, there's no putting the genie back in the bottle here, but he could still keep his distance, and now that I am attached, now that there is a real baby to consider, I don't want co-parenting for us. I want the happily ever after.

When I'm getting ready for the party, I shove a pillow up the empire waist dress just to see how it will look with my belly consuming my body, and I love how it looks. I've been so tentative about getting excited, but now I want to let the ideas run away with me. I want to go to the store and buy all the onesies and a cute crib and all the things.

There's a knock at my door that surprises me into dropping the pillow, but when I glance at the clock, I see that it's just about time for Eloise to show up. I quickly grab the pillow and throw it on the couch before opening the door.

Eloise is in a short dress that hits just above her knees and is tight against her sinful curves. Her dress is also black, per the dress code. We're to mourn the marriage but celebrate their next chapter. I include myself in this, but sometimes rich people do the weirdest things.

"Are you husband hunting?" I tease as she readjusts her cleavage.

"So, you think it's too much?" She turns a critical eye on what I'm wearing, which is leaps and bounds more conservative.

"No, do you want me to go change?" I offer, thinking of a black bandage dress I could put on.

"No, you don't have to," she says, but I can hear from her voice that she wants me to. I'm already walking toward my bedroom to change before she can say anything else.

"When do you leave for Scotland?" I call, tossing my old dress off.

"Tomorrow, actually. Thanks again for setting it up!"

I'm quick about changing dresses, and honestly, I love how great my tits look in this dress. It's a better look for me, and anyway, my days of wearing dresses like this are numbered, at least for the next several months.

The black dress creates a diamond-shaped cutout over my cleavage and hugs each and every curve I have. I can try to blame all the pasta and gelato, but I know the truth, and it's a secret truth that only I know until I can tell Ken.

The 'daddy' onesie I have sitting in my nightstand feels like a beacon. It's the only thing I've let myself buy, because I figure it will be a good way to tell him.

"We're going to be late!" Eloise calls.

"Being late is *fashionable*," I point out.

When I step out, Eloise grins. "*Now* can we go?"

Ken, gracious man that he is, agreed to close his bar down so his ex could pay him handsomely to use it for their party. It rubbed me the wrong way, that she was still exercising this control over him, but he seemed okay with it.

Leslie has transformed the bar into a chic club with draped fabric and lights hanging from the ceiling. There is uplighting casting the room in blues and purples, drowning out the original brick work.

Dare I say it, I even see normal glassware being used for drinks. A waiter passes Eloise and I with four glasses. Much as I want to drink every glass on his tray, I need to do better. I take one just to give the illusion of having something to drink. If this were an ordinary situation, I would have told Eloise at my apartment, but it feels wrong telling anyone else before telling Ken. It's the only reason I didn't call my friends to come over so I could tell them.

"Miss Seaborn!" Leslie greets, approaching Eloise and I with a huge grin. Ken is right behind her with his hands shoved in his pockets. When his brown eyes meet mine, I feel my panties melt off.

If I could, I would jump him right here. He's dressed immaculately in a black tuxedo that fits his cut figure so well. I want to feel him up and tug the bowtie off and run my hands through his hair. Tonight, I want to claim him in front of everyone here. Shout it from the rooftops that he's the father of my baby.

"I was shocked it still fits!" Leslie calls as she walks over.

It draws my attention away from Ken, which is probably for the best, because I'm sure the lust in my gaze is apparent. If the tent in Ken's pants is any indication, he's feeling it too.

I turn my gaze to Leslie. The woman is wearing white. Not only that, but the dress looks familiar.

"What fits?" Eloise asks, taking the focus off how Ken and I were eye-fucking each other.

"My old wedding dress! I had modifications made, of course. Shortened it and got rid of the sleeves, but I was shocked that it fit well enough to wear tonight! We spent all that money on it, so I'm glad I get to wear it again, even if just for nostalgia purposes."

My head nearly does a complete 360 turn before I plaster on my most winning smile, the one I use for press events or when at work. I'm not sure why, but I feel hot and green with jealousy all of a sudden.

"Leslie." My voice is high enough to break glass and both Ken and Eloise wince. I look to Ken for some sort of hint or guidance or something, but he only shrugs his shoulders and shakes his head as little as he can to get the point across.

"And this is Eloise, right? So glad you both could make it. No beau to bring around?"

"Nope," I say simply. I hate this, I hate this, I hate this. I get it, but I also hate it.

The four of us make an awkward group, not least of all because Ken is looking at me like he wants to rip my dress off me and claim me on the floor of his bar in front of everyone. Maybe we can sneak away. He has to have an office of some kind here. All I need is one orgasm, like I'm a junkie and he's my fix.

"Well, I'm sure there will be some eligible men around here I can connect you with," Leslie offers, but Ken surprises us all with his reaction.

"No, absolutely not."

I catch the reddening of his cheeks when he realizes what he's done.

"What I mean is, this isn't the place for that. Leave Ainsley and Eloise alone."

Eloise isn't even paying attention. She's wandered off to look at some sort of sign nearby.

Leslie, to her credit, only nods at her ex. "I'm sorry if I made you uncomfortable. Please, mingle and have fun." It's hard to miss how she glances between me and Ken before looping her arm around his and trying to lead him off.

It feels like a punch to the gut to be dismissed so easily. Finally out of their snare, I look around for where Eloise has disappeared to. Against one wall is a projection of photos of Ken and Leslie, each one systematically ripped apart before moving onto the next one.

"This is so weird," she whispers, leaning against me.

"This is so Leslie," a familiar voice says behind me.

I turn around, relieved to find Apple. Her smile is close-lipped, tinged with sympathy but bathed in warmth. She knows the rules. No acting familiar, like we've met before, though it kills me because I want to tug her in for a hug.

"Yeah?" I ask, looking at her.

"She's always done everything by a full measure. Their wedding, god, release of doves when they kissed, eight-foot cathedral train, sixteen bridesmaids. If Tobias had been born then, I'm sure she would have made him toddle down the aisle, side by side with Timmy, who was able to make it to the nuptials. He was three at the time and halfway down the aisle, he started screaming. There were too many eyes on him. Thankfully, Howie was already standing at the altar, trying to coax him down, but it was Ken who marched to him, scooped him up, and held him for almost the entire ceremony."

"He loves those boys," I remark wistfully, wondering what it will be like with our baby. *Our baby.* That thought keeps stunning me. Maybe at some point it will just be a fact, but it still feels so new that thinking about it is just downright strange.

"He does." Apple hip checks me. "They loved you too. They won't stop raving about some game you played with them while Mom and I went to the spa. Toby keeps looking in cabinets wondering if Monster Ainsley is lurking there."

Eloise looks up at me. "Already you're the monster aunt?"

"I'm so sorry, I didn't even introduce you two. This is Apple, Ken's sister, and this is Eloise, my paralegal."

They shake hands before Apple blindly reaches behind her for a man in a tux, pulling him toward her. He manages to get off an apology before turning to his wife. He's handsome and it takes me a minute to remember meeting him with Ken a few months ago. Dressed up like this, it's hard to reconcile the casual man with the one in a tux before me now.

"This is Howie."

"Senator Howard Bishop," Eloise stammers, nearly dropping her drink.

Amusement lights his blue eyes, but he reaches out his hand to her for a shake.

"This is Eloise and Ainsley," Apple finishes, gesturing at us both.

When he looks at me, some of the facade melts and I get to see the real Howie, not Howard. "Monster Ainsley? You're going to have to tell me what game you played, because Tobias will not stop asking to play it, and he says I play it wrong. Even Timmy has been talking about it, and that kid won't talk about anything. It's so nice to meet you both."

Eloise has stopped functioning and is just staring. He must be used to this because he doesn't comment.

"It was really just hide and seek. I'd take some makeup with me and apply it while I was hiding, which isn't easy, so of course I came out a little monstrous-looking. I told them I'd cook them up if they weren't fast enough at finding me."

"Kids really do just need simple things," Apple muses, linking her arm with her husband. She turns her focus back to me. "I'm glad you and Ken talked. I told him he was being an asshole to flip out about you maybe considering a bid for partner."

Howie, again, fails to show a single emotion on his face. "Partner? I thought you were..." Howie gestures at me, and then just around the room. I get what he's trying to say. Apple elbows her husband and shakes her head.

"Yes, my office wanted me on the partner track," I explain, totally skating over the new job and the pregnancy.

"Good thing we're going to a new firm," Eloise says, taking a mini quiche from a passing server.

"New firm? Ken didn't say anything! Congratulations!" Apple does hug me this time, ignoring what should and shouldn't be done.

"That's because I haven't had a chance to tell him yet. It all happened this week and then you and your mother came to town."

"And I ruined it?" Apple exclaims

"No, no, not at all." I wave her off impatiently. "It's just we had other things to talk about. So just don't mention it to Ken yet."

"Then tell me, what kind of law do you do?" Howie asks, moving it away from my talk of this secret.

"I do divorce mediations, but at your wife's insistence, my new firm is actually willing to talk to me about doing some pro bono work in the family law sector. I'm sure there are families in need who can use the same assistance as my wealthier clientele."

"You're absolutely right." Howie takes a deep breath, like he's about to start in on something, but Apple squeezes his arm with a shake of her head.

"So, are you really going to run for president?" Eloise blurts, finally catching her wits.

I try to glance around surreptitiously for a waiter with water, but all they have are cocktails.

Howie winks. "You'll just have to wait and see."

Apple shakes her head. "He means no. There will be no presidential election if this man wants to ever be inside his wife again." The threat in her voice tells me this is not the first time she's had to level this threat. The look on Howie's face tells me this isn't the last time she's going to have to say it.

"In other news, did you hear how the Crown Princess of Mondelia is marrying an American?" I interject, trying to steer the conversation away from what looks like a common fight between the couple.

"Princess Aurelia? She's gorgeous. We should be so lucky to have one of our citizens be a part of their court. They've been so closed off in terms of international relations, maybe this will be good," Apple says with a smile.

"I heard that Prince Luciano is very open to international relations with the female sex," Eloise adds with a coy smile.

Apple fake clutches at her pearls. "I will have you know I am a very devoted married woman and would never take him up if he were to offer me a ride on his disco stick." She gives a big dramatic wink.

"This is the real reason I can't run for president. My wife will have been recorded saying she would ride the prince of a foreign nation like a horse at the rodeo."

"Who is my sister riding?" Ken asks, stepping behind me. He's standing too close, so close I want to melt into him and stay there. To an outside observer, he is standing what could be inappropriately close, but given the volume in the space, it's permissible.

What is probably not permissible is how his hand has found

its way to the back of my thigh and is inching further and further up. His body is blocking the show from an outsider catching a glimpse as his finger dips between my legs to find my sex.

Ken's breath is hot against my neck as he presses his hips forward so I can feel his arousal against my ass. I press back into him, eager for the friction.

"Your sister is talking about the Prince of Mondelia." Howie keeps his eyes very pointedly on his brother-in-law's face, ignoring the shenanigans happening under my skirt.

"Prince Luc, right? I heard he's coming to the US as part of some tour for his sister's engagement. You would think they would be touring Mondelia." Somehow, Ken's voice is even, and I hate him for it. I nearly gasp when he slides a second finger into me. How I wish I could have a drink just to distract me.

"I'm sure they'll do that too," Apple adds.

Ken's breath tickles the fine hairs on the nape of my neck when he whispers. "I'm glad you wore these heels. I would be lying to you if I said I didn't have to rub one out in my office when you got here. There was something about your defiance when you walked in here, like you knew you owned me."

My knees nearly buckle under the weight of the filth he's whispering to me. I'm left to this sweet torture, feeling him move inside me.

A waiter moves in front of us, holding out passed hors d'oeuvres. Ken waves them off with a shake of his head, but I grab one and shove it into my mouth so I can moan under the cover of eating the bacon-wrapped scallop.

"They're good, but not that good," Apple says, biting into hers.

Howie covers his laugh with a cough.

I'm a little bit grateful when Leslie and Roberta walk over to our group. Ken slips his hand out of me, pinching my bare ass before putting his hand in his pocket.

There is another woman with the two of them, and Leslie doesn't hesitate to introduce us.

"Mom, I want you to meet Ainsley Seaborn. She's the woman who handled our divorce. It's because of her that the whole process was as seamless and quick as possible. We should do a celebratory shot!"

Her mother is already coolly regarding me and how close I'm standing to Ken. It feels like she can see every dirty secret written on my face.

"I'm Celeste. Did you bring your husband to the event?"

I purse my lips. "No husband." I don't owe this woman shit.

"What a shame for a beautiful woman such as yourself to be alone in the world."

"Mother, leave the poor woman alone."

"It's fine," I say. "What's next for you, Leslie?"

"I'm going to London. I'm hoping for a fresh start. I have friends and a job and an apartment lined up. I just needed to get all my stuff out of the apartment here first."

Ken interrupts before the questions turn to what's next to him. "Can I get you a refresh on your drink, Ainsley?"

"No, I'm fine," I promise.

"And Kenneth, what is next for you? Are you going to try to find someone to impregnate? Maybe you've already got a serious new girlfriend?" I don't miss how Celeste's gaze moves to me before back to Ken, her brown eyes seeming to notice too much.

"No serious girlfriends for me. I've been with Leslie so long, I would like to see what my options are before settling down again."

I feel my whole heart clench at his words. I know that this is just supposed to be for show and just for this event. This is all pretend until we can reveal our relationship to the greater group at large. I hate that we have to hide, but saying shit like that just rubs me the wrong way. There were other answers he could have given, especially in front of me, that didn't have to hurt my feelings.

"It would be foolish to jump into something so soon after your divorce. The woman warming your bed will always wonder if she's just a rebound. You'll want time to find the right woman to mother the child you want badly enough to end a marriage over." Celeste's words are cutting, but I have to pretend like this is a normal conversation, so I tear up the strips of napkin I'm holding.

If Ken would let me at this bitch, I would level her. But I can't. I have to bite my tongue to avoid asking her what she would know about a rebound when her face looks like a constipated dried-out pussy bitch. It takes a deep breath for me to reign in the unkind things I have to say about this woman in my head. Honestly, though? If it weren't for Ken trying to keep me his secret there would be nothing for her to say because I am a goddamned catch of a woman.

I wish Ken and I had been given a chance to talk before tonight because I need to know why he thinks I need to be treated like his dirty little secret. I can understand complicated family dynamics, but I'd love getting to shove in this woman's face that not only has Ken moved on with a fucking bomb ass boss bitch, but I'm pregnant too, so she can go fuck herself.

There is no more napkin to tear apart, but Apple nudges one toward me.

Leslie seems to sense the tension because she jumps in. "Ken, be a dear and get those Lick My Pussy Shots. You remember? The ones we found on our honeymoon!" She widens her eyes like she's pleading.

Ken's hand grazes the small of my back. "Sure, Les."

I want to ask Ken for water, but he's gone before I can voice the request. My glass of champagne looks more and more tempting the more we stand around but Ken is back just as quickly as he left.

"That was speedy, Kenneth," Celeste remarks, once again studying the distance between us.

"I do own the bar, Celeste. I can ask people to do things for me." His tone is biting.

Roberta jumps in quickly. "Celeste, I heard your vineyard had a bad year because of the forest fires in California. I was so sorry to hear about it from Leslie."

I want to kiss this woman for saving me from the tedium that is Leslie's mother. I zone out a little as we wait for the shots to show up. There is a lot of catch-up between the families, and Eloise and I are content to let them all chat.

When Eloise excuses herself to go to the bathroom, I follow her, glad for the opportunity to get away and circulate. I don't blame Leslie or her mother, but I need a chance to breathe.

I'm the first one out of the bathroom, and I'm surprised when a hand grabs my arm and pulls me away. For one heart-sinking moment, fear grabs me, but then I look up into Ken's eyes. His grip is nearly bruising as he half-drags, half-leads me to a door. He pushes it open, placing me in front of him as he locks the door behind him.

Ahead of me is a stairwell that I take my cue to walk up.

There is a second door at the top that he reaches around me to key in. Just as I suspected, there is an office here for Ken.

The door is barely closed behind me when he's on me, not hesitating to pull my body against his. He walks me backward until the backs of my legs hit something sturdy and firm. I don't look back to confirm; Ken's arm sweeps behind me, sending papers flying off the desk, onto the floor. He doesn't ask, he just grabs my hips, lifting me up and placing me at the perfect height. There is no foreplay. There is just urgent desire as he pulls his cock free.

"Ken, we need to talk," I try as he kisses down my neck.

He pauses for a bare moment. "Is it going to change anything right now? Have you gotten married since I saw you last?" He watches me for just a moment, studying my face to see if maybe I've changed my mind.

"No."

"Then I don't care." There is a roughness as he shoves my dress up and rips my panties off.

Heat suffuses my whole body at the dominance he's expressing. And, okay, sure. I can wait to tell him. It's not like it's going to change anything in the next five minutes.

"You better not make me look like a mess out there," I demand, unsurprised that I sound breathy.

"Ainsley, you're going to take what I give you and you're going to walk out into that party with my come dripping between your legs, knowing that you are mine. Are you even aware of the eyes on you tonight? I'm pretty sure Leslie wishes she was up here having her way with you, but you are *mine*." He hauls me to the edge of the desk, and I yelp in surprise. It turns to a pure moan when he thrusts in me.

I want to lean closer to him as he pounds away at me, but he keeps pushing me back so he can watch my body, watch my breasts move with each jerk of his hips. He doesn't use any of the finesse I know he has. He just jackhammers his body against mine, and it does the trick. I can't get enough of feeling him move inside me.

"Oh god, Ken," I grit out, my moan starting low and growing louder as his hip movements bring me closer to completion. I shatter, my mind emptying of all thought before his movements become jerkier and he clutches my hips closer. His head drops forward, his body bowing so his forehead rests against my breastbone. We're both breathing heavily, slicked with sweat.

"I have to go out there and give a stupid speech, as if I don't have the best thing in my life already right here."

"Ken," I start. I have to tell him; holding this secret is getting to be too much for me.

The intercom on his phone crackles. "Ken, Leslie is looking for you to start the toasts."

Pressing me back down onto the desk, he grabs the phone. "Thanks, Lyle. I'll be right there. Don't let her know I was in my office."

I can't help but feel like a dirty little secret. I know I'm not. There is a reason that we have to be so secretive, but it feels wrong all of a sudden. If I'm honest with myself, Ken's reasoning is making less and less sense, and I feel a little dirty, but not in the *this is so hot* way. I'm still trying to sort through these feelings when Ken pulls out of me and makes quick work of fixing his clothes.

"I'm going to head down first. I have my own bathroom through there." He points the way for me before kissing me on the forehead and leaving me in the room alone.

I grip the sink in the bathroom, trying to get these raging emotions under control. Ken loves me, I know that. Except, do I? He hasn't said it. I know I haven't said it either, but I'm also not dragging him away from my friends and family for a quickie only to pretend like I'm nothing more than a business acquaintance. I know we said we were going to take it slow, but for fuck's sake, I'm the mother of his child, and he may not know that yet, but I deserve more respect. Celeste may be his ex-mother-in-law, but he didn't even raise a defense on my behalf to her. He didn't apologize to me for it. He just stuck his cock in me, got off, and ran off to be with Leslie.

When I get back downstairs, the party is still in full swing, and only Ken and I and maybe Lyle know what happened upstairs. It feels dirty knowing that his come is inside me while his ex-wife mills around, thanking people for their attendance. It was supposed to feel like the good kind of dirty, but it no longer does.

Honestly, I just want to go home. This stopped being fun before the party even started, and listening to people give reverse toasts about Ken and Leslie makes the few things I have had to eat sink to the bottom of my stomach like lead.

"Are you okay?" Apple asks, gently touching my forearm.

"I'm fine."

Lyle thankfully gave me a glass of water without complaint. There was no recognition in his eyes when he handed it over, which I was genuinely thankful for. Not like having to talk to the guy you screwed at the bar of the guy you're currently screwing during his divorce party. There are honestly so many different people getting screwed, I can't even keep track.

"You look green, but not with envy."

"Thanks, Apple."

"Well, should I lie? I'm sure Ken wouldn't mind you lying on the couch in his office."

I think of what we were just doing in his office, and I shake my head. "No, I think I'm going to head out." A quick glance around the room tells me that Eloise is otherwise preoccupied. She's sitting in a booth with someone I don't recognize. I shoot her a quick text that I'm leaving.

"Do you want me to tell Ken anything?"

"Ask him to call me when he's ready for me to not be his secret girlfriend."

Apple opens her mouth, but I'm done listening and waiting. Ken knows how to find me.

Twenty

KEN TEXTED me late the night of the party, but I ignored it. I ignored it because I'm honestly mad at him. It's bullshit for him to treat the mother of his *child* like she's no one. As if he didn't haul me up to his office to give me a screaming orgasm in the middle of the party.

I'm mad mostly at myself because I should have more self-respect than to still even talk to Ken after how he completely disregarded me in front of his family and his ex. That should have been his moment to show off how much better his life was with me than with her.

These are the reasons that I cried into a pint of ice cream when I got home and called my friends begging for validation that I'm not really a terrible person even if I have unkind thoughts about someone.

Sunday morning, I'm still ignoring Ken's texts, including the one from ten last night when he asked me to call him, until I can talk myself down. I want to *rage* at him for how he treated me, but I know that having a conversation like that is not going to help anyone. So, I'll talk to him on Monday.

There is a thundering knock on the door that stirs me from where I doze on the couch.

"Who is it?" I call, knowing the answer. My father is the only person in the world that knocks like he's the FBI come to serve a warrant.

"Your father. Open the door or I will use my key."

I grumble and shove the blankets off. When I pull the door open, he has his fist raised to pound on it again.

"What are you doing here?" I ask, stepping aside to let him in. "And I gave you that key for emergencies. Letting yourself in when I don't answer the door fast enough to your liking does not an emergency make."

The back of his hand gently presses against my forehead. "Are you feeling okay? You look peaky. And not hearing from my daughter in two weeks to be stood up for a dinner date we had does make an emergency."

Shit. I forgot to cancel with him after the whirlwind of finding out about the baby and the party last night.

"I'm fine. Just tired."

"Do you even know what day it is?" he asks, looking genuinely concerned.

"Sunday."

He gazes at me doubtfully. After toeing off his shoes, he goes and pulls at my curtains.

"No!" I cry out, but it's too late and he's letting the early morning sun into my space. I wince at the sun, trying to cower away from it like a vampire shoved into the light.

"You're not going to burst into flame, but if I have to smell you any longer, I might. Go shower. Now."

I sniff my armpit and grimace.

"I do not smell," I object. It's an order, and the thirteen-year-old that lives inside me whenever I'm around my father rears her petulant head at being told what to do. But I feel a wave of nausea rise in the back of my throat, and I look at the clock with a frown. Ten-thirty, right on time.

Covering my mouth before I vomit all over my entryway, I actually listen to my father and shower. After throwing up.

When I emerge, I'm annoyed at how much better I feel from that simple act. I don't blow dry my hair, leaving it down and damp, but I do pull on a tight pair of leggings and an oversized shirt from the bottom of my hamper. On second glance, it's one of Ken's and I have to bury the wave of tears that threaten me. These emotions are unreal. How can I be mad and sad all at once?

"Now, how do you feel?" my father asks when I step into my living room.

"Better," I grumble. The apartment looks totally different. In the thirty minutes it took me to shower and dress, he cleaned, throwing out the food and bottles that have been sitting out for far too long.

"You need a pet, or something to get you out of bed. I'm pretty sure you're going to need a new couch because that one has a mold the shape of your body in it."

I look at where he's pointing and he's right.

Rude. It's more because it's old than because I haven't moved from the same spot since Friday night. Sleeping alone in bed felt wrong after how I left things with Ken.

"I'm just having a rough week. I start a new job this week."

"I heard. That's also why I'm here. Both Sean and Eloise contacted me separately. They're concerned about you."

I feel my lower lip quiver.

"Daddy," I start, but burst into tears, the whole horrible story spilling from my lips before I can stop myself. I give him the clean version of events, the version that doesn't involve a threesome and sex in a bar and, of course, the baby. No one knows about this little pea that's growing inside me.

"So, are you going to let this jerkoff ignore you?"

"What?" I look up from the glass of water my dad got me, confused.

"My Ainsley, the little girl I raised, has told teachers to suck her non-existent cock when told she couldn't do something because she was a girl or she was too small. When they said you were too short for the basketball team, you went out of your way to prove them wrong. When they told you that you weren't smart enough for AP Calculus, you worked twice as hard to get into that class. Are you going to tell me that one jerkoff who doesn't know a good thing when he has it is going to stop you from being happy?"

I wipe at my own eyes. "But I love him." Even admitting as much to my father without first telling Ken feels wrong, but it feels like the only reasonable thing I can say.

"Does he love you too?"

"I don't know. He hasn't said it, and I thought maybe he did, but the way he ignored me Friday night? I feel too fragile. I feel like one of those logic puzzles. I'm all jumbled and I don't know how to make the pieces fit back together."

"That's okay, too. You don't have to fit the pieces back together. You just need to find a way for them to work. If you want this to work with him, you will find your way to him, but you have big feelings you need to sit with. Let's go get brunch, get a manicure, and call it a daddy-daughter day? I can get us tickets to watch some good old-fashioned baseball, and it can be like old times."

"I think that sounds like a good idea," I agree, holding back a tide of emotions.

Sean's words come back to me. Combined with my dad's advice, I know that I need to pull up my big girl panties and reach out to Ken. It feels a little cowardly, but I just text him with a simple message.

> Call me when you're ready to admit to our relationship.

"You look like shit."

I glance up from my new desk at Sean, who is leaning against the doorway with his hands in his pockets. He cuts a trim figure in his suit, only he doesn't have a jacket on, just a gray vest over his crisp white button-down.

I'm not sure starting work was the best idea, but I texted Sean and he got me set up. With no questions asked. All I've been doing today is staring at my phone, hoping to see something from Ken. He hasn't texted since Saturday night when he asked me to call him, and it stings. I know I've been giving him the cold shoulder, and even though it's not logical, I want him to keep trying.

"Who wears three piece suits anymore?" I ask, leaning back in my chair. I gesture at one of the two seats in my office. I feel bad getting a head start on Eloise, but I need something to occupy my time. My emotions are all over the place about Ken not responding to my text. Every hour on the hour, I tell myself to fuck him, he's not worth it, and that there are other fish in the sea. Then on the half hour, I cry as discretely as I can, wondering how I'm going to do this without him.

"Distinguished gentlemen wear three piece suits. I was going to offer to take you to lunch for celebratory drinks, but you're looking green around the gills."

"I thought I covered it up well enough with my make-up. It's been a rough weekend."

His eyebrows raise, and he steps into my office, closing the door. The space I'm in is nearly twice the size of my old office, and I have windows this time instead of being crammed in an inner office with only fluorescent lights. I have my window closed for now, but I have to keep alternating between opening it and closing it again. I'm either suffocated by the lingering perfume of the former tenant of my office or I'm drowning in the smell of garbage outside.

"Do you want to tell me about it?"

"No, it doesn't paint me in a particularly professional light, and being new and all, I would like to at least maintain that façade as long as I can."

Sean doesn't sit in a chair but leans against my desk on my side.

"Ainsley, this is me. You know I'm not just some co-worker. We've been through a lot."

I lean over and open my window, wrinkling my nose at him. He's not wrong. After his wife died, I spent a week at his house, making sure he ate and that there was someone to answer his phone. I didn't want to overstep, but his mom called me and begged me to keep an eye on him after he stopped answering her calls.

"I'm–" No. I still can't tell him before I tell Ken, as much as I want to confide in a friend. "I think the guy I was seeing and I sort of broke up. It was an ambiguous situation to begin with, and then he told me that we couldn't admit to dating in front of his ex, but I was good enough for a quickie in his office."

"You never took breaking up this hard, even when I left you for Olive. Are you sure that the ex is an ex?"

"Positive. I handled their divorce. And anyway, it was only one time. You broke up with me *once*," I point out, but it's working. He's getting my mind off of Ken.

"Yeah, and it was catastrophic. I was the catch of your life. That sort of ending ruins people. Anyway, what? Do I smell? I promise I showered after the gym this morning."

"Of course, you're one of those people that goes to the gym before work," I scoff. "It's your cologne or whatever. It's giving me a headache."

The teasing smirk that had been on Sean's face slips away when I complain about his cologne. I can see it in the way he looks at me that he knows and he has no idea what to do about it. It's that moment of knowing that passes between the two of us that has me biting my lip hard enough that I taste blood.

"If you need anything, you know I'm here. It's why I texted your father this weekend to check in on you."

I scowl. "This is why I don't tell you anything."

"Ainsley, this is why you *have* to tell me things. I'm worried. I've never seen you in a business setting outside of a skirt and heels. You're wearing yoga pants and two different sneakers. That's not to say you can't wear yoga pants, but...I know you." His voice softens as he looks at me, and I hate the genuine concern on his face. He reaches out a hand and softly brushes his thumb across my cheek. I need this gesture, but I need it from Ken.

"I'm just off my game. I'll be better, I promise."

Twenty-One

FOR THE NEXT week and a half, I hold up my end of the bargain. After the yoga pants catastrophe, I make sure I'm put together for the office. It's a good thing too, because the next day we went out to lunch with the partners as a get-to-know-you, and I would have been mad at myself going into that looking anything less than my best.

I don't have many clients yet, but in my first week, I've managed to collect a handful, with several contacting me from my old firm. Whoever is addressing my absence is telling clients exactly where they can find me, so I'm relieved to know that I'll have some work to throw myself into.

Anything to get my mind off Ken. I keep checking my phone to see if he's texted me. Hearing nothing is killing me. I don't understand *why* he hasn't reached out and that's what's bothering me the most. In the grand scheme of things, I expected what happened to be a tift for a few days and then we would have amazing make-up sex and I would tell him about the baby.

The worst is, it's for such a stupid reason that I haven't reached back out to him. It's my pride that has me deleting my text to him every time I try. Why should I be the one to text him again? I threw down the gauntlet first. When we were trying to fix things after Italy, I reached out first. I'm still waiting for him to respond to my text this time. I put the ball in his court, *again*. It's his turn to prove that I'm not just a rebound girl.

I spend the week dreaming up my pro bono clinic and all the ways I can help lower income families in New York City. I pour through my old law books and look up other facets of family law. When the attorney who manages trusts and estates stops by to welcome me, I offer him all the help I can.

Eloise returns from her Scottish vacation without a Scottish Lord by her side, and I'm both glad and disappointed. I'm thankful that she does not mention the divorce party, both of us choosing to ignore any mention of Ken. For now, I have put what happened in a box and it will live in the box until I have to face it. This might not be the healthiest of coping mechanisms, but for now, it's what I'm going to do.

It's been almost two weeks since the divorce party, and my resolve is breaking down. The longer I go without saying anything to Ken, the more it feels like I'm intentionally keeping the pregnancy from him instead of just trying to find the right time to say something.

When I get into work on Thursday, there is a solitary rose sitting on my desk with a note attached to it. I lift the flower and inhale deeply before reading the note.

How shall I list all the ways I love thee?

I scowl at the note before tapping the flower against my lips. I have no idea what to make of this note that is so obviously from

Ken. I have to assume that he knows where I'm working now because of Eloise or maybe even Apple, though I never told her the name of the firm.

At eight-thirty, Eloise knocks on my door, holding a basket of lemons with a single rose protruding from the basket.

"What?" I ask with a laugh as she places it on my desk.

"I was hoping you knew."

I spy a familiar slant of writing on a note attached to the basket and pull it off, running my fingers over indented letters.

I can't smell lemons without remembering the feel of your body. I love how open and free you were while we were in Italy.

I blush furiously. Grabbing a single lemon, I lift it to my nose, trying to see if the same memories are triggered. My mouth waters at the thought of him moving inside me and having his cock in my mouth.

Still mad, I push the basket to Eloise. "Throw them in the kitchen. Maybe people want lemon in their tea and water. Maybe someone will make a nice lemonade."

"Do you want to tell me what this is about?" she asks, lifting the basket again.

"I have the feeling we will find out by the end of the day."

The gifts and letters continue throughout the day, full of memories and moments, and true to Ken's word, all the things he loves about me. When he sends me my favorite latte at nine, he tells me that he loves my pre-coffee grumpiness. When he sends me lunch from a sushi place near my new office, he tells me he loves how I always try a different kind of sushi. Sean is at least there for me to give that to him.

"I'm thinking I'll accept your sushi as thanks for getting you this killer job." He takes the tray of rolls and dives in while I dig into a smoothie bowl.

"Enjoy it while it lasts," I snark, looking over at the paperwork in front of me. Like Eloise, Sean has taken up a post in my office and I'm unsure if it's because he's looking out for me or for his own curiosity.

"No cute little love note with this one?" He digs around in the bag and pulls out a small note. Whatever the card says turns Sean scarlet all the way to his ears. "I'll let you read this one."

He hands it over to me, and I see why.

Italy was only the beginning. We didn't properly join the mile high club. Maybe on a flight to Tokyo...

My office fills with roses and gifts all day long. I'm already counting down to the end of the day when there is a gentle knock on my door. I look up, startled to see one of my new bosses. I jump to my feet, dropping the box of confetti-pink leather four-and-a-half-inch Christian Louboutin shoes to the floor.

"Were those Louboutin?" Marie asks while walking into my office. She's short, like me, and I know she appreciates a good heel. Her long, black hair is pulled away from her face in a complex braid, leaving her perfectly round face on display. In the time I've known her, she's never hidden her feelings, letting them play out on her face for anyone to see. Some people, mostly men, would complain about that, say it's a weakness in business, but I disagree. Marie lets her adversaries know when she has them by the balls and when she's disgusted by the shit they pull.

"They are," I confirm, lifting them off the ground and placing them on my desk for her to admire.

"Not my color, but that heel...these are naked heels."

I snort, "Naked heels?"

"Yeah, you are not meant to wear clothes in those shoes. They are for you and your lover to enjoy. Your lover, who is very clearly groveling." Marie gestures around the room at all the gifts that cover each surface.

I keep expecting a text from Ken that it's time for us to talk this out, but maybe I need to be the one to take action now. Ken's note with the shoes agreed with Marie's sentiment, that he loves my love of shoes and how I look wearing just those. Not that it stopped him from sending me bras and underwear and garters and lingerie that cost nearly twice as much as the shoes.

"He is groveling," I confirm, not sure if I'm also confirming he's my lover. There's a set of hardcovers sitting on a chair, a series I was loving while we were in Italy and its Italian translation.

Eloise knocks on the door sheepishly, holding a single rose that looks painfully fake. "Sorry to interrupt. This just came for you." She hands me the rose, eyeing the note tied to it.

Not wanting to split my focus from my boss, I set it aside, even if it kills me.

"No, no, I'm invested now. Go ahead and read it," Marie orders, grabbing a chocolate from the box of chocolate caramels Ken also sent.

I look at her then the flower.

I will love you until the last petal falls. I'm sorry, Ainsley. I love you and I was wrong.

I'm more mad at how I'm swooning without hearing these words directly from him. I need to hear him tell me to my face that it was wrong of him to hide me and make me act like we weren't together. I'm not just some fuck buddy he can bring into his office, make me scream through my orgasm, and then go out to his party and pretend like I'm just his lawyer.

I toss the flower aside, into the pile of other flowers that sit right next to my cracked window.

"Still not forgiven?" Marie asks, poking at the bag of makeup, full of the things for my usual nightly routine. Either he had help or he was that attentive when we were in Italy, and that makes me angrier that he could notice so much and do what he did to me.

"No," I say, knocking his other notes into the trash. "Was there something you needed?"

"I wanted to let you know I have a client in the conference room for you."

I jump to my feet, smoothing down my black dress. "Right, I'm sorry, do you have their names? Is it a divorce?"

"Didn't say. Just that they needed an attorney and heard you were the best. It doesn't do well to have my newest hire upstaging me." Marie winks, nearly leading me on a leash out of my office. I dig around under the things on my desk for my notepad and grab the nice pen Ken sent, only because it was the first one I saw. The note accompanying that trinket was that he loved the swoops and swirls in my handwriting, which is the same as it was when I was twelve. Sometimes I even still dot my *i*'s with a heart.

Since I'm still finding my way, Marie leads me to the conference room. "I'll leave you to it," she says with a wink before continuing to her office.

I take a deep breath in and push into the conference room.

"Hi, I'm Ainsley Seaborn..."

The rest of my spiel dies on my lips because Ken is standing in the middle of the room, surrounded by flowers. Their scent is thick and cloying, and I nearly stagger back a step. I cover my mouth, trying to keep my nausea at bay.

"I fucked up" is the first thing out of his mouth.

I want to push past him and open a fucking window, but it's blocked. There must be over a hundred flowers in here. This is a nightmare.

I want to confirm that he did fuck up, but opening my mouth might result in me vomiting, and I refuse.

When I don't say anything, Ken takes this as approval to push forward. He wipes his hands on his jeans before pulling a paper out of his pocket. "Sometimes being around you makes me think and feel a lot of things, so I wrote them down so I didn't miss anything. Because I don't want to miss anything with you. I love everything about you, and I've been miserable without you."

I take a small breath in through my mouth but don't let go of the door handle.

When I'm still nonverbal, he pushes forward. "Right. Losing you was my worst nightmare come true. I talked a lot to my therapist and my mom and my sister about what happened. My mom and sister both wanted me to apologize to you right away, and I wanted to too, but I also wanted to give you space. It was never about me wanting to distance myself from you. It was about wanting to distance you from Celeste and Leslie. When you left, I realized that I had fucked up, and when you didn't answer my initial texts, I knew that you needed space. I just hope I didn't give you too much space."

"Why didn't you *ask* me what I needed?" I'm able to get these words out but need to keep my mouth closed after. Speaking up may have been a strategic mistake.

I'm grinding my teeth and digging my nails into my palms, hoping to draw blood at this point. His words are barely penetrating the haze of the smell. Did he buy out every florist on the goddamned island? It feels like there are at least a thousand roses in here.

"Because I thought I knew what you wanted. I thought that you were punishing me for still talking to Leslie. I should have been asking you what you needed from me instead of assuming and listening to my own fears. Apple is the one that told me that you were probably mad about what Celeste was saying. It's not that I thought you were a rebound and weren't important enough to introduce to everyone. I thought I was protecting you. I meant what I said. I still want this. I still want you. I still want that future we talked about."

The future that involves me being the mother of his child.

The mother of his child.

It's that thought that has me grabbing the trash can that is thankfully right next to the door so I can throw up. I drop hard to my knees, purging everything in my system. Ken is right there, gathering my long locks up and twisting them at the base of my neck so he can run a soothing hand along my spine.

I reach up and wipe at a tear that I tell myself is from throwing up and not at all the emotions he's spent the day stirring. The tears keep coming, and I retch again, gripping the trash can like it's my last lifeline.

"Was the sushi place not good? It looked like it had decent ratings on FoodNow!"

"No, you asshole, it wasn't the sushi. I'm pregnant," I tell him miserably, sinking to the floor completely. I turn to look up at him, hating a little bit how I blurted it out. All my plans for telling him with the onesie are gone.

Ken's expression looks like a combination of surprised, stricken, and awed all at once. He swallows hard, his Adam's apple bobbing.

"What?" he asks, shaking his head, and he looks so befuddled that I have to hold in my laughter. All these giggles at inappropriate times are going to get me into so much trouble at some point in the next eight months.

"I'm in the family way. I'm pregnant."

Ken drops back onto the floor, a crease appearing on his forehead. "How?"

I punch him in the shoulder gently. How? As if he and I didn't have sex regularly for a month. "When a mommy and a daddy love each other very much...I'm pregnant with *your* child. I found out the day after we made up from Italy."

Ken rushes forward, kissing me and hauling me onto his lap. I let out a surprised yelp as he cradles me to him, pressing his head into the crook of my neck. He's whispering something, but I can't make it out, and I realize it's because he's crying.

I smooth his hair down as he rocks me in his lap until he can take a deep breath.

Ken leans back so he can look me in the face. He holds my cheeks, pushing my hair back clumsily. I'm honestly expecting him to be mad that it took me this long to tell him. Only, there is no anger or contempt on his face.

"You're going to be the most amazing mother. Not because you're strong and going to prove to anyone and everyone that you can do this on your own, but because you're smart and kind and stubborn and the most wonderful creature I've ever seen walk the earth. You should make me grovel and worship you until you're happy and comfortable and secure in knowing how I feel about you."

"You're just saying these things because I'm pregnant," I point out, grabbing both of his wrists to pull them from my face.

"No, you can look at the paper I took notes on. I did all that before I knew you were pregnant. If I could go back, I would do it all so differently."

"Hindsight has that effect on people."

Ken thrusts the paper into my hand so I can clearly see how he has outlined all the ways that he loves me. I see why he says he needed the paper to stay on target, because even though he has a list of the things he wants to say, there are branches off the items with more things. Next to his entry about how grumpy I am without coffee, he points out that he loves that I will take coffee any way it's presented and he loves how unapologetic I am about that. He has a post-it over that about how I treat shitty diner coffee like it's the most expensive blend there is.

Tears spring to my eyes, and I sniffle, but that was a mistake because I smell the flowers and have to fight the urge to retch again.

"I'm going to prove it to you, and I'll do it in any way you let me. I'll rub your feet and massage away your stretch marks. I'll do the two a.m. run to Between the Buns for your favorite burger and fries. I'll do whatever it takes, and if you want me to spend the next month finding presents, I'll do it. Name your price."

I cup his cheek gently. "There is no price, Ken. I just want to be loved. And for my child, *our* child, to feel loved unconditionally. If you just want to be the sperm donor the way we were sort of angling at the beginning, we can do it that way."

"I don't just want to be a sperm donor, Ainsley. I want to be all-in with you. I thought this–everything today–told you that. I am so in love with you that I want to quote cheesy movies about you being the lamb and me being the lion. I want us to have a functional, loving relationship where we communicate instead of hiding from each other and making assumptions about each other's feelings. I spent too long having to keep what I really want to myself and I'm tired of it. I love you. I want to be with you. I already told you that eventually I want to marry you."

"How can you say that? You just got out of a divorce." The hint of the flowers hits me, and I get out of his lap quickly. "Can we go somewhere and talk? The smell is too much."

Ken jumps to his feet, brushing the hair from my face, and I know gestures like that are going to make me melt to him.

"Of course. I'll take care of this, and then I'll meet you in your office?" He sounds hopeful, but I shake my head.

"Yes to getting rid of the flowers, but we should go back to my place and talk."

"Done. I'll help carry everything back to your place too."

I hate how unsure both of us sound about this. With a nod, I leave him in the conference room and open it to find Eloise at Addison's desk, trying to seem like she wasn't eavesdropping at all. It's a blur of a movement, but I think Sean was out there too and ran back into his office. He all but confirms it when he tries to wander out casually.

"Do you need something, Ainsley?" he asks me, like I'm at his office door for a reason.

I scowl at him. "No, but I'm heading out for the day. There are flowers in the conference room if anyone wants. Addison, please send an email." Ken steps out behind me, closing the door while holding the waste basket I was sick in.

Taking the small crowd in stride, Ken asks where the bathroom is. When no one jumps to tell him, I direct him outside our office and across the hall.

"You guys are awful spies, really."

"Did he grovel enough?" Sean asks, following Eloise and I to my office.

"What do you know about it?" I ask suspiciously.

"Someone had to help him get all those flowers in. I'm right next to the conference room. It was a little hard to miss."

Once I step into my office, ushering Eloise and Sean in with me, I close the door and turn on them.

"Did either of you have anything to do with today's events?"

"What? No!" both of them try to say, but it doesn't pass muster.

"Et tu, Brute?" I say, pointing a finger in each of their faces.

"I may have called him last week," Sean confesses, sharing a guilty look with Eloise. I would ask how he would even know to call Ken, but that exchange between them is all the evidence I need. It might be circumstantial at this point, but I'll make them fold.

When there is another knock on my door, I whip it open in a flurry. "What now?!" I demand.

"Just stopping by to see if the apology worked." Marie chuckles.

"I'm guessing you were in on this as well?"

"Who do you think let him in to place that first flower?"

"I appreciate the help, but boundaries."

Marie's expression hardens as she steps in and closes the door, so now my office has four of us in it. She looks suspiciously at Sean and Eloise, then back at me. "I didn't fuck up did I? He's not one of those ultra charming bastards that you managed to get free of and I let him back in your life?"

Seeing how serious she is, I immediately set the record straight. "No." I'm firm, shaking my head, but this puts things into perspective, at least somewhat. "It's nothing like that. Today's just been a whirlwind, like our romance, and if you weren't my boss, I would love to regale you with the full story, but as it is, you sign my paychecks and I only *just* started working here."

"Maybe next month you can tell me. I think that's a sufficient amount of time to share all the dirty details."

"In the grand scheme of things, your fight wasn't that bad. Really, it was more of a non-fight," Eloise adds unhelpfully, and I cut her a withering glance.

"You're already in the doghouse, ma'am," I remind her.

Eloise throws her hands up. "Oh, who gives a shit? Does he deserve to grovel for twice as long as you were together? Absolutely, but he has worshiped the ground you walked on since you met, pretty much. He spent the entirety of the divorce party looking at you. So no, I won't butt out of this. I love you too much to let you use one fight to end your relationship. I'm pretty sure I had to referee worse fights way more often between you and Charlie."

"You and good old Chuck fought?" Sean asks, amused.

I had forgotten he was standing there for a moment and glare at him too. "Fighting would have required him to actually be home. It was more like passive aggressive voicemails and calls between assistants."

"Yeah, his assistant Ashley actually took me out for drinks during a particularly bad exchange over him missing Thanksgiving. She's really sweet. I'm thinking I should give her a call now that he has a less sucky job."

"Besides the point," I snap.

There is a tentative knock on my door, but I don't need to open it to know that it's Ken on the other side. "Weezy, hold my calls for the rest of the day. I'm going to try to clean up this mess." I gesture at the gifts all over my office. "And the meddling from you pesky kids ends now."

Marie opens the door, and it is a testament to how awesome of a boss she is that she hasn't fired me on the spot for being nothing less than a train wreck my first few weeks of employment. She must have really wanted me here to be so completely forgiving.

Ken steps aside to let everyone out, but Sean lingers, his hand gently touching my waist as he leans in to whisper in my ear, glaring at Ken.

"Is he watching?" Sean asks, his lips barely moving. Ken is definitely watching with a mixture of annoyance and resignation. I glance away, giving just a little nod. "If you say the word, I'll call Chucky up and end this man with no questions asked."

"That's conspiracy," I whisper back, but I'm grateful to have him in my corner.

"You wouldn't rat me out. I know it. Does he look sufficiently regretful to have risked you?"

I survey Ken and confirm that he looks decidedly unhappy. It's not just for the moment, with Sean being so close to me. It's how his clothes look rumpled, like he's pulled them from the dryer after they've been sitting there for days. It's how his beard has grown in again during our time apart. Ken looks the part of a man barely holding it together after nearly losing the woman that he loves. I nod again.

"Good," Sean whispers one last time before kissing my cheek and leaving my office. When he gets to the door he pauses in front of Ken, placing a hand on his chest. "Do better to deserve her." There is a not-so-subtle threat in his words.

I should tell him to leave it. A better woman wouldn't encourage Ken's jealousy the way I have, but I'm not a better woman, and I'm going to make sure Ken realizes how close he came to losing me. To losing us.

"I will, I promise," Ken replies, but it's not for Sean, it's for me. It's so I see how serious he is about making this whole situation work.

When it's just the two of us again, Ken surveys the damage, including the bottle of my favorite wine that I now cannot enjoy. But in nine months? I absolutely will be drinking it then.

"How can I help?" Ken asks as I shuffle things around, trying to pile them. When I pick up the stack of books, he lunges toward me, plucking them from my hands.

"You can help by not taking things out of my hands. Mostly, I just need to gather it all together and try and condense it enough for both of us to carry. Anything that doesn't fit, I'll take home tomorrow."

"You shouldn't carry anything too heavy," Ken practically scolds, placing stuff into a box that Eloise had the foresight to bring in earlier.

"I'm pregnant, not weak. You were just praising me for how strong I am, but I can't pick up three books?"

"I think you are strong. I'm sorry, should I be ashamed that knowing you're carrying my child has brought out my inner caveman? Be glad I'm not throwing you over my shoulder and locking you in your apartment. I know you're capable, and strong. I know you could and probably should clobber me if you had the chance. It doesn't change the fact that I want to take care of you." He crosses to me, taking my laptop and placing it back on my desk so he can pull me against him. I want to hesitate, but my body clings to him like a melted marshmallow. He places his palm to my chest, right over my heart. "You have so much love to give, and I know that our child will want for nothing. You're going to bring smiles and laughter into their life and show them exactly what love is."

Emotion grips me, and I give in too easily. I lean up and press my lips against his, sweetly at first, then with need as the heat of a thousand fires licks up my spine before flooding me with desire between my legs. My traitorous body opens to him, but he doesn't take the bait. His hand on my waist tightens, but he doesn't push it further than the kiss. Just as quickly as the feeling came over me, it's gone and I feel so embarrassed.

"Now I'm the one that's sorry," I say, trying to pull out of his grip, but he won't let me go.

"Look at me, Ainsley," he orders, but I look anywhere but him. He presses his hips against me, and I can feel his erection thick and needy against my thigh, and I want to whimper with the feel of him. I know what it's like when he slides into me, slick with my arousal. I finally look at him, and I can see my own lust reflected in his eyes. "I want you. I want you more than you can understand, and I think it goes back to that primal caveman you've woken inside me. I want to hear you scream my name so that Sean guy hears how I've claimed you for me. But right now, we need to work on our communication and making your feel secure that I want more than just sex from you."

Conflicting emotions arise in me. I want to be mad at him not just for knowing me so well, but also because he's right that if we're going to try to make a run for this, we need a more solid base than the lust that got us here. There is also nothing sexier than a man who is willing to put my emotional well-being above his hard-on, which only makes me want him more. This man is everything to me, and I want to have my way with him right now.

"Mhm," I confirm, slowly drawing out of his grip.

Ken chuckles. "Please, Ainsley, don't test my resolve. Feeling your body against mine has me imagining all the wonderful things I want to do to you. So please, stop tempting me. I will give in."

"If you need me to protect your virtue, then I suppose I must. Besides, it's only my second week at work. Getting caught fucking on my desk is a bad idea."

"Not that it's going to get you laid, but we should get going."

With that settled, Ken and I gather what we can before

hopping into a cab. We're both in desperate need of reassurance from the other that we hold hands the whole way, and I have absolutely no problem with it.

I want us to talk more, but I'm dead on my feet when we get home. I'm such miserable company that I don't even manage to get fully undressed before falling asleep.

I'm surprised to find I'm alone in bed, but I'm tucked in and wearing one of Ken's old shirts that was still lying around.

Outside my bedroom, I can hear someone moving around, and I can only guess that it's Ken. I hope it's Ken, otherwise it can be any number of my friends that have keys to my apartment.

When I emerge, Ken turns to face me, holding a spatula and a pan.

"I'm glad you're up."

"How long was I out for?" I sit at the kitchen table and watch him.

"An hour and a half. I was torn between letting you sleep and waking you up. On the one hand, I wanted you to get your rest. On the other hand, if you slept any longer you weren't going to sleep tonight."

"Sounds like you put a lot of thought into it. What did you do while I slept?"

"Went grocery shopping, did some reading about pregnancy, began to look at apartments close by."

"Close by?" I ask.

Ken slides a plate in front of me, and I stare at it, unable to bring myself to look up at him. He sits beside me and takes my hands into his. "I'm not assuming anything right now. We were just talking about taking it slow before the party and now you're pregnant. I'm not assuming that this means that you're looking to get married tomorrow, but I do want to make this work somehow, eventually."

"Move in," I rush the words out quickly, and Ken, to his credit, doesn't flinch at my outburst.

"Are you sure?"

"Don't act like I don't know my own mind. I want you here. Co-parenting and pretending like we could never be more to each other than just that wasn't going to work. There was always and is always going to be something between us. I don't want to deny it. I don't want to put off what is inevitable. Move in. We can figure the rest out from there."

"I don't want you to feel like you're stuck with me moving in."

"Stay here," I plead, feeling on the verge of desperation.

"We should take this slow." He sounds pained saying it.

"No, we should have taken it slow. At this point, I'm carrying your child. Slow was three months ago. I'm not going to want someone else. You have ruined me for other men. I want our child to have a family, not two split houses. I want them to be able to crawl into bed with us when they have a nightmare, and I want them to go ask you for something after I already told them no. I want to be there to watch you teach them how to cook, and I want them to learn from us what a happy, healthy, functional relationship looks like.

"So, say yes. Say yes to staying here. We don't have to share a bed, because you were right earlier. We have so, so much to work through, but I want to work through it knowing that the end result will be you having to sleep on the couch when I'm too pregnant and uncomfortable to get up. I don't want to have to call you and wonder where you are when I go into labor. I want to know that I'll have my partner with me, every step of the way." I lick my lips. "Say yes," I whisper desperately.

Tucking my hair behind my ear, Ken leans down and kisses me. Within that kiss is the hundreds of hello kisses and goodbye kisses we've shared and missed and are going to share. It's full of his own desperate yearning for the vision I saw.

Lust is so easy for us, the sex, the desire. But being real and laying my heart open like that, being afraid he would say no even though he was begging me for the same chance earlier, was terrifying. Ken groans as he kisses me deeply, washing away any insecurity that I had. It feels like our entire existence has come down to this moment, this moment of choosing to try to make this work.

"Are you sure this is what you really want?"

"I swear to all that is holy, if you second-guess me again, you're just going to always sleep on the couch."

This next kiss is bruising in all its power. We've been apart for two weeks too long. Our desperation to connect drives me to start to pull Ken's shirt off, but he stops me, pulling away. His lips brush my forehead.

"If you're serious, then we have plenty of time to work back up to that. I don't want to push this too fast."

His restraint wrecks the last of mine, and I press him back against the counter.

"I thought you said something about wanting to fulfill my every craving."

Ken looks like he wants to devour me on the spot, but still he's holding back. We're both breathing heavily, waiting to see if the other will snap.

"Fuck it," he snarls, scooping me up. My legs lock around his hips as he grips my ass and hauls me to my bedroom.

For all the strength and power he's exuding in this moment, he's so gentle with me as he lays me down on the bed. My body short-circuits as he reaches between my legs almost tentatively and feels how wet my pussy is.

"Oh god, Ainsley, you're fucking soaked for me." His eyes are hooded, but I can feel him watching me. Ken's hands move from between my legs to my hips so he can reach under my shirt, pulling my panties off. In one easy, careless move, he has them off me and thrown over his shoulder.

"Don't think this means we don't have a lot to work on," I warn. "But I need you. I need you inside me, stretching me." My words are nearly incoherent as he pushes my shirt up so my whole body is bared to him.

I push up on my elbows so he can finish shedding my clothes. Once the shirt is off, he throws that on the floor too before he grabs the hem of his shirt and similarly discards it.

Ken sits on his haunches, just watching the panting I'm already doing before we've even really gotten started. "I'm never going to stop doing everything I can to deserve you."

He kisses my toes, which makes me giggle, until he's slowly but surely moving up my body, starting with my legs. Ken is all soft touches and tender kisses, slowly building the tension. Lips on the crease of my hip and up my soft belly that I know in a few months will be swollen with child.

My eyes tear at the tenderness, and I have to turn my head away to stop the tears from flowing. Ken is worshiping me as he works up to my face and when he realizes I'm crying, he goes still. This hot, coiling tension between us cools immediately.

"Ainsley, talk to me. Did I do something wrong?" Ken's body hovers over mine in a one-armed plank. Impressed is one word for it, but I can't take that emotion on when so many others are fighting within me.

"No, no, I just. This time feels different, and just keep going, I'm fine, I promise. I want this. I want us."

Ken kisses the tears one my face, finally collapsing beside me.

"How about we snuggle tonight, and we can revisit my wearing you down tomorrow?"

My lower lip slips out into a pout as I start to cry more fully before I nod, burying my face in his chest, knowing that even as the pendulum of my emotions swings, I am at home in his arms.

Twenty-Two

EVERY STEP of this process of getting Ken formally moved into the apartment makes me feel like I'm going to have this baby before I even see my doctor again. I focus on taking things one day at a time, and moving day feels like it takes all month, mostly because his boxes are all over the place because he refuses to actually let me lift anything.

During one of his trips down, there is a knock on the door. I'm stranded in the middle of the chaos but try to maneuver my way to the door.

"It should still be unlocked," I say, pulling the door open, but I'm struck dumb by who is on the other side. "Daddy."

"Yeah, buttercup?" Ken replies, approaching the door behind my dad. When he realizes I wasn't talking to him, he drops the box he was carrying.

From the way my father turns red all the way to the tips of his ears, he must be thinking that I call Ken this in bed, and now I'm turning red. I've called Ken 'dad' and 'daddy' just to try them out, the same way he's starting to try out 'mom' and 'momma.' It doesn't feel natural yet, but maybe it will when I start showing.

"Sir," Ken greets, trying to play it cool. He bends over and picks up the box he was carrying, though I can hear it rattling around more than I did earlier. Hopefully whatever is inside wasn't fragile.

My father clears his throat. "Ainsley?" he questions, waiting for an explanation.

"Dad, this is Ken. Ken, this is my father." I watch them greet each other apprehensively.

My father is blatantly sizing Ken up before glancing beyond me at the boxes in the apartment. Our limited plan was to just throw everything in the guest room and sort it out from there since it will eventually have to be turned into a nursery.

I stagger back at the thought of a nursery. My apartment is spacious for a couple, but a family? When it was just going to be me and a child, that was one thing, but now that baby makes three...

Ken drops the box a second time, pushing my father out of the way to get to me. "Ainsley?" Ken questions, worry thick in his voice.

"I'm fine," I tell him, waving him off. "I just, there is so much stuff, I don't know what to do."

We discussed telling people I was pregnant, but I wanted to wait to tell anyone else. I know the statistics. I know that this could maybe never come to fruition. I want to guard my heart against possible disappointment.

My father looks from Ken to me and back to Ken again. "Kenneth Baker? 2.9 GPA at Vanderbilt, played the cello all through college. Spent the summer between your junior and senior year at your family home in Italy before you had to come home early after your girlfriend accused you of cheating. Met Leslie Studebaker at a bachelor party and thought it was fate because your last name was in hers, 'like you were meant to be.' Purchased your bar six years ago and managed to turn a floundering establishment around. That Ken?" My father looks at me, proud of himself.

"Uhm, yes," Ken confirms, confused.

"Did you do this shit to Charlie, too?" I demand.

"I didn't have to. I knew all of Charlie's skeletons because I knew his father."

"Wait, you ran a background check on me?" Ken says, finally realizing that this is how my father knows all this information.

"After hearing how you broke my daughter's heart? I had to know just how many people would come asking questions when you disappeared."

Ken laughs, like it should be a joke, but my father's face doesn't budge. "Oh, you're serious."

"Why wouldn't I be? You dangled something my daughter wanted in her face and rather than giving her the carrot, you gave her the stick." I know he doesn't mean it as a double entendre, but I'm only human and I snicker. It earns me a stern look from my father, who must be doing his best to lay down the law. "I have half a mind to break your kneecaps for making her feel like she meant nothing to you. I've done worse to men for less."

"You're right," Ken confirms, wrapping an around my shoulders.

I tuck myself into his side, trying to convey to my father that he should let this one go. "Dad, we've made up." I hope my tone and narrowed eyes are convincing.

When he opens his mouth, Ken cuts him off.

"I know what a mistake I made. Ainsley and I are trying to work it out and respectfully ask that you not intervene. If I fuck this up again, I'll gladly write a farewell letter to my family, telling them not to ask questions when I disappear. I've been in love with your daughter for a while now, and almost losing her only made me realize that I don't want to live another day without her."

I swoon and blame the pregnancy hormones, but who am I kidding? Ken's been proclaiming his love for me with his words, with his mouth, with his actions since finding out about the baby.

My father clears his throat. "I was going to ask if you needed help moving your boxes in, but I thank you for that confirmation."

"No, Dad, you were not going to ask that, but sure, Jan," I tease, stepping out from Ken's side so my dad can some inside.

"I resent that accusation, but just tell me how I can help." My father rolls up his sleeves, ready to dive in wherever we need him.

We get a system working, and in an effort to encourage further male bonding, I disappear to grab some beer for them. When I get back, they're both pouring over an open box filled with sports memorabilia.

"I remember this ball!" my father exclaims, holding up a baseball in a clear plastic container. They don't even acknowledge my return, they're so engrossed in what they're looking at and talking about.

"Should I even bother setting these out?" Ken asks, gesturing at the box. Part of him bringing everything into the apartment was an effort for him to consolidate what he has. His cello has a place of honor in the corner that we already set aside for him. He's trying to evaluate what he still wants from his old apartment.

It's startling to know that there is so much more.

"No, I don't think so."

I haven't even started to propose the idea of us needing a bigger place. I think a three-bedroom is a necessity, at the least. There are so many important conversations we need to have. It was one thing to talk in the abstract. Now that a future together is a more tangible thing, we need to decide things, like how many children we want and where we are going to live.

Do we send them to private school? Get a nanny? Breast milk or formula?

Ken crowds my space, pressing me against the fridge, pulling me from the downward spiral of thoughts.

"Where did you go?" he whispers, nudging my forehead with his nose so I have to look up at him. If my father saw him right now, he might choose to overlook the fact that we're trying to make it work.

"Nowhere," I say, unconvincingly, looking past his head.

He kisses me, hard, finally snapping me back into the present.

"Want to try that again? You said we need to communicate better." He cups my cheek.

"You smell," I point out, wrinkling my nose at him.

Ken grinds against me, for effect, and I giggle. "You usually like it when I smell. You usually like what I'm doing that causes me to smell."

I bite my lip, thinking of our bodies slick with sweat as we move together.

My father clears his throat. "You're blocking the beer you so kindly got." There is a hint of amusement in his eyes, and I know that whatever transpired while I was out getting the beer earned Ken a temporary stay of execution.

I blush, stepping out of the way to grab drinks for my father and Ken.

"I'll get started on cooking dinner. Are you going to stay with us, Lucius?" Ken asks, moving into the kitchen and pulling out the different pots and pans he might need.

"If that's okay with Ainsley, then I think that sounds terrific. What are you making?"

I think my father is trying to stay so he can get as much first-hand information about Ken as he can.

Ken's gaze swings to me, checking what I'm craving. They haven't been intense yet, but he's catering to my every whim.

"Can enchiladas be on the menu?" I ask, moving to the table to start clearing off some of the stuff Ken has designated as castoff.

"Anything you want, buttercup, it's yours. Can you give us a second, Lucious? I just want to run something by Ainsley." Ken gently leads me into my bedroom, or rather, our bedroom now.

"If you think you're getting a quickie, you're sorely mistaken. But you need to be quick and we should do it in the bathroom."

Ken laughs. "I did not bring you in here to screw your brains out. I do believe your father when he says he will kill me if I hurt you. Why am I not surprised your father is mafia-adjacent?"

"He is not," I object, but wave him on. "If we're not in here for you to blow my mind, what did you want?"

"I want you to talk to me and tell me where you went before. Something big was on your mind."

I press a chaste kiss to Ken's lips. "I was overwhelmed for a minute. There's a lot changing really fast. It's not a bad thing at all, there's just a lot of decisions that need to be made, and it was one thing when having a baby was something that was in the abstract and sometime in the future, but now we are on a ticking clock, and I think having you move in just sort of...brought it to a head. Like, do we want to get a nanny that speaks another language? Should I breastfeed? Should we find out the baby's sex beforehand?"

"I think raising our kids to speak Italian would be nice since we're going to probably go there often, but I also support other languages, like Spanish and Mandarin. If you want to breastfeed, do it. If you don't, don't. Fed is best and that's all that matters. I have no preference on finding out the sex. It would be cool to know in advance. It would also be fine not to know in advance."

"I don't."

Ken tugs me closer, resting his hands on my waist. "Don't what?"

"Want to know. I don't want to know before they're born."

He nods. "Then we don't find out. I know it feels like we're crunched for time, but we will figure this out. We have an army of people who love us and who will love this little pea. There will be growing pains, there will *always* be growing pains now, but I know we can figure it out together. Okay?"

"Okay," I agree.

Ken sweeps me into a deep kiss, holding my body against his until I feel steady enough to go back out.

When we emerge, my dad is already in the kitchen with all the pots and pans out. Ken tries to shoo him away as he pulls all of the ingredients out.

While the three of us are eating dinner, I think I can see my future playing out right. I can see my father coming over for meals and watching our child, possibly more children. Our family will flourish and grow with the support of our parents and siblings and friends.

This child will be loved by everyone in their life.

Ken and I are staring at the sonogram picture as I try to ignore the mess around me. We need to talk about moving. Ken has too many things and our aesthetic doesn't match. My cotton candy pink apartment is at odds with his postmodern furniture. He keeps trying to claim that it belonged to Leslie and she just didn't want to move it, but I notice how he keeps trying to replace my side table with his, and I will not be fooled.

"Clearly, they have Uncle Reginald's nose," Ken says, wielding the tiny picture like it's irrefutable.

"I don't think they even has a nose yet, but that is definitely my father's chin," I say with a laugh. It's hard not to be this kind of ridiculous when you feel so on top of the world. After securing it to our fridge with a magnet, I turn to Ken with a grin on my face.

"What?" he asks, eyeing me with an eyebrow raised.

"I love you," I tell him finally.

If he could melt into the ground, I think he would.

"I love you too, Ainsley Seaborn, warts and all."

"What warts?" I demand, scowling.

He grabs my hips and pulls me to him. "This one, and this one, and this one." He peppers kisses all along my face and neck until I giggle and am reliant on him for support.

His arms lock around me, firm and strong, pulling me up and lifting me when I get to the very tips of my toes. My legs hook around his hips and he carries me deeper into the apartment, back to the bed we share.

Our kisses change. They're slow and languid, like we have all the time in the world to make love to each other. His hands are deft, undoing button after button on my blouse, bearing me to him.

He's gentle as his mouth traces a line down my body, pausing at each breast. I arch my back into him as his tongue laps around my nipple before blowing cool air onto it. My hands grab his head, fisting in his thick hair. He repeats this with the other nipple, being gentle but tantric as his fingertips graze my body. I can feel my pulse all over my body as it throbs with the need to feel him. It's been a month since we've been together. A month since I felt him move inside me, and I'm ready to end the drought.

I struggle with the zipper on my skirt, my fingers nearly shaking before I give up and just hike it up. Ken chuckles, kissing my belly button and then the soft curve of my abdomen.

"I'm going to take my time loving you for the rest of our lives, Ainsley Seaborn. Be patient."

I hate how soft his voice is and how badly I want to tell him to fuck that and fuck me. "Right, and I will love slow sex…another time. But right now, I want you. I need you. I need this connection."

He pulls the zipper down the side of my skirt with an aching slowness that nearly sets me panting. "Ainsley, there is nothing I want more than to be buried inside you, but I want to feel every inch of you. I want to watch the moment I enter you and when you suck your bottom lip in as you get close. And I want to burn the image of you clenching around my cock into my retinas. So, I'm going to go slow, and later tonight, after I've had my fun, you can have yours."

Ken peels my skirt down my legs before he takes off his own clothes, taunting me. There is another surprise when he finds that I'm not wearing any underwear. He doesn't remark on it, just presses a kiss to my pussy before teasing his way back up to my mouth.

He isn't wrong about watching my face as I feel every inch of him slide into me. It's already pulling aching sounds from my throat as I want to set the pace faster. Once he's seated inside me fully, we're both panting from the effort to not speed this up, to not fuck each other's brains out. It's not our usual speed, but I like it. I like having this moment.

He slides back out of me just as slowly, and I cant my hips up to meet him with the same speed. Soon we're settling into this slow friction.

"God, you feel so fucking good," Ken groans, pressing his head into my shoulder.

"You started this. I'm so fucking close, finish it," I beg.

Ken complies, upping the tempo just a little with a slow thrust in but a quick pull out. He grabs my hips, lifting them just a little, and I cry out as I give in to the emotion, give in to the feelings until there is nothing but the two of us and our orgasms.

Ken finds his own release as I do, my body clenching around him until he's spent. He rolls onto his side, pulling me with him. He stays inside me until both of our breathing has calmed.

"There is nothing greater than us," he whispers to me, placing his large hand over my abdomen. The emotions coursing through me are so potent, I want to bottle them so I can remember this feeling forever.

It becomes painfully obvious that the apartment isn't going to cut it. Getting Ken's things out of storage was a tremendous mistake. I'm constantly tripping over boxes, and it's making me crazy. We've been living like this for a month now, and I'm going to lose my shit.

So, I ask Ken to meet me at an address one day before he goes to work. He agrees without complaint.

It's only five-thirty, but the day is sweltering, and I check my watch again to see how late Ken is. It's only been five minutes, but I'm pregnant and hot all the time. I don't need to be baking in the sun too.

"Sorry, sorry. I went into the bar to accept a delivery because the new bartender already said they were going to be late." He kisses me on the lips, and as much as I am melting into the pavement, I won't do it out here. It's way too hot.

"It's fine. I just wanted to talk to you about something."

The neighborhood we're in is quiet. It's only one avenue off Central Park West, and there are brownstones lining the street. I walk up one of the stoops and enter the code into the lock box before turning the key and letting us in.

Ken eyes me but waits for me to explain as I walk us into the foyer. The blast of the AC is enough to make me shiver. Ken gallantly reaches to warm me, but I glare at him. It was a welcome shiver. He is not going to steal this chill from me. This is my cold air and my cold air alone.

The wood floor has a herringbone pattern, which I highlight as I lead him around the house on my own little guided tour, pointing at all the original molding.

"Ainsley, what are we doing here?" he asks as we ascend the stairs to the second level. We've already been through the dining room and the formal living room and the large eat-in kitchen. The house is from the late 1800s, so it doesn't have the modern open concept of my apartment, but it's got amazing history and bones.

I don't answer him right away, leading him to one of the bedrooms that I happen to know isn't the master. This isn't my first time inside this house. I push open the door to a mostly empty room.

"I figured this could be the nursery." I gesture at the bassinet that sits alone in the middle of the room. Out the window is the view of the outside garden area.

"Ainsley..." Ken says slowly, pulling my hips to him.

"Kenneth..." I echo.

"Did you buy this house?"

"No, but I want to. I want us to buy it together. There are six bedrooms, so plenty of space if we want more kids. And there is space for Apple and Howie and the boys to visit. I want us to start our family...here. And if you're worried about the finances, I know other marital law attorneys I trust to draw up a fair agreement about splitting the place."

"Already kicking me out?" he asks slyly, pulling me to him.

"Only if you keep denying me those tart heart candies I like so much."

"They're out of season! You eat them faster than I can find them," he scolds with a laugh. He reaches out and rubs my belly, knowing that there is a little life growing behind it.

"So, you want to do it? Buy this place, together? I can't do the apartment anymore. I could buy this place myself, too."

"No, we're going to do this like we're going to do everything else for the rest of our lives: together."

Twenty-Three

FOUR MONTHS LATER

I'M LEANING BACK in the folding chair I've been provided with, trying to find a comfortable position, but it's impossible. The baby gives a swift kick in retaliation for all the shifting.

"You tell them, little pea!" I concur, rubbing the spot it hit.

"Do you want me to go get you something more comfortable to sit on?" Sean asks, glancing at me from his own metal folding chair.

"I want you to open the damn doors so we can see if this is even going to work," I grumble, reaching for my water and chugging. It's a mistake to drink so much, but I'm so damn thirsty. Already, I can feel my bladder beg for release.

"Just smile for me," Ken pleads with his phone out, snapping photos of where I'm seated. This school gymnasium is not what I expected, but it's just a beginning.

Marie has been my biggest advocate at the firm, especially with my community outreach program. It's why all of my colleagues are sitting here, ready to help anyone who needs it. We're each at different tables with our laptops and a few student volunteers who agreed to run back and forth to the copy room in the coaches' office to help keep the paperwork moving.

"I am not smiling for you," I scowl and then give him a cheesy grin, just to satisfy him. "Why are you even here?"

"This is a big moment for both of my babies. Besides, if I wasn't here, I'm sure you would get swept up and miss your own gender reveal," Ken says pointedly.

"We already know my gender," I gesture at my stomach. "Besides, why does anyone care what bits the baby has? So long as there are ten fingers and ten toes and two lungs and a healthy heart..."

"I've got to stop you there. Now you're getting greedy," Ken teases, kissing the top of my head.

Eloise runs into the room with a cushion in her hands. "Eloise to the rescue!" she calls. "One of the secretaries upstairs has sciatica, and if I didn't have to listen to her tell me about it for thirty minutes, I would have been back sooner."

Both Ken and Sean jump to help me up, which I grumble about, but I'm a short woman and the baby has consumed my entire person. It's fine, I'm fine. I'm perfectly fine waddling into meetings with clients for whom pregnancy is a point of contention in their divorce.

"Are we ready to open the doors?" Marie asks, inspecting every table as if she hasn't done this four times already.

"Yes, please," I plead. Once Marie is out of earshot, I lean over to Eloise. "Man my table, I have to pee."

Ken chuckles and walks with me.

"I'm proud of you, you know," he tells me as we walk.

"Oh?" I say, as if surprised. He hasn't been shy with his lavish praise and I'm thankful for it. There are nights when I feel like a boat or a balloon about to float away, but Ken will rub my feet or look at me like he wants to tear my clothes off and I'll feel better, even if it's temporary until the next thing sets me off.

"Yeah, not only are you growing a baby, but you managed to

get this small pilot program up and running while buying a house, selling your apartment, and growing your own divorce book."

It has been a rough four months. I wanted to see this happen before I was benched with the baby. A few hours on a Saturday in one school district was the answer, and I'm still nervous about how it's going to work out.

"You're just saying that because you want a blow job." I shoulder-bump him and he chuckles.

"Always, but I'm serious about this. You're incredible. You need to know that."

"You remind me every day."

It turns out I did need Ken there to keep me on task to get to the gender reveal party on time. The turnout was way higher than expected, and Eloise and Addison had to collect contact information for anyone we couldn't get to. I spent all day listening to couples tell me about how they have tried but just can't afford a divorce attorney, and so I help however I can, promising to be their ally during this time.

I'm about to beckon over another mother who wants me to look over her pre-existing divorce paperwork when Ken shakes his head at Eloise. My paralegal is fast on the intercept, moving to woman.

"I'm going to have to take your information," I can hear Eloise tell her as Ken pulls me out of my chair.

"I need to help," I tell him, trying to keep the whine out of my voice.

"And you will. But, buttercup, this is a marathon, not a sprint. You can't help everyone in one day. Let Eloise do the intake and you can do the hard part later."

I scowl but hug Eloise before leaving.

As we approach the door, I take a moment to pause, looking at all of my colleagues sitting at their tables, ready to help the community on a gorgeous September Saturday. They work hard and should be able to enjoy the day, but they're here, ready to do better.

My friends and family are all at The Boathouse in Central Park for a combination gender reveal and baby shower. I didn't want to have to exclude my father or Ken's nephews from any celebration, and doing it like this was the best way to appease all parties.

Ken and I stopped by our townhouse so I could change into a tie-dye blue and pink dress for just this occasion. It's got an off-the-shoulder peasant sleeve and has so much space in it for me to move around comfortably. My attempts to not buy larger maternity clothes are getting thwarted each day. Even with Ken measuring my stomach every week, it's hard to believe I'm still getting bigger.

Roberta is the first person to rush me, holding me close. Since we finally broke the news about the baby, she's been visiting the city periodically to check in on us. She knows we're both working and is determined to make sure the house is ready for the baby. All the things I was worried about not knowing, like covering all eight thousand outlets? She's taking care of.

"How is my grandbaby doing?" she asks, talking not to me but directly to my stomach. I smooth my hand over my bump with a big grin.

"Somersaults at all hours, and they have the hiccups constantly," I tell her. I know that today is going to be a big day for me and the bump, so I'm trying to relax into the idea of having hands all over me.

"Mother, leave Ainsley alone. She *just* walked in," Apple moans, coming in for a hug and tugging me close. I feel a tiny hand press to my stomach and look down to see Tobias, who has left a chocolatey handprint on my dress.

"Baby!" he exclaims before nuzzling it with his nose.

"I'm so sorry!" Apple cries, pulling her son back before rushing to get something to clean the handprint off.

Ken is watching me closely, but I shrug as if to say, *What can you do?*

We make the rounds, greeting friends and family and coworkers. Charlie and Elia hang back with Taryn and Vivian. I want to go to them and sit quietly and watch the room, but today I'm the center of attention. I hate it. This is why I'm only having one party, and why we waited to do the gender reveal.

When I have a chance to breathe, my friends are waiting off to the side with a glass of water, which I greedily gulp down.

"Seems rude to have all these things a pregnant woman can't eat. Whose idea was it to get sushi?"

"Tobias," Apple says, sliding into our circle. "I had the paperwork on my desk and Tobias checked off a ton of boxes."

"That explains the caviar and vodka ice luge," I say with a laugh.

"That was actually your father," Vivian corrects.

"Of course." My belly laughs are contagious, and everyone wants a piece of my belly.

"How are you *feeling?*" Taryn asks, shoveling a piece of sushi into her mouth.

I scowl. "Like my tits hurt and all I want to do is have sex, all the time."

It's the gospel truth. I've been insatiable, wanting to feel Ken. No amount has been good enough. Ken has had quite the time trying to keep up with all of my cravings. He hates when I bring up the time he actually fell asleep while I was riding him, but it's something he will never live down.

Charlie coughs into his drink, looking to Ken. "Want to get a drink with me?" he asks, trying to lead Ken away from the all-female talk.

"I know how that is," Apple says. "Until Tobias, I was trying to get Howie to have sex with me everywhere we went. When I was pregnant with Tobias, I would want it, but by the time Howie was done taking off his pants, I was passed out," she adds.

Ken turns to Charlie. "I would love that drink."

I smile, watching the two of them walk off. I'm surprised Taryn didn't bring her boyfriend, but I'm not going to push it. I'm glad she ended things with Brad, who would have been pretty awkward to have around today. I'll need to remember to ask her how things are going with this new guy. Perhaps tomorrow during brunch I can give her the tenth degree.

When it's time for us to do the gender reveal, Ken takes my hand and leads me over to the adorable three-tier cake with two tiny ducks on the top. Along the side of the cake it says, "Waddle it be..."

I chuckle, wrinkling my nose. "I feel like I should be offended?" I ask the crowd, pointing at the little ducks. "Are you trying to say there is something wrong with how I'm walking?"

There are polite laughs around the room while Ken loops his arm around my shoulder. Vivian reaches over to hand both of us large party poppers with a string we're to pull. The confetti will explode with the color of the baby's sex.

It took a lot of cajoling to convince me to do this. Ken was the one that got through to me that I'll have to accept sooner rather than later that it's not going to be about what I want. The only possible answer I had as to why he was such a pushover about this was because his mother asked about it daily.

If having this party made her stop asking, it was worth it.

"Before we pop the cannons, I want to take a moment to thank you all for your support of Ainsley and I," Ken says and kisses the top of my head. "This hasn't been the most straightforward of roads to get to this point. There were bumps along the way and growing pains, and the most delightful of surprises." Ken places his palm on my stomach, beaming at me.

Charlie clears his throat, drawing Ken to being back on task. Ken winks at him before continuing. "Being with Ainsley has opened up a whole new level of happiness and love in my life that makes me wake up with a smile on my face. I'm excited for the family that we're going to be starting, and we can't wait for everyone to meet our little one."

"Obviously, Ken stole my thunder and beat me to the punch," I say. "It means so much for me to know that our little one already has so many people who care about them so much to be here and celebrate with us. I've been told it takes a village and some amazing aunts to raise a child. I know that our kid will be loved so completely, regardless of their sex or gender."

"Quit stalling!" Apple shouts from the back, and I laugh.

Ken counts us down. "Three...two...one..."

We pull the string and there is a loud pop before green confetti fills the air. Cheers erupted when we pulled the string, but they die down quickly with murmurs of confusion echoing through the room.

"Ainsley and I want to keep the sex of our baby a surprise," Ken says. "This is us formally rebuking any attempts to pressure us into decisions. Keep trying and it won't end well." He looks very pointedly at his mother, who has the decency to look ashamed.

My friends whoop and holler, keeping moods buoyant.

When we're able to get away for a moment, I pull Ken aside. He looks around the coat closet I've sequestered us in and smiles at me.

"You planned that," I accuse.

"Wasn't it worth it to see my mother's face?"

Fighting a smile, I shake my head. "Of course, it was. But you let me rail at you for *weeks* over this."

"I did. And I can't take total credit for the idea. Vivian was the one who suggested the different colored confetti cannons. Apparently, the store she got them from got a kick out of it too." Ken brackets my waist, his thumb sweeping along the sides of my belly. "I will always put you and our baby first. Yesterday, today, and tomorrow."

I press up to the tips of my toes from my ever-fashionable sneakers to kiss him. Our lips meet, and he presses down to meet me all the way so I'm on solid footing. The kiss holds the promise of his words and so much more for us. My hands twist in his hair, and I'm elated, knowing that I've found the other half of my heart.

Epilogue

I'M BARELY awake when I feel a hand trace down the side of my hip with probing touches. My breathing must change because that same hand delves between my legs, where I'm already soaked from the dirty dream I was having.

Ken brushes his lips against my neck, pressing his hips against my ass so I can feel his erection against me.

I stifle my moan by biting my lip. It's awkward to roll over but I manage it so I can watch Ken's face as I grip his erection. Even after all this time, it heats my blood to watch his eyes flutter closed as I touch him.

Mornings like this are rare, and I enjoy the quiet, but I want to enjoy my husband more. I'm impatient, always impatient, and I push him onto his back.

"Someone is needy," Ken chides as I straddle him.

"Someone needs to orgasm right now or it's going to be a horrible, no good, very bad day."

Ken reaches between my legs so he can guide himself inside me, and I sink slowly over him as he takes me all the way in. His hands rest on my stomach, the real reason I'm in control right now.

Two more months and I'll be able to see my feet again. We make love slowly. Ken holds my hips as I rock on him, slowly drawing my orgasm out. I want to scream my release, but Ken doesn't let me, clamping his hand over my mouth as I moan his name, trying to stay quiet. Our house guest wouldn't appreciate being woken like this...again. Roberta is staying with us until the baby arrives, and we're thankful to have her, but sometimes, I just want to moan as loudly as I want.

Ken pistons his hips up until I have to cover his mouth with my hands. It's not the energetic sex we once had, but I'll take what I can get.

I roll off him because when I'm this pregnant, it's really the only move I'm capable of.

"Good morning," I say sleepily, leaning toward him for a kiss.

Mornings like this, where we make love and kiss slowly, are what I live for.

"Good morning. How did you sleep?" Ken tugs my shirt all the way up so he can kiss my belly good morning too. Another thing I live for.

"Creature of the Night was... well, a creature of the night," I complain.

Ken palms my stomach, obviously wondering if our morning activities have woken the beast. They have not. If anything, my movements soothed it.

"It's because they know that daddy was out late and they wanted to make sure you could give me a kiss when I came home."

"What was that about, anyway?" I ask, tracing circles on my stomach, which elicits a response. I'll never get used to seeing the baby move from the outside.

"Nothing. Charlie came in." Ken is cut off by our bedroom door being thrown open. I twist to see what the commotion is, but it's hard not to know.

Ayala launches herself on the bed, a mess of wispy thin, blonde hair in her face.

"Careful of momma's tummy, little pea," Ken scolds as our three-year-old throws herself between us.

"Sorry, baby," she says sweetly before kissing my belly.

My heart melts as I push the hair out of her face. "What are you doing up?" I ask, knowing it's only going to get her started.

And, boy, does it. She tells us all about how she woke up early and went to Gamma's room because she knows she's supposed to let momma sleep. She tells the story Gamma told her about Italy, and how she wants to fly a boat. This week her dream profession is ferryboat captain, and once we're able to travel again, we're going to take her to Positano just so she can take the ferry to Capri all day. Who knows what she'll want to be by then, but we'll indulge her in that too.

Ken keeps glancing at me with that moony-eyed expression as he alternates between listening to our daughter and watching my mouth. He needs to stop because otherwise I'm going to want to jump him again.

If I thought we had a lot of sex before, I was so mistaken. It's how Ken claims he knew I was pregnant this time, because all I wanted to do was fuck.

There is a light knock on my door that has us looking up. "Sorry to intrude, but someone was hungry." Roberta walks in, holding Atticus in her arms. Our ten-month-old is squirming in his grandmother's arms.

She approaches us, handing our son to Ken, who settles him nicely into our little cuddle puddle.

"Now all we're missing is the dog," I joke, kissing Atticus's little chubby cheek. The baby giggle soothes something in my soul.

"He wasn't interested in the bottle?" Ken asks, a twinge of disappointment in his voice.

We've been trying to wean Atticus as we get closer to the new baby coming, but he's been fighting us. He's as stubborn as his mother. Shocking.

"No. I'll leave you to it. You want me to take Ayala?" she asks as if our equally strong-willed daughter will go anywhere she doesn't want to. I can complain about my mother-in-law all I want, but she's been heaven sent as we get ready for baby three.

"We're good here. Thanks, Roberta."

She closes the door behind her, and we settle in. Ken stacks pillows for me so I can lean back, propped up just enough so I can relax as Atticus latches and goes to town.

Ayala doesn't skip a beat, chatting as Ken gets up to grab a brush so he can try and tame her thin wisps into a braid.

"Jealous?" I ask Ken as Atticus tangles his tiny fist into my shirt.

"Always. I can't wait till I can play again." He winks like the cad he is.

"You are the one that keeps knocking me up," I point out. The gap between Ayala and Atticus was the longest gap between babies. With this new little monster, Ken knocked me up as soon as he was able to. Not that I'm complaining.

"You're the one that's irresistible. Besides, I think you enjoy it. Everyone knows just who you belong to." Ken wiggles his eyebrows.

"You're a scoundrel."

"What's a scandawl?" Ayala pipes up, and both Ken and I laugh.

"What time is everyone getting here?" I ask, pulling the plates out of the cabinet and setting them aside while Ken and his mom make breakfast.

"Would you sit down?" Ken scolds as I reach on my tiptoes, thanks to my belly getting in the way.

"I'm fine," I tell him, my fingers glancing the plate. Roberta takes the spatula from Ken so he can move over to help me.

"If you wanted to get up close and personal with me, all you had to do was ask," he teases, reaching around me.

"Kenneth, all I want to do is get up close and personal with you, but your mother is here and we have guests coming."

"We can cancel. You didn't want a sprinkle, anyway."

He's not wrong, but my friends wanted this as an excuse to get together so they can drink Ken's mimosas all morning and the boys can watch sportsball together. Apple and Howie might even be making a trip here, but I have no idea. It started as an idea from Taryn and then grew into something I couldn't control.

"You cannot cancel," Roberta warns as she starts to plate and cut up pancakes for my children.

Our dog, Crackle, is pacing under the children's chairs, knowing it's only a matter of time before something falls into his domain. The small rescue might be the ugliest animal I've ever seen, but Ayala loves him to pieces and he's a part of our family, even if he is missing half an ear and only has three legs.

"Apple and the boys are coming, and they're excited to play with the littles," Roberta continues. "The caterers should be here in an hour. Your friends are supposed to come at noon."

Ken pushes me into a chair, helping me relax in it until the catering staff comes in to set up. He then shoos me upstairs with the children to get them ready for the party. Mostly, I fight with Ayala about the three outfits we got for her to choose because all she wants to do is wear the green tea-party dress Uncle Charlie got her from England. I keep Atticus in the sweeper onesie that Taryn got him as a joke. Ever since he started crawling, he's been picking up everything on the floors. He might as well clean while he's at it.

With Roberta minding the kids so I can get ready, Ken draws me into our custom shower so I can let each and every part of my body get massaged. I let Ken pamper me, washing my hair and my body.

"Sit," he orders, guiding me to the shower bench.

"I'm fine on my feet."

"Ainsley, just sit on the bench so I can eat you out," Ken insists, slowly pushing me down.

"Only if you fill me up first," I counter.

"You drive a hard bargain, but it's your day. You can have me any way you want."

He moves inside me, cupping my breasts as I come violently around his cock and then again on his mouth. It's the reason we're forty-five minutes late to a party in our own home.

"You never told me why Charlie stopped by the bar last night," I remind Ken just as we're about to leave our room.

"Oh, I'll let him tell you." There is a mischievous glint to Ken's eye.

When we emerge downstairs, Elia, Taryn, and Vivian are sitting at my kitchen island, each with a drink in front of them, but I notice one of their drinks lacks the telltale bubbles from champagne. When she's ready to say something, I know she will.

Ken kisses my temple and heads in the direction of voices in our backyard, with Crackle getting underfoot.

"Where are the boys?" I ask, grabbing a bottle of water. The caterers, thankfully, were just there to set up Sterno trays and leave.

"Out back. Ken got a new grill and they wanted to check it out. They're also currently responsible for your children, so there is that," Elia answers.

"And Roberta?" I draw my friends into our living room, so I can drop onto a more comfortable chair.

"Out front talking to Apple. I think she just got here," Taryn volunteers.

"Sean is managing the clinic today. I'm going to tell you, though, he's going to make you cut back your hours," Eloise warns as she joins us from the bathroom.

"It's *my* clinic," I whine.

"And you're also about to pop with your twelfth child. He's got it. You know he won't take the clinic from you. He just wants to make you take it easy. Something about nesting?"

"I'll show him nesting," I grumble.

When the boys come inside, I smile at how Ayala is carried in on the hip of her godfather. I'm pretty sure she hasn't stopped talking since she came into our room this morning. Charlie gives me a wink before dropping onto the couch next to Elia, holding his two favorite girls.

"Go ahead. Tell her," Ken urges.

"Oh my god, are you pregnant?" I ask, moving to sit up more, but failing.

"Weren't you the one scolding me once upon a time about assuming any woman over thirty is pregnant?" Eloise chides.

"Yes, but *I'm* pregnant, so babies are on my mind all the time."

"Not to be the hater, but you're *always* pregnant," Taryn points out with a laugh, her ring flashing on her hand.

"Talk about a breeding kink," Vivian mutters, sipping her drink.

"It's a family thing. Competition is fierce," Apple confirms, rubbing her own smaller bump, a girl finally, arriving just in time for the presidential primaries.

"My children are very fertile," Roberta confirms with a laugh.

My father rubs his nose. "Can we please move off the topic of my daughter's sex life? I would hate for my grandchildren to grow up fatherless if I think about it too much."

Charlie wipes a fake bead of sweat off his face for dodging *that* bullet.

"Okay, but the real news isn't all that exciting," Elia says. "We've decided to sell the condo. Even though it's only a mile away, we're tired of being the only ones on the other side of Central Park, so we're buying a brownstone just a few blocks away."

"We wanted to be closer to this little monkey," Charlie teases, tickling Ayala's side until she giggles, and he hugs her to him. "And the apartment was just..."

Elia and Charlie share a look.

"It was time to move on," Elia finishes for him. "And this way, it will be easier for playdates with Bonsai and Mochi."

"Mochi, Mochi, Mochi!" Ayala chants, jumping up.

We spend time catching up as the rest of our guests arrive, while Ayala and Atticus jump around between their loving aunts and uncles.

It's moments like these that I wish I could freeze in time, surrounded by the people I love who I know love me back. It's watching my son fall asleep in my friends' arms. It's seeing their spouses let Ayala paint their nails.

Ken is curled close around me, his hand resting on my stomach, where our newest family member kicks to a steady beat, eager to join the fray with all these people who will love them just as dearly as Ken and I already do.

Acknowledgments

This book has been a true labor of love, and I'm thankful to everyone who helped me get through the drafting process.

I want to thank first and foremost Kayla and Jenn C. for reading the early version of this book, and for giving me your honest feedback on it. Without it, I don't know what would have become of Ainsley and Ken's story, but you helped make it better.

For Amanda and the impeccable Lady Holly Patina, Editorial Assistant/Supervisor, your guidance in these books has never steered me wrong. Thank you for helping to polish this diamond in the rough.

To Katie, Tracy, and Hannah, for keeping me going.

Michael, Michael, Michael. You're the best person in my life. You never fail to lift me up even on my darkest days. My writing career wouldn't happen without your consistent encouragement.

To my parents and sister for never failing to believe in me. I love you.

For my readers, if this is your first story of mine or you've been here awhile, thank you for coming along on this journey.

Interested in Romantasy?

Check out the Game of God's series - a Hades and Persephone re-imagining. Start Daphne Hale's story with The King's Game - available now!

About the Author

Nicole Sanchez has been writing stories on any scrap of paper she could get her hands since before middle school. She lives in New Jersey with her high school sweetheart and love of her life along with their two quirky cats. When she isn't writing or wielding the Force, she can be found traveling the world with her husband or training for her next RunDisney Event.

For more books and updates:

Newsletter

Website

Facebook Reader Group

Also by Nicole Sanchez

Love in the Big Apple Series:
Central Park Collision
Las Vegas Luck
Madison Avenue Mediator

Game of Gods Series:
The King's Game
The Queen's Gamble
The Royal Gauntlet

Anthologies:
Billionaires and Babes Charity Anthology
Getting Witchy With It Charity Anthology
No Going Back: Sultry in the City Anthology

Made in the USA
Middletown, DE
20 July 2023

35297415R00176